In Bed with a Highlander

Maya Banks

BALLANTINE BOOKS • NEW YORK

In Bed with a Highlander is a work of fiction. Names, characters, places, and incidents are the products of the author's imagination or are used fictitiously. Any resemblance to actual events, locales, or persons, living or dead, is entirely coincidental.

A Ballantine Books Mass Market Original

Copyright © 2011 by Maya Banks
Excerpt from *Seduction of a Highland Lass* copyright © 2011 by Maya Banks

Published in the United States by Ballantine Books, an imprint of The Random House Publishing Group, a division of Random House, Inc., New York.

BALLANTINE and colophon are trademarks of Random House, Inc.

This book contains an excerpt from the forthcoming book *Seduction of a Highland Lass* by Maya Banks. This excerpt has been set for this edition only and may not reflect the final content of the forthcoming edition.

ISBN 978-0-345-51947-4
eBook ISBN 978-0-345-51948-1

Cover design: Lynn Andreozzi
Cover illustration: Alan Ayers

Printed in the United States of America

www.ballantinebooks.com

19 18 17 16 15 14 13 12 11 10

Ballantine Books mass market edition: September 2011

"Will you tell me what it is I want to know now?" he asked. To be fair—and he was a fair man—he wanted to give her the opportunity to confide her identity before he related his own knowledge.

She thrust her chin upward in the show of defiance he now expected from her and shook her head. "Nay. I will not. You cannot order me to trust you. Why, that's the most ridiculous thing I've ever heard."

He sensed she was warming up for a full-length diatribe, so he did the one thing he knew would silence her.

He rapidly closed the distance between them, curled his hands around her upper arms, and hauled her upward. His lips found hers in a heated rush, her gasp of outrage swallowed up by his mouth.

She went rigid against him, her hands shoving between them in an attempt to push him away. He brushed his tongue over her lips, tasting her sweetness, demanding entrance into her mouth.

Her second gasp came out more as a sigh. Her lips parted and she melted into his chest like warm honey. She was soft all over, and she fit him like his sword fit his hand. Perfectly.

He pushed inward, sliding his tongue over hers. She went rigid again, and her fingers curled into his chest like tiny daggers. He closed his eyes and imagined them digging into his back as he thrust between her thighs.

Lord, but she was sweet. Nay, bedding her would be no hardship at all. The image of her swollen with his child flickered through his mind, and he found himself very pleased with the image. Very pleased indeed.

When he finally pulled away, her eyes were glazed, her lips deliciously swollen, and she swayed like a sapling in the wind.

She blinked several times and then frowned sharply. "Why did you do that?"

"It was the only way to silence you."

She bristled with outrage. "Silence me? You took liberties with my . . . my . . . my lips in order to silence me? That was very impertinent of you, Laird. I won't allow you to do it again."

He smiled and folded his arms over his chest. "Aye, you will."

Her mouth gaped open in astonishment and then worked up and down as she struggled to speak. "I assure you I won't."

"I assure you that you will."

By Maya Banks

In Bed with a Highlander
Seduction of a Highland Lass
Never Love a Highlander
Never Seduce a Scot
Highlander Most Wanted

For Kim Whalen, who believed in this book from the very beginning and who told me she would absolutely find a home for it. You did just that.

For Lillie, who is such an invaluable support in so many ways. You make my reader heart so very happy with our book dishing, and you're unwavering support of my stories is something I'll always be grateful for.

To Fatin, who is like a mama lion. You take such good care of me. I love you for that!

And finally to my family for trekking all over Scotland with me. For the missed trains, the ridiculous roundabouts, the horrible food, and one of the best times of my life. Love you all so much.

CHAPTER 1

Mairin Stuart knelt on the stone floor beside her pallet and bowed her head in her evening prayer. Her hand slipped to the small wooden cross hanging from a bit of leather around her neck, and her thumb rubbed a familiar path over the now smooth surface.

For several long minutes, she whispered the words she'd recited since she was a child, and then she ended it as she always did. *Please, God. Don't let them find me.*

She pushed herself from the floor, her knees scraping the uneven stones. The plain, brown garb she wore signaled her place along the other novices. Though she'd been here far longer than the others, she'd never taken the vows that would complete her spiritual journey. It was never her intention.

She went to the basin in the corner and poured from the pitcher of water. She smiled as she dampened her cloth, and Mother Serenity's words came floating to mind. *Cleanliness is next to Godliness.*

She wiped her face and started to remove her gown to extend her wash when she heard a terrible crash. Startled, she dropped the cloth and whirled around to stare at her closed door. Then galvanized to action, she ran and flung it open, racing into the hall.

Around her, the other nuns also filled the hall, their

dismayed murmurs rising. A loud bellow echoed down the corridor from the abbey's front entrance. A cry of pain followed the bellow, and Mairin's heart froze. Mother Serenity.

Mairin and the rest of the sisters ran toward the sound, some lagging back while others shoved determinedly ahead. When they reached the chapel, Mairin drew up short, paralyzed by the sight before her.

Warriors were everywhere. There were at least twenty, all dressed in battle gear, their faces unwashed, sweat drenching their hair and clothing. But no blood. They hadn't come for sanctuary or aid. The leader held Mother Serenity by the arm, and even from a distance, Mairin could see the abbess's face drawn in pain.

"Where is she?" the man demanded in a cold voice.

Mairin took a step back. He was a fierce-looking man. Evil. Rage coiled in his eyes like a snake waiting to strike. He shook Mother Serenity when she didn't respond, and she warbled in his grasp like a rag doll.

Mairin crossed herself and whispered an urgent prayer. The nuns around her gathered in a close ball and also offered their prayers.

"She is not here," Mother Serenity gasped out. "I've told you the woman you seek is not here."

"You lie!" he roared.

He looked toward the group of nuns, his gaze flickering coldly over them.

"Mairin Stuart. Tell me where she is."

Mairin went cold, fear rising to a boil in her stomach. How had he found her? After all this time. Her nightmare wasn't over. It was, indeed, just beginning.

Her hands shook so badly that she had to hide them in the folds of her dress. Sweat gathered on her brow, and her gut lurched. She swallowed, willing herself not to be sick.

When no answer was forthcoming, the man smiled,

and it sent a chill straight down Mairin's spine. Still staring at them, he lifted Mother Serenity's arm so that it was in plain sight. Callously, he bent her index finger until Mairin heard the betraying pop of bone.

One of the nuns shrieked and ran forward only to be backhanded down by one of the soldiers. The rest of the nuns gasped at the bold outrage.

"This is God's house," Mother Serenity said in a reedy voice. "You sin greatly by bringing violence onto holy ground."

"Shut up, old woman," the man snapped. "Tell me where Mairin Stuart is or I'll kill every last one of you."

Mairin sucked in her breath and curled her fingers into balls at her sides. She believed him. There was too much evil, too much desperation, in his eyes. He had been sent on a devil's errand, and he wouldn't be denied.

He grasped Mother Serenity's middle finger, and Mairin rushed forward.

"Charity, nay!" Mother Serenity cried.

Mairin ignored her. "I'm Mairin Stuart. Now let her go!"

The man dropped Mother Serenity's hand then shoved the woman back. He stared at Mairin with interest, then let his gaze wander suggestively down her body and back up again. Mairin's cheeks flamed at the blatant disrespect, but she gave no quarter, staring back at the man with as much defiance as she dared.

He snapped his fingers, and two men advanced on Mairin, grabbing her before she could think to run. They had her on the floor in a split second, their hands fumbling with the hem of her gown.

She kicked wildly, flailing her arms, but she was no match for their strength. Would they rape her here on the chapel floor? Tears gathered in her eyes as they shoved her clothing up over her hips.

They turned her to the right and fingers touched her hip, right where the mark rested.

Oh nay.

She bowed her head as tears of defeat slipped down her cheeks.

" 'Tis her!" one of them said excitedly.

He was instantly shoved aside as the leader bent over to examine the mark for himself.

He, too, touched it, outlining the royal crest of Alexander. Issuing a grunt of satisfaction, he curled his hand around her chin and yanked until she faced him.

His smile revolted her.

"We've been looking for you a long time, Mairin Stuart."

"Go to hell," she spat.

Instead of striking her, his grin broadened. "Tsk-tsk, such blasphemy in the house of God."

He stood rapidly, and before Mairin could blink, she was hauled over a man's shoulder, and the soldiers filed out of the abbey and into the cool night.

They wasted no time getting onto their horses. Mairin was gagged then trussed hand and foot and tossed over the saddle in front of one of the men. They were away, the thunder of hooves echoing across the still night, before she had time to react. They were as precise as they were ruthless.

The saddle dug into her belly, and she bounced up and down until she was sure she was going to throw up. She moaned, afraid she'd choke with the gag so securely around her mouth.

When they finally stopped, she was nearly unconscious. A hand gripped her nape, the fingers easily circling the slim column. She was hauled upward and dropped unceremoniously to the ground.

Around her, they made camp while she lay shivering in the damp air. Finally she heard one say, "You best be seeing to the lass, Finn. Laird Cameron won't be happy if she dies of exposure."

An irritated grunt followed, but a minute later, she was untied and the gag removed. Finn, the apparent leader of this abduction, leaned down over her, his eyes gleaming in the light of the fire.

"There's no one to hear you scream, and if you utter a sound, I'll rattle your jaw."

She nodded her understanding and crawled to an upright position. He nudged her backside with his boot and chuckled when she whirled around in outrage.

"There's a blanket by the fire. Get on it and get some sleep. We leave at first light."

She curled gratefully into the warmth of the blanket, uncaring that the stones and sticks on the ground dug into her skin. Laird Cameron. She'd heard talk of him from the soldiers who drifted in and out of the abbey. He was a ruthless man. Greedy and eager to add to his growing power. It was rumored that his army was one of the largest in all of Scotland and that David, the Scottish king, feared him.

Malcolm, bastard son of Alexander—and her half brother—had already led one revolt against David in a bid for the throne. Were Malcolm and Duncan Cameron to ally, they would be a near unstoppable force.

She swallowed and closed her eyes. The possession of Neamh Álainn would render Cameron invincible.

"Dear God, help me," she whispered.

She couldn't allow him to gain control of Neamh Álainn. It was *her* legacy, the only thing of her father's that she had.

It was impossible to sleep, and so she lay there huddled in the blanket, her hand curled around the wooden cross as she prayed for strength and guidance. Some of the soldiers slept while others kept careful watch. She wasn't fool enough to think she'd be given any opportunity to escape. Not when she was worth more than her weight in gold.

But they wouldn't kill her either, which granted her an advantage. She had nothing to fear by trying to escape and everything to gain.

An hour into her vigil of prayer, a commotion behind her had her sitting straight up and staring into the darkness. Around her, the sleeping soldiers stumbled upward, their hands on their swords when a child's cry rent the night.

One of the men hauled a kicking, wiggling child into the circle around the fire and dropped him on the ground. The child crouched and looked around wildly while the men laughed uproariously.

"What is this?" Finn demanded.

"Caught him trying to sneak one of the horses," the child's captor said.

Anger slanted Finn's features into those of the devil, made more demonic by the light of the fire. The boy, who couldn't be more than seven or eight years old, tilted his chin up defiantly as if daring the man to do his worst.

"Why you insolent little pup," Finn roared.

He raised his hand, and Mairin flew across the ground, throwing herself in front of the child as the fist swung and clipped her cheek.

She went reeling but recovered and quickly threw herself back over the child, gathering him close so she could cover as much of him as possible.

The boy struggled wildly under her, screeching obscenities in Gaelic. His head connected with her already aching jaw, and she saw stars.

"Hush now," she told him in his own language. "Be still. I won't let them hurt you."

"Get off him!" Finn roared.

She tightened around the little boy who finally stopped kicking and flailing. Finn reached down and curled his hand into her hair, yanking brutally upward, but she refused to let go of her charge.

"You'll have to kill me first," she said cooly when he forced her to look at him.

He dropped her hair with a curse then reared back and kicked her in the ribs. She hunched over in pain but was careful to keep the child shielded from the maniacal brute.

"Finn, enough," one man barked. "The laird wants her in one piece."

Muttering a curse, he backed away. "Let her keep the dirty beggar. She'll have to turn loose of him soon enough."

Mairin snapped her neck up to glare into Finn's eyes. "You touch this boy even once and I'll slit my own throat."

Finn's laughter cracked the night. "That's one crazy bluff, lass. If you're going to try to negotiate, you need to learn to be believable."

Slowly she rose until she stood a foot away from the much larger man. She stared up at him until his eyes flickered and he looked away.

"Bluff?" she said softly. "I don't think so. In fact, if I were you, I'd be guarding any and all sharp objects from me. Think you that I don't know what my fate is? To be bedded by that brute laird of yours until my belly swells with child and he can claim Neamh Álainn. I'd rather die."

Finn's eyes narrowed. "You're daft!"

"Aye, that might be so, and in that case I'd be worried one of those sharp objects might find its way between your ribs."

He waved his hand. "You keep the boy. The laird will deal with him and you. We don't take kindly to horse thieves."

Mairin ignored him and turned back to the boy who

huddled on the ground, staring at her with a mixture of fear and worship.

"Come," she said gently. "If we snuggle up tight enough, there's plenty of blanket for the both of us."

He went eagerly to her, tucking his smaller body flush against hers.

"Where is your home?" she asked when he had settled against her.

"I don't know," he said mournfully. "It must be a ways from here. At least two days."

"Shh," she said soothingly. "How did you come to be here?"

"I got lost. My papa said I was never to leave the keep without his men, but I was tired of being treated like a baby. I'm not, you know."

She smiled. "Aye, I know. So you left the keep?"

He nodded. "I took a horse. I only meant to go meet Uncle Alaric. He was due back and I thought to wait near the border to greet him."

"Border?"

"Of our lands."

"And who is your papa, little one?"

"My name is Crispen, not 'little one.'" The distaste was evident in his voice, and she smiled again.

"Crispen is a fine name. Now continue with your story."

"What's your name?" he asked.

"Mairin," she answered softly.

"My papa is Laird Ewan McCabe."

Mairin struggled to place the name, but there were so many clans she had no knowledge of. Her home was in the highlands, but she hadn't seen God's country in ten long years.

"So you went to meet your uncle. Then what happened?"

"I got lost," he said mournfully. "Then a McDonald

soldier found me and intended to take me to his laird to ransom, but I couldn't let that happen. It would dishonor my papa, and he can't afford to ransom me. It would cripple our clan."

Mairin stroked his hair as his warm breath blew over her breast. He sounded so much older than his tender years. And so proud.

"I escaped and hid in the cart of a traveling merchant. I rode for a day before he discovered me." He tilted his head up, bumping her sore jaw again. "Where are we, Mairin?" he whispered. "Are we very far from home?"

"I'm not sure where your home is," she said ruefully. "But we are in the lowlands, and I would wager we're at least a two days' ride from your keep."

"The lowlands," he spat. "Are you a lowlander?"

She smiled at his vehemence. "Nay, Crispen. I'm a highlander."

"Then what are you doing here?" he persisted. "Did they steal you from your home?"

She sighed. " 'Tis a long story. One that began before you were born."

When he tensed for another question, she hushed him with a gentle squeeze. "Go to sleep now, Crispen. We must keep our strength up if we are to escape."

"We're going to escape?" he whispered.

"Aye, of course. That's what prisoners do," she said in a cheerful tone. The fear in his voice made her ache for him. How terrifying it must be for him to be so far from home and the ones who love him.

"Will you take me back home to my papa? I'll make him protect you from Laird Cameron."

She smiled at the fierceness in his voice. "Of course, I'll see to it that you get home."

"Promise?"

"I promise."

* * *

"Find my son!"

Ewan McCabe's roar could be heard over the entire courtyard. His men all stood at attention, their expressions solemn. Some were creased in sympathy. They believed Crispen to be dead, though no one dared to utter that possibility to Ewan.

It wasn't something Ewan hadn't contemplated himself, but he would not rest until his son was found—dead or alive.

Ewan turned to his brothers, Alaric and Caelen. "I cannot afford to send every man in search of Crispen," he said in a low voice. "To do so would leave us vulnerable. I trust you two with my life—with my son's life. I want you each to take a contingent of men and ride in different directions. Bring him home to me."

Alaric, the second oldest of the McCabe brothers, nodded. "You know we won't rest until he is found."

"Aye, I know," Ewan said.

Ewan watched as the two strode off, shouting orders to their men. He closed his eyes and curled his fingers into fists of rage. Who dared take his son? For three days he'd waited for a ransom demand, only none had been forthcoming. For three days he'd scoured every inch of McCabe land and beyond.

Was this a precursor to an attack? Were his enemies plotting to hit him when he was weak? When every available soldier would be involved in the search?

His jaw hardened as he gazed around his crumbling keep. For eight years he'd struggled to keep his clan alive and strong. The McCabe name had always been synonymous with power and pride. Eight years ago they'd withstood a crippling attack. Betrayed by the woman Caelen loved. Ewan's father and young wife had been killed, their child surviving only because he'd been hidden by one of the servants.

Almost nothing had been left when he and his brothers had returned. Just a hulking mass of ruins, his people scattered to the winds, his army nearly decimated.

There had been nothing for Ewan to take over when he became laird.

It had taken this long to rebuild. His soldiers were the best trained in the highlands. He and his brothers worked brutal hours to make sure there was food for the old, the sick, the women, and the children. Many times the men went without. And silently they grew, adding to their numbers until, finally, Ewan had begun to turn their struggling clan around.

Soon, his thoughts could turn to revenge. Nay, that wasn't accurate. Revenge had been all that sustained him for these past eight years. There wasn't a day he *hadn't* thought about it.

"Laird, I bring news of your son."

Ewan whipped around to see one of his soldiers hurrying up to him, his tunic dusty as though he'd just gotten off his horse.

"Speak," he commanded.

"One of the McDonalds came upon your son three days ago along the northern border of your land. He took him, intending to deliver him to their laird so he could ransom the boy. Only, the boy escaped. No one has seen him since."

Ewan trembled with rage. "Take eight soldiers and ride to McDonald. Deliver him this message. He will present the soldier who took my son to the entrance of my keep or he signs his own death warrant. If he doesn't comply, I will come for him myself. I will kill him. And it won't be quick. Do not leave a word out of my message."

The soldier bowed. "Aye, Laird."

He turned and hurried off, leaving Ewan with a mix of relief and rage. Crispen was alive, or at least he had been. McDonald was a fool for breaching their tacit peace agreement. Though the two clans could hardly be considered allies, McDonald wasn't stupid enough to incite the wrath of Ewan McCabe. His keep might be crumbling, and his people might not be the best-fed clan, but his might had been restored twofold.

His soldiers were a deadly fighting force to be reckoned with, and those close enough to Ewan's holdings realized it. But Ewan's sights weren't on his neighbors. They were on Duncan Cameron. Ewan wouldn't be happy until the whole of Scotland dripped with Cameron's blood.

CHAPTER 2

Mairin gazed wearily at the looming keep as they rode through the final stone skirt and into the courtyard. Thoughts of escape deteriorated as she stared helplessly at the massive holding. It was impenetrable.

Men were everywhere, most of them training, some tending to repairs on portions of the inner wall, others taking a rest and drinking water from a pail close to the steps of the keep.

As if sensing her fatalistic thoughts, Crispen looked up, his green eyes bright with fear. Her arms were looped around his body, her hands tied together in front of him, and she squeezed him to try to reassure him. But 'twas God's truth, she was shaking like the last leaf in autumn.

The soldier leading her horse pulled up, and she had to fight to stay in the saddle. Crispen steadied them by grabbing onto the horse's mane.

Finn rode up beside them and yanked Mairin from the horse. Crispen came with her, screeching his surprise as he tumbled from her grasp to the ground.

Finn lowered her down, his fingers bruising her arm with his grip. She wrenched away and reached with her bound hands to help Crispen stand.

All around them, activity ceased as everyone stopped

to take stock of the new arrival. A few of the keep's women stared curiously at her from a distance, whispering behind their hands.

She knew she must look a fright, but she was more concerned with what would happen when Laird Cameron arrived to view his captive. God help her then.

And then she saw him. He appeared at the top of the steps leading into the keep, his gaze sharp as he sought her out. The rumors of his greed, of his ruthlessness and ambition, led her to expect the very image of the devil. To her surprise, he was an exceedingly handsome man.

His clothing was immaculate, as though it had never seen a day on the battlefield. She knew better. She'd mended too many soldiers who'd crossed paths with him. Soft leather trews and a dark green tunic with boots that looked too new. At his side, his sword gleamed in the sunlight, the blade honed to a deadly sharpness.

Her hands automatically went to her throat, and she swallowed rapidly against the knot forming.

"You found her?" Duncan Cameron called from the top of the steps.

"Aye, Laird." Finn thrust her forward, shaking her like a rag doll. "This be Mairin Stuart."

Duncan's eyes narrowed, and he frowned as though he'd suffered disappointment in the past. Had he been looking for her for so long? She shivered and tried not to allow her fear to overwhelm her.

"Show me," Duncan barked.

Crispen moved toward her just as Finn hauled her against him. She slammed into his chest with enough force to knock the breath from her. Another soldier appeared at his side, and to her utter humiliation, they tossed up the hem of her dress.

Duncan descended the steps, his face creased in concentration as he neared. Something feral sparked in his eyes, and they lighted in triumph.

His finger caressed the outline of the brand, and he broke into a broad grin. "The royal crest of Alexander," he whispered. "All this time you were thought dead, Neamh Álainn lost forever. Now you are both mine."

"Never," she gritted out.

He looked startled for a moment and then he stepped back, scowling at Finn. "Cover her."

Finn yanked down her clothing and released her arm. Crispen was back at her side immediately.

"Who is this?" Duncan thundered when he laid eyes on Crispen. "Is this her brat? Does she claim him? It cannot be!"

"Nay, Laird," Finn was quick to say. "The child is not hers. We caught him trying to steal one of our horses. She champions him. Nothing else."

"Get rid of him."

Mairin wrapped both arms around Crispen and stared at Duncan with all the force of her hatred. "You touch him and you'll regret the day you were born."

Duncan blinked in surprise and then rage suffused his face, flushing it to near purple. "You dare, you *dare* to threaten me?"

"Go ahead, kill me," she said calmly. "*That* would serve your purpose well."

He lashed out and backhanded her across the cheek. She fell to the ground, her hand snapping up to cup her jaw.

"Leave her alone!" Crispen cried.

She lunged for him, pulling him down until he was cradled in her arms. "Shhh," she cautioned. "Do nothing to anger him further."

"I see you have regained your senses," Duncan said. "See to it they don't leave you again."

She said nothing, just lay there on the ground, holding

Crispen as she stared at Duncan's unmarred boots. *He must never work*, she thought. Even his hand was soft against her cheek. How could a man who rose to power on the broken backs of others have such strength?

"Take her inside and give her to the women to bathe," Duncan said in disgust.

"Stay near me," she whispered to Crispen. She didn't trust Finn not to hurt him.

Finn hauled her to her feet and half dragged, half carried her inside the keep. Though the outside gleamed, the inside was dirty and musty and smelled of days-old ale. Dogs barked excitedly, and she curled her nose as the odor of feces assaulted her nostrils.

"Upstairs with you," Finn snarled, as he shoved her toward the stairs. "And don't be trying anything. I'll have guards posted outside your door. Make it quick. You don't want to keep the laird waiting."

The two women given the task of seeing to Mairin's bath viewed her with a mixture of sympathy and curiosity as they briskly washed her hair.

"Do you be wanting the lad to bathe as well?" one asked.

"Nay!" Crispen exclaimed from his perch on the bed.

"Nay," Mairin echoed softly. "Leave him be."

After they rinsed the soap from Mairin's hair, they helped her from the tub and soon had her dressed in a beautiful blue gown with elaborate embroidery around the neck and sleeves and again at the hem. She didn't miss the significance of being dressed in Duncan's colors. How easily he considered her his conquest.

When the two women offered to arrange her hair, Mairin shook her head. As soon as it was dry she'd braid it.

With a shrug, the women departed the room, leaving her to await her summons from Duncan.

She sat down on the bed next to Crispen, and he snuggled into the crook of her arm.

"I'm getting you dirty," he whispered.

"I don't care."

"What are we going to do, Mairin?"

His voice shook with fear, and she kissed the top of his head.

"We'll think of something, Crispen. We'll think of something."

The door flew open, and Mairin instinctively shoved Crispen behind her. Finn stood there in the doorway, his gaze triumphant.

"The laird wants you."

She turned to Crispen and cupped his chin until he looked directly into her eyes. "Stay here," she whispered. "Don't come out of this room. Promise me."

He nodded, his eyes wide with fright.

She rose and went to where Finn stood. When he reached for her arm, she yanked it away. "I'm capable of walking unaided."

"Uppity bitch," he bit out.

She preceded him down the stairs, her dread growing with each passing second. When she saw the priest standing next to the fire in the great hall, she knew that Duncan was taking no chances. He'd marry her, bed her, and seal her fate and that of Neamh Álainn.

As Finn shoved her forward, she prayed for strength and courage for what she must do.

"There's my bride now," Duncan said, as he turned from his conversation with the priest.

His smile didn't reach his eyes, and he studied her intently, almost as if he were warning her of the consequences if she refused.

God, help me.

The priest cleared his throat and focused his attention on Mairin. "Are you willing, lass?"

Silence fell as all awaited her response. Then slowly, she shook her head. The priest swung his gaze to Duncan, a look of accusation in his eyes.

"What is this, Laird? You told me you both wished this marriage."

The look on Duncan's face had the priest backtracking. The priest hastily crossed himself and positioned himself a safe distance from Duncan.

Then Duncan turned to her, and her blood ran cold. For such a handsome man, he was, in that moment, very ugly.

He stepped toward her, grasping her arm above the elbow, squeezing until she feared her bone would snap.

"I'll ask this only once more," he said in a deceptively soft voice. "Are you willing?"

She knew. She knew that when she uttered her denial, he would retaliate. He might even kill her if he saw his path to Neamh Álainn shattered. But she hadn't stayed sequestered all these years only to yield at the first sign of adversity. Somehow, someway, she must find a way out of this mess.

She lifted her shoulders, infusing the steel of a broadsword into her spine. In a clear, distinct voice, she uttered her denial. "Nay."

His roar of rage nearly shattered her ears. His fist sent her flying several feet, and she huddled into a ball, gasping for breath. He'd hit her so hard in the ribs that she couldn't squeeze breath into her lungs.

She raised her shocked and unfocused gaze up to see him towering over her, his anger a tangible, terrible thing. In that moment, she knew she'd chosen right. Even if he killed her in his frenzy, what would her life be like as his wife? After she bore him the necessary heir to Neamh Álainn, he'd have no further use for her anyway, and he'd just rid himself of her then.

"Yield," he demanded, his fist raised in warning.

"Nay."

Her voice didn't come out as strong as before. It came out more of a breathy exhalation than anything, and her lips trembled. But she made herself heard.

In the great hall, the murmurs rose, and Duncan's face swelled, his cheeks purpling until she thought he might well explode.

That shiny boot kicked out, connecting with her body. Her cry of pain was muted by the next blow. Over and over, he kicked, and then he yanked her up and drove his fist into her side.

"Laird, you'll kill her!"

She was barely conscious. She had no idea who uttered the warning. She hung in his grasp, every breath causing her unbearable pain.

Duncan dropped her in disgust. "Lock her in her chambers. No one is to give her any food or water. Nor that brat of hers. We'll see how soon it takes her to yield when he starts whining of hunger."

Again, she was hauled upward with no regard to her injuries. Each step up the stairs was agony as she bounced against the hard stone. The door to her chamber opened, and Finn threw her inside.

She hit the floor, battling for consciousness with every breath.

"Mairin!"

Crispen huddled over her, his little hands gripping her painfully.

"Nay, don't touch me," she whispered hoarsely. If he touched her, she was sure she'd faint.

"You must get to the bed," he said desperately. "I'll help you. Please, Mairin."

He was near tears, and it was only the thought of how he'd survive in Duncan's hands if she died that prevented her from closing her eyes and praying for peace.

She roused herself enough to crawl toward the bed,

each movement sending a scream down her spine. Crispen bore as much of her weight as he could, and together they managed to haul her over the edge of the bed.

She melted into the straw mattress, hot tears slipping down her cheeks. Breathing hurt. Crispen settled next to her, his warm, sweet body seeking comfort she couldn't offer.

Instead, his arms went around her, and he hugged her to his little body. "Please don't die, Mairin," he begged softly. "I'm scared."

"Lady. My lady, wake up. You must wake up."

The urgent whisper roused Mairin from unconsciousness, and as soon as she turned, seeking the annoyance that disturbed her, agony flashed through her body until she gasped for breath.

"I'm sorry," the woman said anxiously. "I know you're badly injured, but you must hurry."

"Hurry?"

Mairin's voice was slurred, and her brain was a mass of cobwebs. Beside her, Crispen stirred and gave a start of fright when he saw the shadow standing over the bed.

"Aye, hurry," the impatient voice came again.

"Who are you?" Mairin managed to ask.

"We haven't time to talk, Lady. The laird is in a drunken sleep. He'll think you too badly hurt to escape. We have to go now if you are to make it. He plans to kill the child if you don't yield."

At the word *escape*, some of the cobwebs vanished. She tried to sit up but nearly cried out when pain knifed through her side.

"Here, let me help you. You too, lad," the woman said to Crispen. "Help me with your lady."

Crispen scrambled over the bed and slid off the edge.

"Why are you doing this?" Mairin asked when they both helped her sit up.

"What he did was a disgrace," the woman murmured. "To beat a lass as he did you. He's mad. You've been his obsession. I fear for your life no matter whether you yield or not. He'll kill the boy."

Mairin squeezed her hand with the little strength she had. "Thank you."

"We must hurry. There is a bolt-hole in the next chamber. You'll have to leave alone. I can't risk taking you. At the end, Fergus waits for you with a horse. He'll put you and the lad on it. It'll pain you, aye, but you'll have to endure. 'Tis your only way out."

Mairin nodded her acceptance. Escape in agony or die in comfort. Didn't seem like such a difficult decision.

The serving woman cracked open the door of the chamber, turned back to Mairin, and put a finger to her lips. She motioned to the left to let Mairin know the guard was there.

Crispen slid his hand into hers, and again she squeezed to comfort him. Inch by breathless inch, they crept by the sleeping guard in the darkness of the hall. Mairin held her breath the entire way, afraid if she let out so much as a puff, the guard would wake and alert the keep.

Finally they reached the next chamber. Dust flew and curled around her nose as they stepped within, and she had to squeeze her nostrils to keep from sneezing.

"Over here," the woman whispered in the darkness.

Mairin followed the sound of her voice until she felt the chill emanating from the stone wall.

"God be with you," the serving woman said as she ushered Mairin and Crispen into the small tunnel.

Mairin stopped only long enough to squeeze her hand in a quick thank-you, and then she urged Crispen into the narrow passageway.

Each step sent a fresh wave of agony through Mairin. She feared her ribs were broken, but there was naught that could be done about it now.

They hurried through the darkness, Mairin all but dragging Crispen behind her.

"Who goes there?"

Mairin halted at the man's voice but remembered that the woman had said Fergus awaited them.

"Fergus?" she called softly. " 'Tis I, Mairin Stuart."

"Come, Lady," he urged.

She rushed to the end and stepped onto the cold, damp ground, wincing when her bare feet made contact with rough pebbles. She gazed at their surroundings and saw that the bolt-hole exited the back of the keep where there was only a skirt between the keep and the hillside that jutted skyward.

Wordlessly, Fergus melted into the darkness, and Mairin ran to catch up to him. They moved along the bottom of the hillside and headed for the dense population of trees at the perimeter of Duncan's holding.

A horse was tied to one of the trees, and Fergus quickly freed him, gathering the reins as he turned to Mairin.

"I'll lift you up first and then the lad." He pointed into the distance. "That way is north. God be with you."

Without another word, he lifted her, all but tossing her into the saddle. It was all she could do not to fall off. Tears crushed her eyes and she doubled over, fighting unconsciousness.

Help me please, God.

Fergus lifted Crispen, who settled in front of her. She was glad he wasn't riding behind her because, God's truth, she needed something to hang on to.

"Can you manage the reins?" she whispered to Crispen as she leaned into him.

"I'll protect you," Crispen said fiercely. "Hold on to me, Mairin. I'll take us home, I swear it."

She smiled at the determination in his voice. "I know you will."

Fergus gave the horse a slap, and it started forward. Mairin bit her lip against the scream of pain that battled to erupt. She would never make it even a mile.

Alaric McCabe drew up his horse and held his fist up to halt his men. They'd ridden all morning, searching endless trails, tracking hoofprints to no avail. All were dead ends. He slid from the saddle and strode forward to view the disturbance in the soil. Kneeling, he touched the faint hoofprints and the flattened grass to the side. It looked as though someone took a fall from a horse. Recently.

He scanned the immediate area and saw a footprint in a patch of bare soil a few feet away, then lifted his gaze toward the area the person had headed. Slowly he rose, drew his sword, and motioned for his men to spread out and circle the area.

Carefully, he stepped through the trees, watching warily for any sign of ambush. He saw the horse first, grazing a short distance away, the reins hanging, the saddle askew. He frowned. Such disregard for the care of a horse was surely a sin.

A slight rustle to his right swung him around, and he found himself staring at a small woman, her back wedged against a huge tree. Her skirts jumped like she had a litter of kittens hidden underneath, and her wide blue eyes were full of fear—and fury.

Her long black hair hung in disarray to her waist, and it was then he noticed the colors of her tunic and the coat of arms embroidered at the hem.

Rage temporarily blinded him, and he advanced, his sword held in an arc over his head.

She flung an arm behind her, shoving something farther between her and the tree. Her skirts wriggled again, and it was then he realized she shielded a person. A child.

"Stay behind me," she hissed.

"But Mair—"

Alaric froze. He knew that voice. His fingers shook, for the first time in his life his hand unsteady around the hilt. Hell would be a cold place indeed before he ever allowed a Cameron hand on his kin.

With a snarl of rage, he charged forward, grasped the woman by the shoulder, and hurled her aside. Crispen stood against the tree, his mouth open. Then he saw Alaric and all but leapt into his arms.

The sword fell to the ground—another sin of neglect—but in that moment Alaric didn't care. Sweet relief staggered him.

"Crispen," he said hoarsely, as he hugged the boy to him.

A shriek of rage assaulted his ears just as he was hit by a flying bundle of woman. So surprised was he, that he stumbled backward, his hold on Crispen loosening.

She wedged herself between him and Crispen and landed a knee to his groin. He doubled over, cursing as agony washed over him. He fell to one knee and grabbed his sword just as he whistled for his men. The woman was demented.

Through the haze of pain, he saw her grab a resisting Crispen and try to run. Several things happened at once. Two of his men stepped in front of her. She halted, causing Crispen to slam into her back. When she started in the opposite direction, Gannon raised his arm to stop her.

To Alaric's astonishment, she swiveled, grabbed Crispen, and fell to the ground, her body huddled protectively over him.

Gannon and Cormac froze and looked to Alaric just as the rest of his men burst through the trees.

To further confuse the hell out of all of them, Crispen finally wiggled out from underneath her and threw himself on top of her, scowling ferociously the entire time at Gannon.

"Don't you hit her!" he bellowed.

Every one of his men blinked in surprise at Crispen's ferocity.

"Lad, I wasn't going to hit the lass," Gannon said. "I was trying to prevent her from fleeing. With you. God's teeth, we've been searching for you for days. The laird is worried sick over you."

Alaric strode over to Crispen and plucked him off the huddled woman. When he reached down to haul her upright, Crispen exploded again, shoving him back.

Alaric stared at his nephew with an open mouth.

"Don't touch her," Crispen said. "She's badly hurt, Uncle Alaric."

Crispen chewed his bottom lip, and it looked for the world like the lad was going to break down and cry. Whoever the woman was, it was obvious Crispen didn't fear her.

"I won't hurt her, lad," Alaric said softly.

He knelt down and brushed aside the hair from her face and realized she was unconscious. There was a bruise on one cheek, but otherwise she didn't look injured.

"Where is she hurt?" he asked Crispen.

Tears filled Crispen's eyes, and he wiped hastily at them with the back of his grubby hand.

"Her stomach. And her back. It hurts her fierce if anyone touches her."

Carefully, so as not to alarm the boy, Alaric pulled at her clothing. When her abdomen and back came into view, he sucked in his breath. Around him, his men alternately cursed and murmured their pity for the slight lass.

"God in heaven, what happened to her?" Alaric asked.

Her entire rib cage was purple, and ugly bruises marred her smooth back. He could swear one of them was in the shape of a man's boot.

"He beat her," Crispen choked out. "Take us home, Uncle Alaric. I want my papa."

Not wanting the boy to lose his composure in front of the other men, Alaric nodded and patted him on the arm. There would be plenty of time to get the story from Crispen later. Ewan would want to hear it all.

He stared down at the unconscious woman and frowned. She had offered her body for Crispen's, and yet she wore the colors of Duncan Cameron. Ewan would be beyond control if Cameron had any involvement in Crispen's disappearance.

War. At long last, war would be declared.

He motioned for Cormac to tend to the lass, and he reached for Crispen, intending that the boy ride with him. There were several questions he wanted answered on the ride home.

Crispen shook his head adamantly. "Nay, *you* take her, Uncle Alaric. She has to ride with you. I promised her that Papa would keep her safe, but he's not here so you have to do it. You *have* to."

Alaric sighed. There was no reasoning with the boy, and right now he was so glad he was alive, he'd cede to his ridiculous demands. Later he'd bend the brat's ear about not questioning authority.

"I want to ride with you, too," Crispen said, his gaze nervously going to the woman.

He inched closer to her as if he couldn't stand the idea of being separated from her.

Alaric looked skyward. Ewan hadn't taken a firm enough hand with the boy. That was all there was to it.

And so Alaric found himself astride his horse with the

woman draped across the saddle in front of him, her body shielded in the crook of one arm, while Crispen sat on his other leg, his head nestled against her bosom.

He glared at his men, daring even one of them to laugh. Hell, he had to relinquish his sword for the duty of carrying the two extra persons, never mind their weight didn't equal that of a single warrior.

Ewan just better be damn grateful. He could decide what was to be done with the woman just as soon as Alaric dumped her into Ewan's lap.

CHAPTER 3

As soon as they crossed over the border onto McCabe land, a shout went up that echoed through the hills, and in the distance, Mairin heard the cry taken up and relayed. Soon, the laird would know of his son's return.

She twisted the reins nervously in her fingers as Crispen all but bounced off the saddle in his excitement.

"If you keep gathering those reins, lass, you and the horse are going to end up back where you came from."

She glanced guiltily up at Alaric McCabe, who rode to her right. His admonishment had come out as a tease, but God's truth, the man scared her. He looked savage with his unkempt, long dark hair and the braids dangling on each side of his temples.

When she'd awakened in his arms, she'd nearly tossed them both out of the saddle in her haste to escape. He'd been forced to pry both her and Crispen from their perch against him, and he'd put them both on the ground until the entire thing could be sorted out.

He hadn't been pleased by her stubbornness, but she had Crispen solidly on her side, and having extracted a promise from Crispen to tell no one her name, they'd both stood mute when Alaric demanded answers.

Oh, he'd blustered and waved his arms. Even threatened to choke the both of them, and in the end he'd muttered blasphemies against women *and* children before resuming their journey to bring Crispen home.

Alaric had then insisted she ride with him at least another day, because he said, in no uncertain terms, the likelihood of her sitting a horse by herself in her condition was nil, and it was a sin to abuse a good horse with an inept mount.

The journey that would normally last two days took them three, thanks to Alaric's consideration of her condition and their stopping frequently to rest. She knew Alaric was considerate because he *told* her. Numerous times.

After the first day, she was determined to ride without Alaric's assistance, if for no other reason than to wipe the smugness from his expression. He obviously had no patience for women, and, she suspected, with the exception of his nephew, whom he obviously loved, he had even less patience with children.

Still, given the fact that he knew nothing about her, only that Crispen championed her, he had treated her well, and his men had been politely respectful.

Now that they neared Laird McCabe's stronghold, fear fluttered in her throat. She would no longer be able to keep silent. The laird would demand answers, and she would be obligated to give them.

She leaned down to whisper close to Crispen's ear. "Do you remember your promise to me, Crispen?"

"Aye," he whispered back. "I'm not to tell anyone your name."

She nodded, feeling guilty for asking such a thing from the boy, but if she could pretend to be of no importance, just someone who happened upon Crispen and saw him safely back to his father, perhaps he would be grateful enough to provide a horse and maybe some food, and she could be on her way.

"Not even your father," she pressed.

Crispen nodded solemnly. "I'll only tell him you saved me."

She squeezed his arm with her free hand. "Thank you. I could ask for no better champion."

He turned his head back to grin broadly at her, his back puffing with pride.

"What are the two of you whispering about?" Alaric demanded irritably.

She glanced over to see the warrior watching her, his eyes narrow with suspicion.

"If I wanted you to know, I'd have spoken louder," she said calmly.

He turned away muttering what she was sure were more blasphemies about annoying females.

"You must make the priest weary with the length of your confessions," she said.

He raised one eyebrow. "Who says I confess anything?"

She shook her head. The arrogant man probably thought his path to heaven was already assured, and that he acted in accordance to God's will just by breathing.

"Look, there it is!" Crispen shouted as he pointed eagerly ahead.

They topped the hill and looked down at the stone keep nestled into the side of the next hill.

The skirt was crumbled in several places, and there was a detail of men working steadily, replacing the stones at the wall. What she could see of the keep above the outer walls looked blackened by an old fire.

The loch spread out to the right of the keep, the water glistening in the sunlight. One of the fingers meandered around the front of the keep, providing a natural barrier to the front gate. The bridge across it, however, sagged precariously in the middle. A temporary, narrow path over the water had been fashioned to the side, and it would only allow one horse at a time into the keep.

Despite the obvious state of disrepair to the keep, the land was beautiful. Scattered across the valley to the left of the keep, sheep grazed, herded by an older man flanked by two dogs. Occasionally one of the dogs raced out to herd the sheep back into the imaginary boundary, and then he'd return to his master to receive an approving pat on the head.

She turned to Alaric, who'd pulled to a stop beside her. "What happened here?"

But he didn't answer. A deep scowl creased his face, and his eyes went nearly black. She gripped the reins a little tighter and shivered under the intensity of his hatred. Aye, hatred. There could be no other term for what she saw in his eyes.

Alaric spurred his horse, and hers followed automatically, leaving her to grab onto Crispen to make sure neither of them fell.

Down the hill they rode, Alaric's men flanking her protectively on all sides. Crispen fidgeted so hard in the saddle that she had to grip his arm so he wouldn't jump out of his skin.

When they reached the temporary crossing, Alaric halted to wait on her.

"I'll go in first. You follow directly behind me."

She nodded her understanding. It wasn't as if she wanted to be the first into the keep anyway. In some ways, this was more frightening to her than arriving at Duncan Cameron's keep because she didn't know her fate here. She certainly knew what *Cameron* had in mind for her.

They rode over the bridge and through the wide, arched entryway into the courtyard. A great shout went up, and it took her a moment to realize that it was Alaric who'd made the sound. She looked over to see him still astride his horse, his fist held high in the air.

All around her, soldiers—and there were hundreds—

thrust their swords skyward and took up the cry, raising and lowering their blades in celebration.

A man entered the courtyard at a dead run, his hair flying behind him as his stride ate up the ground below him.

"Papa!" Crispen cried, and scrambled out of the saddle before she could prevent him.

He hit the ground running, and Mairin stared in fascination at the man she assumed was Crispen's father. Her stomach knotted, and she swallowed, trying not to allow herself to panic all over again.

The man was huge, and just as mean looking as Alaric, and she didn't know how she could think it, when there was so much joy on his face as he swung Crispen into his arms, but he frightened her in a way that Alaric did not.

The brothers were very similar in build and stature. Both had dark hair that fell below their shoulders, and both wore braids. As she looked around, though, it became apparent that all his men wore their hair the same way. Long, wild, and savage looking.

"I'm so glad to see you, lad," his father choked out.

Crispen clung to the laird with his small arms, reminding Mairin of a burr stubbornly clinging to her skirts.

Over Crispen's head, his gaze met Mairin's, and his eyes immediately hardened. He took in every detail about her, she was sure, and she twisted uncomfortably, feeling horribly picked apart under his scrutiny.

She started to get down from her horse because she felt a little silly when everyone around her was dismounting, but Alaric was there, his hands reaching up to effortlessly pluck her from the horse and set her down on the ground.

"Easy, lass," he cautioned. "You're healing well, but you need to take care."

He sounded almost concerned, but when she looked

up at him, he wore the same scowl he always wore when he looked at her. Irritated, she scowled right back. He blinked in surprise, then pushed her toward the waiting laird.

Ewan McCabe looked a lot more threatening now that Crispen was out of his arms and back on the ground. She found herself backing up a step only to collide with the mountain that was Alaric.

Ewan looked first at Alaric, bypassing her as if she were invisible, which was just fine with her.

"You have my thanks for bringing my son home. I had every confidence in you and Caelen."

Alaric cleared his throat and nudged Mairin forward.

"You have the lass to thank for Crispen's return. I merely provided the escort."

Ewan's eyes narrowed as he studied her further. To her astonishment, his eyes weren't the dark, fierce orbs she'd thought, but rather they were an odd pale green. When he scowled, though, his face darkened to a thundercloud, and who could possibly think his eyes were anything but a matching black?

Startled by this revelation—and if she were avoiding the inevitable confrontation with the laird, who could blame her?—she turned abruptly and stared up into Alaric's eyes. He blinked then glared at her like he thought she was daft—and she was pretty sure he did think so.

"Your eyes are green, too," she muttered.

Alaric's scowl turned into a look of concern. "Are you sure you didn't suffer a blow to the head you didn't tell me about?"

"You will look at me," Ewan roared.

She jumped and whirled around, taking an instinctive step back and landing once again against Alaric.

He muttered an expletive and hunched over, but she

was too worried about Ewan to see what Alaric was cursing over.

Her courage had run out, and her determination not to feel pain, not to allow her spine to wither, promptly died a brutal death.

Her legs shook, her hands shook, and pain speared through her sides, making her gasp softly with each breath. Sweat beaded her forehead, but she wouldn't allow herself to back down any further.

The laird was angry—at her—and for the life of her she couldn't discern why. Shouldn't he be grateful to her for saving his son? Not that she'd really done anything heroic, but he didn't know that. For all he knew, she could have battled ten men on Crispen's behalf.

It wasn't until he stared back at her in astonishment that she realized she'd babbled her entire thought process aloud. The entire courtyard had gone silent and looked at her as if she'd pronounced a curse on all of them.

"Alaric?" she murmured, not turning away from the laird's gaze.

"Aye, lass?"

"Will you catch me if I faint? I don't think a fall to the ground would be good for my injuries."

To her surprise, he grasped both of her shoulders and held her tightly. His hands trembled the slightest amount, and he made the weirdest sound. Was he laughing at her?

Ewan advanced, his astonishment replaced by that dark scowl again. Did no one in the McCabe clan ever smile?

"Nay, we don't," Alaric said in amusement.

She snapped her lips shut, determined she wouldn't say another word, and prepared herself for the laird's censure.

Ewan stopped a single foot in front of her, forcing her

to crane her neck upward to meet his stare. It was hard to be brave when she was sandwiched between two hulking warriors, but her pride wouldn't allow her to throw herself at his feet and beg for mercy. Even if she currently thought it was the best idea. Nay, she'd faced down Duncan Cameron and survived. This warrior was bigger and meaner, and he could probably squash her like a bug, but she wouldn't die like a coward. She wouldn't die at all if she had anything to say about it.

"You will tell me who you are, why you're wearing Duncan Cameron's colors, and how the hell my son came into your possession."

She shook her head, backed up against Alaric, only to hear him curse again as she stepped all over his feet, and then quickly stepped forward again, remembering, belatedly, her vow to be courageous.

Ewan frowned even harder, if that was possible. "You defy me?"

There was a note of incredulity in his voice that she might find amusing if she weren't bathed in pain and about to shake right out of the gown that offended the laird so.

Her stomach boiled, and she prayed she wouldn't throw up on his boots. They weren't new and shiny like Duncan's, but somehow she thought he'd take great offense anyway.

"I don't defy you, Laird," she said in an even voice that made her proud.

"Then give me the information I seek. And do it now," he added in a deadly soft voice.

"I . . ."

Her voice cracked like ice, and she swallowed back the nausea that rose in her throat.

She was saved by Crispen, who could obviously stand still no longer. He burst forward, inserting himself between her and his father, and wrapped his arms around her legs, burying his face in her bruised abdomen.

A low moan escaped her, and she reflexively put her arms around Crispen to pull him away from her ribs. She would have slithered straight to the ground if not for Alaric grasping her arms to steady her again.

Crispen turned in her grasp and stared up at his father who looked to be battling extreme shock and burning impatience.

"Leave her alone!" Crispen exclaimed. "She's hurt, and I promised you'd protect her, Papa. I *promised*. A McCabe never breaks his word. You told me."

Ewan looked down at his son in astonishment, his mouth working up and down as the veins in his neck bulged.

"The lad is right, Ewan. The lass is sorely in need of a bed. A hot bath wouldn't be remiss."

Surprised by Alaric's support, but more grateful than she could possibly express, she chanced another look at the laird only to see him gape incredulously at Alaric.

"Bed? *Bath*? My son has been returned to me by a woman wearing the colors of a man I loathe more than life, and all anyone can suggest is that I give her a bath and a bed?"

The laird looked precariously close to exploding. She stepped back, and this time, Alaric accommodated her by moving aside so she could put distance between her and Ewan.

"She did save his life," Alaric said evenly.

"She took a beating for me," Crispen shouted.

Ewan's expression wavered, and he stared again at her as if trying to see for himself the extent of her injuries. He looked torn, as if he really wanted to demand that she cooperate, but with both Crispen and Alaric staring expectantly at him, he snapped his lips shut and took a step back himself.

His muscles bulged in his arms and neck, and he took several breaths as if he were working to keep his patience. She felt sympathy for him, she truly did. If it were her child, she'd demand, just as he had, every detail. And if it were true—and Ewan had no reason to lie—that Duncan Cameron was his mortal enemy, she could well understand why he looked at her with such mistrust and hatred. Aye, she understood well his dilemma. It didn't mean she was suddenly going to cooperate, however.

Gathering her nerve, and hoping she didn't sound boastful, she looked the laird in the eye. "I did save your son, Laird. I would be most appreciative of what aid you could provide. I won't ask for much. A horse and maybe some food. I'll be on my way and no longer a bother."

Ewan no longer stared at her. Nay, he turned his face heavenward as if praying for either patience or deliverance. Maybe both.

"A horse. Food."

He said the words, still looking up at the sky. Then he slowly lowered his head until those green eyes scorched the breath right out of her.

"You aren't *going* anywhere, lass."

CHAPTER 4

Ewan stared at the woman before him, and it was all he could do not to shake her senseless. The little chit had audacity, he'd hand her that. He didn't know what hold she had on his son, but he'd soon get to the bottom of it.

Even Alaric seemed under her spell, and while he could understand it, because Lord, the lass was bonnie, it annoyed him that his brother sought to defend her against him.

She turned her chin up farther in defiance and the light caught her eyes. Blue. Not just blue but a brilliant hue that reminded him of the sky in spring just before summer took hold.

Her hair was bedraggled but the curls hung all the way down to her waist, a waist he could span with his hands. Aye, his hands would fit nicely in the curve between her hips and her breasts, and if he slid his hands up just a bit, he'd cup the generous swell of her bosom.

She was beautiful. And she was trouble.

She was also in pain. She hadn't faked that.

Her eyes dimmed and he got a better view of the shadows that surrounded them. She was trying valiantly to hide her discomfort, but it radiated from her in almost discernible waves.

Her questioning would have to wait.

He raised his hand and motioned toward one of the women gathered on the perimeter.

"See to her needs," he ordered. "Have a bath drawn. See that Gertie prepares her a plate of food. And for God's sake, give her something other than Cameron's colors to wear."

Two of the McCabe women hurried forward and each took an arm of the woman still standing by Alaric.

"Careful now," Alaric cautioned. "Her injuries are still paining her."

The women removed their hands and instead gestured toward her to precede them into the keep. She looked nervously around, and it was clear she had no desire to go in. She tucked her bottom lip between her teeth until Ewan was sure she'd draw blood if she didn't cease.

Ewan sighed. "I'm not ordering your death, lass. You asked for a bath and food. Are you questioning my hospitality now?"

She frowned, and her eyes narrowed as she gazed sharply at him. "I asked for a *horse* and food. I've no need of your hospitality. I'd prefer to be on my way as soon as possible."

"I've no horses to spare, and furthermore, you aren't going anywhere until I've sorted this entire matter out. If you have no wish for a bath, I'm sure the women would be happy to show you into the kitchens so you can eat."

He finished with a shrug that signaled he didn't care whether she bathed or not. That had been Alaric's idea, but didn't all women jump at the chance to wallow in a tub of hot water?

She pursed her lips as if to argue but evidently decided restraint was a better idea. "I'd like a bath."

He nodded. "Then I suggest you follow the women upstairs before I change my mind."

She turned, muttering something under her breath

that he didn't catch. His eyes narrowed. The contrary lass was sorely trying his patience.

He looked around for his son only to see him running behind the women toward the keep.

"Crispen," he called.

Crispen turned around, anxiety over being kept from the woman etched on his small brow.

"Come here, son."

After another moment's hesitation, he launched himself toward Ewan, and Ewan caught him up in his arms once more.

His heart raced frantically as the sheer relief of holding his son again overwhelmed him. "You frightened ten years off me, lad. Don't ever scare your father like this again."

Crispen clung to Ewan's shoulders and burrowed his face into Ewan's neck.

"I won't, Papa. I promise."

Ewan hung on to him far longer than necessary, until Crispen wiggled to be set free. He hadn't thought to see his son again, and if Alaric was to be believed, he had the woman to thank for it.

He looked over Crispen's head to Alaric, demanding answers from his silent brother. Alaric shrugged.

"If you're wanting answers from me, you're looking to the wrong person." He gestured impatiently at Crispen. "He and the lass refused to tell me anything. The cheeky little brat demanded I return them both to you so that you could protect her."

Ewan frowned and looked Crispen in the eyes. "Is this true, son?"

Crispen looked decidedly guilty, but determination sparked in his green eyes. His lips twisted mutinously, and he tensed as if he expected Ewan to launch into a tirade.

"I gave my word," Crispen said stubbornly. "You said a McCabe never breaks his word."

Ewan shook his head wearily. "I'm beginning to regret telling you of things a McCabe doesn't do. Come, let's sit in the hall so you can tell me of these adventures of yours."

He leveled a glance at Alaric, silently commanding his presence as well. Then he turned to Gannon. "Take your men and ride north to find Caelan. Tell him Alaric has returned Crispen home. Return as quickly as you can."

Gannon bowed and hurried away, shouting orders as he went.

Ewan set Crispen down but kept a firm grip on his shoulder as he herded him into the keep. They walked into the hall amid a chorus of cries and exclamations. Crispen was soundly hugged by every passing woman and slapped on the back by the men of the clan. Finally Ewan waved them away so they were left alone in the hall.

Ewan sat at the table and patted the space next to him. Crispen hopped onto the bench while Alaric sat across the table from them.

"Now tell me what happened," Ewan commanded.

Crispen looked down at his hands, his shoulders drooping.

"Crispen," Ewan began gently. "What else did I tell you McCabes always do?"

"Tell the truth," Crispen said grudgingly.

Ewan smiled. "Indeed. Now begin your tale."

Crispen sighed dramatically before saying, "I snuck out to meet Uncle Alaric. I thought I'd wait at the border and surprise him when he came home."

Alaric glared across the table at Crispen, but Ewan held up his hand.

"Let him continue."

"I must have gone too far. One of the McDonald soldiers took me and said he was going to take me back to his laird to ransom me."

He turned pleading eyes on Ewan. "I couldn't let him do that, Papa. It would shame you, and our clan can't afford a ransom. So I escaped and hid in the cart of a traveling merchant."

Ewan tensed in rage at the McDonald soldier, and his heart clenched at the pride in his son's voice.

"You could never shame me, Crispen," Ewan said quietly. "Now go on with your story. What happened next?"

"The merchant discovered me after a day and he chased me out. I didn't know where I was. I tried to steal a horse from men who were camping but they caught me. M—I mean she saved me."

"Who saved you?" Ewan demanded.

"*She* saved me."

Ewan swallowed his impatience. "Who is *she*?"

Crispen fidgeted uncomfortably. "I can't tell you. I promised."

Ewan and Alaric exchanged frustrated glances, and Alaric raised one eyebrow as if to say I told you so.

"All right, Crispen, what exactly did you promise?"

"That I wouldn't tell you who she was," Crispen blurted. "I'm sorry, Papa."

"I see. What else did you promise?"

Crispen looked puzzled for a moment, and across the table, Alaric smiled as he caught on to the direction Ewan was headed.

"I just promised I wouldn't tell you her name."

Ewan stifled his grin. "All right, so continue with your story. The lady saved you. How did she do this? Was she camping with the men you tried to steal the horse from? Were they escorting her to a destination?"

Crispen's brow creased as he struggled with whether

he could divulge such information without breaking his promise.

"I won't ask her name again," Ewan said solemnly.

Looking relieved, Crispen pursed his lips and then said, "The men took her from the abbey. She didn't want to be with them. I saw them bring her into the camp."

"God's teeth, she's a nun?" Ewan exclaimed.

Alaric shook his head adamantly. "If that woman is a nun, then I'm a monk."

"Can you marry a nun?" Crispen asked.

"Why on earth would you ask a question like that?" Ewan demanded.

"Duncan Cameron wanted to marry her. If she's a nun, he can't, can he?"

Ewan straightened and shot Alaric a fierce look. Then he turned to Crispen, trying to keep his reaction calm so that he didn't frighten his son.

"The men you tried to steal the horse from. Were they Cameron soldiers? Were they the ones who took the woman from the abbey?"

Crispen nodded solemnly. "They took us to Laird Cameron. He tried to make . . . her . . . marry him, but she refused. When she did, he beat her badly."

Tears welled in his eyes, and he made a fierce expression to hold them back.

Again, Ewan glanced over at Alaric to judge his reaction to the news. Who could this woman be that Duncan Cameron wanted her badly enough to steal her from an abbey? Was she an heiress sequestered there until her marriage?

"What happened after he beat her?" Ewan prompted.

Crispen swiped at his face, leaving a trail of dirt over his cheek.

"When she came back to the room, she could barely hold herself up. I had to help her to the bed. Later a woman woke us and said that the laird was in a drunken sleep and that he planned to threaten me to make her do what he wanted. She said we had to escape before he awoke. The lady was afraid but promised me she'd protect me. And so I promised her that I would take us here to you so that you could protect her. You won't let Duncan Cameron marry her, will you, Papa? You won't let him hurt her again?"

He gazed anxiously up at Ewan, his eyes so earnest and serious. He looked so much older than his eight years in that moment, as if he'd taken on a great responsibility, one far greater than his age warranted, but one he was determined to follow through with.

"Nay, son. I won't allow Duncan Cameron to harm the lass."

Relief flooded Crispen's expression and suddenly he looked extremely weary. He swayed in his chair and leaned over on Ewan's arm.

For a long moment, Ewan stared down at his son's head, resisting the urge to run his fingers through the unruly tresses. Ewan couldn't help but feel a surge of pride at the way Crispen had fought for the woman who'd saved him. According to Alaric, Crispen had bullied Alaric and his men the entire way back to the McCabe keep. And now he was bullying Ewan into keeping a promise Crispen had made in the McCabe name.

"He's asleep," Alaric murmured.

Ewan carefully ran his hand over his son's head and held him solidly against his side.

"Who is this woman, Alaric? What is she to Cameron?"

Alaric made a sound of frustration. "I wish I could tell you. The lass wouldn't say a word to me the entire time she was with me. She and Crispen were as tight-lipped as two monks with vows of silence. All I know is that when I found her, she was severely beaten. I've never seen a lass abused as she was. It turned my stomach, Ewan. There's no excuse for a man to ever treat a woman such as he did. And yet, as badly injured as she was, she took on me and my men when she thought we were a threat to Crispen."

"She said nothing the entire time she was with you? Let nothing slip? Think, Alaric. She had to have said something. It simply isn't a woman's nature to be silent for prolonged periods of time."

Alaric grunted. "Someone should tell her that. I'm telling you, Ewan, she said nothing. She stared at me like I was some kind of toad. Worse, she had Crispen acting like I was the enemy. The two whispered like conspirators and glared at me when I dared intervene."

Ewan frowned and drummed his fingers on the solid wood of the table. "What could Cameron want with her? Furthermore, what was a highland lass doing in a lowland abbey? Highlanders guard their daughters as jealously as gold. I can't see a daughter being packed off to an abbey days away."

"Unless the lass was being punished," Alaric pointed out. "Maybe she was caught out in an indiscretion. More than one lass has been wooed between the sheets outside the sanctity of marriage."

"Or maybe she was a difficult harridan her father despaired of," Ewan murmured, as he remembered how difficult and recalcitrant she'd been just moments ago. That scenario he could believe. But again, she would have had to have committed an egregious sin for a father to send her so far away.

Alaric chuckled. "She's spirited all right." Then he sobered. "But she protected Crispen well. She put her body between him and others more than once, and she suffered greatly for it."

Ewan mulled on that truth for a long moment. Then he looked up at Alaric again. "You saw these injuries?"

Alaric nodded. "I did. Ewan, the bastard kicked her. There were imprints of a boot on her back."

Ewan cursed, the sound echoing across the hall. "I wish I knew what her connection to Cameron was. And why he wants her badly enough to abduct her from an abbey and beat her senseless when she refused to marry him. Why he'd then think to use my son to sway her."

"It would have worked, too," Alaric said in a grim voice. "The lass is very protective of Crispen. If Cameron had threatened him, she would have consented. I'm positive of that."

"This presents a problem for me," Ewan said quietly. "Cameron wants her. My son wants me to protect her. The lass only wants to be gone. And then there is the mystery of who she is."

"If Cameron discovers her whereabouts, he'll come for her," Alaric warned.

Ewan nodded. "So he will."

The brothers' gazes met and held. Alaric nodded his acceptance of Ewan's silent declaration. If Cameron wanted a fight, the McCabes would be more than willing to give him one.

"What about the lass?" Alaric finally asked.

"I'll make that determination once I've heard the whole story from her," Ewan said.

He was confident that he could be a reasonable man, and once she saw how reasonable, she'd cooperate fully.

CHAPTER 5

Mairin awoke with the knowledge that she wasn't alone in the tiny chamber she'd been sleeping in. Her nape prickled and she carefully opened one eye to see Ewan McCabe standing in the doorway.

Sunlight peeked through the window, penetrating the gap in the furs. The light somehow made him more ominous than if he stood cloaked in darkness. In the light, she could see how big he was. He made a menacing portrait, framed by the doorway he barely fit through.

"Pardon the intrusion," Ewan said in a gruff voice. "I was trying to locate my son."

It was then, as she followed his gaze to the bundle beside her, that she realized Crispen had crawled into her bed during the night. He was snuggled firmly into her side, the covers pulled tight to his neck.

"I'm sorry. I didn't realize . . . ," she began.

"Since I tucked him into my bed last night, I'm sure you didn't realize," he said dryly. " 'Tis apparent he made the move during the night."

She started to move, but Ewan held up a hand. "Nay, don't wake him. I'm sure you both need your rest. I'll have Gertie hold the morning meal for you."

"T—Thank you."

She stared helplessly up at him, unsure of what to do

with his sudden kindness. Yesterday he'd been so fierce, his scowl had been enough to frighten a man out of his boots. After a short nod, he backed out of the room and closed the door behind him.

She frowned. She didn't trust such an about-face. Then she glanced down at the sleeping boy next to her, and her frown eased. Gently, she touched his hair, marveling at how the limp curls framed his face. In time, it would be as long as his father's.

Perhaps the laird had calmed in the face of his son's safe return. Maybe he was even feeling grateful and was sorry for his gruffness.

Hope tightened her chest. He might be more amenable to giving her a mount and supplies. She had no good idea where to flee, but given that Duncan Cameron appeared to be Ewan McCabe's sworn enemy, it wasn't a good idea for her to remain there.

Sadness tugged at her heart and she squeezed Crispen closer to her. The abbey that had been her home for so long, and the comforting presence of the sisters, was no longer available to her. She was without a home and safe harbor.

Closing her eyes, she whispered a fervent prayer for God's mercy and protection. Surely He would provide for her in her hour of need.

When she next awoke, Crispen was gone from her bed. She stretched and flexed her toes then immediately winced as pain snaked through her body. Even a hot bath and a comfortable bed hadn't completely rid her of her discomfort. Still, she could move considerably better than she had the day before, and she was certainly well enough to sit a horse on her own.

Throwing aside the furs, she braced her feet on the stone floor and flinched at the chill. She rose and went to the window to throw back the covering to allow the sunlight to stream in.

The rays slid over her like liquid amber. She closed her eyes and turned her face into the sun, eagerly soaking up the warmth.

It was a beautiful day as only a spring day in the highlands could be. She stared over the hillsides, basking in the comfort of seeing home for the first time in many long years. In truth, there'd been many days when she'd despaired of ever seeing heaven again. Neamh Álainn. Beautiful heaven. One day she'd gaze upon her legacy— her child's legacy. The only part of her father she'd ever have.

She curled her fingers into tight fists. "I will not fail," she whispered.

Not wanting to waste any more time above stairs, she donned the simple gown one of the serving women had left for her. The neckline was embroidered with a feminine chain of flowers, and in the middle, in green and gold, was what she assumed was the McCabe coat of arms. Glad to be wearing something other than Duncan Cameron's colors, she hurried toward the door.

When she neared the bottom of the stairs, she hesitated, feeling suddenly unsure of herself. She was saved from making an awkward entrance into the hall when one of the McCabe women saw her. The woman smiled and hurried over to greet her.

"Good afternoon. Are you feeling better today?"

Mairin winced. "Is it afternoon already? I didn't mean to sleep the day away."

"You needed the rest. You looked fair to dropping yesterday. My name is Christina, by the way. By what name do you call yourself?"

Mairin colored, feeling suddenly foolish. She wondered if she should make up a name, but she hated the idea of lying.

"I can't tell you," she murmured.

Christina's eyebrows shot up, but to her credit she didn't react further. Then she reached for Mairin's arm and tucked it into hers.

"Well then, lady, let's take you into the kitchens before Gertie feeds your meal to the hounds."

Feeling relieved that Christina hadn't pressed her, she allowed the girl to drag her into the kitchen where an older woman stood tending a fire in the pit. Mairin had expected a matronly woman, and why, she was't sure. Shouldn't women charged with the cooking be motherly?

Gertie was bone thin, and her gray hair was pulled into a tight knot at her nape. Strands escaped on all sides until they flew about her face, giving her a look of wildness. She pinned Mairin with a sharp glance that peeled back several layers of Mairin's skin.

"About time you got up and around, lass. No one stays abed here for that long unless they're dying. I don't expect you're dying since you're standing before me looking hale and hearty. Don't make a habit of it, or I won't hold the morning meal for you again."

Taken aback, Mairin's first instinct was to laugh, but she wasn't sure whether the other woman would take offense. Instead she folded her hands solemnly in front of her and promised never to do so again. A vow she felt comfortable making since she didn't plan to spend another night in the McCabe keep.

"Have a seat then. There's a stool in the corner. You can take your meal there. No sense messing up the table in the hall again for one person."

Mairin meekly obeyed and made quick work of the trencher of food. Gertie and Christina watched as she ate, and Mairin could hear them whispering when they thought Mairin wasn't looking.

"Wouldn't tell you her name?" Gertie exclaimed loudly.

She turned in Mairin's direction and uttered a *hmmph*. "When people won't give their name, 'tis because they have something to hide. What are you hiding, lass? Don't be thinking our laird won't find out. He's too precise to take such nonsense from a slip of a lass like yourself."

"Then I'll discuss the matter with your laird and only your laird," Mairin said firmly. She hoped that by injecting enough strength into her voice she'd make the other woman back down. Gertie just rolled her eyes and resumed tending her fire.

"Can you take me to him?" Mairin asked Christina as she rose from the stool. "I really must speak to him right away."

"Of course, Lady," Christina said in her sweet voice. "I was instructed to take you to him the moment you finished eating."

The food Mairin had just consumed swirled in her gut like sour ale.

"Are you nervous?" Christina asked as they descended the steps from the keep. "You have no reason to be. The laird seems gruff, and he can be stern when crossed, but he's fair and very evenhanded with our clan."

The part that Christina left out was that Mairin wasn't part of the McCabe clan, which meant that any policies about fair and evenhanded didn't apply. But she had saved Crispen, and it was obvious that the laird loved his son. She held on to that thought as they rounded the corner into the courtyard.

Mairin's eyes widened at the site of so many men training. The clash of swords and shields nearly deafened her, and the afternoon sun striking the metal made her squint and wince. She blinked and focused her gaze away from the reflections dancing through the air. When she realized what she was seeing instead, she gasped.

Her hand fluttered to her chest, and her vision went a

bit blurry. It wasn't until her tortured lungs begged for mercy that she realized she was holding her breath. She sucked in a mouthful of air, but that didn't help her light-headedness.

The laird was sparring with another soldier in only his boots and trews. His bare chest gleamed with a sheen of sweat, and a trickle of blood slid down his side.

Oh merciful heavens.

She watched in fascination, unable to make herself tear her gaze away, no matter that it was surely a sin to ogle in this fashion.

The laird was broad shouldered. His massive chest sported several scars. A man didn't get to be his age without acquiring battle scars. Badges of honor to highlanders. A man without them was considered weak and without courage.

His hair clung damply to his back and his braids swung about him as he pivoted in the dirt to parry another thrust by his opponent. His muscles strained and bulged as he swung the heavy sword about his head and slashed downward. At the last moment, his opponent threw up his shield, but he still buckled under the blow.

The younger man went sprawling, his own sword clattering to the ground. He did have the presence of mind to cover himself with the shield as he lay there panting softly.

The laird frowned but extended his hand down to the younger soldier. "You lasted longer this time, Heath, but you're still allowing emotion to rule your actions. Until you learn to control that temper of yours, you'll prove an easy mark in battle."

Heath scowled and didn't look appreciative of his laird's criticism. He ignored Ewan's outstretched hand and scrambled to his feet, his face red with anger.

It was then that the laird looked up and saw Mairin standing there with Christina. His eyes narrowed and she felt pinned by the force of his stare. He motioned for his tunic, which Alaric tossed to him from the side. After hastily pulling it over his bare chest, he motioned for Mairin to come forward.

Feeling strangely disappointed that he'd put the tunic back on, she edged closer, all but dragging her heels in the dirt. It was silly. She was a grown woman, but in front of this man, she felt like an errant child about to be called to task.

Guilty conscience. A good confession would clear that up.

"Come walk with me, lass. We have much to discuss."

She swallowed and snuck a peek at Christina, who performed a curtsy in the laird's direction before turning and heading back the way they'd come.

His teeth flashed into a grin. "Come," he said again. "I don't bite."

The flash of humor caught her unawares and she smiled broadly, quite unaware of its effect on the men who saw it.

"Very well, Laird. Since you've offered me such reassurance, I'll take the risk and accompany you."

They walked from the courtyard and took a path that led up the hillside that overlooked the loch. At the top, the laird stopped and stared out over the water.

"My son says I have much to thank you for."

She folded her hands in front of her, gathering a bit of the material of her gown in her fingers. "He's a good lad. He helped me as much as I helped him."

The laird nodded. "So he told me. He brought you to me."

Mairin didn't like the way he said the last. There was too much possession in his voice.

"Laird, I must depart today. If you cannot spare a horse, I understand. I'll leave on foot, though I would appreciate an escort to your border."

He turned to her with an uplifted eyebrow. "On foot? You wouldn't make it far, lass. You'd be tossed over someone's saddle and spirited away the moment you left my land."

She frowned. "Not if I'm careful."

"As careful as you were when you got yourself abducted by Duncan Cameron's men?"

Heat rose in her cheeks. "That's different. I wasn't expecting . . ."

Faint amusement glittered in his eyes. "Does anyone ever expect to be abducted?"

"Aye," she whispered.

"Tell me something, lass. You appear to be someone who firmly believes in a promise. I'd wager you expect people to remain true to their word."

"Oh aye," she said fervently.

"And you exacted a promise from my son, is this not so?"

She looked down. "Aye, I did."

"And you expect him to keep that promise, do you not?"

She squirmed uncomfortably but nodded even as guilt filled her.

"As it turns out, Crispen also exacted a promise from me."

"What promise?" she asked.

"To protect you."

"Oh."

She didn't know what to say to that. Somehow she had just maneuvered herself into a trap. She knew it.

"I'd say 'tis hard to protect a lass if she's out running all over the highlands on foot, wouldn't you say?"

She scowled, unhappy with the direction this conversation was headed.

"I release you from his promise," she declared.

He shook his head, a smile lifting the corners of his

mouth. Shocked, she stared transfixed at the change such a gesture wrought on his features. My, but he was quite handsome. Really handsome. And he looked younger, not as hardened, though she'd seen the scars, so she knew he was anything but soft. Nay, he was a warrior. There was no telling how many men he'd killed in battle. Why, he could probably snap someone's neck with his fingers. Certainly hers.

The thought had her reaching up to cover her throat.

"Only Crispen can release me from that promise, lass. As I'm sure he told you, a McCabe always keeps his word."

Glumly, she remembered Crispen saying just that. She also remembered his vow to her that his father would protect her. She'd been too bent on self-preservation to really give thought to what that meant.

"Are you saying I can't leave?" she whispered.

He seemed to consider her question for a moment, his gaze never straying from her. He stared until she squirmed under his scrutiny.

"If I knew you had a safe place to go, then of course I'd allow you to go. To your family perhaps?"

She wasn't going to lie and say she had family, so she said nothing at all.

The laird sighed. "Tell me your name, lass. Tell me why Duncan Cameron was so adamant that you marry him. I've promised Crispen I'd protect you, and I will, but I can't do so unless I have all the facts."

Oh dear, he was going to get all gruff again when she refused to obey his command. He'd been ready to throttle her the day before. A night's sleep probably hadn't tempered the desire, no matter how patient he seemed to be at the moment.

Instead of openly defying him as she'd done yesterday, she stood mute, hands still folded in front of her.

"You realize, I'll find out soon enough. It would be

better on you if you simply told me what I want to know now. I don't like to be kept waiting. I'm not a patient man. Particularly when those under my command defy me."

"I'm not under your command," she blurted before she could think better of it.

"The moment you stepped onto my land, you came under my command. My son's promise put you solidly under my care and protection. My promise to my son solidified that. You *will* obey me."

She raised her chin, staring directly into those piercing green eyes. "I survived at Duncan Cameron's hands. I'll survive at yours. You can't make me tell you anything. Beat me if you must, but I *will* not tell you what you want to know."

Outrage sparked in his eyes, and his mouth gaped open. "You think I'd beat you? Do you think me the same manner of man as Cameron?"

The fury in his voice had her stepping back. She'd struck a nerve, and anger rolled off the laird's shoulders in thunderous waves. He all but snarled his question at her.

"I did not intend any insult. I do not know what manner of man you are. I've only made your acquaintance for a short time, and you must admit, our meeting has been less than amicable."

The laird turned away, his hand going to his hair. She didn't know if he intended to pull it in frustration or to prevent himself from wrapping those fingers around her neck.

When he turned around, his eyes blazed with purpose, and he advanced on her, closing the distance between them. She took another rapid step back, but he was there, looming over her, bristling with outrage.

"Never, *never* have I treated man or woman in the manner Cameron treated you. Dogs are treated with better regard than that. *Never* make the mistake of comparing me with him."

"A—Aye, Laird."

He raised his hand, and it was all she could do not to flinch. How she stood so stoic, she didn't know, but it seemed important she didn't show fear that he'd strike her. Instead, he touched a strand of her hair that whispered down her cheek.

"No one will hurt you here. You will trust me."

"You can't command someone to trust you!"

"Aye, I can, and you will. I'm giving you until tomorrow to decide you trust me enough to tell me what I want to know. I am your laird, and you will obey me as everyone else here obeys me. Is that understood?"

"That . . . that's ridiculous," she sputtered, forgetting her fear of angering him further. "That's the most absurd thing I've ever heard."

She turned her back to him, telling him without words what she thought of his dictate. As she stomped away, she missed the amused smile that settled over Ewan's face.

CHAPTER 6

Mairin spent the afternoon studying the keep's defenses and looking for a possible escape route. The laird hadn't given her any choice in the matter. While she kept a sharp eye peeled to the goings-on around her, she also considered the matter of just where she would travel.

Duncan would scour the other abbeys. That was too obvious a choice to make. Her mother's people hailed from the western isles, but her mother had disassociated herself from her clan even before she'd become the king's mistress.

And truthfully, she couldn't count on them not knowing of Neamh Álainn. She'd find herself married off to the first man who had knowledge of her inheritance. She needed time. Time to consider the best course.

Mother Serenity had been working with Mairin to form a list of possible candidates for marriage. Mairin hadn't wanted a warrior, but she'd recognized the need to have one as her husband. From the moment she claimed her legacy, her husband would have to spend the rest of his life defending it from greedy, power-hungry men.

Wasn't that the way of the world, though? Only the strong survived, and the weak perished.

She frowned. Nay, that wasn't true. God protected the

weak. Perhaps that's why he made warriors, so they could protect women and children. Which meant Duncan Cameron could only be of the devil.

With a sigh, she planted her hands down on the sun-warmed ground, intending to push herself to her feet so she could return to her room to best plot her escape. Before she could fully rise, she saw Crispen running up the hillside, waving his hand to her.

She sank back to the ground and waited for him to catch up to her. His face split into a wide grin and he flopped onto the ground beside her.

"Are you feeling more yourself today?" he asked politely.

"I feel much better. I've been moving about to work out the soreness."

He snuggled into her side. "I'm glad. Did you speak to Papa?"

Mairin sighed. "I did."

Crispen beamed up at her. "I told you he would take care of everything."

"Indeed you did," she murmured.

"So are you staying?"

The hopeful expression on his face made her heart melt. She wrapped her arm around him and squeezed tight. "I can't stay, Crispen. You must know that. The are men besides Duncan Cameron who would me if they knew who I was."

Crispen's face crinkled until his nose twitched.

"'Tis complicated," she murmured. "I wis different, but Mother Serenity always told m to make the best with what we have."

"When will you leave and where will y see you again?"

Here she had to tread lightly. She Crispen running to his father with ne ture. Now that she'd made the decisi own, she didn't want the laird interfering with his demand to trust him. She nearly snorted at that notion. He might be able to command his clan to trust him, and she was sure it did, but a woman in her position couldn't afford to trust anyone.

"I don't know yet. Departures take planning."

He turned his chin up so that he was looking up into her eyes. "Will you tell me before you leave so I can say good-bye?"

Her heart ached at the idea of leaving the lad she'd grown so fond of over the past days. But she wouldn't lie and tell him she would when she knew well that she wouldn't be announcing her departure to anyone.

"I can't promise, Crispen. Perhaps we should say our good-byes now so that we're sure to say everything we want to say."

He rose up and flung his arms around her, nearly knocking her back to the ground.

"I love you," he said fiercely. "I don't want you to go."

She hugged him to her and pressed a kiss to the top of his head. "I love you, too, dearling. I'll always keep you close in my heart."

"Promise?"

She smiled. "That I can promise, and I do."

"Will you sit by me for the evening meal tonight?"

Since she didn't plan to leave until everyone else was abed, his request was reasonable enough. She nodded, and he beamed back at her.

A shout went up from the courtyard that Mairin and Crispen heard all the way up the hillside. She turned in the direction of the noise to see a procession of soldiers wearily parading over the bridge and into the keep.

Crispen launched himself from her hold and ran several steps before stopping. " 'Tis Uncle Caelen! He's back!"

"Of course you must go greet him," Mairin said

He ran back to her and grabbed her hand, attempting to pull her up. "You come, too."

She shook her head and pulled her hand away. "I'll just stay here. You go ahead. I'll be along in a little while."

The last thing she needed was to make the acquaintance of yet another McCabe brother. She shuddered. He was probably just as infuriating as Ewan and Alaric.

Ewan arrived to greet Caelen just as Caelen slid from his horse and strode in Ewan's direction.

"Is it true? Has Crispen been returned?" Caelen demanded.

"Aye, 'tis true. Alaric brought him home yesterday."

"Well, where is the little brat?"

Ewan smiled just as Crispen tore through the courtyard shouting "Uncle Caelen" at the top of his lungs. Caelen went white and staggered backward before righting himself and catching the mass of wiggling boy that hurled himself into Caelen's arms.

"God be praised," Caelen breathed. "You're alive."

Crispen threw his arms around Caelen's neck and hung on for dear life. "I'm sorry, Uncle Caelen. I didn't mean to frighten you and Papa. But don't worry, Mairin took good care of me."

Ewan's eyebrows went up. Beside him Alaric also took note of Crispen's slip.

Caelen scowled over Crispen's head at Ewan. "Who the hell is Mairin?"

Crispen went rigid in Caelen's arms, and then he struggled until Caelen finally put him down. He turned stricken eyes toward Ewan, torment in his gaze.

"Oh nay, Papa, I broke my promise. I broke it!"

Ewan reached for his son and squeezed his shoulder reassuringly. "You didn't mean to, son. If it'll make you feel better, I'll order Alaric and Caelen to forget it immediately."

"And you, Papa?" Crispen asked anxiously. "Will you forget it as well?"

Ewan suppressed a chuckle and then glanced at his brothers. "We will all three endeavor to forget."

"Will someone tell me what the blazes is going on?" Caelen demanded. "And does it have anything to do with the strange woman sitting on the hillside?"

Ewan followed Caelen's gaze to where Mairin sat on the hill that overlooked the keep. Trust Caelen to have immediately observed a stranger in the keep. He was exceedingly cautious about who gained access. A lesson learned the hard way.

"She's not staying," Crispen said unhappily.

Ewan turned sharply toward his son. "Why do you say that?"

"She said she couldn't."

"Ewan? Am I going to have to beat the information from you?" Caelen asked.

Ewan held up his hand to silence Caelen. "Did she say anything else, Crispen?"

Crispen frowned and opened his mouth but then shut it promptly again, his lips forming a tight, mutinous line. "I already broke my promise," he muttered. "I shouldn't say anything else."

Ewan sighed and shook his head. This whole bloody mess was enough to give him a giant ache in his temples. God save him from stubborn, secretive females. Worse, she'd completely won his son's heart, and she couldn't leave the keep fast enough.

He frowned at that thought. It wasn't as though he wanted her to stay. He didn't want Crispen hurt, but neither did he want the hassle of a difficult woman or the trouble she brought with her.

"Why don't you run along so I can properly welcome your uncle home. I have much I need to discuss with Caelen and Alaric."

Instead of looking offended, Crispen's eyes glimmered with relief. He turned and headed straight back up the hill toward where Mairin had sat. Only now she was gone. Ewan glanced around for the direction she'd taken, but she was nowhere to be seen.

"Mairin? Who the hell is Mairin and what does she have to do with Crispen? Furthermore, what is she doing *here*?"

Ewan jerked his thumb in Alaric's direction. "He brought her."

As expected, Alaric immediately denied his part in the whole mess. Ewan held back his laughter at the weariness in Alaric's voice.

Caelen was close to losing his patience, not that he had much, so Ewan told him everything he knew. Alaric filled in some of the information, and when they were done, Caelen looked at Ewan in disbelief.

"She would tell you nothing? And you allowed this?"

Ewan sighed. "What would you have me do, beat her as Cameron did? The lass will come around. I've given her until tomorrow to decide to trust me."

"And what will you do when she refuses tomorrow?" Alaric smirked.

"She won't refuse me."

"The important thing is we have Crispen back," Caelen said. "What the woman does or says is irrelevant. If Cameron comes looking for a fight, I'll be more than happy to give him one and then we'll send the woman on her way."

"Come, 'tis getting dark and Gertie will have dinner waiting. She doesn't like to serve a cold meal and well you know it," Ewan said. "Leave the matter of Mairin to me. The two of you needn't concern yourself over it."

"As if we'd want to," Caelen muttered, as he shouldered past Ewan.

CHAPTER 7

Mairin gathered her shawl closer around her body and crept over the crumbling wall of the stone skirt. She'd chosen the pathway closest to the loch because fewer guards were posted on that side. After all, an enemy could hardly come barging over the water to attack.

The spring air had a decided nip, and suddenly the decision to leave the warmth of her small chamber didn't seem so wonderful.

The evening repast had been a stressful event. She'd taken one look at the laird's youngest brother and thought better of her promise to sit next to Crispen at the table. He scowled at her, and it wasn't as if she hadn't been treated to scowls from the other McCabe brothers, but there was a darkness to Caelen's frown that unnerved her.

She'd uttered an excuse about not feeling well and had immediately retreated above stairs. Undaunted by her departure, Crispen brought a plate of food to her door, and the two of them had sat cross-legged in front of the fire to eat.

Afterward, she pleaded fatigue and sent Crispen on his way. And she waited. For hours she listened for the sounds of the keep to diminish. When she was sure everyone was abed, or at least safely ensconced in their quarters, she snuck down the stairs and out the entrance that faced the loch.

She breathed easier when she entered the shelter of the trees that divided part of the loch from the keep. Here she could move with relative obscurity and follow the loch until she was away.

A great splash startled her, and she turned in the direction of the water. She went still, holding her breath as she peered through the trees toward the inky black water. There was barely a moon this night, and only a slim light was cast onto the rippling surface.

It was enough for her to see that three men were taking a late swim. It was also enough for her to see *who* was taking the swim. Ewan McCabe and his brothers were diving into the loch, and God have mercy on her, they didn't have a stitch of clothing on.

She immediately covered her eyes with both hands, mortified beyond all measure that she'd just seen the backsides of three grown men. Were they mad? The loch had to be incredibly cold. She shivered at the mere thought of just how icy such a swim would be.

For several minutes she sat, hunkered down by a tree, hands covering her eyes until finally she eased them away only to see Ewan McCabe come walking from the water. Her eyes rounded in shock, and her hands hung limply at her sides as she stared, transfixed by the sight of a fully naked man. He stood, drying himself with a cloth, and each stroke only drew attention to his muscled body. And . . . And . . . she couldn't even bring herself to *think* about the area between his legs.

When she realized she was staring quite unabashedly at his . . . his . . . *manhood,* she promptly clapped both hands over her eyes again and sank her teeth into her bottom lip to stifle the squeak that threatened to spill out.

Her only hope was that they would finish their swim and go back to the keep. She couldn't risk moving about in the trees and attracting attention, but neither did she want to sit here staring immodestly.

Heat suffused her cheeks, and though she kept her eyes firmly covered, the image of Ewan McCabe without clothing burned through her mind with astonishing clarity. No matter what she did, she couldn't rid herself of the memory of him walking from the water—completely and utterly naked.

It would take at least three confessions to atone for this much sinning.

"You can look now. I assure you I am fully clothed."

The laird's dry voice slid with agonizing precision over her ears. Mortification billowed over her, and her cheeks grew so tight with humiliation that all she could think to do was sit there, hands still covering her eyes. Maybe if she wished really hard, when she opened her eyes, the laird would be far, far away.

"Not likely," came the amused reply.

She dropped one hand to her mouth, which is where it should have been all along so nothing stupid slipped out, like the fact that she'd just wished the laird to be a great distance away.

Now that she had one eye uncovered, she chanced a look at him to see that he was indeed clothed. With that established, she let her other hand slip down as she looked nervously at the laird.

He stood, legs apart, arms crossed over his chest, and, predictably, he was scowling.

"Want to tell me what you're doing skulking around in the dark?"

Her shoulders sagged. Apparently she couldn't even muster a good escape. How was she to know he and his brothers liked taking idiotic swims so late?

"Do I have to answer that?" she mumbled.

The laird sighed. "What part of me telling you that you weren't leaving my protection did you not understand? I don't take kindly to those under my authority blatantly disregarding my orders. If you were one of my soldiers, I'd kill you."

The last didn't sound like a boast. He didn't even say it with any flair, so she was sure it wasn't said to impress her. Nay, it was God's truth, and that served to scare her even more.

Some demon prompted her to deny his claim. "I'm not under your authority, Laird. I'm not sure how you came to that notion, but 'tis quite untrue. I'm not under anyone's authority, save God's and my own."

The laird smirked back at her, his teeth glinting in the low moonlight. "For a lass determined to make her own way, you've done a poor job of it."

She sniffed. "That's very uncharitable of you to say."

"It doesn't make it any less true. Now if we're done with this conversation, I suggest we return to the keep, preferably before my son vacates my chambers and goes to seek you out in yours. He seems to have a certain affinity for sleeping with you. I don't like to imagine his reaction when he finds your bed empty."

Oh, that was simply unfair, and the laird well knew it. He was manipulating her emotions and striving to make her feel guilt for leaving Crispen. She frowned sharply at him to let him know of her displeasure, but he ignored her and took her arm in his strong fingers.

She had no choice but to allow him to herd her back in the direction of the keep. He marched her around the stone skirt and through the courtyard where he paused to issue a sharp command to his guard that she was not to be allowed to escape again. Then he proceeded into the keep, and to her further dismay, insisted on escorting her all the way back to her chamber.

He opened her door and thrust her inside. Then he stood in the doorway, glaring ferociously at her.

"If you intend to intimidate me with mean looks, you're destined to fail," she said airily.

His eyes went heavenward for a moment, and she could swear he was counting under his breath. He took a second, as if trying to collect his flagging patience, which amused her, considering he didn't seem to possess any.

"If I have to bar the door, I will. I can be a very accommodating man, lass, but you've sorely tried my will. I've given you until tomorrow to trust me with whatever you're hiding. After that, I can promise you won't like my hospitality any longer."

"I don't like it now," she said crossly. She waved her hand in his direction. "You can leave. I'll only be going to bed now."

His jaw ticked, and his fingers flexed at his sides. She wondered if he was imagining those fingers around her neck. He looked to be contemplating such a thing right that very moment.

Then, as if to contradict her command, he stalked forward until he loomed forbiddingly over her. His jaw still twitched, and his eyes narrowed as he stared down at her.

He touched his fingertip to the end of her nose. "You don't make the rules here, lass. I do. It would be in your best interests to remember that."

She swallowed, suddenly very overwhelmed by the sheer size of him. "I will endeavor to remember."

The laird gave a short nod then turned on his heel and left the room, slamming the door with a bang.

Mairin flopped onto the straw mattress and sighed in disgust. *That* had not gone the way she intended. She was supposed to be well away from McCabe land by now, or at the very least to the border. Her plan had been to venture north, because there was nothing for her to the south.

Now she was stuck in the keep with an overbearing laird who thought he could command her trust as easily as he commanded his soldiers. He'd find out on the morrow that she wasn't so easily bent to another's will.

CHAPTER 8

"Laird! Laird!"

Ewan frowned and looked up from the table to see Maddie McCabe rush into the room, her face flushed with exertion.

"What is it, Maddie? I'm in talks here."

Maddie ignored the reprimand and stopped just a few feet away. She was so agitated, she wrung her hands.

"With your permission, Laird, there is something I must tell you." She glanced surreptitiously around and then confided in a low whisper, "Privately, Laird. 'Tis very important!"

An ache began in Ewan's temples. So far, the morning had been filled with dramatics. The evening before as well, as he remembered his encounter with Mairin. The lass hadn't showed herself as of yet, and he was sure she was being purposely difficult. As soon as he was finished with Alaric and Caelen, he planned to confront her and tell her that her time was up.

Ewan raised his hand and gestured for his men to leave. He caught Alaric's and Caelen's gazes and nodded for them to stay. Anything Maddie had to say could be said in front of them.

As soon as the rest of his soldiers filed out, Ewan returned his attention to Maddie.

"Now, what is so important that you'd interrupt a meeting with my men?"

" 'Tis the lass," she began, and Ewan groaned.

"What now? Has she refused to eat? Has she threatened to throw herself from her window? Or perhaps she's disappeared?"

Maddie sent him a puzzled look. "Of course not, Laird. She's above stairs in her chamber. I brought her morning meal myself."

"Then what about her?" Ewan growled.

Maddie let out a breath as if she'd run the entire way. "May I sit, Laird? For truly, 'tis not a short tale I'll be telling you."

Caelen rolled his eyes while Alaric looked bored. Ewan gestured her to sit.

She settled down and pressed her hands into a single fist before setting it on the table before her.

"The lass is Mairin Stuart."

She dropped the announcement as if she expected Ewan to react in some way.

"I know the lass's name is Mairin. I hadn't known her family name, but 'tis a common enough name in the highlands. The question is how did you gain this information? She's refused to tell anyone who she is. If Crispen hadn't let it slip, I wouldn't have known myself."

"Nay, she didn't tell me. I knew, you see?"

"Nay, I don't see. Perhaps you better tell me," Ewan said patiently.

"When I went up to bring her meal, I came in on her dressing. It was all quite awkward, and I apologized of course, but before she covered herself, I saw the mark."

Maddie's voice rose again and she sat forward, her eyes gleaming with excitement.

Ewan stared expectantly at her, waiting for her to continue. Lord, but the woman did love a good story. His brothers sat back, resigned to Maddie's colorful retelling.

"The lass is *Mairin Stuart*," she said again. "She bears the royal crest of Alexander. I saw it, branded on her leg. She's the heir to Neamh Álainn."

Ewan shook his head. "That's a bunch of nonsense, Maddie. 'Tis naught but a legend circulated on the tongues of bards."

"What legend?" Alaric asked as he sat forward. "I've heard of no such legend."

"That's because you never listen to bards," Caelen said dryly. "You're much too busy during festive times tossing up the skirts of some wench."

"And you listen to these poets and singers?" Alaric mocked.

Caelen shrugged. "'Tis a good way to keep abreast of the current gossip."

Maddie's eyes gleamed as she turned her attention to Alaric. "The story goes that King Alexander had a child after his marriage to Sybilla, a daughter. And that at her birth, he had his royal crest branded on her thigh so that her identity could never be questioned. Later, he bequeathed Neamh Álainn to her firstborn child." She leaned forward and whispered, "'Tis said, he did so so that she would be sure to secure a good marriage since she was a bastard born child and her mother was baseborn."

Alaric snorted. "'Tis a well-known fact that Alexander never sired a daughter. He had no legitimate children and only one bastard son. Malcolm."

"He *did* sire a daughter. A daughter named Mairin Stuart. And she's just above stairs in her chamber," Maddie insisted. "I'm telling you I saw the mark. I am not mistaken in this."

Ewan remained silent as he mulled Maddie's remarks and those of his brothers. He wasn't entirely sure he believed any of this nonsense, but it would certainly explain why Duncan Cameron was so determined to marry the lass, and it would also explain why she was desperate to escape.

"Why not just acknowledge the lass?" Alaric argued. "A bastard of the king would have no trouble securing a sound marriage. Any number of men would line up, if for no other reason than to seek favor with the crown."

"He didn't want anyone to know," Maddie said. "I can remember some years ago hearing the whispers that circulated. Alexander waited a full five years before making his bequest to the lass. He valued his marriage to Sybilla, and Malcolm was born *before* their marriage. It isn't known how he explained the bequest, but soon after his death, rumors began going around about the existence of the lass."

"With Malcolm still imprisoned, the existence of another descendent of Alexander could brew support for Malcolm's followers," Ewan said thoughtfully. "It could, in fact, be a large reason for Cameron's determination to wed her. Taking over her inheritance would give him more power than he currently wields. Much more power. Scotland could be at war again, and David would face a renewed threat. With Alexander having sired not one, but two possible contenders to the throne, David's position would be weakened. He can't afford another lengthy war that will only divide Scotland once again."

"A bastard cannot inherit," Caelen reminded him. "This would never be accepted."

"Think, Caelen. If Duncan Cameron had control of Neamh Álainn, he would be unstoppable. It would matter not the circumstances of Alexander's children's births. With that kind of wealth and power, if Cameron chose to ally himself with Malcolm, either could seize power."

"Are you saying you believe this rubbish?" Alaric asked in astonishment.

"I'm not saying anything. Yet," Ewan said calmly.

"Don't you see, Laird?" Maddie burst in, excitement bubbling into her voice. "She's the answer to our prayers. If *you* marry the lass, then your heir would inherit Neamh Álainn. 'Tis said she brings a rich dowry to her marriage in addition to the bequest of the lands for her firstborn."

"Marry her?"

The question was all but shouted by all three brothers. Ewan's mouth gaped open, and he stared at Maddie in astonishment.

Maddie nodded emphatically. "You have to admit, 'tis a sound plan. If you marry her, Duncan Cameron very well can't."

"There is that," Caelen pointed out.

Alaric turned to Caelen, his expression questioning. "Now you're going along with this madness?"

Ewan held up his hand to silence them. The throbbing in his head had escalated to a full-blown ache. He leveled a stare at Maddie, who had been listening to everything with rapt attention.

"You may go now, Maddie. I fully expect that everything that has been said here will remain strictly confidential. If gossip gets about the keep, I'll know where it originated."

Maddie rose and dropped a curtsy. "Of course, Laird."

She hurried off and then Ewan turned to his brothers.

"Tell me you aren't considering this madness," Alaric cut in before Ewan could get a word out.

"What madness do you think I'm considering?" Ewan asked mildly.

"Marriage. Believing that the lass is the bastard daughter of Alexander, which makes her the niece of our current king. Not to mention half sister of the man who spent ten years trying to usurp David from the throne. And would do so again given the least opportunity."

"What I believe is that the lass and I are due for a long conversation. I intend to see this mark for myself. Given the relationship between our father and Alexander, I've seen his royal seal on more than one occasion. I'd know if the mark on her leg is the true one."

Caelen snorted. "And you think she's going to lift her skirts for you to see this brand? She's more likely to knee you in the testicles for the offense."

"I can be persuasive when the situation calls for it," Ewan drawled.

"This, I'd love to see," Alaric said.

Ewan raised his eyebrows. "You'll see nothing of the sort. If I catch you even looking like you want a glimpse under Mairin Stuart's skirts, I'll pin you to the wall with my broadsword."

Alaric raised his hands in defense. "Forget I said anything. You're awfully touchy about a lass you claim annoys you to no end."

"If the lass is who Maddie says she is, I aim to marry her," Ewan said grimly. "Our clan needs the coin her dowry would provide."

Simultaneously, his brothers' mouths dropped. Caelen cursed loudly and Alaric shook his head and sent his eyes heavenward.

"Think about what you're saying," Caelen said.

"I believe I'm the only one who *is* thinking," Ewan returned. "If 'tis true that her firstborn inherits Neamh Álainn, think about what this would mean for our clan. We would control the choicest lands in the whole of Scotland. No longer would we sit here dreaming about the day we take our revenge on Duncan Cameron. We would decimate him and his name. He would be obliterated from history. Our name would be avenged. The

McCabe clan would be second only to the king. No one, and I mean no one, would ever have the power to destroy us as Duncan Cameron nearly did eight years ago."

His fist came down on the table, and his entire body trembled with rage.

"I made a vow on our father's grave that I would not rest until our clan was restored to its full glory and that I would make Duncan Cameron pay for his crimes against us."

Caelen's face went cold, and Ewan could see the pain flare to light in his brother's eyes. But he nodded, his lips set into a fine line. "In this we agree."

"Neamh Álainn lies to the north with only McDonald between us. If we form a strong alliance with him, we would control a vast portion of this region."

Excitement stirred in Ewan's veins as the plans of the last eight years came to life in his mind. Finally he saw a way to fulfill his vow to his father.

"The lass is courageous and she's fiercely protective of Crispen. She'd make him a fine mother, as well as the rest of the sons she'd bear me. In return, I'd give her my protection, and she'd never have to worry about Duncan Cameron again."

"It isn't us you have to convince," Alaric said with a twist of his lips. "'Tis the lass you have to persuade. Caelen and I stand beside you always. You well know that. My loyalty is to you. Always. It extends to the woman you marry, no matter who she may be. She *is* a very courageous lass. I saw that for myself. And if she brings with her a dowry like Neamh Álainn, then I see no downside in marrying her."

Caelen nodded, but he said nothing about Mairin. Ewan didn't expect him to. It would surprise Ewan greatly if Caelen ever allowed himself to trust another woman again. If he ever sought to breed sons, Ewan felt pity for the woman Caelen would marry. Once, Caelen had given himself unreservedly. The folly of youth. He'd vowed never to do so again.

Ewan put his hands down on the table and pushed himself to his feet. "It would appear I have much to discuss with Mairin Stuart. Alaric, I want you to send out an escort for Father McElroy. He's up at the McDonalds' administering last rites to one of their sick. I'll need him here to perform the wedding. If the lass is who Maddie says she is, I don't want to delay. We'll marry immediately."

CHAPTER 9

Ewan stopped outside Mairin's chamber and smiled at the proximity to his own private quarters. She probably wouldn't be pleased if she knew how close he'd placed her. He knocked to be polite, but he didn't wait for her answering summons before opening the door and entering the chamber.

Mairin whirled from her position at the window, her unbound hair flying about her shoulders. The furs were pulled aside to allow the sun to shine in, and she posed an enchanting portrait with the light reflecting the brilliant hue of her eyes.

Aye, she was indeed a bonnie lass, and it would be no hardship to marry her and get her with child. In fact, now that he'd decided on a course of action, he looked forward to the prospect of Mairin in his bed.

She looked indignant over his intrusion, but before she could launch the reprimand he was sure was forthcoming, he held up a hand. The lass had no respect for his authority over her, but that was a matter that would quickly change. When she was his wife, he'd take great delight in advising her of her duty to him and, most important, her obligation to obey him without question.

"Will you tell me now what it is I want to know?" he asked. To be fair—and he was a fair man—he wanted to give her the opportunity to confide her identity before he related his own knowledge.

She thrust her chin upward in the show of defiance he now expected from her and shook her head. "Nay. I will not. You cannot order me to trust you. Why that's the most ridiculous thing I've ever heard."

He sensed she was warming up for a full-length diatribe, so he did the one thing he knew would silence her.

He rapidly closed the distance between them, curled his hands around her upper arms, and hauled her upward. His lips found hers in a heated rush, her gasp of outrage swallowed up by his mouth.

She went rigid against him, her hands shoving between them in an attempt to push him away. He brushed his tongue over her lips, tasting her sweetness, demanding entrance into her mouth.

Her second gasp came out more as a sigh. Her lips parted and she melted into his chest like warm honey. She was soft all over, and she fit him like his sword fit his hand. Perfectly.

He pushed inward, sliding his tongue over hers. She went rigid again, and her fingers curled into his chest like tiny daggers. He closed his eyes and imagined them digging into his back as he thrust between her thighs.

Lord, but she was sweet. Nay, bedding her would be no hardship at all. The image of her swollen with his child flickered through his mind, and he found himself very pleased with the image. Very pleased indeed.

When he finally pulled away, her eyes were glazed, her lips deliciously swollen, and she swayed like a sapling in the wind.

She blinked several times and then frowned sharply. "Why did you do that?"

"It was the only way to silence you."

She bristled with outrage. "Silence me? You took liberties with my . . . my . . . my lips in order to silence me?

That was very impertinent of you, Laird. I won't allow you to do it again."

He smiled and folded his arms over his chest. "Aye, you will."

Her mouth gaped open in astonishment and then worked up and down as she struggled to speak. "I assure you I won't."

"I assure you that you will."

She stamped her foot, and he stifled his laughter at the fury in her eyes. "You've gone daft! Is this some trick? An attempt to seduce me into telling you who I am?"

"Not at all, Mairin Stuart."

She recoiled in shock. If he had any doubts about the validity of Maddie's claims, he didn't now. Mairin's reaction was too genuine. She was utterly horrified that he knew the truth.

She quickly came to the same realization that she'd given herself away, because she didn't attempt to deny it. Tears welled in her eyes and she turned away, her fist going to her mouth.

An uncomfortable sensation knotted his chest. The sight of her distress unsettled him. The lass had suffered enough, and now she looked as though she was utterly defeated. The light had vanished from her eyes the moment he'd uttered her name.

"Mairin," he began and gently touched her shoulder. She trembled underneath his touch, and he realized she shook with quiet sobs. "Lass, don't cry. 'Tis not as bad as that."

"Nay?" She sniffed and shrugged away from his hand, moving closer to the window again. She bowed her head and her hair fell over her face, obscuring it from his view.

He wasn't any good with tears. They discomfited him. He was much more comfortable when he was inciting her anger. So he did the one thing he knew would infuriate her. He ordered her to stop crying.

As predicted, she turned on him, spitting like a cornered kitten.

"I'll cry if I want to. You will cease ordering me about!"

He raised an eyebrow. "You dare to issue *me* orders?"

She flushed, but at least she wasn't crying any longer.

"Now tell me about this brand on your thigh. Your father's crest. I'd like to see it."

She went crimson and she backed up a step until her back met with the ledge of the window. "I will not do something so indecent as to show you my leg!"

"When we're married, I'll see more than that," he said mildly.

"Married? *Married*? I'm not marrying you, Laird. I'm not marrying anyone. Not yet anyway."

It was the *yet* that intrigued Ewan. Clearly the lass hadn't totally discounted the notion of marriage, and she seemed levelheaded enough, so she had to realize the importance of marrying. She could hardly bear an heir to Neamh Álainn if she never married.

He sat on the bed and stretched his legs outward. This might take awhile, and he might as well be comfortable.

"Tell me why not *yet*. Surely you've given thought to marriage."

"Aye, I've given it thought. I've thought about little else over the years," she blurted out. "Have you any idea how the last ten years have been for me? Living in fear, having to hide from men who'd force me to their will so that they'd gain from their marriage to me. Men who would plant their seed in my belly and discard me the moment I gave birth.

"I was but a child when I was forced into hiding. A *child*. I needed time to formulate a plan. Mother Serenity suggested I find a man, a warrior, with the strength to protect my heritage, but also a man with honor. Someone who would treat me well," she whispered. "A man who would cherish the gift I would bring to our marriage. And me."

He was struck by the vulnerability in her voice. The dreams of a young woman sounded strong in the tale she spun. It wasn't practical, but when he looked at her, he understood that she'd been desperate and afraid, and she'd clung to the hope of finding such a man among all the ones who'd do just as she said. Marry her, impregnate her, and discard her when she no longer served a purpose.

He sighed. She wanted to be loved and cherished. He couldn't offer her those things, but he could offer her his protection and his regard. It was far more than Duncan Cameron would give her.

"I'll never hurt you, lass. You'll have the respect due you as wife to the laird of the McCabe clan. I'll protect you and any child you bear me. You wanted a man who had the strength to defend your legacy. I'm that man."

She turned wounded eyes on him, skepticism bright in her gaze. "Not to offer insult, Laird, but your keep is crumbling around your ears. If you can't defend your own, how can you expect to defend a holding such as Neamh Álainn?"

He stiffened at the insult, intended or not.

"You cannot be angry over such an observation," she rushed to say. "'Tis my right to question the qualifications of the man I would marry and in whose hands I would place my life."

"I have spent the last eight years fortifying my troops. There is not a larger, better-trained force in all of Scotland."

"If that is correct, why then does your keep look as if it has sustained crippling damage in a battle?"

"It did," he said bluntly. "Eight years ago. Since then

my focus has been on keeping my clan fed and my men trained. Repairs to the keep have been a much lower priority."

"I had not desired to marry anyone yet," she said in a mournful voice.

"Aye, I can understand that. But it seems you no longer have a choice. You've been discovered, lass. If you think Duncan Cameron will give up when a holding such as Neamh Álainn is at stake, you're daft."

"There's no need to be insulting," she snapped. "I'm not daft."

He shrugged, growing impatient with the direction of the conversation. "The way I see it, you have two choices. Duncan Cameron. Or me."

She paled and twisted her hands in agitation.

"Perhaps you should give it some thought. The priest should arrive within two days. I'll expect an answer by then."

Ignoring the dazed look in her eyes, he turned and walked from the chamber. He paused at the door and turned to pin her with a stare.

"Don't think to try to escape again. You'll find I have no patience for chasing disobedient lasses all over my lands."

CHAPTER 10

Marry the laird. Mairin paced the interior of her chamber until she thought she might go mad. She stopped at the window and stared out, inhaling the soothing spring air. It was a warm afternoon with only a gentle bite of a chill.

Making a decision, she gathered her shawl and hurried from the room. No sooner had she stepped from the keep than one of the McCabe warriors fell into step beside her. She peeked cautiously up at him and remembered that he'd been one of the men with Alaric the day they'd found her and Crispen. She searched her memory for his name, but the whole event had been one big blur to her.

She smiled, thinking he only wanted to offer her greeting, but he continued in step with her as she rounded the corner of the keep and headed in the direction of the hole in the skirt.

Before she could lift her dress hem and climb over the crumbling rock face, the soldier gallantly took her hand and assisted her over the side.

She stopped and he nearly bumped into her, so close was he following behind. She whirled around and tilted her neck so she could look him in the eyes.

"Why are you following me?"

"Laird's orders, my lady. 'Tis unsafe for you to walk about the keep unescorted. I am charged with your protection when the laird himself is not with you."

She snorted and put one hand on her hip. "He fears me escaping again and you've been put to the task of making sure that doesn't happen."

The soldier didn't so much as blink.

"I have no intention of leaving the keep. The laird has informed me of the consequences of such an action. I'm merely out for a walk and a bit of fresh air, so there's no reason for you to leave your other duties to escort me."

"My only duty is to your safety," he said solemnly.

She gave a disgruntled sigh. She was sure the laird's men were every bit as thickheaded and stubborn as he was. It was probably a requirement.

"Very well. By what name are you called?"

"Gannon, my lady."

"Tell me, Gannon, are you my permanent watch guard?"

"I share the duty with Cormac and Diormid. Next to his brothers, we are the laird's most senior men."

She picked her way over the stones protruding from the ground as she made her way up the hillside toward the grazing sheep.

"I can't imagine that's a duty any of you would welcome," she said wryly.

"'Tis an honor," Gannon said gravely. "The laird's confidence is great. He wouldn't entrust the safety of the mistress of the keep to just any of his soldiers."

She stopped and whirled around, clamping her lips shut to prevent the shriek from escaping. "I am not the mistress of this keep!"

"You will be in two days' time, just as soon as the priest arrives."

She closed her eyes and shook her head. She'd never

been a drinker of spirits, but right now an entire tub of ale would be welcome.

"The laird does you a great honor," Gannon said, as if sensing her disquiet.

"I'm thinking 'tis the other way around," Mairin muttered.

"Mairin! Mairin!"

She turned to see Crispen running up the hill as fast as his legs would carry him. He shouted her name the entire way and nearly knocked her off her feet when he crashed into her. Only Gannon's steadying hand prevented her fall.

"Careful, lad," Gannon said with a smile. "You'll knock the lass over if you aren't careful."

"Mairin, is it true? Is it true?"

Crispen positively wiggled in his excitement. His eyes shone like twin stars and he clutched at her arms, alternately hugging and squeezing her.

She grasped his shoulders and carefully pried him away from her. "Is what true, Crispen?"

"You're marrying Papa? You'll be my mother?"

Anger descended with breathtaking speed. How could he? How could the laird do this to Crispen? It would break his heart if she denied it. The laird's manipulation shocked her. She'd thought him more honorable than that. Arrogant, aye. Even determined and focused. But she hadn't imagined him acting so deceitful and stirring the emotions of a young child.

Furious, she rounded on Gannon. "Take me to the laird."

"But, my lady, he's with the men. He's never to be disturbed during training unless 'tis a matter of great urgency."

She advanced on him, thrusting her finger into his chest. She accentuated her words by poking him. He was forced to take a step backward, his gaze wary.

"You will take me to him at once or I'll turn this entire keep upside down to find him. Believe me when I say, this *is* a matter of life and death. *His* life and death!"

When she saw the determined denial in Gannon's eyes, she threw up her hands, let out a huge sigh of exasperation, and turned to head down the hill. She'd find the laird herself. If he was training with his men, it meant he was in the courtyard where such training took place.

Remembering Crispen, and that she had no wish for him to hear what it was she had to say to the laird, she turned and pointed her finger sharply at Gannon.

"You keep Crispen with you. Do you hear?"

His mouth gaped open at her command, and he stared alternately at her and at Crispen as if unsure what to do. He finally bent down, said something to Crispen, then pushed him in the direction of the sheep herder.

Mairin turned and stomped down the hill, angrier with each step. She nearly tripped over a rock and fell flat on her face, but Gannon caught her elbow.

"Slow down, my lady. You're going to injure yourself!"

"Not myself," she muttered. "Your laird, more likely."

"Pardon? I'm sorry. I didn't hear you."

She bared her teeth and shrugged out of his grasp. She blazed around the corner of the keep and into the courtyard. The heavy clang of swords, mixed swear words, and the smell of sweat and blood rose sharp in her ears and nose. She surveyed the mass of training men until she finally found the source of her fury.

Before Gannon could stop her, she waded into the fray, her gaze focused solely on the laird. Around her, shouts went up. She thought one man fell as she passed, but she couldn't be sure because she didn't pause in her quest.

Halfway there, the laird stopped his activity and

turned to stare. When he saw her, his brow creased and he scowled. Not just his usual show of displeasure. He was furious. Well, that was fine, because so was she.

Only when she stopped barely a foot in front of the laird did Gannon catch up to her. He was out of breath and looking at the laird like he feared for his life.

"Your pardon, Laird. I couldn't stop her. She was determined—"

The laird's angry gaze found Gannon and he arched an eyebrow in blatant disbelief. "You couldn't stop one slip of a lass from marching across a courtyard where any one of my men could have killed her?"

Mairin snorted in disbelief but when she turned so she could survey the men who were now all standing in silence, she swallowed. Each carried a weapon, and if she'd stopped to think about it at the time, she'd have realized that going around the perimeter would have been a much better idea.

They were all scowling at her, proving her theory that the laird demanded surliness and pigheadedness from his men.

Determined to show no remorse for her mistake, she turned back to the laird and pinned him with the full force of her glare. He might be angry, but she was far more so.

"I have not given you an answer, Laird," she all but yelled. "How could you? How could you do something so . . . so . . . underhanded and dishonorable?"

The scowl on his face morphed into an expression of complete astonishment. He gaped at her with such incredulity that she wondered if he'd perhaps misunderstood. So she hastened to inform him of precisely what she was so furious about.

"You told your son that I was going to be his mother." She walked up to him, stabbing her finger into his chest. "You gave me two days. Until the priest arrived. Two days to make my decision, and yet you inform the entire keep that I'm going to be the new mistress." By then, she was beating him solidly with her hand.

The laird glanced down at her fingers as if he were about to shoo an annoying insect. Then he looked back at her, his eyes so icy that she shivered.

"Are you quite finished?" he demanded.

She took a step back, the initial rush of her fury subsiding. Now that she'd vented her rage, the reality of what she'd done slapped her full in the face.

He advanced, giving her no opportunity to put any distance between them.

"Don't you ever, *ever* question my honor. If you were a man, you'd already be dead. As it is, if you ever speak to me as you've done just now, I can guarantee you that you will not like the consequences. You are on my lands, and my word here is the law. You are under my protection. You will obey me without question."

"Not bloody likely," she muttered.

"*What*? What did you say?" He roared the question at her.

She glanced serenely up at him, a bland smile on her face. "Nothing, Laird. Nothing at all."

His gaze narrowed and she could see his hands twitching again like he'd love nothing more than to throttle her. She was beginning to think it was an affliction of his. Did he go around wanting to choke the life out of everyone or was she special in that regard?

"I'm afraid 'tis an urge that is entirely original to you," the laird barked.

She clamped her mouth shut and closed her eyes. Mother Serenity had vowed one day Mairin would regret her propensity to blurt out her least little thought. Today just might be that day.

By now the scowls of his men had been replaced with looks of open amusement. She didn't appreciate being the source of that amusement so she gave them a scowl of her own. It only served to make them twitch more as they battled their mirth.

"I will say this but once," the laird said in a menacing voice. "I have spoken of our prospective marriage to no one save the men I sent to escort Father McElroy back to my lands and those I charged with your protection. I would give the priest a reason for ushering him here with such haste. You, however, have now broadcast our impending nuptials to my entire clan."

She glanced uneasily around to see that quite a crowd had gathered. They stared upon her and the laird with undisguised interest. Indeed, they were hanging on every word.

She pinched her lips into a bow and stared unflinchingly up at the laird, who was still bristling with outrage.

"Then how does your son know? And why do I have an escort who informs me his duty is to see to the mistress of the keep?"

"Are you accusing me of speaking an untruth?"

His voice was deathly quiet, so low that no one save her could hear, but the tone sent a surge of fear straight to her toes.

"Nay," she said hastily. "I would merely like to know how so many people know of a marriage that may or may not take place if you've told no one."

His eyes narrowed. "First, the marriage *will* take place. Just as soon as you've regained your senses and realize that 'tis the only sensible option left to you."

When she would have opened her mouth to dispute his assertion, he shocked her by clamping his hand over her mouth.

"You will be silent and allow me to finish. I have doubts that you've ever been able to hold your silence for more than a moment in your entire lifetime," he grumbled.

She huffed but his hand tightened on her mouth.

"I can only assume that my son overheard me speaking to my men of our marriage. If you would have but cautioned him to hold his tongue, he would not have repeated it beyond his question to you. But now, you've announced our marriage to the entire clan. Some might even consider it a proposal. In which case, I accept."

He finished with a grin and then stepped back, releasing his hold on her mouth.

"Why . . . you . . . ," she sputtered. She worked her mouth up and down but nothing would come out.

A cheer went up from the crowd assembled.

"A wedding!"

Congratulations were shouted. Swords were raised. Men beat on the backs of their shields with the hilts of their swords. Mairin winced from the noise level and stared helplessly up at the laird. He stared back, arms crossed over his chest, a satisfied smile carving his too-handsome face.

"I did not ask you to marry me!"

He was undaunted by her vehemence. "'Tis customary to seal a betrothal with a kiss."

Before she could tell him what she thought of that daft idea, he hauled her against him. She hit his chest and would have bounced off if he hadn't held her firmly in place.

"Open your mouth," he demanded in a husky voice that sounded oddly tender given his degree of anger.

Her lips parted and he slid his tongue sensuously over hers. Her senses scattered in the wind. For a moment she quite forgot everything but the fact that he was kissing her and he had his tongue inside her mouth. Again.

And he'd just announced to his clan that they were marrying. Or maybe she had. Realizing that the longer he kissed her in front of God and everyone, the harder a time she'd have denying his claim, she gave him a mighty

shove and nearly fell on her behind. To her mortification, Gannon caught her and held her up while she
swiped at her mouth with the back of her arm.

Oh, but the laird looked smug now. He had a satisfied
grin on his face as he watched her and waited.

"Kiss? I won't kiss you. I want to hit you!"

She spun around and fled. The laird's laughter followed her the entire way.

"Too late, lass! I already kissed you."

Back in her chamber, which she should have never
left, Mairin resumed her pacing in front of the window.
The man was impossible. He would drive her daft inside
a day. He was controlling, overbearing. Arrogant.
Handsome. And he kissed like a dream.

She groaned and smacked a hand to her forehead. He
didn't kiss like a dream. He did it all wrong anyway. She
was quite certain Mother Serenity had never said anything about tongues when kissing. Mother Serenity had
been quite descriptive in her talks with Mairin. She
hadn't wanted her to go ignorant to her marriage bed,
and above all things, Mairin would one day marry.

But tongues? Nay, Mother Serenity had nothing to say
on the matter of tongues. Mairin would have remembered such a thing, surely.

Mairin had assumed that the first time the laird had
kissed her it was an aberration. A mistake. After all, her
mouth had been open. It stood to chance his tongue
might slip inside if he, too, had his mouth open.

She frowned at the thought. Could Mother Serenity
have been mistaken? Surely not. She was knowledgeable
about all things. Mairin trusted her implicitly.

But the second time? It was no coincidence, because
this time he'd commanded her to open her mouth, and
like a simpleton, she'd gaped her mouth open and let
him slide his tongue over hers.

Just the memory had her shivering. It was . . .

It was undignified. That's what it was. And she'd tell him so if he ever tried to do it again.

Feeling marginally better now that she had that matter squared away, she turned her thoughts to the pressing issue of marriage. Hers.

It was true that the laird filled a lot of the criteria that she and Mother Serenity had come up with. He was undoubtedly strong. He seemed awfully possessive of those he considered under his protection. It was true he had a large army. One had only to look at the numbers in the courtyard and how hard they trained.

The marriage would be equally, if not more, beneficial to him. Aye, she'd have his protection, and he had the might to defend a holding such as Neamh Álainn, but he gained wealth and land that was rivaled only by that of the king.

Did she trust him to hold such power?

She hadn't meant to impugn his honor. She'd been angry, but she didn't really believe that he was a dishonorable man. If she did, she'd be trying a lot harder to escape. Nay, she was giving serious consideration to his proposal. Or her proposal. Or whoever had issued it.

She hadn't come into contact with many men in her lifetime. Only at an early age before she'd been taken to the abbey in the middle of the night and sequestered there for many years. But she remembered the fear and the absolute knowledge that her life would be immeasurably changed if she fell into the wrong hands.

She didn't feel that fear with Ewan McCabe. Oh, she feared him, but she didn't fear mistreatment from him. He'd had ample opportunity—and desire—to strangle her, and yet he'd held his temper each time. Even when he wasn't convinced of her role in his son's abduction and rescue, he hadn't made a single move to harm her.

She was fast coming to the conclusion that he was all bluster.

The thought made her smile. The McCabe men did like to frown. But Alaric had stood with her even after muttering blasphemies against her and all women. Caelen . . . well, so far they had a mutual agreement to avoid each other. Now *he* frightened her. He didn't much like her, and he didn't care if she realized that or not.

Was she insane for considering marriage to the laird?

She stood by the window and watched as shadows darkened the rolling hills that surrounded the keep. In the distance, dogs barked as they brought in the sheep. The purple hue of dusk had settled over the land. Low to the ground, light fog rose, covering the hills like a mother tucking in her child for the night.

This would be her life. Her husband. Her keep. Her clan. No longer would she fear that at any moment she'd be found and forced to marry a brute of a man who cared naught for anything but the riches she'd bring with the birth of an heir.

She would have a life, one she'd nearly given up hope of ever having, and she'd have a family. Crispen. The laird. His brothers. His clan.

Oh, but the longing was fierce inside her.

She turned her eyes heavenward and whispered a fervent prayer. "Please, God. Let this be the right decision."

CHAPTER 11

The lass was submerged in a full tub of water, head thrown back, eyes closed, and an expression of sheer bliss curved the contours of her face.

Ewan watched from the door, silent so he didn't disturb her. He should make his presence known. But he didn't. He was enjoying the unimpeded view far too much.

Her hair was pinned atop her head, but loose tendrils drifted down the slim column of her neck, clinging damply to her skin. His gaze drifted along the lines of those strands. He was particularly fascinated by the ones that rested on the curves of her breasts.

Bonny breasts she had. As bonny as the rest of her. She was all soft curves and lines, pleasing to the eye. She shifted, and for a moment he thought he was caught, but she never opened her eyes. She arched just enough that the pink tips of her nipples lifted through the water.

His mouth went dry. His cock went rigid and strained against his trews. He curled and uncurled his fingers, unsettled by the fierce reaction she stirred within him.

He was hard and aching. Want was fierce within him. There was nothing to prevent him from charging across the room, yanking her from the tub and laying her on the bed. She was his to take. From the moment she'd set foot on his lands, she was his. Whether she married him or not.

Still, the perverse part of his nature wanted her to come to him. He wanted her to accept her fate and bind herself to him of her own accord. Aye, the taking was far more satisfying when the lass was willing. Not that he couldn't have her willing in a matter of seconds . . .

A frightened gasp echoed across the room. He frowned as he stared into her open eyes. He didn't want the lass afraid of him.

She didn't stay afraid for long.

Sparking with outrage, she bolted to her feet. Water sloshed over the side of the wooden tub and sluiced down her body, accentuating each of those delectable curves he had just been admiring.

"How dare you!"

She stood, trembling in the water, not a stitch of clothing to obstruct a complete view of her body. Ah, she was a delectable sight, spitting fury, her breasts thrust proudly out. Dark curls nestled at the apex of her legs, guarding the sweet mysteries that lay beneath.

And then, as if realizing she'd given him a lot more to look at by bolting to her feet, she let out a squeak and promptly dropped back into the tub. Both arms covered her chest and she hunched forward, hiding as much of herself as possible.

"Get out!" she roared.

He blinked in surprise and then grinned his appreciation of her bellow. She might be a slip of a thing, and she looked deceptively harmless, but she was a force to be reckoned with. Just ask his men, who were all understandably wary around her now.

She ordered Gannon, Diormid, and Cormac around relentlessly. At the end of the day he was treated to a list of complaints about their duties to guard—and placate—their mistress. Cormac had the idea that she should take over the training of their troops. Ewan thought she had a vicious streak and that she was merely retaliating over the fact that they'd been given the task of looking after her.

She was not above ordering around those who stumbled into her path either. And if questioned, she merely gave everyone that sweet, innocent smile and told them that according to their laird, she would soon be the mistress of the keep. Accordingly, it was their duty to take their instructions from her.

The problem was most of those instructions bordered on the absurd. She'd run everyone ragged for the last two days, and Ewan was here to tell her to cease. Father McElroy was due at any moment. One, she would give him her answer, and two, she would stop making his men look like haggard women by the end of the day.

It was shameful for warriors to whine as much as his men.

"I've already seen everything there is to see," Ewan drawled.

A blush worked over her cheeks and she glared her disapproval at him.

"You shouldn't have come in without knocking. 'Tisn't proper."

He lifted an eyebrow and continued to stare at her though he knew it discomfited her. The same demon that provoked her to drive his men to madness prompted him to give her a little of that back.

"You were sound asleep in the tub, lass. You weren't going to hear an army if it passed through."

She snorted and shook her head in denial. "I never sleep in the tub. Why, I could drown. That would be stupid, and I am never stupid, Laird."

He grinned again but didn't argue the fact that she had been soundly asleep when he'd entered the chamber. He cleared his throat and went on to the matter at hand.

"We need to speak, lass. 'Tis high time you give me an answer. The priest should be here at any moment. You've done enough mischief. 'Tis a serious matter we've to decide."

"I'll not speak to you until I'm out of the tub and dressed," she said with a sniff.

"I could help you with the matter," he said, without so much as flinching.

"That's very considerate . . ." She broke off as she became aware of what he'd offered. Her eyes narrowed and she hugged her arms tighter around her legs. "I won't budge until you leave this room."

He sighed more to stifle the laughter that threatened than to show exasperation. "You have but a moment before I return. I suggest you make haste. You've kept me waiting long enough."

He could swear she growled as he turned to walk out the door. He grinned again. She was proving to be a worthy bride and mistress to the McCabe clan. He might have expected a woman in her circumstances to be a frightened mouse, but she was as fierce as one of his warriors. He was looking forward to peeling back the many diverse layers she'd presented and getting to the woman underneath. The very beautiful, soft lass that he'd already seen glistening and wet.

Lord, but she was beautiful. And damn if he wasn't eager to get her in front of the priest.

Mairin lunged from the tub and wrapped one of the furs tightly around her. Casting furtive glances over her shoulder, she stood in front of the fire as she hastened to dry herself enough that she could put her gown back on. It would be just like the laird to walk back in before she finished dressing.

Her hair still quite wet, she pulled her clothing on and then sat in front of the fire to dry and comb her hair. She shivered when the window fur fluttered against a particularly stiff burst of wind and the cooler air blew over her damp hair.

When the knock sounded, though she'd expected the laird, she jumped and turned to see the door open to admit him. His eyes raked over her like hot coals, and suddenly she didn't feel a chill at all. In fact, it was decidedly warmer in her chamber now.

She stared silently, mouth dry, and, for the first time, without words. There was something different about him, and she wasn't sure what, or that she wanted to know. He studied her—nay he wasn't studying her. He was devouring her with his eyes. Like he was a hungry wolf closing in on a kill.

She swallowed at the image that thought invoked, and she covered her neck with her hand as if to protect her from his teeth.

He didn't miss the gesture and amusement gleamed brightly in his eyes. "Why are you afraid of me now, lass? You've shown no fear of me from the beginning. I can't imagine that I've done anything now to change that."

" 'Tis over," she said quietly.

He cocked his head to the side and then he moved closer to her, settling his large frame on the small bench in front of the fire.

"What's over, lass?"

"Time," she muttered. "I've run out of time. I was a fool for not being better prepared. I waited too long, 'tis God's truth. I should have selected a husband long before now, but it was so peaceful at the abbey. I was lured into a false sense of security. Mother Serenity and I always spoke of the future, but with each passing day, the future loomed ever nearer."

He shook his head and she glanced down at him, puzzled by his refusal.

"You did just right, Mairin. You waited."

Confused, she wrinkled her nose and asked, "What did I wait for, Laird?"

He smiled then, and she saw the arrogance etched in every facet of his face. "You waited for me."

Oh, but the man knew how to ruin her mood. 'Twas the truth, she thought he did it apurpose. She sighed, for it did her little good to continue to deny his suit. She knew and he knew that she'd marry him. There was no other choice. But he wanted the words, so she'd give him the words.

"I'll marry you."

His eyes gleamed in triumph. She thought he'd tease her some more, perhaps tell her it was high time she'd come to her senses. But he did none of those things. He kissed her.

One moment he was a respectable distance away. The next he was so close that she was enveloped by his scent.

He took her chin and tipped it up so he could fit his mouth to hers. Warm—nay, hot—and getting hotter with each passing second, his lips moved over hers like velvet.

It was an impressive feat that he could kiss her and all her senses fled. For a man who was constantly reminding her to come to hers, he seemed to take great delight in making them flee again.

His tongue rasped across her lips, and when she kept them tightly closed, he turned light and coaxing. He teased the seam of her mouth, licking and then nibbling. This time he didn't order her to open her mouth, and despite her determination not to do so, she found herself sighing in utter bliss.

As soon as her lips parted, his tongue slipped inside, probing and stroking with delicate precision. Each caress incited a deep response, one that she was at a loss to explain. How could kissing make her breasts go tight and other parts of her body tingle and swell until she felt near pain?

He evoked a restless, cagey feeling that made her want to squirm right out of her skin. And when he raised his hands to slide them up her arms, she shivered, trembling all the way down to her toes.

When he pulled away, she was dazed and she stared at him in absolute confusion.

"Ah, lass, what you do to me," he whispered.

She blinked rapidly as she attempted to gather herself. This was a time when she needed to be solemn and sage. Offer something about how their marriage would be strong and based on mutual respect.

But none of those things would form in her mind. Quite simply, his kisses reduced her to a blithering idiot.

"You don't kiss the correct way," she blurted out.

Mortified that this was all she could manage to say, she closed her eyes and prepared herself for his censure.

When she reopened them, all she saw was deep amusement. The man looked fair to laughing. Her eyes narrowed. It was obvious he needed instruction on the matter.

"And what, pray tell, is the correct way?"

"You must keep your mouth closed."

"I see."

She nodded to reinforce her statement. "Aye, there are no tongues involved in kissing. 'Tis undignified."

"Undignified?"

Again she nodded. This was going better than she imagined. He was taking her instructions quite well.

"Mother Serenity told me that kisses are for the cheek or the mouth, but only in very intimate situations. And they shouldn't last overlong. Just enough to convey the proper emotion. She never mentioned anything about a tongue. It can't be proper for you to kiss me and stick your tongue inside my mouth."

His lips twitched in a suspicious manner. He even put a hand to his mouth and rubbed firmly for several moments before he lowered it and said, "And your Mother Serenity is an authority on kissing, is she?"

She nodded vigorously. "Oh aye. She told me everything I needed to know for the eventuality of my marriage. She took her duty very seriously."

"Perhaps you should instruct me personally on this kissing matter," he said. "You could show me the way of it."

She frowned but then remembered this was the man she was taking as her husband. In that case, she supposed it was entirely proper, and even expected, that she should offer instruction in the matter of loving. It was very decent of him to be so understanding and to offer to correct the matter immediately. Why, they were going to get along quite well.

Feeling much better about her impending nuptials, she leaned forward and pursed her lips, prepared to show him the way of it.

As soon as her lips touched his, he grasped her shoulders and hauled her even closer.

She felt swallowed up. Consumed. Like he was absorbing her very essence.

And despite her stern lecture and patient instruction, he used his tongue.

CHAPTER 12

"Wake up, my lady! 'Tis your wedding day."

Mairin pried open her eyes and groaned at the sight of the women crowding into her small chamber. She was exhausted. Her late-night escape attempts and the time spent pacing her chamber had caught up to her. After last night's conversation with the laird, she'd fallen into a deep sleep.

One of the women threw aside the furs covering the window, and sunlight speared through Mairin's eyeballs with razor-sharp clarity.

Her moan was louder this time and it set off a titter of laughter through the room.

"Our mistress doesn't sound excited to be marrying our laird."

"Christina, is that you?" Mairin grunted out.

"Aye, lady. 'Tis I. We're having hot water brought up for a bath."

"I bathed last evening," Mairin said. Perhaps it would gain her an extra hour of sleep.

"Oh, but a bath on your wedding morning is a must. We'll wash your hair and work sweet-smelling oils into your skin. Maddie makes them herself and they smell divine. The laird will be most appreciative."

The laird wasn't uppermost on her mind this morning. Sleep was.

Another giggle raced around the room, and Mairin realized that once again, she'd given voice to her thoughts.

"And we've brought you a gown to be married in," another of the women said.

Mairin looked over, trying to remember the name of the young woman who was beaming excitedly at her. Mary? Margaret?

"Fiona, my lady."

Mairin sighed. "Sorry. There are so many of you."

"I took no offense," Fiona said cheerfully. "Now would you like to see the gown we've fashioned for you?"

Mairin shoved herself up to her elbow and stared through bleary eyes at the assembled women. "Gown? You sewed a gown? But I agreed to marry the laird only last evening."

Maddie didn't look the least bit apologetic. She smiled broadly at Mairin as they held up the gown for her to see. "Oh, we knew it was only a matter of time before he persuaded you, lass. Aren't you glad we began sewing? It took two solid days of round-the-clock sewing, but I think you'll be happy with the result."

Mairin stared at the beautiful creation in front of her. Tears crowded to the surface, and she blinked to keep them at bay. "'Tis beautiful." And it was. It was rich green brocade and velvet with gold-trimmed sleeves and hem. Around the bodice were intricately embroidered designs with gold threads that shone in the sunlight.

"I've never seen anything to rival it," she said.

The three women beamed back at her. Then Maddie went over to the bed and yanked the covers back. "You don't want to keep the laird waiting. The priest arrived at dawn this morning, and the laird is quite impatient to have the ceremony done."

"Nay, of course not," Mairin said dryly. "It wouldn't do to keep the laird waiting."

For the next hour, the women washed, scrubbed, and rubbed Mairin from head to toe. By the time she was done with the bath and laid out on the bed for them to work in the scented oils, Mairin was perilously close to falling into unconsciousness.

They'd washed and dried her hair and then brushed it until it crackled and shined. It fanned over her back, satiny fine. Mairin had to admit, the women knew how to make a woman feel her best on her wedding day.

"All done," Christina announced. " 'Tis time for the dress and then you're off to your wedding."

Just then a knock sounded on the door and Gannon's voice boomed through the heavy wood.

"The laird wants to know how much longer."

Maddie rolled her eyes and then went to yank open the door, though she kept her body between Gannon and the inside of the room so he wouldn't look on Mairin's nakedness.

"You tell the laird we'll have her down as soon as we can. These things can't be rushed! Would you have the lass not looking her best on her wedding day?"

Gannon muttered an apology and then backed away, promising he'd relay the news to the laird.

"Now then," Maddie said as she returned to Mairin. "Let's get this gown on you and then downstairs to the laird."

"They've been at it for hours," Ewan muttered. "What could possibly take so long?"

"They're women," Alaric said, as if that explained everything.

Caelen nodded and turned up his mug to drain the last of his ale.

Ewan sat in his high-backed chair and shook his head. His wedding day. There was a marked difference in this day and the day he'd wed his first wife.

He hadn't thought of Celia except in passing for quite some time now. Some days he had difficulty conjuring the image of his young wife to mind. The years had passed, and with each year, she'd faded more from his memory.

He'd been a much younger man when he'd wed Celia. She, too, had been young. Vibrant. He remembered that much. She always had a ready smile. He'd considered her a friend. They'd been childhood playmates before training had become his life. Years later, their fathers had seen fit to ally themselves and marriage between the clans made sense.

She'd borne him a child in their second year of marriage. By the time the third year rolled around, she was dead, his keep was in ruins, and his clan nearly decimated.

Aye, their wedding day had been a joyous occasion. They'd feasted and celebrated for three days. Her face had been alight with joy, and she'd smiled the entire time.

Would Mairin smile? Or would she come to their marriage with those same wounded eyes she'd had when she arrived?

"Where is she, Papa?" Crispen whispered beside him. "Do you think she changed her mind?"

Ewan turned to smile at his son. He stroked his hand over the lad's hair in a reassuring manner. "She's just getting dressed, son. She'll be here. She gave her word, and as you know, she puts great store in keeping her word. Women like to look their best on their wedding day."

"But she's beautiful already," Crispen protested.

"That's true," Ewan said. And it was. The lass wasn't just beautiful, she was enchanting. "But they like to look extra special for just such occasions."

"Does she have flowers? She should have flowers."

Ewan almost laughed at the look of consternation on Crispen's face. His son was more nervous than he. Ewan wasn't nervous. Nay, he was just impatient and ready to have it done with.

"You don't have flowers?" Crispen asked.

Ewan looked down at his son. Crispen looked so appalled that Ewan frowned.

"I didn't give flowers any thoughts. But perhaps you're right. Why don't you go take up the matter with Cormac."

Across the room, Cormac had evidently been listening in on the conversation. He looked as appalled as Crispen had, and he hastily took a step back. But Crispen was too fast and was immediately in front of the man, demanding that they go collect flowers for Mairin.

He shot Ewan a disgruntled look as he allowed himself to be tugged from the great hall.

"What the hell is taking them so long?" Caelen demanded. He shifted restlessly in his chair and spread out his long legs as he slouched lower. "This is a waste of a good training day."

Ewan chuckled. "I wouldn't consider my wedding day to be a waste of time."

"Of course you wouldn't," Alaric said. "While the rest of us are out sweating, you'll be enjoying a warm, sweet lass."

"He'll be sweating," Caelen said slyly. "Just not in the way the rest of us are."

Ewan held up his hand to staunch the bawdy talk before it caught on with the rest of the men. The last thing he needed was his prospective bride to walk in and be embarrassed to her toes.

Just then Maddie burst in, her cheeks rosy and her chest heaving as she tried to catch her breath.

"She's coming, laird!"

Ewan glanced over at the priest, who was enjoying a

mug of ale, and motioned him up. As Mairin rounded the corner, the entire hall stood in acknowledgment of her presence.

Ewan was momentarily struck dumb. The lass wasn't just beautiful. She was utterly magnificent. Gone was the shy, somewhat awkward young woman and in her place was a lady with all the bearing of a descendent of royalty. She looked just like the princess she was.

She swept into the room, head held high, a look of serene calm on her face. Her hair was partially pulled into a knot just above her nape and the rest hung loose to her waist.

There was such a regal air about her presence, that Ewan suddenly felt unworthy.

Crispen burst into the room holding a wad of flowers so tightly that the stems were already limp and the flowers wilting as he flopped them about. He ran to Mairin and thrust them into her hands, petals scattering to the floor.

Her expression completely changed. Gone was the super-composed, cool woman. Her eyes warmed and she smiled tenderly down at his son. She leaned down to brush a kiss across his brow.

"Thank you, Crispen. They're absolutely beautiful."

Something twisted in the region of Ewan's heart.

He stepped forward until he was just behind Crispen. He reached down to frame his hands over his son's shoulders as he stared into Mairin's blue eyes.

"The priest is waiting, lass," he said gruffly.

She nodded then glanced down at Crispen. "Will you come with us, Crispen? After all, you're very much a part of this ceremony."

Crispen puffed out his chest until Ewan thought he might burst. Then he slipped his hand into Mairin's. Ewan reached for the other, and she handed her flowers off to Maddie before sliding her fingers through his.

It felt right. Here was his family. His son and the woman who would be mother to him. He tugged her toward the waiting priest, as his two brothers came forward to flank Ewan and Mairin.

There in the protective hold of his family, he and Mairin exchanged their vows. She never wavered. Never gave any hint that she was anything but willing. She stared the priest in the eyes and then turned to look into Ewan's, as she recited her promise to honor and obey.

When the priest declared them married, Ewan leaned in to seal their troth with a kiss. She hesitated a mere moment and then whispered, "You will not use your tongue!"

His laughter rang out over the hall. His clan looked eagerly for the source of his laughter, but he had eyes only for his new bride.

He found her lips, so sweet and warm, and took his time as he ravaged her mouth. And, oh aye, he used his tongue.

When he broke away, she glared ferociously up at him. He grinned and reached for her hand, pulling her against him as they turned to face his clan. Then he held her hand high in the air and presented her as the new mistress of the keep.

The roar of his clan echoed so loudly in the hall that Mairin winced. But she stood proudly beside Ewan, a delighted smile curving her lips.

One by one, his men came to kneel and offer their pledge to their new mistress. At first, Mairin looked baffled by the show of loyalty. She twitched as if she would have liked to disappear through the flooring.

Ewan smiled as he watched her come to terms with her new position. She'd led a sequestered life. Now, for the first time, she was stepping into her destiny.

When the last soldier bowed before Mairin, Ewan

took her elbow to guide her toward the table where Gertie and the kitchen maids were busy setting out the trenchers for the wedding feast. In the corner, a small group of talented musicians gathered to play a set of lively tunes. After the feast there would be dancing and merriment until the bedding ceremony at sundown.

Ewan shared his place at the head of the table with Mairin. He wanted her seated beside him in a position of honor.

He called for a chair to be placed adjacent to his, and when the trenchers were laid and the first course served, he offered her the choicest bites from his serving.

Seemingly delighted by his regard, she allowed him to offer her tender bites of meat from his dagger. She smiled up at him so dazzlingly that for a moment he forgot to breathe. Shaken by the effect she had on him, he nearly knocked over the mug containing ale.

Alaric and Caelen sat on either side of Ewan and Mairin. After the last of the people sitting at the main table had been served, Alaric rose from his seat and asked for silence. Then he held up his goblet and glanced down at Ewan and Mairin.

"To the laird and his lady!" he called. "May their marriage be blessed with health and many sons."

"Or daughters," Mairin muttered so low that Ewan almost didn't catch it.

His mouth twitched as he listened to the rest of his clan roar agreement. He raised his goblet and inclined his head in Alaric's direction.

"And may our daughters all be as beautiful as their mother."

Mairin gasped softly and turned shining eyes on Ewan. Her smile lit up the entire room. To his utter shock, she suddenly bolted up, grabbed his face between her hands, and gave him a lusty kiss that curled his toes.

The room erupted in a chorus of cheers. Even Caelen

looked amused. When Mairin pulled away, Ewan was hard-pressed to remember his own name.

She scooted closer to him, pressing her soft curves to his side. His body reacted immediately. He was instantly hard, and his current position prevented him from shifting to alleviate the growing discomfort. If he adjusted, he would unseat Mairin, and he didn't want her to move away from him.

So he sat and grew more uncomfortable by the moment.

Midway through the feast, the flute player began a particularly merry tune. It was lively and fast and dozens of feet began a rhythmic tapping on the floor. Mairin clapped her hands together and let out a sound of pure delight.

"Do you dance, lass?" Ewan asked.

She gave a wistful shake. "Nay, there was never dancing in the abbey. I'm probably clumsy at it."

"I'm not exceedingly graceful myself," Ewan said. "We'll muddle through it together."

She gifted him with another smile and impulsively squeezed his hand. He made a sudden vow that no matter how foolish he looked, he would dance with her as long as she wished it.

"Laird, Laird!"

One of his watchmen ran into the hall, sword drawn. He searched Ewan out and immediately set out for the end of the table. Ewan rose, his hand automatically going to Mairin's shoulder in a protective gesture.

The soldier was out of breath when he came to a halting stop a mere foot from where Ewan stood. Alaric and Caelen shot up from their seats and waited for the news.

"An army approaches, Laird. I received word but a moment ago. They carry Duncan Cameron's banner. They come from the south and were two hours from our border at last report."

CHAPTER 13

Ewan cursed long and hard. Alaric's and Caelen's expressions grew stormy, but something else glimmered in their eyes. Anticipation.

Ewan found Mairin's hand again and gripped it so tight that she winced from the pain of it.

"Gather the troops. Assemble in the courtyard. Wait for me," Ewan commanded.

He started to drag Mairin from the table when Alaric called out. "Where in the hell are you going, Ewan?"

"I have a marriage to consummate."

Openmouthed, Mairin found herself hauled toward the stairs. Ewan bounded up the steps, and she was forced to run to keep pace, or be dragged behind him.

He shoved her into his chamber and slammed the door behind him. She watched in befuddlement as he began stripping out of his clothing.

"Take off your dress, lass," he said, as he tossed aside his tunic.

Completely bewildered, Mairin sagged onto the edge of the bed. He wanted her to undress? He was busy pulling his boots off, but it was her duty to undress him. He didn't have the right of it at all.

Thinking to instruct him on his error, she rose and

hurried over to stay his progress. For a moment, he halted and stared at her as if she were daft.

" 'Tis my duty to undress you, Laird. 'Tis the wife's duty," she corrected. "We're married now. I should undress you in our chambers."

Ewan's gaze softened and he reached out to cup her cheek. "Forgive me, lass. This time will be different. Duncan Cameron's army approaches. I don't have the time to woo you with sweet words and a soft touch." His forehead creased and he grimaced. "It will have to be a quick bedding."

She looked up at him in confusion. Before she could question him further, he began tugging at the laces on her dress. When he didn't immediately have the bodice undone, he pulled impatiently.

"Laird, what are you doing?" she stammered out.

She gasped in surprise when the material ripped and fell over her shoulders. She tried to lift the dress back up, but Ewan pushed downward, leaving her in only her undergarments.

"Laird," she began, but Ewan hushed her by taking her shoulders and pressing his lips to hers. As he maneuvered her to the bed, he managed to divest her of the rest of her clothing.

His trews hit the floor, and she felt something hot and hard brush against her belly. When she looked down and saw what it was, her mouth gaped open and she stared in horror at the jutting appendage.

He captured her chin and directed her gaze upward again. As his mouth covered hers, he lowered her to the bed until she lay on her back and he hovered just above her, his arm pushed into the bedding to prevent his full weight from bearing down on her.

"Spread your legs, Mairin," he rasped against her lips.

Confounded by the entire experience, she relaxed her thighs and then squeaked in dismay when Ewan's hand slipped between her legs and stroked his thumb through the delicate folds.

His mouth slipped down the side of her neck. Chill bumps raced over her shoulders and to her breasts as his lips fastened against the flesh just below her ear. It was oddly exciting and it stirred breathless feelings of . . . she wasn't sure how to describe any of it. But she liked it.

"I'm sorry, lass." His voice was heavy with regret. "I'm so damned sorry."

She frowned as she gripped his shoulders. His body moved over hers, covering her with his heat and hardness. What was he sorry for? It didn't seem appropriate to offer apology in the middle of loving.

She felt him, hard as steel, as he probed between her thighs. It took a moment for her to realize what he was probing with. Her eyes flew open and her fingers dug into his skin.

"Ewan!"

"Forgive me," he whispered.

He thrust forward, and the hazy euphoria she'd experienced just moments before disappeared as pain tore her in half when he ripped through her body.

She cried out and pounded his shoulders with clenched fists. Tears slipped down her cheeks and he swept them away with his mouth as he rained kisses over her face.

"Shhh, lass," he crooned.

"It hurts!"

"I'm sorry," he said again. "I'm so sorry, Mairin. But I can't stop. We must finish this."

He moved tentatively, and she hit him again. He'd torn her in two. There was no other explanation for it.

"I haven't torn you apart," he said gruffly. "Be still a moment. The pain will go away."

He withdrew, and she flinched as her body tugged tightly at him. Then he pushed forward again, and she whimpered at the fullness.

A shout in the hallway made her go rigid. Ewan cursed and then began moving again. She lay there in shock, unable to process or put a name to the uncomfortable sensation that welled within.

Once, twice, and once again he pushed into her, and then he tensed against her and held himself so still that she could hear the violent thud of his heartbeat.

Just as suddenly, he rolled away, and she felt sticky wetness between her legs. Not having any idea what it was she was supposed to do next, she lay there trembling as her husband hurried to dress.

After he pulled on his boots, he returned to the bed and slipped his arms underneath her. Maybe now he would offer the tender words a husband was supposed to say after loving. But he simply picked her up and cradled her in his arms for a moment. Then he carried her to the bench in front of the fire and set her down.

She blinked and watched as he stripped the linen from the bed and examined the bloodstain in the middle. Curling it into his hand, he glanced over at her, his eyes brimming with apology.

"I must go, lass. I'll send one of the women to tend you."

He left the chamber, shutting the door behind him, and Mairin stared after him in complete disbelief over what had just transpired.

A moment later, Maddie bustled in, sympathy burning bright in her eyes.

"There, there, lass," Maddie said, as she gathered Mairin in her arms. "You look too pale, and your eyes are much too wide. I'll have hot water brought up to you. 'Twill soothe your aches and pains."

Mairin was too mortified to ask Maddie any of the questions swirling around her mind. She sat there, numb to her toes, while the battle cry rose from the courtyard and then the sound of hundreds of horses thundering across the land drowned out everything else.

Then her gaze flickered across the discarded dress on the floor. He'd torn her dress. Her wedding dress. After every other bewildering thing that had occurred this day, the dress shouldn't have upset her so. But tears welled in her eyes, and before she could call them back, warm trails trickled down her cheeks.

Maddie left her to replace the linens on the bed. She bustled around the chamber, though it was clear she had no task to do.

"Please," she whispered to Maddie. "I just want to be alone."

Maddie eyed her dubiously, but when Mairin reinforced her request, Maddie reluctantly turned away and left the chamber. Mairin stayed on the bench for a long moment, her knees huddled to her chest as she stared into the dwindling fire. Then she got up to wash the stickiness from her body. When she was done, she crawled onto the bed and huddled underneath the clean linens, too tired and distraught to worry over Duncan Cameron's army.

Ewan led his men over the hilltops and down the steep southern boundary of their lands, his two brothers flanking him. Another rider had ridden furiously to give Ewan an update. Cameron's men were approaching without delay.

There would be no time to stage a surprise attack, and in truth, Ewan had no desire for one. He rode with the might of his entire army, save only a contingent that remained behind to guard the keep. There was no doubt they'd be outnumbered, but the McCabe soldiers made up in might what they lacked in numbers.

"They're just over the next hilltop, Laird," Gannon said as he drew up his horse in front of Ewan.

Ewan smiled. Revenge was at hand.

"Let's greet Cameron on the next rise," Ewan said to his brothers.

Alaric and Caelen raised their swords into the air. Around them, the shouts of their men echoed sharply across the land. Ewan spurred his horse and they raced down the hill and began the climb to the next. When they topped the rise, Ewan called a halt as they stared down at the assembled might of the Cameron army.

Ewan scanned the Cameron soldiers until finally his gaze lighted on his prey. Duncan Cameron sat high in his saddle, dressed in full battle regalia.

"Cameron is mine," he shouted to his men. Then he glanced sideways at his brothers. " 'Tis time to deliver a message."

"Kill them all?" Alaric asked mildly.

Ewan's nostrils flared. "Every last one."

Caelen rotated his sword in his hand. "Then let it be done."

Ewan gave the battle cry and urged his horse down the hill. Around him, his men took up the cry and soon the valley echoed with the thunder of horses. The McCabes descended like avenging hellfire, their savage cries enough to frighten the souls of the dead.

After a faltering hesitation, when it wasn't clear whether they meant to attack or run, Cameron's men surged forward. They met in a clash of swords at the bottom of the hill. Ewan slashed through the first two men he encountered with a deft swing of his sword. He could see the surprise—and the fear—in the eyes of Cameron's men. They hadn't expected to encounter a fighting force such as Ewan's, and Ewan derived unholy satisfaction from that fact.

He glanced quickly to check on his men. He needn't have worried. Caelen and Alaric were cutting a swath through Cameron's men while the rest of his soldiers dispatched their foes with expert speed and agility.

Ewan set his sights on Cameron, who still hadn't dismounted his horse. He stood back, watching his men and barking orders. Ewan single-mindedly cut a path through Cameron's men until only two soldiers stood between him and Cameron.

He dispatched the first with a slice through the man's chest. Blood gleamed crimson on his sword as he swung it around to meet the last obstacle to his goal. The soldier glanced warily at Ewan and then back at Cameron. He raised his sword as if to meet Ewan's advance, but at the last moment he turned and fled.

Ewan's lips curled into a satisfied smile at the sudden fear in Cameron's eyes.

"Get off your horse, Cameron. I'd hate to spill the blood of a steed as fine as he."

Cameron raised his sword, gathered the reins in his other hand, and kicked his horse forward. He charged at Ewan, letting out a bloodcurdling cry.

Ewan deflected the blow and twisted his sword, lifting Cameron's right out of his hands. It went sailing through the air and landed with a sickening thud into one of the fallen bodies a short distance away.

Ewan spun to meet the next charge, but Cameron never slowed. He spurred his horse to faster speeds and raced across the terrain. Away from his men and from the battle.

As Ewan turned to battle another foe, he snapped his teeth together in fury. Coward. Bloody coward. He'd deserted his men and left them all to die while saving his own arse.

Ewan gave the order for his men to finish it, and he began working his way back toward his brothers. The Cameron soldiers were woefully outmatched.

The remaining commander of Cameron's ill-fated

army evidently came to the same conclusion. He yelled retreat, and his men didn't just retreat. They fled.

The commander, unlike Cameron, wasn't a coward. He didn't flee. He urged his men to beat a hasty retreat and he fought valiantly at their rear, offering his protection—as pathetic as it was—so they could escape to safety.

Ewan signaled his men to give chase, and he turned his sights on the commander.

When Ewan bore down on him, he saw the resignation on the older man's face. Ewan raised his sword and stalked forward. The commander took one step back, then brought his sword up, prepared to battle to the death.

Ewan swung his sword in a great arch and the blades met with a resounding clang. The older man was weakening. He already had a wound and he was losing blood. On Ewan's second strike, he knocked the sword from his opponent's hand and it hit the ground with a clatter.

Death stared back at Ewan from the depths of the man's eyes. The commander knew it and accepted it as only a warrior could. He sank to his knees and bowed his head in front of Ewan, in acknowledgment of defeat.

Ewan stared down at him, his throat working against the anger that swirled so fierce within him. Had this been what his father had done just before Cameron cut him down? Had his father fought to the bitter end? Or had he known, as this man knew, that defeat was inevitable?

For a long moment, Ewan held his sword above his head, and then he slowly lowered it and looked around at the dying battle. Cameron's men were scattered across the landscape. Some dead. Some dying. Some fleeing on foot, while others ran their horses into the ground to escape Ewan's soldiers.

He whistled for his horse, and the commander looked

up, surprise glittering in the eyes that had just been shadowed by imminent death.

When Ewan's horse obediently stopped a mere foot away, Ewan reached back for the sheet bearing Mairin's virgin blood. He spread it out like a banner, the ends blowing in the wind. Then he wadded it into his hand and thrust it into the commander's face.

"You will take this back to Cameron," Ewan said through gritted teeth. "And you will bear my message."

The commander slowly took the linen and then nodded his acceptance of Ewan's dictate.

"You will tell Duncan Cameron that Mairin Stuart is now Mairin McCabe. She is my wife. The marriage has been consummated. Tell him that Neamh Álainn will never be his."

CHAPTER 14

By the time Ewan and his men rode back into the courtyard, it was well past midnight. They were dirty, bloody, tired, but jubilant over such an easy victory.

A celebration would ensue, but Ewan didn't feel like celebrating. Duncan Cameron had escaped Ewan's retribution and it burned like sour ale in his belly. He wanted the bastard on the end of his sword, now not only because of what he'd done eight years before, but because of what he'd done to Mairin.

He gave orders to his men to increase the watch. There was much to be done in light of his marriage to Mairin. The keep's defenses would have to be strengthened, and new alliances, such as one with the McDonalds, were more important than ever.

Even with all of that weighing down on him, his primary thought lay with Mairin. He regretted the haste in which he'd bedded her. He didn't like guilt. Guilt was for men who made mistakes. Ewan didn't like the idea of making mistakes or admitting his failures. Aye, but he'd failed the lass and he was at a loss as to how to make it up to her.

He took the time to bathe in the loch with the other men. If it weren't for the fact that a sweet lass lay in his bed, he'd have crawled beneath the covers in his boots and not worried over the mess until morning.

After washing the dirt and blood from his body, he quickly dried and mounted the steps to his chamber. Eagerness drove him. Not only did he want to show the lass a little tenderness, but he burned for her. Before, he'd only tasted of her sweetness. Now he wanted to feast on it.

He quietly opened his chamber door and stepped inside. The room was cloaked in darkness. Only the coals from the fire gave light as he crossed to the bed. She was nestled in the middle of the bed, her hair spread out like a veil of silk. He slid one knee onto the bed and leaned over her, prepared to wake her, when he saw the lump on the other side of her.

Frowning, he peeled back the cover to see Crispen nestled in her arms, his head laying on her bosom. A smile eased his frown when he saw how she had both arms wrapped protectively around him. The lass had taken her role as Crispen's new mother very seriously. They were tucked in as tight as two kittens on a cold night.

With a sigh, he eased down beside her, resigning himself to the fact that he wouldn't awaken his wife with kisses or touches this night.

He moved in close until her back was cradled against his chest. Then he curled one arm around both her and Crispen, as he buried his face in Mairin's sweet-smelling hair.

It was the fastest he'd ever fallen asleep in his life.

He was careful not to wake Mairin or Crispen when he rose just a few hours later. He dressed in the darkness and got his boot caught on something as he tried to walk toward the door. He reached down and picked up the offending material and realized it was Mairin's dress that she'd worn when she wed him.

Remembering that he'd torn it in his haste to bed her, he stared down at it for a long moment. The image of Mairin's wide, shocked eyes and the hurt reflected in them made him frown.

It was just a dress.

Curling it in his hand, he took it with him as he made his way below stairs. Even at the early hour, the keep was already stirring with activity. Caelen and Alaric were just finishing eating and looked up when Ewan entered the hall.

"Marriage has turned you into a slugabed," Caelen drawled. "We've both been up for an hour."

Ignoring his brother's jibe, Ewan took his seat at the head of the table. One of the serving women hurried out with a trencher of food and set it in front of Ewan.

"What the hell are you holding, Ewan?" Alaric asked.

Ewan glanced down to see he was still carrying Mairin's dress tightly clenched in his hand. Instead of answering Alaric, he called the serving girl back.

"Is Maddie about yet?"

"Aye, Laird. Would you like me to fetch her?"

"At once."

She dipped a curtsy and hurried out to do his bidding. Mere moments later, Maddie hurried in.

"You called for me, Laird?"

Ewan nodded. "Aye." He thrust the dress toward the woman, and with a surprised look, she took it. "Can you repair it?"

Maddie turned the material over in her hands, examining the place where the material had rent.

"Aye, Laird. 'Twill only take a needle and thread. I could have it done in no time."

"See that you do. I'd like for your mistress to have it whole again."

Maddie smiled, and her eyes sparkled with a knowing look that annoyed him. He scowled at her and motioned her away. Still grinning, she tucked the dress under her arm and left the hall.

"You tore her wedding dress?" Caelen smirked.

"You certainly have a way with the wenches," Alaric said, shaking his head. "You haul her up the stairs for perhaps what was the fastest consummation on record, and you tear her wedding dress in the process."

Ewan's nostrils flared. "She's not a wench. She's your sister now and you should speak of her with respect as your mistress and wife to your laird."

Alaric held up his hands in surrender and leaned back in his chair. "No offense was intended."

"Touchy, isn't he?" Caelen said.

Ewan's glare silenced his youngest brother. "We have much to do today. Alaric, I need you to be my emissary to McDonald."

Both Alaric and Caelen shot forward in their seats, incredulity etched on their faces.

"What? Ewan, the bastard tried to abduct your son," Alaric growled.

"He denies knowledge of his soldier's actions and vows that his soldier acted on his own accord. The soldier is dead now," Ewan said flatly. "He won't be a threat to my son ever again. McDonald wants an alliance. 'Tis to his advantage to call us friend. I've denied him until now. But his lands would join ours to Neamh Álainn. I want you to make it happen, Alaric."

"So be it," Alaric said. "I'll leave within the hour."

Alaric strode from the hall to prepare for his journey. Ewan quickly finished his meal and then he and Caelen quit the hall and went to where his men were training.

They stood in the courtyard, watching as the other soldiers sparred and went through their training exercises.

" 'Tis imperative that Mairin be under constant guard," Ewan said in a low voice to Caelen. "Duncan Cameron won't give up just because I've wed her. There is much to be done, and Mairin must remain inside the keep under careful watch."

Caelen shot Ewan a wary glance. "Don't think to saddle me with such a chore. She's your wife."

"She's the future of our clan," Ewan said in a dangerously soft voice. "You would do well to bear that in mind when you tell me what you will and won't do. I expect your loyalty to me to extend to her."

"But a nursemaid, Ewan?" Caelen asked in a pained voice.

"All you have to do is keep her safe. How hard can that be?" Ewan asked. He motioned to his senior commanders when they finished the current round of sparring.

He instructed Gannon, Cormac, and Diormid on his expectations that Mairin be watched over at all times.

"As you wish, Laird. She won't like it much," Gannon said.

"I'm not concerned with what she won't like," Ewan countered. "My concern is keeping her safe and with me."

The men nodded their agreement.

"There's no need to alarm her. I don't want her to feel unsafe on my land. I want her guarded well but I want it to appear that 'tis just the way of things."

"You can count on us to keep Lady McCabe safe, Laird," Cormac vowed.

Satisfied that his men understood the importance of keeping close watch on Mairin, Ewan summoned his messenger and penned a missive to the king informing him of his marriage to Mairin and requesting the release of her dowry.

For the first time in many years, hope beat a steady

rhythm in his chest. Not for vengeance. Nay, he'd always known that the day would come when he would repay the wrongs done to his clan. With Mairin's dowry his clan would prosper once again. Food would be plentiful. Supplies would be on hand. They would cease eking out their existence under spartan conditions.

Despite Ewan's intention to spare a moment to speak with Mairin—he wasn't entirely sure about what—the day passed in a blur of activity. He'd thought to gauge her mood and offer reassurance that Duncan Cameron's men had been dispatched. Aye, she'd feel better and more secure, and she damn sure wouldn't doubt his ability to protect her or his keep any longer.

An incident with his men prevented Ewan from dining with Mairin, and by the time he trudged up the stairs to his chamber, he was tired, but at least he was clean after a dip in the loch.

He nudged the door open to see that she was already abed, her soft, even breathing signaling her slumber. He started forward, intent on waking her, when he saw that once again, Crispen was snuggled against her. He sighed. Tomorrow he would make it a point to tell her that Crispen was to sleep in his own chambers across the hall.

He never got the chance to make his point. From the moment Mairin awoke, he never seemed to gain the opportunity to speak with her. Toward afternoon, he grew impatient and issued a direct summons for her to appear before him.

When it went unanswered, he sent Cormac to fetch her, since Diormid was guarding her. Cormac returned with the news that Mairin was visiting the cottages of the other women and would speak to her laird later.

Ewan scowled, and Cormac seemed uncomfortable telling his laird that his bride had refused him.

Clearly they were going to have to discuss matters far more important than where his son slept. Namely, the idea that she had the right to refuse a direct order from Ewan.

He made it a point to eat dinner with Mairin that evening. She looked tired and nervous. Her gaze kept darting toward him when she thought he wasn't looking, as though she feared him lunging across the table and hauling her to his chamber.

He sighed. He supposed it wasn't an unreasonable fear given what had occurred on their wedding day. Some of his irritation fell away. The lass was skittish. It was up to him to allay her fears and soothe her worries.

Protection was something he could readily offer. His loyalty to the woman he called wife would be unwavering. She'd never want for anything he could provide as long as he lived. Those were things that the warrior in him readily embraced. But things like tenderness and understanding? Sweet words meant to soothe away worries? The mere idea appalled him beyond measure.

His thoughts must have been expressed on his face because Mairin sent him a startled look and then she immediately rose and excused herself from the table. Without waiting for his permission to leave, she murmured something to Crispen. The lad stuffed his mouth full of food and hastily shoved away from the table. He took her hand and they left the hall in the direction of the stairs.

Ewan's eyes narrowed as he realized just what it was she was doing. She was purposely taking Crispen into their bed in an effort to avoid Ewan. If he weren't so annoyed, he might have been impressed by her craftiness.

He himself pushed away from the table and rose with a nod to Caelen. He'd rather go off to war than go up those stairs and face a situation with his new wife that he had no inkling of how to resolve.

A good start would be to issue a stern lecture on obeying his orders. After that, he would simply command her to cease being so skittish around him.

Feeling confident about his plan of action, he went up to his chamber and opened the door. Mairin whipped around, surprise written in her eyes.

"Is there something you need, Laird?"

He lifted an eyebrow. "Can I not retire to my own chamber?"

She flushed and gathered Crispen to her skirts. "Aye, of course. You don't usually come to bed so early. That is, I hadn't expected you to . . ."

She trailed off, her blush deepening. She pressed her lips firmly together as if refusing to say another word.

He couldn't resist teasing her. "I hadn't realized you were so familiar with my sleep habits, lass."

Her blush disappeared and she glared her displeasure.

Determined to set her straight on several issues, he crooked his finger at Crispen, and when he grudgingly separated himself from Mairin and approached his father, Ewan put his hands on Crispen's shoulders.

"Tonight you'll sleep in your own chamber."

When Mairin would have protested, he silenced her with a stern look. Crispen also wanted to argue, but he was too disciplined for that. Most of the time.

"Aye, Papa. May I kiss Mama good night?"

Ewan smiled. "Of course."

Crispen hurried back over to Mairin and allowed her to sweep him into a hug. She kissed the top of his head and then squeezed him tight. Crispen returned and stood solemnly in front of Ewan.

"Good night, Papa."

"Good night, son."

Ewan waited until his son had left the room before turning back to Mairin. Her chin went up and defiance sparked in her eyes. She was preparing for battle. The thought amused him but he smothered the smile that threatened. It was God's truth, he'd smiled more since her arrival than he had in his life.

"When I issue you a summons, I expect you to heed it," he said. "I expect—nay, I *demand*—obedience. I won't accept defiance from you."

Her mouth took on a pinched look. At first he thought he'd frightened her again, but on second look, he saw she was furious.

"Even when your demands are ridiculous?" she asked with a sniff.

He raised an eyebrow at that. "My asking you to present yourself to me is ridiculous? I had matters to discuss with you. My time is valuable."

She opened her mouth and then promptly shut it again. But she muttered something under her breath that he didn't catch.

"Now that we have that matter resolved, while I appreciate your devotion to my son, he has his own chamber that he shares with other children of the keep."

"He should sleep with his mother and father," she blurted.

"Aye, there will be times when that is indeed the case," Ewan agreed. "But right after our marriage is not one of them."

"I fail to see what being newly married has to do with it," she muttered.

He sighed and tried to rein in his impatience. The lass was going to be the death of him.

"'Tis hard to bed my wife if my son is sharing the bed with us," he drawled.

She looked away and twisted her hands in front of her. "If 'tis all the same to you, I'd rather not have you . . . bed me."

"And how do you plan to become pregnant, lass?"

Her nose wrinkled and she cast him a cautious but

hopeful look. "Perhaps your seed has already taken root. We should wait to see if that is the case. 'Tis truth you've no skill at loving, and 'tis obvious I've none as well."

Ewan's mouth gaped open. He was sure he hadn't heard correctly. No skill? His mouth closed then fell open and then he snapped it shut with the force of his incredulity.

She shrugged. " 'Tis a well-known fact that a man is either skilled in matters of loving or matters of war. 'Tis obvious that fighting is your skill."

Ewan winced. The little wench was shredding his manhood. His cock positively shriveled under her criticism. Anger warred with exasperation until he saw the tremble of her lower lip and the trepidation in her eyes.

He sighed. "Ah, lass, 'tis true I bedded you with all the skill of a stable boy with his first woman."

Her cheeks flushed a delicate pink, and he kicked himself for his coarseness. He dug his fingers into his hair.

"You were a virgin. 'Tis unlikely anything I could have done would have made it good, but there is a lot I could have done to make it more pleasant."

"I would have liked pleasant," she said wistfully.

He cursed. How badly had he hurt her? He knew he hadn't given her the pleasure or patience she deserved. At the time, all he'd known was that he had to consummate the marriage with all haste. There hadn't been time to seduce a shy virgin. Only now his shy virgin had turned into a stubborn, unwilling wife.

"Mairin, the marriage wasn't valid until I bedded you. I couldn't risk having something happen before I had the chance to bed you. If you'd been captured, Cameron could have taken you and petitioned to have our marriage set aside. He would have bedded you and got you with child to strengthen his claim."

Her lip trembled and she cast her eyes downward to where her fingers twisted nervously at her skirts.

He took advantage of her momentary distraction and closed in. He reached down and took her hands in his. She was small and soft. Delicate. The idea that he'd been too rough, that he'd hurt her, unsettled him.

He should suffer no guilt for taking his wife. Her duty was to provide him pleasure, however he saw fit to take it. But the memory of her tear-filled eyes was a fist to his gut.

"It won't be like that from now on."

She raised her eyes to his and her brow wrinkled in confusion. "It won't?"

"Nay, it won't."

"Why?"

He tempered his irritation and reminded himself that she needed a gentle hand right now.

"Because I'm quite skilled in loving," he said. "And I plan to show you."

Her eyes widened. "You do?"

"I do."

Her mouth rounded, and she tried to take a step back. He held her hands tightly in his and pulled her back until she bumped into his chest.

"In fact, I intend to show you how very skilled I am."

"You do?"

"I do."

She swallowed and stared into his eyes, her own, wide and confused. "When do you plan to do this, Laird?"

He bent and swept his mouth over hers. "Right now."

CHAPTER 15

Mairin put her hands on Ewan's chest to steady herself, else she would have fallen under his relentless assault on her senses. She sighed and leaned farther into his kiss, not even protesting when his tongue slid sensuously over her bottom lip as he coaxed her to open.

The man might not be skilled in loving, but she could drown in his kisses. Maybe he'd be amenable to continue kissing and forego the rest.

"Kiss me back," he murmured. "Open your mouth. Let me taste you."

His words slid like velvet over her skin. She shivered as her breasts plumped and swelled. An ache began deep in her body, in parts that didn't bear mentioning. How was he able to incite such a response when all he was doing was kissing her?

His palms glided up her waist and then up over her shoulders and up her neck until he framed her face. The heat from his touch branded her. It felt as though she'd have permanent marks on her cheeks from his fingers, and yet he was exquisitely gentle, the tips glancing over her skin like tiny winged creatures.

Unable to deny the probing of his tongue, she relaxed her mouth and allowed him to slide inside. Warm and rough. So very sinful. It was a decadent sensation, one she was certain she should deny herself, but she couldn't.

The temptation to taste him back was strong. So strong that it beat an incessant rhythm at her temples, in her mind, at her very core. Shyly she brushed her tongue over his lips. He groaned and she immediately pulled back, afraid she'd done something wrong.

He hauled her right back and captured her mouth once again in a ravenous fashion that left her breathless.

"Do it again," he whispered. "Taste me."

From the sound of it, he hadn't disliked her touching him with her tongue. Tentatively she licked over his lip again. He relaxed his mouth against hers, opening so she had access.

Feeling braver, she boldly pushed forward, hot and wet. She shivered from the sheer carnality of something so simple as a kiss. She felt naked and vulnerable, as if she was spread out and underneath him as he slaked his lust over and over. Only this time she burned for him. She wanted him over her, his body covering hers. She felt twitchy and anxious, like her skin was too tight.

"This time I'll undress you as I should," he whispered, as he walked her back toward the bed.

Her mind was dim and she was slow sorting through her muddled thoughts. She frowned, knowing he didn't have the right of it again. Was she forever going to have to instruct him?

"I should undress you. 'Tis my duty," she said.

He grinned. " 'Tis only your duty when I say it is. Tonight I fully intend to undress you and enjoy every moment. You deserve a slow wooing, lass. This will be your wedding night all over again. If I could go back and do it all differently, I would. But I'll give you the next best thing. I'll give you tonight."

The promise in his voice shook her to her toes. She blinked as he lowered her dress over one shoulder and then followed a line down her neck and over the curve of her arm with his lips.

Each inch of her skin he uncovered, he kissed, sliding downward until her dress fell away, leaving her nearly bare under his gaze. Each layer pooled at her feet, until she was naked.

"You're beautiful," he husked, his warm breath whispering over the chill bumps that dotted her flesh.

He cupped one breast, palming it so the pale globe plumped upward. Her nipple contracted and beaded so tight that it sent tiny shards of lightning through her belly.

Then he bent and flicked his tongue over the erect nub, and her knees promptly buckled. She landed on the bed with a soft bounce, and he chuckled lightly as he followed her down.

With a gentle nudge, he had her on her back and he loomed over her, so big and strong. He stared so unabashedly at her nakedness that she reached for the covers, something, anything, to make her not feel so vulnerable.

He stayed her hand with his, his gaze tender as he met hers. "Nay, don't cover yourself, lass. You're an exquisite sight. Unrivaled by any woman I've ever seen." He trailed a finger over the curve of her waist to her hip and then back up again until he rubbed over her taut nipples. "You're skin is as soft as the finest silk. And your breasts . . . they remind me of ripe melons just waiting to be tasted."

She tried to suck in air but her lungs burned from the effort. Each breath felt tight. She panted shallowly, feeling more light-headed by the minute.

He backed away from the bed, and for a moment, she panicked. Where was he going? But he began shedding his clothing in a much more impatient manner than he'd divested her of hers. He kicked off his boots and then ripped off his tunic and trews, tossing them across the room.

Looking at him was inevitable. She couldn't have glanced away if she wanted. There was something intensely mesmerizing about the rugged, work-honed contours of his body. Scars, some old, some much newer, traced paths over his flesh. There wasn't a single bit of spare flesh to be seen. Muscles tightened his chest and even his abdomen, where so many men went soft with age. Not her warrior. This was a man honed in the fires of battle.

With a nervous swallow, she dropped her gaze to the juncture of his legs, curious to see the part of him that had caused her such pain before. Her eyes widened at the sight of him jutting so hard and . . . big. She began backing up toward the bed before she even realized what she was doing.

"Don't be frightened," he murmured, as he lowered himself over her. "I won't hurt you this time, Mairin."

"You won't?"

He smiled. "I won't. You're going to like it."

"I will?"

"Aye, lass, you will."

"All right," she whispered.

He kissed her lips, warm and so tender. It was a ridiculous notion, but he made her feel so very protected and cherished. She now had two very conflicting views on loving because this . . . this was very nice.

He continued to kiss her, sliding his mouth down the line of her jaw and then lower to her neck and the tender flesh just below her ear. He paused a moment and sucked wetly before grazing his teeth over her pulse point.

"Oh!"

She felt him smile against her neck, but he never removed his mouth. Instead he trailed lower to her chest until he was precariously close to her breasts. Remembering her reaction when he put his tongue on her nipple, she found herself arching into him.

He didn't tease, and for that she was thankful. She was strung so tight that she feared what was going to happen to her. His lips closed around one nipple and he sucked hard. Her back bowed and her hands flew to grip his hair. Oh saints, but this was a wondrous sensation.

He suckled, in turns hard, and then gentle and rhythmic. His tongue circled sensitive flesh, and his teeth nipped ever so lightly, coaxing the bud to an even harder point.

"Sweet. So sweet," he said, as he moved his mouth to her other breast.

She sighed, though the sound came out more as a garbled utterance than a breathy exclamation. The chill of the chamber no longer bothered her. She felt rather like she'd been lying in a meadow on a warm summer day, allowing the sun's rays to melt her to her bones.

Aye, boneless was an apt description.

As he suckled at her breast, his fingers glided down her belly, caressing for a moment before he carefully worked his way down to the juncture of her thighs. The moment his finger slid through her folds, she tensed.

"Shhh, lass. Relax. I'm only going to bring you pleasure."

His finger found a particularly sensitive spot and he began to rub lightly and then rotate in a circular motion. She gasped and then squeezed her eyes shut as she was bombarded by the most intense pleasure. Just as he'd promised.

There was a curious tightening as her body drew up. Her muscles clenched. Precarious. That's how she felt. Like she was about to fall off a very high peak.

"Ewan!"

His name fell from her lips, and in the recesses of her

blurry mind, she realized this was the first time she'd used it.

He released her nipple and her hand tightened in his hair. The she realized she was still clutching his head with a death grip. She let go and let her hands fall to the bed. But she needed to grab something.

He pressed his tongue to her midline and slowly worked a damp trail to her belly. Her stomach heaved as her breaths came faster. He traced a lazy trail around her navel and then to her utter shock, he went lower, moving his body down the bed as he worked ever closer to the place where his fingers had caressed.

He wouldn't. Surely such a thing wasn't at all decent.

Oh, but he did. . . .

His mouth found her heat in a lusty, carnal kiss that made every muscle in her body twitch and convulse as if she'd been struck by lightning.

She should tell him he shouldn't. She should tell him he couldn't. She should offer instruction on the proper way to do things, but dear heaven, she couldn't think anything at all beyond don't stop.

Please don't stop.

"I won't, lass," he murmured against her most intimate flesh.

Her legs had gone stiff and unyielding around him, and he gently forced them back apart.

"Relax."

She tried. Oh, but she tried, but his mouth was making her daft. And then his tongue found her, so hot and erotic. A wash of indescribable pleasure soared through her belly as he lapped at her entrance. Her vision blurred and she twisted her fingers into the covers until they were bloodless and all sensation fled.

She had no control of her body any longer. She arched mindlessly, and her legs shook, the tremors working to her thighs until she was a mass of quaking flesh.

"Ah, you're ready for me, lass."

His voice deepened to a hoarse, almost desperate tone. She chanced a look down to see him staring at her, his eyes bright and savage looking.

"I am?" she breathed.

"Aye, you are."

He moved up her body with speed that surprised her. He cupped her bottom with one hand and settled his body between her legs. She could feel him, hot and unbelievably hard, nestled against her opening.

Then he leaned down and fused his mouth to hers. This time she didn't hesitate, nor did she think to instruct him on the proper way of kissing. She opened her mouth and devoured him before he ever had the opportunity to demand she did so.

"Hold on to me," he rasped out between hot, openmouthed kisses.

She wrapped her arms around his broad shoulders and dug her fingers into his back. She kissed him. She tasted him. She absorbed him, breathing him in with each gasp for air.

Before she even realized he had moved, he had lifted his hips and slid inside her the barest of inches. She stretched to accommodate him and then wondered how she'd been able to do so.

He kissed her again and then rested his forehead to hers, their eyes so close, all she could see was the thin ring of green that surrounded the dark pupils.

"Relax," he said again. "I won't hurt you."

She raised her lips to meet his. This time their mouths met in a delicate dance, the tenderest of touches. "I know."

And she did know. Somehow, she knew that this was different. There was no rush. No unpleasant shock to her senses. Her body melded to his, surrendering to his power and his need. To her need.

His hips moved forward with infinitesimal slowness. She opened around him as he slid deeper. The fullness overwhelmed her, but it wasn't pain or surprise that rocked her body.

"Almost there," he whispered.

Her eyes widened as he went even farther and then he stopped, lodged so deeply within her that she couldn't breathe. He surrounded her, gathering her in his arms, holding her close as he began moving, a slow, seductive rhythm that had her mad with want.

The muscles in his back rippled and bulged. Her fingers danced across his flesh in a frantic pattern as she sought purchase. Something to anchor herself with when she was adrift in a storm.

His movements increased, faster and more forceful. Their sighs caught and mingled in the air heavy with the scent of their loving.

"Wrap your legs around me," he directed. "Hold me tight, lass."

She wrapped her entire body around him until she was sure they were so inexorably entwined that they'd never come apart.

The burning sensation increased until she stirred restlessly, frantic for . . . release. Breathing hurt, so she didn't, and her chest protested, but she held on, reaching for something she had no sense of.

And then she came apart, unraveling like the threads in an unfinished tapestry. She screamed, or tried to, but Ewan's mouth closed over hers, and he swallowed her frantic cry.

She had no control of her body. She couldn't think. Could only feel, helpless to do anything but lie in Ewan's arms as he murmured soft words against her ears.

Utterly bewildered by what had occurred, she fixed unfocused eyes on her husband as an expression of agony creased his face. He gave one more mighty thrust, seating himself deeply within her body. Then he slumped over her, pressing her into the mattress as he gave her his seed.

She nestled her face into the hollow of his throat, so sated and completely boneless that she considered staying in bed for the next year. Ewan rested over her for a long moment before finally easing his weight from her and rolling to the side.

He gathered her into his arms and stroked her hair. Then he pressed a kiss to her temple and let his cheek rest against the side of her head.

Her befuddled mind couldn't make sense of what had just happened. Only one thing struck strongly in her mind.

"Ewan?" she whispered.

It took him a moment to respond. "Aye, lass?"

"I was wrong."

He stirred, rubbing his face against her cheek. "What were you wrong about?"

"You're very skilled at loving."

He chuckled and then hugged her tighter to him. Yawning broadly, she snuggled deeper into his arms and closed her eyes.

CHAPTER 16

When Mairin awoke, she was momentarily disoriented. She blinked away the fuzziness. Her head still felt muggy but her body, while only a little stiff and sore from her bruises, was surprisingly warm and sated. Limp, like she'd enjoyed a prolonged soak in a steaming tub of water.

Light pierced through the window that no longer had the fur covering it, and the sun's height told her she'd slept far later than she'd intended.

Gertie wouldn't be pleased, and Mairin would have to wait for the noon meal. For that matter, it might be noon already.

The night came back to her in a rush. Heat centered low in her abdomen and scorched higher until her cheeks were flaming. She sat up, then realized she was completely nude. She grabbed the bed coverings and clutched them to her chin, then dropped them in disgust.

She was alone in the bedchamber. No one was going to see her. Still, she scrambled from the bed and hastily donned her clothing.

Her hair was in disarray and a quick feel of her cheeks told of the flush that was still there. She probably looked like a hot coal.

She'd actually told the laird that he wasn't skilled at

loving. Aye, he'd showed her differently. He'd done things that she hadn't imagined two people ever doing. His mouth . . . and his tongue.

She flushed all over again and closed her eyes in mortification. How could she ever face him again?

Mairin adored Mother Serenity. She trusted her above all others. The abbess had been good to Mairin. And patient. Aye, she'd had the patience of Job when it came to instructing Mairin and answering all the questions Mairin had plied her with. But it was becoming increasingly clear that perhaps the abbess had left out a lot about loving. And kissing.

Mairin frowned as she pondered just how different the teachings of the older woman had been from the startling reality of bedding. If the abbess had been wrong about kissing . . . and loving . . . what else could she be wrong about? Mairin felt suddenly ignorant and woefully uninformed.

Never one to stew in her own ignorance, she decided that she would just have to seek out instruction on the matter. Christina . . . well, she was too young. And unmarried. Gertie frightened Mairin with her sharp retorts. Besides, she'd probably just laugh at Mairin and shoo her out of the kitchens. Which left Maddie. She was older and certainly more worldly. Plus, she had a husband, so surely she could offer insight into loving and who had the wrong of it.

Feeling better about her plan, she brushed the tangles out of her hair and braided it so she didn't look like she'd just spent the night indulging in loving. Then she headed out of her chamber and descended the stairs.

To her chagrin, Cormac was waiting in the hall. As soon as she entered, he rose and fell in step beside her. She shot him a disgruntled look, but he merely smiled and offered her greeting.

Deciding not to offer him any encouragement, she instead pretended he wasn't there and went toward the kitchens to brave Gertie's wrath. When she got to the doorway, the ruckus within made her pause.

There was an awful clanging and banging of pots and Gertie's voice rose above the din as she screeched her displeasure at one of the kitchen maids.

Maybe it wasn't the time to try to cajole a late breakfast from the cranky cook.

"Uh, Cormac?"

"Aye, my lady."

"Is it close to time for the noon meal? I confess I slept over late this morning. I didn't at all sleep well last night," she rushed to say. She didn't want to give Cormac the idea that her lateness was due to anything else.

He smothered a smile with the back of his hand and then summoned a more serious expression. She glared at him for his thoughts were plainly written in his smug look.

"He probably boasted to everyone," she muttered.

"Your pardon, my lady?" Cormac said as he leaned forward.

"Nothing."

"'Tis approaching the noon meal. Perhaps another hour at most. If you like, I'll ask Gertie for a plate if you're hungry now."

Her stomach growled at the suggestion of food, but a wary glance at the kitchen when another crash sounded decided the matter for her.

"Nay, I can wait. I have other things to do."

She set off at a determined pace, hoping Cormac would take the hint and leave off. But he dogged her steps, keeping pace with her as she descended the steps of the keep.

She was greeted by a blast of sunshine that warmed her despite the chill. She hadn't remembered the shawl that Maddie had left for her, and she was loath to go back up the stairs to fetch it. Unless . . .

She turned and gifted Cormac with a sweet smile. "I left my shawl in the laird's chamber and there is still a chill to the air. Would you mind ever so much fetching it for me?"

"Of course not, my lady. It wouldn't do for you to take a chill. The laird would be most unhappy. Wait right here and I'll have it for you in just a moment."

She stood demurely until the moment he disappeared back into the keep and then she set off at a brisk walk, careful to avoid the courtyard. On the way, she stopped two women and asked if they knew where she could find Maddie. After being told that Maddie was in her cottage after her morning duties, Mairin hurried toward the row of neat cottages that lined the left side of the keep.

When she reached Maddie's door, she took a deep breath and knocked. A moment later, Maddie opened the door and seemed surprised to see Mairin standing there.

"My lady! Is there something I can help you with?"

Mairin glanced over her shoulder to make sure Cormac wasn't breathing down her neck.

"There is. That is, I hoped there is something you could instruct me on," Mairin said in a low voice. "In private."

Maddie stepped back and motioned Mairin inside. "Of course. Do come in. Would you like refreshment? I was warming some rabbit stew over the fire. My husband does like a nice hot bowl of stew for his luncheon, but he won't be here to eat for a little while yet."

Remembering her missed breakfast and her rumbling belly, Mairin sniffed appreciatively of the air and the wonderful smell emanating from Maddie's kitchen.

"If 'tis not too much trouble. I did oversleep this morning," Mairin said mournfully.

Maddie smiled and gestured for Mairin to follow her into the small area that housed the hearth for cooking. "I heard Gertie was in quite a temper this morning."

Mairin nodded. "'Tis the truth I feared for my life if I ventured in after missing the morning meal."

Maddie pulled out a chair and ushered Mairin into it and then set about dishing up some of the stew into a bowl. She handed it to Mairin and then took her own seat across the table.

"Now, my lady, what is it you would like me to instruct you on?"

Before Mairin could open her mouth, a knock sounded at the front door. Maddie frowned but got up to see about the summons. A moment later she returned with Christina and Bertha, whose eyes rounded when they saw Mairin sitting at Maddie's table.

"Oh, my lady," Christina exclaimed. "We were just coming to see if Maddie knew of your whereabouts. Cormac has the entire keep in an uproar trying to find you."

Mairin let out a sigh. "I persuaded him to fetch my shawl so I could seek Maddie's advice about something. 'Tis a private matter, you see, and not appropriate for Cormac's ears."

Bertha grinned broadly. "Then we needn't tell him where you are."

Mairin nodded her appreciation and fully expected the two women to depart, but both sat down at Maddie's table, and Bertha leaned forward in interest.

"What is it you wish instruction on, my lady? We're all willing to help. You're our mistress now."

"Our lady said it was a private matter," Maddie scolded.

Mairin nodded. "Aye. A delicate matter, indeed."

Warmth traveled into her cheeks and she was sure her face was afire.

"Ah, a woman's matter," Bertha said knowingly. "You can tell us, lass. We're very discreet."

Maddie nodded her agreement while Christina looked on in puzzlement.

"Well," Mairin began reluctantly. "Perhaps it would be better to gain more than one perspective on the matter. 'Tis the truth I'm a bit confused at the conflicting information. You see, Mother Serenity instructed me on the ways of loving."

"Oh dear Lord," Bertha muttered. "Lass, tell me you didn't receive *all* your instructions from an aging abbess."

Startled, Mairin stared back at the other woman. "Why aye, Mother Serenity is knowledgeable in all things. She wouldn't lie to me. I think perhaps I may have confused some of her instructions. There were so many, you see."

Maddie shook her head and made a *tsk*ing sound through her teeth.

"Tell us what you want to know, child. I can assure you that your Mother Serenity, while well intentioned, couldn't possibly have told you the whole of it."

"Well, she instructed me on kissing, and the laird—" She broke off, mortified at the idea of saying aloud what was in her thoughts.

"Go on." This time Christina piped in and leaned forward, her eyes round with curiosity.

"Well, he used his tongue. Mother Serenity never said anything about the use of one's tongue in kissing. She was quite explicit in the matter."

Maddie and Bertha chuckled and exchanged knowing glances.

"Tell me, lass, did you enjoy the laird's kisses?" Maddie asked.

Mairin nodded. "'Tis the truth I did, and I have to

admit, I used my own. It was quite . . . breathless. I don't understand it at all."

"Kissing with tongues?" Christina's eyes went wide.

Maddie frowned at Christina and then made a shooing motion with her hands. "Lass, you're far too young for this conversation. Why don't you go stand outside and keep watch for Cormac."

Mairin noted Christina's crestfallen look but she didn't argue. Christina stood and left the room. Only when the sound of the front door closing reached them did Bertha and Maddie return their attention to Mairin.

"Is that all you were wanting to know?" Maddie asked.

Mairin shifted in her seat and wondered if she shouldn't abandon the entire notion and return to the keep so Cormac could lecture her for her desertion.

"There now, lass," Bertha said in a kindly voice. "Ask us what you want. We won't be telling tales on you."

Mairin cleared her throat. "Well, I might have told the laird that he was unskilled at loving."

Both women looked so appalled that Mairin regretted blurting out that tidbit. Then they burst into laughter. They laughed so long and hard that they wiped tears streaming down their cheeks.

"And how did the laird take this?" Maddie gasped out between wheezes.

"Not very well," Mairin grumbled. "I did later tell him I was wrong."

Bertha grinned. "Ah, you were, were you?"

Maddie nodded approvingly. "Proved you wrong, did he? You can't hold your wedding day against him, lass. It was your first time. Not much he could have done would have helped in that regard. Better to get it done with and over, I say."

"But he . . ."

"He what?" Bertha asked.

"It was indecent," Mairin muttered.

Maddie stifled her laughter with a hand, but her eyes danced merrily. "But you liked it, aye?"

"Aye," Mairin admitted. "He did things. . . ."

"What sort of things?"

"Well, he used his mouth." Mairen leaned forward and whispered, "Down there. And on my . . ."

"Your breasts?" Bertha asked.

Mairin closed her eyes in mortification and nodded.

Both women chuckled and leaned back in their chairs.

"Sounds like the laddie has the right of it then," Maddie said, approval firm in her voice. "You're a lucky lass to have a skilled man in your bed. Not every woman does."

Mairin frowned. "They don't?"

Bertha shook her head. "Now don't be telling anyone I told you so, but my Michael, well, it took him a few years before he developed any skill. If it weren't for a few discussions with some ladies older than I, I'm not sure we would have ever gotten it right."

"Oh, aye, 'twas the same with my Ranold," Maddie said. "He was always in such a hurry. It wasn't until I threatened to withhold my charms that he made an effort to work on his skills."

Mairin's head was spinning at the women's chatter. Such intimate matters didn't seem to bother the other two women whatsoever. Mairin on the other hand was ready for the earth to swallow her up.

Maddie reached across the table and put her hand over Mairin's. She squeezed and offered Mairin a smile. "Let me give you some advice, lass. If you don't mind an old woman offering it."

Mairin slowly nodded.

" 'Tis not enough for your man to be skilled in matters of loving. You need to have some skills yourself."

Bertha nodded vehemently. "Aye, 'tis the truth. If you

keep your man satisfied in the bed chamber, he won't have any cause to stray."

Stray? Mairin looked at them in horror. "Are you suggesting that the laird wouldn't be faithful?"

"Nay, of course we wouldn't disparage the laird. But 'tis a fact, 'tis better to be safe than sorry. You want your laird to be well satisfied. Men are far more amenable when they're sated from loving."

Maddie slapped Bertha on the shoulder and laughed. "Aye, now that's the truth. The best time to ask a boon is just after a rousing bout of loving."

Amenable was good. Mairin liked the idea of that. And now that the disturbing thought of Ewan's fidelity had entered her head, she couldn't shake it. Surely he wouldn't?

"What things should I know?" Mairin asked.

"Well, you said he used his mouth. You know, down there," Bertha said with a twinkle in her eyes. "You can do the same to him, lass. 'Tis guaranteed to drive him wild."

Mairin was sure her absolute ignorance was reflected in her expression. And her horror. She started to say something, but the image of what Bertha was describing hit her square between the eyes and she couldn't shake it.

"How . . . ?" She couldn't even finish the question. What was she supposed to ask?

"You've shocked the lass," Maddie said reproachfully.

Bertha shrugged. "No point in dillydallying around the point. The lass has to learn from someone. Her Mother Serenity certainly didn't do her any favors."

Maddie put her hand back over Mairin's. "What Bertha means is that a man likes being kissed . . . down there. On his cock."

Bertha snorted. "Tell her right, Maddie. A man likes to be suckled."

Mairin was sure the blood leeched right out of her cheeks. Kissed? Suckled?

"You liked it well enough, didn't you, lass?" Bertha asked. "A man is no different. He likes to be touched and caressed with a lass's hands, mouth, and tongue."

It was true enough that Mairin did enjoy Ewan's touches. And his kisses. He was skilled with his tongue. Aye, she liked his tongue, even if he did indecent things with it.

"Putting my . . . my . . . mouth on his . . ." She couldn't bring herself to say the word. " 'Tisn't decent, surely!"

Bertha rolled her eyes and Maddie laughed.

"There's little decency to good loving," Maddie said sagely. "If 'tis decent, it isn't much fun."

Bertha nodded, her lips compressed as her head bobbed up and down. "Nothing wrong with a nice, dirty romp."

Mairin could scarcely believe what she was hearing. She was going to have to think on this matter. Before she could thank Maddie and Bertha and be on her way, a pounding on the door startled the women.

Maddie rose and went to the door, Mairin and Bertha right behind her. Mairin had a very good idea who was at the door, but when Maddie opened it, it was worse than Mairin had feared.

It wasn't Cormac waiting to lecture her. Ewan stood with Caelen, arms crossed over his chest, a scowl darkening his features. Christina stood to the side, her eyes apologetic.

"Care to explain yourself?" Ewan demanded.

CHAPTER 17

Instead of answering her husband, Mairin turned to Maddie and Bertha and offered a polite curtsy. "Thank you both for your counsel."

When she turned around again, Ewan was still glaring holes in her while Caelen looked annoyed that he'd been summoned on the errand to locate Mairin. She tried to walk past Ewan as she exited Maddie's cottage, but he didn't budge. She shoved but he was an immovable object.

Finally she stepped back. "You wished to speak with me, Laird?"

Ewan emitted a loud sigh and then took her arm in his not-so-gentle grasp. Mairin offered a wave to the women as Ewan hauled her along beside him. She stumbled and had to run to keep up, else she'd find herself dragged across the ground by her fuming husband.

She glanced over her shoulder to see Caelen following close behind. She shot him a disgruntled look in the hopes he'd disappear, but he didn't look impressed with her silent demand for privacy.

Finally Ewan halted some distance from the cottages. He loomed over her like some avenging warrior out for blood. Though she tried to face him bravely, some part of her shrunk to a ridiculous size. He was angry. Nay, angry didn't aptly describe his mood. He was furious.

It took him a few moments and repeated attempts before he was able to get his reprimand out. His mouth opened and snapped shut several times and he looked away as if collecting his temper.

She waited demurely, her hands folded together, and she stared up at him with wide eyes.

"Don't even look at me with those doe eyes," Ewan growled. "You disobeyed me. Again. I've half a mind to lock you in our chamber. Forever."

When she didn't respond to that threat, Ewan blew out his breath.

"Well? What explanation would you like to offer for sending Cormac on an errand and then promptly leaving his escort?"

"I needed to speak with Maddie," Mairin said.

Ewan stared at her for a long moment. "That's it? You disregarded not only my order but acted in complete disregard for your safety because you needed to speak to Maddie?"

"'Twas a delicate matter," Mairin defended.

Ewan closed his eyes and his lips moved in silence. Was he counting? It made no sense to practice mathematics at such a time.

"And you couldn't have had Cormac walk you to Maddie's cottage?"

She looked at him in horror. "Nay! Of course not. It wasn't a matter for a man to hear. 'Twas a private issue and one I had no wish to discuss in front of others."

Ewan's eyes rolled heavenward. "He could have waited outside the cottage."

"He might have overheard through the window," Mairin countered.

"My time is too valuable to spend scouring the keep every time you decide you need to have a private word with one of the women," Ewan declared. "From now on, you'll either have the escort of one of my brothers or my commanders. If you persist in your actions, you'll be confined to your chamber. Is that understood?"

Caelen didn't look any more pleased with Ewan's dictate than she was. It was apparent he was appalled by the duty Ewan had charged him with.

"I said, is that understood?"

Mairin reluctantly nodded.

Ewan turned and pointed at Caelen. "You stay with Mairin. I have immediate matters to attend to."

The annoyed look on Caelen's face didn't sit well with Mairin, so she stuck out her tongue at him as Ewan strode away in the direction of the courtyard.

Caelen crossed his arms over his chest and glared at Mairin. "Perhaps it would be best if you return to the hall for the noon meal."

"Oh, but I'm not hungry anymore," Mairin said cheerfully. "Maddie was kind enough to provide me with a bowl of delicious rabbit stew."

Caelen scowled. "Then perhaps you should go up to your chamber and take a nap. A long nap."

"Mairin! Mairin!"

Mairin turned in the direction of Crispen's voice to see him running toward her with three other children trailing him.

"Mairin, come play with us," Crispen said, tugging at her hand. "We're having races and we need you to judge."

She smiled and allowed herself to be dragged forward by Crispen and his eager friends. They all talked at once, exclaiming over who was the better runner and entreating Mairin to watch each of them as they ran.

Caelen sighed loudly and lengthened his stride to keep up with them, but Mairin didn't pay him any attention.

If he must watch over her at every turn, she would do her best to pretend he wasn't there.

She laughed softly at the idea of pretending a man of Caelen's size could possibly be overlooked. He was as fierce and as muscled as any of Ewan's warriors, and he loomed over her like a giant tree.

Nay, she wouldn't be successful in pretending he wasn't following her, but she could ignore him at least.

A peek at his harried expression made unwanted guilt surge inside her chest. She frowned. She didn't want to feel guilty. Not for wanting a bit of freedom now that she was away from the abbey.

But still, the guilt grew until she was wringing her hands in front of her as she followed Crispen and the other children to an area adjacent to the keep.

She stopped abruptly and whirled around, causing Caelen to nearly run into her. "I've decided to cooperate and allow you to escort me about the keep."

Caelen merely raised an eyebrow in disbelief. "You expect me to believe you're going to meekly submit to Ewan's wishes?"

She shook her head mournfully. "I've been unfair. I offer my apologies. It isn't your fault your laird is unreasonable. Nay, the fault lies with him. You're only doing your duty. I should endeavor to make it easier and not harder for you. I'm well aware of the burden he has given you."

If she expected him to refute the idea that she was a burden, she was sorely disappointed. He merely gazed at her with a bored expression.

"At any rate, I give my word that I won't resort to trickery again," she said solemnly.

She turned back to the children who were arguing over who got to race first. She waded into the fray, laughing and fending off overeager hands.

An hour later, she was exhausted. Who knew children

could drain the life right out of a body? Mairin stopped in her pursuit of Crispen and bent over as she gasped for air in a decidedly unladylike fashion.

The screaming children surrounded her and she turned to find Caelen surveying the goings-on with something that looked very much like a grimace.

"I should make you chase them," she called. "You're supposed to be guarding me."

"Guarding, not herding children," came Caelen's terse reply.

"I think we should attack him," Mairin muttered.

"Oh, let's do!" Crispen whispered.

"Aye, aye!" the children surrounding them chanted.

Mairin smiled as the evil thought coalesced. The image of the warrior on the ground begging for mercy would be a sight to behold.

"All right," she whispered back. "But we must be stealthy about it."

"Like warriors!" Robbie exclaimed.

"Aye, like warriors. Like your fathers," she added.

The boys puffed out their chests, but the few girls who had assembled looked disgruntled.

"What about us, Mairin?" Gretchen, a girl of eight years, asked. "Girls can be warriors, too."

"Nay, they can't!" Crispen said in an appalled voice. "Fighting is for men. Girls are to be protected. My papa said so."

The looks in the girls' eyes were murderous, so to prevent a civil war among the children, Mairin gathered them all close. "Aye, girls can be warriors, too, Gretchen. Here's what we must do."

The huddled together and she whispered her instructions.

The boys weren't happy with their role in the attack. The girls were delighted with theirs. After a quick recounting of their instructions, the girls broke away and skipped toward the keep. As soon as they were past Caelen, they halted and turned back to sneak up on him from behind. Caelen was too distracted by the crowd of rowdy boys approaching him from the front.

He looked suspiciously at Crispen and then over his head to Mairin. She smiled innocently and waited.

Caelen never knew what hit him. Screaming like banshees, the girls hit him from behind. They leapt on Caelen's back and swarmed over him like a horde of locusts.

Shouting his surprise, Caelen went down amid a tangle of arms and legs and squeals of delight. The boys, not to be outdone, added their own war cries and leapt onto the pile.

After his initial surprise and much hollering and shouting, Caelen took his attack with grace. He laughed and wrestled with the children but was finally forced to cry mercy when the girls pinned him to the ground and demanded he surrender.

Caelen threw his arms up and laughingly offered his surrender. Mairin was astounded by the change in the warrior. She wasn't sure she'd ever seen him smile, much less laugh with obvious enjoyment as he tussled with the children. She stared at the goings-on with an open mouth, shaking her head at how good Caelen was with the children. She'd imagined that she'd have to step in rather quickly to defend them against his anger.

The girls were quick to cry victory while the boys protested that they had been the ones to gain Caelen's acquiescence.

"Caelen, Crispen said girls can't be warriors, that 'tis the boys' duty to be warriors and protect the girls," Gretchen said in disgust. "But Mairin said that girls can be warriors, too. Who has the right of it?"

Caelen chuckled. "Crispen is right in that 'tis a warrior's duty to protect his lady and those weaker. However, your mistress makes a very good case for a woman warrior. She may have us all begging for mercy before the month is out."

"I think you speak the truth, brother."

Mairin whirled around to see Ewan and his commanders standing a short distance away, looking in amusement at Caelen's sound defeat at the children's hands.

She swallowed nervously, sure she was about to be handed another stern lecture about her duties, but Ewan walked forward to pick up one of the children and give him a sound dusting off.

Gretchen beamed at Mairin as she sat on Caelen's broad chest. "I want to be a warrior like our laird. Why, I beat up Robbie just last week."

"Did not!" Robbie roared.

"Did so."

To Mairin's horror, Robbie flew at Gretchen, toppling her from Caelen's chest. She needn't have worried, however. The lass obviously hadn't boasted in vain. She flipped Robbie over and was soon straddling him and holding his arms to the ground.

Mairin sighed and went to prevent an all-out war between the girls and the boys. Ewan got there at the same time she did and reached for Robbie as she bent over to pluck Gretchen off the struggling boy.

Pain seared through her side, and then to her shock, an arrow hit the ground right beside the children and embedded deeply into the soil. Why, it had passed just between her and Ewan!

She stared aghast, appalled at how close it had come to hitting one of the children. She whirled around to locate the offending archer but found herself toppled to the ground as Caelen dove over her.

"Leave off!" she exclaimed, as she beat at Caelen's shoulder. "What on earth are you doing? See to the children."

"Quiet!" he barked. "Ewan is seeing to the children's safety."

"This is inexcusable!" Mairin exclaimed. "How could they be so careless? The children could have been killed!"

Caelen covered her mouth and slowly moved his body from hers. He looked around and Mairin could see only Ewan with his arms full of children, as he, too, surveyed the area with sharp eyes. Gannon and Cormac each had a position over the remaining children and they lay still, awaiting their laird's command.

Ewan cursed, and Mairin frowned at him for uttering blasphemies in front of the children. It was another thing she'd take up with him at first opportunity.

Ewan raised his head and bellowed an order. Soon the area swarmed with his men. The children were hustled back toward the keep under heavy guard, as Ewan stood and looked down at Mairin.

Caelen picked himself up from the ground and he and Ewan reached a hand down to slip under her arms. She was hoisted to her feet and she slapped at her skirts, shaking the dust off in a cloud.

Before one of them could do so, she reached down and yanked the arrow from the ground. Then she slapped it against Ewan's chest, her fright giving way to fury.

"How could your men be so careless? They could have killed one of the children!"

CHAPTER 18

Ewan was every bit as furious over the incident as his wife, but he wasn't about to allow her to chastise him in front of his men.

"You will be silent."

Her eyes widened and she took a step back. Good, she was finally realizing her place. But then her eyes narrowed and she scowled ferociously at him.

"I won't be silent," she said in a low voice. "You must have a safe place for the children to play and run free. It won't do for them to be this close to the courtyard if your men can't control their aim."

He took the arrow from her and examined the markings on it. Then he looked up at her again. "Until I know who is responsible, you will cease insulting my men, and me, by thinking we would allow such a thing to happen. You may return to the keep to see to the children. Cormac will escort you."

Hurt flashed in her eyes, but she whirled around and hurried away, her skirts swinging in her haste.

He turned to Gannon, furious over the mishap. "You will find the man who shot this arrow and you'll bring him to me. Not only could he have killed a child, he could have killed my wife."

His fingers curled into a fist at the memory of how

close the arrow had come to Mairin and himself. Though the arrow hadn't struck high enough to have done serious damage to himself, to a lass Mairin's size, it would have been deadly.

His gaze dropped to the ground where Mairin had stood just moments ago. He frowned and dropped to his knee, touching the soil with his fingers. His throat closed in and his heart began to pound. Blood darkened the dirt right next to her footprints. As he followed Mairin's path away, he saw more drops.

"Sweet Jesu," he murmured.

"What is it, Ewan?" Caelen asked sharply.

"Blood."

He shot to his feet and stared after his wife's retreating back. "Mairin!"

Mairin was nearly to the steps leading into the keep when Ewan's roar stopped her dead in her tracks. She winced and turned around. The only problem was the world didn't stop turning when she did.

She swayed precariously and blinked to try to bring everything back to rights. Odd, but her knees shook and felt suspiciously jamlike. Before she knew it, she found herself kneeling on the ground, looking at her husband bearing down on her like an avenging angel.

"Oh dear," she murmured. "I've really angered him now."

But he didn't look angry. He looked . . . worried. He rushed to her and sank to his knees in front of her. Gannon stood just behind the laird, and he, too, looked very concerned. Even Caelen wore something other than his usual look of boredom. His brows were knit together, and he stared at her as if expecting her to react.

"Why are we kneeling on the ground, Laird?" she whispered.

"I need to take you up to our chamber, lass," he said in a tone he might use with a child.

Her brow crinkled about the time pain stabbed through her side as if someone had prodded her with a hot iron. She clutched at her side and bobbled, but the laird caught her by the shoulders with gentle hands.

"But why? Surely you can't . . ." She leaned forward and whispered urgently, " 'Tis not the time for loving, Ewan. 'Tis broad daylight. Why, it isn't much past the noon hour."

He ignored her and then leaned forward and plucked her right off the ground. She landed with a thud against him, which sent another shard of pain through her side. She gasped and the world went a little watery as tears welled in her eyes.

"I'm sorry, lass," he said gruffly. "I did not mean to hurt you."

Perhaps it wasn't a bad idea that he was taking her up to their chamber because it was God's truth she was suddenly so tired that it was quite a task to keep her eyes open.

"If you would stop your shouting, I could go to sleep," she said crossly.

"Nay, lass, don't go to sleep. Not yet. I need you to stay awake until I can assess your injuries."

He then shouted again, this time for someone to fetch the healer. Healer? She didn't need a healer. What she needed was a nice long nap. And she told the laird so.

He ignored her and carried her into their chamber, where he laid her on the bed. She was prepared to close her eyes when he began tugging at her clothing.

Her eyes flew open and she smacked his hands. "What are you doing?"

Ewan looked grim as he stared down at her. "You've been hurt. Now let me take your clothing off so I can see where."

She blinked. "Hurt?" Well, actually, there was a bad pain in her side.

"The arrow must have hit you," he said. "There was blood on the ground where you stood. Do you hurt anywhere?"

"My side. It does ache something fierce, now that you mention it."

When he moved his fingers up her side, she let out a whimper. He grimaced. "Bear with me. I'm sorry, but I have to see what we're dealing with here."

He took a knife from his belt and sliced a large opening in the side of her dress.

"You're forever ruining my clothing," she said mournfully. "Before long, I'll have nothing to wear but my nightdress."

"I'll have a new dress fashioned for you," he muttered.

That cheered her considerably as he made quick work of her clothing with his knife.

He rolled her to the side that wasn't hurting and she felt him tense against her.

"Ah, lass, you've gone and gotten yourself shot by an arrow."

She went rigid. And then she sputtered. "Gotten myself shot? More like one of your men shot me. I'd like to know who it is. I've a mind to take one of Gertie's pots to his backside."

Ewan chuckled. "'Tis not so bad, but you're still bleeding. You'll need stitching."

She went completely still. "Ewan?"

"Aye, lass?"

"Don't let them take a needle to me. Please. You said it wasn't so bad. Can't you clean it and bandage it?"

She hated the pleading in her voice. She sounded weak and silly, but the idea of a needle being plunged into her flesh was worse than an arrow slicing through her skin.

Ewan pressed his mouth to her shoulder and kept it there for a long moment. "I'm sorry, lass, but it has to be done. The cut is too deep and too open for bandaging. The wound needs to be cleaned and closed."

"Will you . . . Will you stay with me?"

He stroked his hand down her arm and then back up and over her shoulder to her cheek. He pushed her hair away from her face and then his hand cupped her nape.

"I'll be here, Mairin."

CHAPTER 19

"What do you mean the healer isn't here?" Ewan asked in disbelief.

Cormac had no love for telling his laird that the healer couldn't be fetched. The dread was there to read on his face.

"Find our healer and bring her here," Ewan said through clenched teeth.

"I cannot, Laird," Cormac said with a heavy sigh. "The MacLaurens lost their healer and Lorna went to help deliver the laird's babe. You gave her permission yourself."

Ewan blew out his breath in frustration. Of course he had. Lorna was a skilled midwife and MacLauren had sent a frantic appeal to Ewan for help when his laboring wife had failed to bring forth a babe in a timely manner. At the time, he'd considered that if any of the McCabes needed the services of a healer, he himself would tend to the need.

Only now his wife needed stitching and it was God's truth he had no liking for the chore.

"Bring me ale, as strong as you can find," he murmured to Cormac. "You might need to ask Gertie where she stocks the blend we keep on hand for injuries and sedation. I need water, needle and thread, and something to bind her wound with. Be quick about it."

When Cormac left, Ewan turned back to Mairin, who lay on the bed, her eyes closed. She was unnaturally pale and it lent an even more delicate look to her features.

He shook his head at the direction of his thoughts. The wound wasn't serious. Certainly nothing she'd die of. Provided he could prevent her from taking a fever.

Gannon and Diormid stood close to the bed, hovering anxiously. While Ewan waited for Cormac to bring the supplies, he turned to his men and spoke in low tones.

"I want every person in the keep questioned. Someone must have seen something. I refuse to believe this was an accident. My men are far too careful. Find out who was practicing with bows and arrows."

"You think someone tried to harm the lass?" Gannon asked in disbelief.

"That's what I'd like to find out," Ewan said.

"I'm sure no one meant to kill me," Mairin said in a bleary voice. " 'Twas an accident, that's all. You may tell your men I forgive them."

"What do you want me to do, Ewan?" Caelen asked, his features drawn into a tight line.

"Remain with me. I'll need help holding her."

Cormac rushed in, his arms full and his fingers clamped tight around a flask of ale. Ewan took the items from Cormac and set them next to the bed.

He didn't want anyone touching Mairin, but he also recognized the impossibility of him being able to do everything. If he was going to do the stitching—and if the healer wasn't able to, no one else was going to do it but him—then he'd need one of the others to hold her steady and make sure he didn't do more damage than good.

He looked up at Cormac. "Go make sure the children are all right. Make sure that Crispen is attended to. He'll worry when he hears what happened to Mairin. Have

Maddie and the other women keep him below stairs until I am done."

Cormac bowed and hurried from the chamber, leaving Ewan and Caelen with Mairin.

Taking the flask in hand, Ewan sat on the bed close to Mairin's head and trailed a finger over her cheek.

"Lass, I need you to open your eyes and drink this."

Her eyelids fluttered and her unfocused eyes found his. He helped her lean up enough so that she could put her lips to the opening. As soon as the liquid hit her mouth, she flinched away, her face drawn into an expression of intense dislike.

"Are you poisoning me?" she demanded.

He held back the chuckle and put the flask close to her mouth again. "'Tis ale. You'll need it to help relax you. It will also help the pain."

She bit her lips and turned worried eyes back to him. "Pain?"

He sighed. "Aye, lass. Pain. I wish it weren't so, but the stitching up will cause you pain. If you drink this down, you won't feel as much. I promise."

"You likely won't feel anything at all after a good taste of that stuff," Caelen muttered.

She wrinkled up her nose and sighed fatalistically as she allowed Ewan to put the ale to her mouth again. To her credit, she drank it down with only minimal gagging and choking. When he lowered the flask, her skin had a greenish hue that made him worry the ale would come back up with the least provocation.

"Deep breaths," he said. "In through your nose. Let it settle."

She flopped back onto the pillow and promptly let out a very unladylike belch followed by a series of hiccups.

"You didn't hear that," she said.

Caelen arched an eyebrow and shot Ewan a look of amusement. "Hear what?"

"You're a good man, Caelen," she said dramatically. "You aren't near as fierce as you look, though if you'd smile on occasion, you'd be quite handsome."

Caelen scowled at that.

Ewan waited several minutes and then leaned over to stare down at Mairin. "How do you feel, lass?"

"Wonderful. Ewan, why are there two of you? I can assure you that one is entirely enough."

Ewan smiled. "You're ready."

"Am I? What am I ready for?"

Ewan dipped one of the cloths into a basin of warm water that Cormac had prepared. After wringing it out, he carefully wiped the now drying blood from Mairin's side. It was only a graze, and in fact, it looked as though the arrow went right between her arm and her side as there was a bloody crease on the inside of her arm as well.

The arrow cut through more of her side, and it was that flesh that needed stitching.

He motioned for Caelen to take position on Mairin's other side. Caelen walked around the bed and carefully pulled her arm away so that her side was bared to Ewan.

"You'll have to hold her," Ewan said patiently. "I don't want her moving when I put the needle to her flesh."

Reluctantly, Caelen anchored her more firmly against his body and held her wrist so that she couldn't flail her arm.

Mairin roused and stared dumbly up at Caelen. "Caelen, your laird will not be pleased to find you in his bed."

Caelen rolled his eyes. "I think he'll understand this time."

"Well, I don't," she said crossly. "It isn't decent. No one should see me in bed except the laird. Do you know what I told him?"

Ewan raised one eyebrow. "Perhaps 'tis best if you keep such matters to yourself, lass."

She ignored him and rambled on. "I told him that he was unskilled at loving. I don't think he was pleased with that statement."

Despite Ewan's glare, Caelen burst into laughter.

"Oh, it isn't polite to laugh at your laird," Mairin said in a solemn voice. "Besides, 'tis not true. I was quite wrong."

Ewan moved a hand to cover her mouth so she wouldn't blurt out anything else in her drunken state. "I think you've said enough."

He ignored Caelen's amused look and signaled that he was ready to begin.

Caelen grimaced, and something remarkably like sympathy flashed in his eyes when Mairin jumped at the first prick of the needle.

A whimper escaped from Mairin when he set the second stitch.

"Hurry," she whispered.

"I will, lass, I will."

In battle his hand never shook. It remained steady around the sword. It had never failed him. Not once. Yet here, doing such a simple task as setting needle to skin, he had to call on every bit of his control to keep his fingers precise.

By the time he tightened the final stitch, Mairin shook uncontrollably beneath his hand. Caelen's fingers were white from the pressure he exerted on her shoulder, and Ewan was sure she'd wear bruises.

"Let her go," Ewan said in a quiet voice. "I'm finished."

Caelen released her shoulder and Ewan waved him from the chamber. After Caelen closed the door behind him, Ewan reached down to touch Mairin's cheek only to find it wet with tears.

"I'm sorry, lass. I'm sorry it was necessary to hurt you."

She opened her tightly closed eyes, and tears shimmered in the blue depths. "It didn't hurt overly much."

She was lying but he felt a surge of pride at her bravado.

"Why don't you get some rest now? I'll have Maddie bring you a tisane for the pain."

"Thank you, Ewan," she whispered.

He leaned down and brushed a kiss across her brow. He waited until she'd closed her eyes before he backed away and retreated from the chamber.

Outside the door, his demeanor swiftly changed from caretaker to warrior.

He went in search of Maddie first and gave her instructions not to leave Mairin's bedside. Then he found Cormac, Diormid, and Gannon in the courtyard questioning his men.

"Have you found anything yet?" he asked.

"We still have the majority of the men to question, Laird. It'll take some time," Gannon said. "There were many men practicing archery, but no one can account for the errant shot."

"This is unacceptable. Someone struck Lady McCabe whether by accident or intent. I want that man." He turned to Diormid. "Were you not supervising the archery? Can you not account for your men?"

Diormid bowed his head. "Aye, Laird, I take full responsibility. Every one under me will be questioned at length. I will find the man responsible."

Ewan shook his head grimly. "I will not have the children of this keep unprotected. 'Tis as Mairin says. They should have a safe place to play and be children without their mothers worrying that they'll be killed by a stray arrow. From now on, the children will play behind the keep on the hillside, far away from where the men train."

"Where they play now is plenty distant from the courtyard," Cormac said with a fierce frown. "What happened today should not have occurred."

"Aye, but it did," Ewan bit back. "I don't want it to ever happen again. You will gather the men after the questioning. I want to address them."

It was well past midnight before Ewan trudged wearily up to his chamber. They'd questioned every single clansman, even the children, and no one could recall seeing anything untoward. The men practicing archery swore that none of them was responsible, and yet the arrow had been a McCabe arrow. There was no doubt about that. Afterward, he'd given his men a dressing down about being more careful in their training. If they couldn't keep the people of their own clan safe from themselves, how were they to protect them from outside threats?

Ewan let himself into his room, and Maddie stirred from her position by the fire.

"How is she?" Ewan asked in hushed tones.

Maddie rose and crept silently to stand in front of Ewan. "She's resting better now. She was in pain before, but after I gave her the tisane, she calmed and was able to rest better. I changed her dressing an hour past. The bleeding has stopped. You did a fine job stitching her, Laird."

"Any sign of fever?"

"Not yet. She's cool to the touch, just restless. I think she'll be just fine."

"Thank you, Maddie. You can retire to your cottage now. I appreciate you sitting with Mairin."

"I was glad to do it, Laird. If you have need of anything else, send for me at once."

She bobbed a curtsy and then walked by him and out the door.

Ewan undressed and slipped into bed beside Mairin, careful not to jar her. As soon as his body touched hers, she stirred and snuggled into his arms like a warm kitten on a cold night. She uttered a deep sigh against his neck and proceeded to wrap her legs around his while throwing one arm over his body.

He smiled. She was a possessive thing in bed. She considered his body her territory and she had no compunction about laying claim whenever he got near. Not that he minded. In truth, there was something about having a warm, sweet lass wrapped around him that appealed to him more than he'd ever thought possible.

He touched one strand of hair, allowing it to curl around the tip of his finger. He wasn't a man ruled by fear, but when he'd realized that Mairin had been shot, he'd experienced a wash of terror unlike anything he'd ever known. The idea that he could have lost her didn't sit well with him.

He could make a lot of excuses, including the biggest, that if she died, Neamh Álainn would never be his. His clan would never be rebuilt. Revenge would never be his. All of those things were true. But the simplest truth was that he hadn't wanted to lose her. None of the other things had even crossed his mind when he'd frantically examined her injuries.

Aye, the lass was getting under his skin. He'd been right about her from the moment he'd first laid eyes on her. She was definitely trouble.

CHAPTER 20

When Mairin awoke, the pain in her head overshadowed the pain in her side. She licked over her cracked lips but it wasn't enough to rid herself of the horrible taste in her mouth.

What on earth had the laird done to her? All she remembered was him ordering her to drink some foul liquid and having to choke it down. Even the memory made her stomach lurch precariously.

She rolled, testing the tenderness in her side, but ran into a warm, snuggly body. She smiled and curled her arm around Crispen and hugged him tight.

He opened his eyes and snuggled closer to her bosom. "Are you all right, Mama?"

"Aye, dearling, I'm perfectly well. I hardly feel a pinch. 'Twas just a little cut."

"I was scared."

His voice wavered and her heart squeezed at the uncertainty in his voice.

"I'm sorry you were afraid."

"Did it hurt? Maddie told me that Papa had to stitch you up. I would think that would hurt a lot."

"Aye, it did, but not overmuch. Your father had a good, steady hand and he was quick about it."

"Papa is the best," Crispen said, with all the confidence a young boy has in his father. "I knew he'd take care of you."

Mairin smiled and kissed the top of his head. "I have need to get out of this bed. I've lain here so long that my muscles are all stiff and sore. Would you like to help me?"

Crispen scrambled from the bed and then made a big show of aiding Mairin to her feet.

"You should go to your chamber and dress for the day. I'll meet you below stairs. Perhaps Gertie will have food for the both of us."

He gave her a huge grin and then scampered off, slamming the door behind him.

Mairin stretched as soon as he was gone, and winced. It truly wasn't bad. She hadn't told a lie. Just a twinge or two when she moved wrong. It certainly wasn't enough to keep her abed.

She turned to retrieve a gown from her wardrobe, when a flash of color caught her eye. Her gaze was drawn to the small table sitting near the window. On top of it lay a neatly folded pile of fabric.

It was her wedding dress. Forgetting all about her injury, she hurried over and delved her fingers into the sumptuous fabric. Then she yanked it upward and allowed the dress to unfold. Why, it was as good as new. There was no evidence of the rend.

She hugged the material to her chin and closed her eyes in delight. It was silly to be so emotional over a dress, but a woman only got married once, didn't she? She frowned. Well, most of the time. She wouldn't think on such matters as the laird dying and leaving her a widow.

She stroked the dress one last time, enjoying the softness as it glided over her fingers. Then she carefully put it away so it would keep until the next time she had an occasion to wear it.

Eager to leave her chamber, she went about pulling her gown on, her gestures awkward as she tried to arrange the dress with as little movement on her left side as possible.

As best she could, she brushed out her hair and left it down, since braiding it was going to be an impossibility one-handed. When she was satisfied that she didn't look quite so haggard, she left the chamber, hoping she wasn't too late for the morning meal.

And it was high time she saw to her duties as mistress of the keep. Surely that would keep her out of trouble with Ewan.

The days since her wedding had passed in a blur, and other than making the acquaintance of other women in the clan, Mairin hadn't done much of anything besides trying to avoid her faithful watchdogs.

Well, enough of all that. It was time to take things in hand. After taking an arrow in the side, she wasn't enthused about venturing out of the keep anyway.

When she entered the hall, she was greeted with looks of horror from her clansmen. Gannon and Cormac were involved in a heated debate, but when they saw her, they broke off and stared as if she'd grown two heads. Maddie, who was passing through as Mairin made her entrance, immediately threw up her hands and rushed over to where Mairin stood.

"My lady, you should still be abed," Gannon exclaimed as he and Cormac also hurried over.

"Aye," Maddie agreed. "You shouldn't be up. I was about to bring up a tray for you to eat in bed."

Mairin raised her hands to silence them. "I appreciate your concern. Truly, I do. But I'm perfectly fine. Staying abed serves no purpose except to drive me daft."

"The laird won't like this," Cormac muttered.

"What has the laird to do with it?" Mairin demanded.

"He should be relieved to know I'm back on my feet and ready to take on my duties as mistress of this keep."

"You should rest, lass," Maddie said soothingly, as she turned Mairin back in the direction of the stairs. "You wouldn't want to aggravate your injury."

Mairin shook off Maddie's hand and turned back to the hall, only to run into Gannon.

"Now, my lady, you should be abed," he said firmly.

"I'm fine," she insisted. "Why, I don't feel a bit of pain. Well, maybe a twinge or two," she added when Cormac shot her a disbelieving look. "But 'tis no reason to stay in bed on such a fine day. I'll even allow you to accompany me," she said to both Gannon and Cormac.

"You'll allow?" Gannon asked with a scowl.

She nodded and smiled serenely. "Aye, I will. I'll be no trouble. You'll see."

"I'll believe that when I see it," Cormac muttered.

"Maddie, I've need of your assistance if you're willing to give it."

Maddie looked confused. "Of course I'll help you, my lady, but I still think you should go above stairs and lie down. Perhaps you can tell me what it is you need assistance with, while you eat your meal in bed."

Mairin faced them all down and let her displeasure show. "There is absolutely no reason for me to go to bed."

"There is every reason, wife."

Cormac's and Gannon's shoulders sagged in relief while Maddie let out a sigh. Mairin turned to see her husband standing behind her, a look of mild annoyance on his face.

"Why is it I can't expect even the least bit of cooperation from you?"

Mairin's mouth fell open. "That's . . . That's . . . well, that's quite a rude thing to say, Laird. You're implying

I'm difficult. I'm not difficult." She whirled back around to face the others. "Am I?"

Cormac looked like he'd swallowed a bug while Gannon found something on the wall to study. Maddie didn't bother trying to be circumspect. She laughed outright.

"Why aren't you in bed, Mairin?" Ewan asked.

She turned back around to face him. "I'm quite well. I'm feeling much more myself today. Well, except for the headache. What was it you made me drink?"

"Something to make you more amenable. I'm tempted to have Gertie prepare you another flask."

She had no response to that.

"Come above stairs with me so I can redress your wound," Ewan said, as he directed her toward the stairs.

"But . . . but I was about to—"

Ewan propelled her up the steps. "Whatever it was you were about to do can wait until I've seen to your injury. If I'm satisfied that you're truly well enough to be up and around, I'll reconsider your confinement."

"My confinement? That's the most ridiculous—"

Ewan stopped and before she could finish her tirade, he planted his mouth over hers in a scorching, toe-curling kiss. It wasn't a tender gesture. It was demanding . . . and passionate, and Lord, she didn't want him to stop.

When he pulled away she had a hard time regaining her senses. They were . . . outside their chamber? She blinked as she tried to remember what brought them here.

"What was that you were saying, lass?"

Her brow furrowed. She opened her mouth then shut it again. "I don't remember."

He grinned and opened the door, pulling her inside the room. He started tugging at her dress and she batted his hands away.

"I won't have you tearing another dress," she muttered.

Ewan sighed. "I had Maddie repair your gown. It was an accident."

Her eyes widened. "You had my dress sewn?"

His lips formed a thin line and he looked away, ignoring her question.

"Laird, you saw to the repair of my dress?"

"Of course not," he said gruffly. " 'Tis a woman's matter. Men don't concern themselves with women's fripperies."

Mairin smiled and then threw herself against Ewan's chest before he could ward her off with his hand. "Thank you," she said, as she wrapped her arms around his waist.

Ewan let out a deep breath and pulled her away from his body, his gaze reproachful. "Lass, when are you going to demonstrate some restraint? You're going to upset your wound again, throwing yourself around like that."

She smiled at his stern face and then leaned up and palmed his face between her hands. Then she pulled him down into a breathless kiss that had her panting and gasping for air within seconds.

She wasn't sure who was more affected. She or he. His eyes glowed, and his nostrils flared as she rocked back onto her feet.

"I'm really quite well, Ewan," she whispered. "Mother Serenity used to avow that God's hand was ever guiding me because no matter how hard I fell or how badly I hurt myself, I always bounced back with amazing speed. My side pains me, aye, but not overly much. 'Tis more of a nuisance than a true pain. There's no reason for me to stay in bed the entire day."

"Remove your dress, Mairin. I'd like to see for myself how you're healing."

With a disgruntled sigh, she loosened the strings of her bodice and carefully peeled away the material. From the corner of her eye, she saw Ewan's expression grow tight as he stared at her bare shoulders.

Fascinated by his intense regard, she took a little more time than necessary to ease the dress down her body. Her hair fell down her back and forward over her breasts. Just the nipples peeked through the strands, and Ewan's gaze was fixed on them.

"Shall I lie down?" she asked softly.

Ewan cleared his throat. "Aye. That's fine. Make yourself comfortable. This won't take but a minute."

She eased down on the bed but watched Ewan from underneath her lashes. While he was thorough in changing the dressing on her wound, his heated gaze dragged over the rest of her body, so tangible that it was like the brush of his hand over her skin.

She stirred restlessly as he finished tying the strip of cloth around her side. The action thrust her breasts forward, brushing against his arm. Her nipples immediately puckered, the rasp of hair over the sensitive tips sending a warm flood of pleasure deep into her body.

"Lass, 'tis not the time for loving," he whispered. "But you tempt me. Aye, you tempt me like no other."

She circled his neck with her arms and they stared at each other for a long, silent moment. His eyes were beautiful and they reminded her of the highland hills in the spring. So green and alive with life.

He lowered his mouth to hers, gently at first, just a simple pressing of mouths together. A gentle smooching sound, flesh meeting flesh. He kissed the corner of her mouth then returned to the middle and then over to catch the other corner.

"You taste of sunshine."

Her chest tightened, and pleasure at the sweet words filled her to bursting.

She could feel him between her legs, hard and pulsing. He strained at his trews, pushing impatiently. She wanted him. Aye, she wanted him badly.

"Ewan," she whispered. "Are you sure 'tis not the time for loving?"

He groaned low in his throat. "Aye, you're a temptress all right."

She lifted her body to fit it to his, unsure of what she was doing, but it felt right. She was hot and flushed and she needed something she was sure only he could give her.

"Kiss me," she murmured.

"Oh, aye, I'll kiss you, lass. I'll kiss you until you beg me to stop."

His lips closed around one taut nipple and pulled as he sucked it farther into his mouth. His hands stroked her body and she arched like a contented cat seeking more of its master's touch.

"Easy, lass," he murmured. "I don't want you to hurt yourself."

Hurt herself? She was going to hurt *him* if he didn't continue kissing her.

He slipped his hands between her thighs and thumbed through the tight curls guarding her sensitive flesh. He brushed over the quivering point even as his fingers sought her moist opening. Despite his warning, she arched helplessly, unable to control her frantic response.

Fire stoked deep within her body and fanned rapidly through her groin, tightening each time his fingers stroked inside. This wasn't how it was done, was it?

She didn't care. Whatever he was doing felt so wondrous that she wanted to beg him never to stop. And she did. Over and over, the words spilling out between fractured sobs.

He sucked at each breast, alternating as he drove her

mindless with his fingers. She was hot and slick around him and she was fast building to an explosive end.

She whimpered and gripped his shoulders as she raised her hips, wanting more. He added a second finger to her sheath at the precise moment his thumb exerted more pressure.

She would have screamed—she did scream—but he raised his mouth from her breast to capture her mouth just as she did and swallowed the savage cry as she came apart in his arms.

Forgotten was her wound, the bandage, any pain or discomfort. There was only wave after wave of intense pleasure until she sagged onto the bed, too limp and weak to do anything more than gasp for air.

He rolled to the side and carefully pulled her into his arms. His lips brushed over her hair and he stroked the tresses with one hand. He caressed and petted every inch of her skin until a wonderful haze surrounded her and enfolded her in its warm glow.

"Sleep, lass," he murmured. "You need your rest."

Too fuzzy and sated to argue, she closed her eyes before she even realized she'd done so. Her last coherent thought was that he was far superior to ale as a sleeping drought.

CHAPTER 21

Mairin let out a lusty yawn and stretched her arms over her head. She was so limber from her bout of loving with Ewan that her side didn't even pain her.

Then she realized that despite her determination to be out and about, she'd spent half the day in her chamber. With a frown, she rose, grumbling under her breath about husbands and trickery.

He'd done it apurpose, she was convinced of it. He'd taken her to their chamber on the pretext of tending her wound and then distracted her with loving. And to think she'd ever thought he wasn't skilled in such matters.

He was too skilled by far.

This time when she left her chamber, Gannon met her directly outside her door. She looked at him in astonishment as he picked himself up off the floor.

"Have you been outside my door all afternoon?"

"Aye, my lady. 'Tis my duty to see to your safety. You have a habit of disappearing, so Cormac and I drew straws to see who would safeguard the chamber door."

She frowned, not liking the idea that she was such a distasteful duty that they were forced to draw straws over the unpleasant task.

She headed toward the stairs, determined to see Maddie without any interference from her husband or her watch guards.

Cormac was in the hall sharing a tankard of ale with a few of the older men of the clan.

"Have you seen Crispen about?" she called to Cormac.

"Nay, my lady. Last I knew of him, he was out playing with the other children. Would you like me to fetch him?"

"Oh nay, let him play. I have no need of him at the moment."

Cormac rose and started in Mairin and Gannon's direction, but she held up her hand. "I am only going to see Maddie. Gannon can escort me. Can't you, Gannon?"

"Aye, my lady. If 'tis all you're planning."

"Of course. 'Tis getting on into the afternoon. 'Twill be dark soon enough."

Gannon relaxed. He nodded in Cormac's direction and then gestured for Mairin to precede him from the hall.

Mairin set out at a brisk pace, determined for anyone who saw her to think she was fully recovered from her accident. By the time she reached Maddie's cottage, she was winded and she leaned against the door for support as she sucked in air.

After recovering her breath, she knocked politely on the door and waited. She frowned when no response was forthcoming.

"Maddie isn't in her cottage, my lady," one of the women sang out from one cottage down. "She's helping Gertie in the kitchens."

"Thank you," Mairin called.

"Would you like to go to the kitchens?" Gannon asked politely.

The thought of encountering Gertie was enough to persuade Mairin she could wait to speak to Maddie. It wasn't as if she could do much of anything today anyway.

She turned in the direction of the keep and came to a

stop and stared at the ruckus right in the middle of the path that split the cottages. Two older men were carrying on quite a spirited conversation, complete with shaking fists and fiercely worded threats.

"What on earth are they arguing about, Gannon?"

"Oh 'tis nothing you need to worry over, my lady," Gannon said. " 'Tis only Arthur and Magnus."

He tried to steer her down the path, but she remained rooted to her spot as the men's voices grew louder.

"Quit yer shouting you old goats!"

Mairin blinked in surprise at the woman leaning out her window hollering at the two men. Arthur and Magnus paid her no mind and continued their argument. It quickly became clear to Mairin that the dispute centered around the mare that stood between the two men, looking quite unimpressed with the goings-on.

"Who does the mare belong to?" Mairin whispered. "And why do they argue so fiercely over it?"

Gannon sighed. " 'Tis an old argument, my lady. And they do enjoy a good argument. If it wasn't the mare, it would be something else."

One of the men turned and started to stomp down the path, shouting all the way that he was going straight to the laird.

Thinking quickly, Mairin stepped in his way and he pulled up just short of running right over her.

"Watch where you're going, lass! Now step aside, if you please. I have business with the laird."

"You'll be respectful and mind your tongue, Arthur," Gannon growled. " 'Tis your mistress you address."

Arthur narrowed his eyes and then cocked his head to the side. "Aye, so it is. Shouldn't you be abed after your mishap?"

Mairin heaved a sigh. The news was all over the keep, no doubt. She had no desire to appear weak when she assumed her duties as mistress. She was already mentally calculating all that needed to be done. With or without Maddie's aid, it was time she stepped into the running of the keep.

"Step aside," Magnus declared. "You have the manners of a jackass, Arthur."

He smiled at Mairin then and offered a sweeping bow. "We haven't been properly introduced. My name's Magnus McCabe."

Mairin returned his smile and was sure to include Arthur, lest he use that as an excuse to start another argument.

"I couldn't help but overhear you arguing over the mare," she began hesitantly.

Arthur snorted. "That's because Magnus has a mouth the size of a mountain."

Mairin held up a hand. "Rather than trouble your laird over such an inconsequential matter, perhaps I can be of help."

Magnus rubbed his hands together and cast a triumphant glance in Athur's direction. "There, you see? The lass will determine who has the right of it."

Arthur rolled his eyes and didn't look impressed with Mairin's offer.

"There is no right or wrong of it," Arthur said matter-of-factly. "The mare is mine. Always has been. Gannon knows."

Gannon closed his eyes and shook his head.

"I see," Mairin said. Then she looked at Magnus. "You dispute Arthur's claim to the mare?"

"I do," he said emphatically. "Two months past, he became enraged because the mare bit him on the—"

"There is no need to say where she bit me," Arthur hastily broke in. "'Tis sufficient to say she bit me. That's all that's important."

Magnus leaned in and whispered. "She bit him on the arse, my lady."

Her eyes went wide. Gannon issued a sharp reprimand to Magnus for speaking to his mistress in such an indelicate fashion, but Magnus didn't look the least repentant.

"Anyway, once the mare bit Arthur, he became so enraged that he turned her loose, slapped her on the flanks, and told the ungrateful . . ." He stopped and cleared his throat. "Well, he told her not to bother ever returning. It was cold out and raining, you see. I took the mare in, dried her, and gave her some oats. So you see, the mare belongs to me. Arthur relinquished all claim to her."

"My lady, the laird has already heard their complaint," Gannon whispered to her.

"And what did the laird decide?" she whispered back.

"He told them to work it out between themselves."

Mairin made a sound of exasperation. "That wasn't particularly helpful."

This would be as good a starting point as any to assert her authority and show her clan that she was a worthy mate to their laird. Ewan was a busy man, and matters such as this should be settled without pulling him into a petty argument.

She turned back to the men, who'd begun bickering again. She held up her hands for silence, and when that didn't work, she put her fingers between her lips and issued a sharp whistle.

Both men flinched and turned to stare at her in astonishment.

"A lady doesn't whistle," Arthur reprimanded.

"Aye, he's right, my lady."

"Oh, so now the two of you are prepared to agree on something," Mairin muttered. "It was the only way to quiet you."

"You wanted something?" Magnus asked.

She folded her hands neatly in front of her, satisfied that she had the perfect plan to solve the argument.

"I'll have Gannon cut the mare in half and give you each an equal portion. 'Tis the only fair way to go about it."

Arthur and Magnus stared at her then looked at each other. Gannon closed his eyes again and didn't say a word.

"She's daft," Arthur said.

Magnus nodded. "The poor laird. He must have been tricked. He's married a daft lass."

Mairin put her hands on her hips. "I am not daft!"

Arthur shook his head, a light of sympathy in his eyes. "Maybe daft is too strong a word. Addled. Aye, maybe a wee addled. Did you suffer an injury to your head recently?"

"Nay, I did not!"

"As a child then?" Magnus asked.

"I am in perfect command of my faculties," she snapped.

"Then why in God's name did you suggest we cut the mare in two?" Arthur demanded. "That's the most daft thing I've ever heard of."

"It worked for King Solomon," she muttered.

"King Solomon ordered a horse cut in half?" Magnus asked in a confused voice.

"Who is King Solomon? He's not our king. I bet he's English. 'Twould be a very English thing to do," Arthur said.

Magnus nodded in agreement. "Aye, all English are daft." Then he turned to Mairin. "Be you English, lass?"

"Nay! Why on earth would you ask something like that?"

"Maybe she has some English blood," Arthur said. " 'Twould explain things."

She gripped her head and felt the sudden, violent urge to pull out her hair by the roots.

"King Solomon suggested a baby be cut in half when two women both claimed to be its mother."

Even Gannon looked appalled. Magnus and Arthur gaped at her and then shook their heads.

"And the English claim we're barbarians," Arthur grumbled.

"King Solomon wasn't English," she said patiently. "And the point was that the real mother would be so horrified over the thought of her baby being killed that she would give the baby to the other mother to spare the child's life."

She looked pointedly at them, hoping they'd understand the moral, but they still stared at her as if she'd spewed a litany of blasphemies.

"Oh, never mind," she snapped. She stalked forward, grabbed the reins from an astonished Magnus, and pulled the hapless mare along as she headed back toward the keep.

"My lady, what are you doing?" Gannon hissed, as he jogged to keep up with her.

"Hey, she's stealing our horse!" Magnus cried.

"Our horse? 'Tis my horse, you dolt."

She ignored the two men as they began bickering all over again.

" 'Tis clear that neither one of them deserves the poor horse," Mairin said. "I'll take her to Ewan. He'll know what to do."

Gannon's expression told her he had no love of taking the horse to his laird.

"Don't worry, Gannon. I'll tell him you tried to stop me."

"You will?"

The hopeful tone in his voice amused her.

She stopped in the middle of the courtyard, suddenly aware that there were no men training and no sign of Ewan.

"Well, where is he?" she asked in exasperation. "Oh, never mind," she said when Gannon failed to immediately respond. "I'll take the horse to your stable master. You do have a stable master, don't you?"

"Aye, my lady, we most certainly do, but—"

"Point me in the direction of the stables then," she said before he could continue. "I really should have familiarized myself with everything on the McCabe lands by now. I've been around the keep and to the women's cottages but beyond that I'm frightfully ignorant. Tomorrow we'll rectify that."

Gannon blinked. "We will?"

"Aye, we will. Now, the stables?"

Gannon sighed and pointed across the courtyard to a pathway leading beyond the stone skirt that sheltered the courtyard. Mairin set off again, leading the mare past the wall.

She followed the worn path until she reached the far side of the keep where she saw an old structure that she assumed must be the stables. There was new wood framing the doorway, but there were also places that looked scorched by an old fire. The roof had been patched and looked to be sturdy enough to hold out the rain and snow.

She was annoyed to see Magnus and Arthur standing in front of the archway that led into the area where the laird's horses were cared for. They watched her warily as she approached, and she scowled to show them the full force of her displeasure.

"You're not getting the horse back," she bellowed. "I'm giving the horse to the stable master so she'll be cared for appropriately."

"I *am* the stable master, you daft lass," Arthur bellowed back.

"You will address your mistress with respect," Gannon roared.

Mairin gaped at Arthur and then turned to Gannon. "Stable master? This . . . This . . . *cretin* is the stable master?"

Gannon sighed. "I tried to tell you, my lady."

"That's ridiculous," Mairin sputtered. "He has as much business running a stable as I do."

"I do a fine job," Arthur snapped. "And I'd do it a lot better if I wasn't having to chase down people who steal my horse."

"You're relieved of duty, sir."

"You can't relieve me of duty!" Arthur screeched. "Only the laird can do that."

"I'm the mistress of this keep and I say you've been relieved," Mairin said belligerently. She turned to Gannon. "Tell him."

Gannon looked a little uncertain, but he stood behind his mistress. She nodded approvingly as Gannon informed the older man that he'd indeed been relieved of duty.

Arthur stomped away muttering all manner of blasphemies while Magnus looked on with a smug smile.

"Is it any wonder the horse bit him on the arse?" Mairin muttered as Arthur disappeared.

She handed the reins to Gannon. "Will you put her into a stall and make sure she's fed?"

Ignoring Gannon's disgruntled look, she turned to head back in the direction of the keep. She was quite pleased with herself. She'd not only managed to escape the confines of the keep without running into her husband, but she'd also handled a difficult situation. Her first duty as mistress of the keep. She smiled and hurried up the steps and entered the great hall.

She waved at Cormac on her way through. "I'm just going up to change for the evening meal. Gannon will be along shortly. He's taking care of a horse for me."

Cormac rose, his brow creased in confusion. "A horse?"

Mairin fairly skipped up the stairs. The day hadn't been a complete waste. In fact, it had been quite lovely.

And she was making strides in her bid to take an active part in the keep's activities. Why, she'd made a decision and hadn't even bothered Ewan over such a trivial matter. It was the least she could do. He had many important duties and the more she could smooth things for him, the more he'd be able to concentrate on those duties.

She splashed water on her face and brushed the dust from her dress. Aye, it had been a good day, and her wound wasn't even paining her.

"Mairin!"

She flinched as the laird's roar carried all the way up the stairs and through her chamber door. He bellowed loud enough to shake the rafters.

With a shake of her head, she picked up her brush and made quick work of the tangles in her hair. If maneuvering her left arm didn't prick at her side, she'd take the time to braid her hair. Maybe by morning.

"Mairin, present yourself at once!"

She dropped her brush and scowled. Lord, but the man was impatient. After one more pat of her dress she headed down the stairs. When she rounded the corner into the hall, she saw Ewan standing in the middle of the room, arms crossed over his chest, a deep scowl etched around his mouth.

To the side stood Arthur and Magnus along with Gannon and Caelen. A few of Ewan's men tarried around the tables, having taken a keen interest in the fuss.

She came to a stop in front of Ewan and smiled demurely up at him. "You summoned me, Laird?"

Ewan's scowl deepened. Then he ran a hand through his hair and looked heavenward. "In the course of the last hour, you've stolen a man's horse and somehow managed to leave me without a stable master. Would you care to explain yourself, lass?"

"I settled a dispute," she said. "And when I discovered that this odious man who clearly abuses his horses was responsible for *your* horses, Laird, I remedied the situation."

"You had no authority to do either," Ewan said tightly. "Your duties are quite simple. Obey me and don't interfere with the running of this keep."

Hurt squeezed her chest. Humiliation tightened her cheeks as she looked from man to man. She saw sympathy in Gannon's expression, but in Caelen's she saw agreement.

Not trusting that she wouldn't further humiliate herself, she turned away and walked rigidly back out of the hall.

"Mairin!" Ewan roared.

She ignored him and increased her pace. She bypassed the stairs and slipped out of one of the doorways leading to the outside.

Odious, impossible, infuriating. All of them. They accused her of being daft, but this was the daftest clan she'd ever come across.

Tears burned her eyes, and she angrily dashed them away. Dusk had fallen over the keep, blanketing it in hues of lavender and gray. The chill nipped at her but she paid no heed, as she hurried across the empty courtyard.

One of the guards on the wall called a warning to her but she waved him off and told him she had no intention of going far. She just needed to be away. Away from Ewan's roaring and the censure in his eyes.

She kept in line with the wall of the keep, making sure to remain inside the stone skirt. There had to be a place somewhere that afforded privacy while still offering safety.

Her solution came in the form of the old bathhouses in the rear of the keep. There was even a bench in the shell of the stone walls. She ducked under a sagging doorway and settled herself on the bench that lined the only wall still standing in its entirety.

Finally, a place away from the rest of the clan where she could have a private weep and lament her husband's disgraceful behavior.

CHAPTER 22

It was important that Ewan not go chasing after his wife, especially in front of his men. It was obvious the lass had no idea what she'd gotten herself into. He'd give her time to cool down and then he would instruct her on the way of things.

He turned back to the men who stood behind him. Gertie was already putting the evening meal on the table, and judging by the smell, it had been a good hunting day for the men assigned to bring fresh meat into the keep.

"Do I have my position back, Laird?" Arthur asked.

Ewan nodded wearily. "Aye, Arthur. You've a fine hand with the horses. However, I've had enough of your incessant bickering with Magnus, and 'tis obvious that it upsets your mistress."

Arthur didn't look happy but he nodded and hurried away to take his seat. Magnus looked as though he wanted to make a jibe at Arthur but Ewan's fierce scowl stopped him. He, too, took his seat—at a table over from where Arthur had sat.

Ewan took his seat and was followed by his men. When Maddie made her way by to fill his trencher, he stopped her.

"When you are finished serving the men, take a tray

up to your mistress. She's in her chamber, and I don't want her to miss the evening meal."

"Aye, Laird, I'll see to it immediately."

Satisfied that his wife wouldn't go hungry and that, for the moment, all arguing was done, he dove into his portion, savoring the taste of the fresh venison.

By letting Mairin get over her upset, chances were that by the time he retired to their chamber, the initial storm would be over. He congratulated himself for his brilliant analysis and had a second helping of the stew.

A half hour later, however, when Maddie hurried into the hall to tell him that his wife was not in their chamber, he realized that his mistake was believing anything would be simple when it came to his impulsive wife.

She made him feel incompetent, and that his efforts to keep her safe were haphazard at best. None of that was true, but it raised his ire because he hadn't felt a moment of self-doubt since he was a lad. He could train and lead an entire army. He could win a battle when he was outnumbered five to one. But he couldn't keep a slip of a lass under control. It defied all reason and was making him daft in the process.

He pushed away from the table and stalked in the direction that Mairin had left. It was obvious she hadn't gone up the stairs, so he continued past to the doorway leading outside the keep.

"Have you seen your mistress?" he called to Rodrick who was up on the wall.

"Aye, Laird. She came by half hour past."

"And where is she now?"

"She's in the bathhouses. Gregory and Alain are watching over her. She's having a good cry, but otherwise, she is well."

Ewan winced and heaved a sigh. He much preferred her spitting like an angry kitten or even indignant and questioning his authority. But crying? He had no use for female tears and even less experience in dealing with them.

He went in the direction of the bathhouses. Gregory and Alain were standing outside one of the walls and they looked vastly relieved when Ewan strode up.

"Thank goodness you're here, Laird. You must make her stop. She's going to take ill with so much crying," Alain said.

Gregory frowned. "It isn't right for a lass to cry so much. Whatever it is you have to promise her, please do so. She's going to drown herself!"

Ewan held up a hand. "Thank you for your protection. You can go now. I'll see to your mistress."

They did a sorry job of hiding their obvious relief. As they left, Ewan heard the light sniffles that came from the inside of the bathhouses. Damn, but he hated the idea of her crying.

He stepped inside the dark interior and glanced around, blinking to adjust to the darkness. He followed the sounds of the sniffling until he found her sitting on a bench along the far wall. She was partially silhouetted by a sliver of moonlight that crept in through the narrow window carved into the stone, and he could see that her head was bowed, her shoulders slumped forward.

"Go away." Her muffled voice filtered through the crumbling bathhouse.

"Ah, lass," he said as he sat beside her on the bench. "Don't cry."

"I'm not crying," she said in a voice that clearly indicated she was.

" 'Tis a sin to lie," he offered, knowing it would get her back up.

" 'Tis a sin to do nothing but yell at your wife, too," she said mournfully. "You promised to cherish me, aye, you did, but 'tis God's truth I don't feel very cherished."

He sighed. "Mairin, you sorely try my patience. I

imagine you'll continue to exasperate me for years to come. I can tell you this won't be the only time I yell at you. If I told you differently I'd be lying."

"You embarrassed me in front of your men," she said in a low voice. "In front of that cretin stable master. He's a toad and shouldn't be allowed near a horse."

Ewan touched her cheek and brushed a long strand behind her ear so he could better see her face. He winced when he felt the dampness of her skin.

"Listen to me, sweeting. Arthur and Magnus have been arguing in one form or fashion since before I was born. The day they stop arguing will be the day we lay them in the ground. They came to me about the horse, but I refused to render a judgment because it kept them focused on the horse. If I gave it to one or the other, then they'd find something else to argue over, and at least the horse is harmless enough."

"I took it away from the both of them," she said. "She may be old but she deserves better than to be argued over by two daft old men."

Ewan chuckled. "Aye, they told me you stole their horse and that you relieved Arthur of his duties."

Mairin twisted in her seat and latched on to Ewan's hand with her own. "How can that deplorable man be your stable master? Why, Ewan, he put his own horse into the cold without food or shelter. You would trust such a man with your own steed? A horse you would go into battle with?"

Ewan smiled at her vehemence. She was a fierce little thing. She'd already come to view his keep as her home and she was taking over with quite the militant attitude.

"I appreciate your determination to ensure we have the best possible care for my horses. But the truth is, Arthur is a magician with horses. Aye, he's hostile and argumentative and he's not very respectful, but he's old and he's been the stable master since my father was laird. He didn't mistreat his mare, lass. I would have taken a whip to him myself if that was the case. 'Twas the story he told to save face after the horse took a bite out of his backside. He's a complete lamb when it comes to the horses. They're his babies, although he'd die before admitting so. He cares more for them than for any other living thing."

Mairin's shoulders slumped and she looked down at her feet. "I made a fool of myself, didn't I?"

"Nay, lass."

She twisted her fingers in her lap. "I just wanted to fit in here. Be a part of a clan. I wanted to have duties. I wanted my clan to respect me, come to me with their troubles. I used to dream of having a home and a family. Not a day went by at the abbey that I didn't imagine what it would be like to live free of fear and to be able to go my own way."

She chanced a look up at him, and he could see the vulnerability shining in her eyes. "That was all just a dream, wasn't it, Ewan?"

His heart turned over in his chest. It was true he hadn't given much thought to her circumstances and how they'd affected her. For all of her adult life, she'd been sequestered at an abbey with only nuns for company and guidance. She'd grown to expect that her life would be hard and uncertain when all she wanted was freedom and someone to cherish her.

So much of her actions and disregard for his authority made sense now. It wasn't as though she set out to blatantly ignore his commands. She was merely feeling her way around and reveling in the first taste of home and family she'd ever experienced. She was spreading her wings and flexing her muscles for the first time ever.

He gathered her in his arms and squeezed affectionately. "Nay, lass, it wasn't a dream. 'Tis no less than you should expect from your new home and clan. You're still finding your way. You'll make mistakes and so will I. This is new for both of us. I propose a bargain. You be patient with me and I promise to try not to yell so much."

She went quiet for a moment and then she turned her chin up until she looked at him again. "That seems fair. I apologize for interfering in things that were not my concern. You were right. 'Tisn't my place."

The hurt and defeat in her voice stirred something deep within him. "Lass, look at me," he said gently, as he tipped her chin upward with his fingers. "This is your home and your clan. You are mistress here and as such your authority is second only to mine. I plan for you to have many years to look forward to making this your home and a place you're comfortable with. There's no need to have everything done in a day."

She nodded.

"You're cold, lass. Come back inside the keep so I can warm you properly."

As he'd hoped, his words made her stir restlessly against him. To give her added incentive, he fused his lips to hers, his heat melting her cold mouth. Ice against fire. In moments, she was returning his kiss with lusty, hot, open-mouthed kisses of her own. Lord, but the lass was a quick study in the art of kissing and using tongues.

He'd spend a lifetime of being indecent in her eyes if she'd only continue kissing him thusly.

"Come," he said haggardly. "Before I take you right here and now."

"You're a lesson in sinning, Laird," she said in her prim, disapproving voice.

He grinned and chucked her cheek in an affectionate manner. "Aye, that may be true, lass, but you're no saint yourself."

Mairin watched her husband as she ate the food that Maddie delivered after Mairin and Ewan retired to their chamber. He looked deceptively lazy, sprawled on the bed, hands behind his head and legs crossed at the ankle.

He'd stripped to just his trews, and she found it hard to concentrate on her food when he was lying there looking so blasted appealing.

As she downed the last of her food, her conversation with Maddie came to mind. She ducked her head, sure that Ewan would see the blush rising on her face, and she had no desire to tell him her thoughts. Not when they were so deliciously indecent.

But now that the thought had stuck in her mind, she studied him from the corner of her eye and wondered if she had the nerve to do as Maddie had described. It stood to reason that if he could make her so mindless with his mouth, the reverse would also be true.

"Are you finished yet, wife?" Ewan drawled.

She glanced down at the empty trencher and slowly set it aside. Aye, this was indeed the perfect time to try her wiles. She nearly giggled at the idea of her *having* wiles. Mother Serenity would be most stern over such a thought.

Not wanting to seem too obvious, she took her time preparing for bed. She undressed with a great deal more care than she usually exerted, her every movement slow and sensual. Twice she peeked to the side to see Ewan watching her, his eyes dark and hooded.

When she was completely nude, she sashayed to the basin of water and made a great production of washing. She turned to the side to give Ewan a good view of her profile, and she heard him suck in his breath when her nipples puckered in the wake of the damp cloth.

Having worked up the sufficient courage and having had enough time to formulate her plan, she tossed aside the cloth and moved toward the bed.

"You're still clothed, husband," she murmured as she stood over him.

Though he still wore his trews, they did nothing to disguise the bulge between his legs. He was hard and getting harder with every passing second.

"Aye, lass, but I can remedy that."

He started to push upward, but she reached down and pressed a hand to his chest.

" 'Tis my duty to undress you."

He settled back onto the bed as her fingers went to the laces of his trews. As soon as she loosened them sufficiently, his erection jutted upward. She wasn't sure she'd ever get used to his size. And she couldn't even fathom how she'd get it in her mouth, but Maddie seemed sure that it was done by plenty of women.

When she had trouble tugging the material over his hips, he lifted them and his hands covered hers as he helped push it down his legs.

When he would have sat up, she once again pushed him down, only this time she followed him down, until her lips were a mere breath from his.

She kissed him, enjoying the feel of his mouth beneath hers. Her hands wandered over his chest, and she marveled at how hard and solid he was. The roughness of his scars contrasted with the bristle of the hair underneath her palms. His nipples puckered and hardened under her touch and she went back, rubbing over them again, fascinated by the reaction that was similar to her own.

"What are you about, lass?" he murmured against her mouth.

She smiled and nuzzled his jaw and kissed her way down to his neck just like he'd done to her. Judging by the sudden tension in his body, he liked it every bit as much as she had.

"I have a theory," she whispered as she hovered just

over one flat nipple. Then she flicked her tongue out and licked the point until it hardened and jutted outward.

Ewan groaned. "What is your theory, lass?"

Placing both hands on his chest, she trailed her tongue down his midline until it dipped into his navel. He flinched and arched upward, his erection prodding at her side.

"My theory is that men might enjoy being kissed . . . down there . . . as much as women enjoy a man's mouth . . . down there."

"Ah hell," Ewan gasped out.

She curled her hand around his thick manhood and tucked the head between her lips.

He sounded like a man taking in his last breaths of life. His body was so tense and bowed that he resembled a wooden beam. His hands flew to the bed and gripped the linens. Oh aye, he liked it.

Emboldened by his obvious enjoyment, she took him deeper, running her hand up and down the shaft as she sucked him farther into her mouth.

"Mairin," he gasped. "Oh sweet heaven, lass. Have mercy."

She smiled and lowered her fingers to stroke his swollen sac. He arched his hips, thrusting even as she took him as deep as she could. He was impossibly hard, so turgid that she wondered how he didn't split his skin.

He throbbed in her hand, hard, yet velvety soft, like a steel sword encased in silk.

"Lass, I can't take much more. You need to stop before I spill in your mouth."

Still gripping him in her hand, she raised her head so she could look into his eyes. Her hair fell forward and he reached up to smooth it from her face, his palm cradling her cheek as he did so.

"Would you like to spill in my mouth?" she asked shyly.

"Ah, Mairin, that's like asking a dying man if he wants to live."

She cupped his face between her hands and lowered her mouth to kiss him. Long and sweet, she licked over his lips and dove inside, brushing her tongue over his, tasting him and teasing.

"I like the idea of tasting you," she whispered.

He cupped her breasts, and as she pulled away, he raised the mounds and lifted his head so that he could feast on her nipples. She leaned heavily on him, her knees weak and shaking under the onslaught. If she gave him half a chance, he'd turn the tables on her seduction.

She pulled away but softened her withdrawal with another kiss, and then she kissed another path down his chest, to his firm belly and then beyond to the nest of hair where his erection jutted hard and bold.

She licked first, tracing the bulging vein on the underside of the thick shaft. When she reached the head, there was already a droplet of liquid seeping from the slit. She lapped gently, sipping at the slightly salty taste of him.

Ewan's breath escaped in one long hiss, and when she lowered her mouth down his length, he seemed to lose all of his carefully cultivated control.

He writhed on the bed, his movements desperate and unmeasured. She held him tight, using her tongue to drive him wild. His hand closed around hers and he pulled upward, his grip tightening as he worked her hand up and down. Realizing what it was he wanted her to do, she began to move her hand in rhythm with her mouth.

"Ah, lass, like that. Just like that," he moaned.

His hand tangled in her hair and then gripped the base of her neck, holding her as his hips hammered upward. She took him to the back of her throat and then hot liquid exploded onto her tongue, filling her mouth in a seemingly unending stream.

It was the most erotic thing she could have ever imagined, and never could she have thought that something so course and basic could have excited her beyond measure, but loving her husband in this fashion drove her as wild as it did him.

She felt powerful and equal, like she could give him every bit as much as he gave her.

He collapsed on the bed and slipped from her mouth. She swallowed the last of his passion and wiped at her lips with the back of her hand. His breaths came ragged and harsh and his gaze slid hotly over her as his chest heaved up and down.

"Come here, lass," he said hoarsely.

He pulled her down on top of him so that their bodies fused, warm and sweaty. He wrapped his arms around her and held her tight as he pressed a kiss to her hair.

Remembering Maddie's assertion that men were much more amenable after loving, Mairin lifted her head until her hair drapped over his chest.

"Ewan?"

His hands smoothed over her shoulders and down to cup her buttocks. He squeezed and kneaded gently as he stared up into her eyes.

"Aye, lass?"

"I would like your promise," she said.

He cocked his head to the side. "What are you wanting me to promise?"

"I realize we're newly married and I don't fully know the way of things, but I've discovered I'm a very possessive woman. I want your promise that you'll be faithful. I know 'tis common for some men to keep a leman—"

She was interrupted by Ewan's scowl. Then he sighed.

"Lass, you've just thoroughly worn me out. Do you mind telling me how on earth I'd have the energy to bed another woman?"

She frowned. That wasn't what she'd wanted to hear.

He sighed again. "Mairin, I took vows. I didn't take them lightly. As long as you prove a good and faithful wife, there's no reason for me to seek out another woman. I wouldn't dishonor you or myself that way. Your loyalty is to me, aye, but my loyalty is to you and any children you bear me. I take my responsibilities very seriously."

Tears crowded her eyes and she leaned down until their foreheads touched. "I'll be faithful to you as well, Ewan."

"You damned well better," he growled. "I'll kill any man who touches you."

"Did you like me kissing you . . . down there . . . ?"

He grinned and raised his lips to smooch hers. "I liked it very much. I may require you to kiss me there every single night before we retire."

She frowned and punched him in the gut. He laughed and sucked inward in mock agony. He grabbed her wrists and rolled, careful not to jar her side. When they were on their sides, locked together, their faces so close she could feel his breath, he touched her cheek and rubbed with the back of his knuckle.

"And now, lass, I'm thinking I have some kissing of my own to do. Complete with tongue."

She sucked in her breath until she saw spots dancing in her vision. "Tongue? Have I told you lately how indecent your tongue is, Laird?"

"It can't get any more indecent than yours just got," he said.

Then he proceeded to show her that indeed, he was far, far more indecent than she could ever dream of being.

CHAPTER 23

Ewan woke to a heavy pounding on his chamber door. Before he could rouse himself enough to answer the summons, the door burst open. Ewan was out of bed in the next instant, his hand on the floor and around the hilt of his sword.

"Jesu, Ewan, 'tis just me," Caelen said. "You were sleeping the sleep of the dead."

Ewan sat back on the bed and first pulled the furs up to shield Mairin's nudity and then to shield his own. "Get the hell out of here," he said irritably.

"If my presence offends your maidenly modesty, I'll turn my back until you dress," Caelen said.

"'Tis not mine I'm worried over," Ewan snarled.

"Well, hell, Ewan, I can't see the lass, nor am I looking. 'Tis important or I wouldn't have breached your chamber."

"Ewan?"

Mairin's sleepy voice rose from the covers, and her head poked out. Her hair was all rumpled, her eyes droopy, and yet somehow she still managed to look adorable. Even though Caelen claimed not to be looking, Ewan caught his brother glancing Mairin's way.

Ewan leaned over and brushed the hair from her face and then kissed her on the forehead. "Listen to me, sweeting. I want you to go back to sleep. You need your rest."

She murmured something he couldn't hear and snuggled back underneath the blankets. He touched her cheek one last time and then rolled out of bed to pull his clothing on.

He ordered Caelen into the hall until he was finished and then put on his boots and picked up his sword. With one final look in Mairin's direction, he strode into the hall where Caelen fell into step with him.

"Sweeting? You need your sleep?" Caelen mimicked. "I think you're missing your scrotum, brother."

Ewan balled his fist and slammed it into Caelen's jaw. Caelen went reeling and had to catch himself on the wall to keep from falling down the stairs.

"Well damn, Ewan. I have to say marriage doesn't agree with you," Caelen said, as he rubbed his jaw.

"I think it agrees with me just fine."

As they entered the hall, Ewan saw Alaric stride in, his clothing dusty and lines of fatigue creasing his face.

"You dragged me from a warm bed for Alaric's arrival?" Ewan asked.

"He said 'twas important. He sent a messenger ahead to summon you to meet him," Caelen defended.

"Ewan," Alaric called as he strode forward.

"What's so urgent that you sent a messenger ahead of you?"

"McDonald is on his way here."

Ewan frowned. "Here? Why? What happened, Alaric?"

"You married. That's what happened. Laird McDonald had every intention of marrying off his daughter to you. He's not pleased to discover that's no longer an option. He's insisted on meeting with you, no matter that you are newly married, as I tried to explain. He informed me that if you wanted this alliance, you would meet with him."

Ewan cursed. "We're in no position to host anyone. We can barely feed our own clan and now we have to host McDonald and his men? We need weeks to prepare for an event such as this, not mere days."

Alaric grimaced and closed his eyes.

"What?" Ewan asked sharply.

"Not days. Day."

More curses blistered Ewan's lips. "Day? When is he arriving?"

Alaric sighed and wiped his forehead wearily. "Why do you think I ran my horse into the ground to get here? McDonald will arrive on the morrow."

"Ewan?"

Ewan whirled to see Mairin standing a short distance away, her gaze questioning.

"May I have permission to speak?"

He lifted a brow, surprised she'd even ask. But he also saw how nervous she appeared as she stared at his two brothers.

He held out his hand, and she hurried over to take it. "You have need of something, Mairin?"

"I overheard, I mean about Laird McDonald coming. Is there trouble?"

Worry shadowed her blue eyes as she stared up at him.

"Nay, sweeting, no trouble. Laird McDonald and I are in talks. 'Tis nothing for you to worry over."

"He'll be here tomorrow?"

"Aye."

She frowned and then squared her shoulders. "There's much to be done, Ewan. Are you going to be difficult about my injury and make me stay abed, or are you going to allow me to do my duty so that I'm not shamed beyond measure when we have important guests?"

"Shamed?"

She huffed in exasperation. "The keep is in no condition for visitors. There's cleaning to do, food to cook, instructions to give. Why, if someone arrived today, they'd think me the most incompetent of any laird's wife. Not only would I be shamed, but you would be shamed as well."

She sounded so appalled over the idea that she would bring shame to him that his gaze softened. He squeezed her hand, which he still held between his own.

"As long as you promise to ease off if you start feeling any pain, I have no issue with you working to ready the keep. However, I expect any of the harder tasks to be taken by the other women. I don't want you doing anything to tear your stitches."

Her smile lit up the entire room. Her eyes danced and she squeezed his fingers. She looked exuberant, like she wanted to fling her arms around him, but she collected herself and let go of his hand.

"My thanks, Laird. I won't let you down."

She bobbed a quick curtsy and hurried off. "Welcome home, Alaric," she called back. Then she stopped and turned, a frown marring her lips. She hastened back over to Alaric and took his hand. "Your pardon. I didn't even think to ask you if you'd had refreshment after your journey. Are you well? We are glad to have you home."

Alaric looked befuddled as Mairin gripped his hand and shook it up and down as she spoke.

"I'm fine, lass."

"Would you like me to have hot water brought up to your chamber so you can take a bath?"

Alaric looked appalled by the suggestion, and Ewan stifled his laughter.

"Uh, nay, the loch will suffice."

Mairin frowned again. "Oh, but the loch is so cold. Wouldn't you prefer hot water?"

Caelen snickered. "Go ahead, Alaric. Have a nice long soak in the tub."

Alaric sent Caelen a quelling stare. Then he smiled gently at Mairin, which was good, because Ewan didn't want to have to admonish his brother for hurting his wife's feelings.

"'Tis very good of you to think of me, but there's no need to have water brought up. I much prefer a swim in the loch over trying to stuff myself into a tub of water."

Mairin smiled brilliantly up at him. "Very well then. If I have your leave, Laird, I'll be on my way. There is much to be done this day."

Ewan motioned for her to go and she rushed away, her feet barely hitting the floor in her haste.

Alaric turned to Ewan with a frown. "What's all this about resting and opening her stitches? What the hell did you do to her?"

"Come," Ewan said. "Let's eat. I'll tell you all that has transpired since you left, and you can fill me in on what happened with McDonald."

Mairin swept through the keep with a purpose, noting what needed to be done and what *could* be done in twenty-four hours' time. Half an hour later, she summoned Maddie and Bertha and informed them that she'd need their help if they had any prayer of pulling off a miracle.

Maddie and Bertha assembled the women of the keep and Mairin addressed them from the top of the steps that led outside to the courtyard.

"Tomorrow we have important guests," she explained to the assembled crowd. "And none of us wants to let our laird down."

There were murmurs of nay and the women shook their heads.

Mairin divided them into groups and divvied up

chores. She even got the children involved. Soon the keep was alive with activity as women rushed to and fro.

Next, Mairin spoke to the men who were assigned to repairs that day. She instructed them to clean the stables and ready stalls for McDonald's horses.

Finally she went in search of Gertie to tackle the matter of food.

The cook wasn't pleased to discover she had to prepare a veritable feast for unexpected guests. She blustered and protested, but Mairin stared her down and told her there was little to be gained by complaining. They couldn't very well starve their guests.

"I'm no miracle worker, my lady," Gertie grumbled. "There isn't enough food to feed our clan, much less a horde of McDonalds."

"What are our options?" Mairin asked tiredly. "What do we have and how can we make it stretch?"

Gertie motioned for Mairin to follow her into the larder. The shelves were frighteningly bare. They were nearly out of staples and the only meat was from the last hunt.

"We're existing hunt to hunt. If the men fail to bring back food, we go without. We have none stored up. If we don't replenish our stocks in the coming months, the winter is going to be a hard one indeed."

Mairin frowned unhappily. Hopefully her dowry would be delivered long before then and the clan wouldn't ever have to go hungry again. It hurt her to imagine the children going without.

She rubbed her forehead and temples as the ache intensified. "What if we send the men out to hunt? If they bring back something this evening, would you have time to prepare for an evening meal on the morrow?"

Gertie rubbed her chin and thoughtfully perused the storeroom. "If they could bring me back a mess of rabbits, I could make a stew and use the few bits of venison we have left over. 'Twould have a good flavor even if there wasn't a whole lot of meat. I can use what flour we have left to make bread, and I can have oatcakes for dipping as well."

"It sounds wonderful, Gertie. I'll go see the laird at once about sending a few of his men out hunting. With any luck, they'll bring home enough to make a huge pot that will last us through the McDonalds' visit."

Gertie nodded. "You do that, lass. I'll start on the bread in the meantime."

Mairin left and went in search of Ewan. She found him in the courtyard overseeing a group of younger men as they went through a series of exercises. Remembering what had happened last time, she waited patiently on the perimeter until Ewan saw her.

She gave a small wave and motioned him over. He spoke a few words to his men and then came over to where she was.

"Ewan, we have need of rabbits. As many as can be gotten. Is there any way you could spare some men for hunting?"

Ewan glanced across the courtyard to where his brothers were engaged in a heated sparring session. Curses rang out from both Caelen and Alaric as they tried valiantly to best the other.

"I'll go myself," Ewan said. "I'll take Caelen and Alaric. We'll bring back the rabbits you need."

She smiled. "Thank you. Gertie will be relieved. She was in a panic over how to feed the McDonalds."

Ewan's eyes went dark and his lip curled. "I'll make sure the clan is provided for. I always have."

Mairin laid a hand on his arm. "I know you will, Ewan. When my dowry arrives, we won't have to worry about what to eat anymore."

He touched her face, palming her cheek for a long moment before letting his fingers trail down to her jaw. "You're a miracle to this clan, lass. We'll be hale and hearty again thanks to you."

She flushed to the roots of her hair, warmed by the tenderness in his touch.

"I'll be going now. Expect us back before sundown."

She watched as he strode across the courtyard and called for Alaric and Caelen. Then she turned and hurried back to the steps of the keep. There was still much to be done in preparation for the McDonalds. She'd be lucky if she slept any this night.

CHAPTER 24

Mairin surveyed the hall with weary appreciation. It was nearly dawn and the women had worked through the night. Those with children, Mairin had sent home the night before, but a small group had stayed on with Mairin to see to the final preparations.

The result was astonishing. Not that Mairin would ever want to do such a thing again in less than a day, but she was well satisfied with the results.

The inside of the keep sparkled. The floors and walls had been washed. The candles in the ceiling fixtures had been replaced with new ones, and light danced shadows along the ceilings.

Sweet-smelling flowers ridded the musty odor of sweat and dirt, and Mairin had taken furs from the bed chambers to line the floor in front of the great stone fireplaces.

The smell of simmering stew had tortured Mairin for the last hours, as Gertie had prepared the rabbits that Ewan and his brothers brought back from the hunt. She was drooling over the idea of a hot piece of crusty bread straight from the oven.

Ewan had tried to get Mairin to take to their bed hours before, but she'd been adamant that the tasks be done since they didn't know exactly when Laird McDonald would arrive.

"It looks wonderful, my lady," Maddie said proudly.

Mairin looked over to where Bertha and Maddie stood and she smiled. "Aye, it does. It looks nothing like before. Even with the repairs that must be done and the damage from the fire, no one can find fault with our work."

Bertha wiped a stray hair from her forehead. "The laird will be proud to welcome guests here. You've performed a miracle."

"Thank you both for giving up your night to help me," Mairin said. "You and Maddie tell the other women to take to their beds and not to worry about rising before noon. The other serving women can take over your duties while you rest."

Both women nodded gratefully and hurried off, leaving Mairin alone in the hall.

Mairin surveyed her handiwork one more time before she turned and trudged toward the stairs. She'd not exactly kept her word to Ewan. Her side pained her considerably, and she hoped she hadn't torn any of the stitches, but the truth of the matter was, the work needed to be done, and it wasn't fair to expect the women of the keep to work long hours if she herself wasn't willing.

She felt great satisfaction in the role she'd taken on. The women had worked long and hard but with a cheerful spirit. They had gone to great lengths to please Mairin, and that in turn pleased her.

For the first time, this felt like home. Her home. And she felt truly a part of the McCabe clan.

She eased into her chamber, but she needn't have bothered. Ewan was awake and dressed and was just finishing putting on his boots.

He frowned when he caught sight of her and immediately stood, his hand going out to steady her when she swayed.

"You put in far too many hours," he admonished. "Are you in pain? Did you tear your stitches?"

She leaned her forehead on his chest, content to remain there for a moment as she collected herself. He swept his hands up her arms to her shoulders and squeezed.

"You're going straight to bed, lass. I won't have any argument. And you aren't to rise until the McDonalds arrive. Are we understood?"

"Aye," she mumbled. She wouldn't even have to pretend to obey that order.

"Come, let me see your wound."

He guided her toward the bed and, with gentle hands, divested her of her clothing.

"'Tis a sin how expertly you rid a woman of her clothing," Mairin grumbled.

He smiled as he turned her to her side. He thumbed over the stitched area and frowned when she flinched.

"'Tis red and swollen. You're not taking proper care, Mairin. If you aren't careful, you're going to end up in bed with a fever."

She yawned broadly and fought to keep her eyes open. "There's too much to do to be abed with fever."

He leaned down and kissed her forehead, leaving his lips there a moment. "You don't feel warm to the touch. Yet. Sleep. I'll have one of the women send up hot water for your bath when I receive word the McDonalds have reached our border."

"That would be nice," she murmured sleepily, but she had already lost her hold on wakefulness and she surrendered to the darkness.

Mairin came awake to a knock at her chamber door. She blinked to brush the heavy veil of sleep aside, but it felt as though someone had poured sand in her eyes.

"Lady McCabe, we have your water for your bath,"

came the call from the door. "The McDonalds will arrive within the hour."

That woke her up.

She shoved aside the bedcovers and hurried to answer the summons. The women carried in pails of water and soon Mairin was immersed in the comfort of hot water. As much as she would have loved to have soaked until the water chilled, she hurried through the washing of her hair.

Two of the maids remained to help dry and brush out her hair. Mairin was fidgety and agitated throughout the process. She was nervous. This was her first real test as the new lady of the keep.

She didn't want Ewan or the McDonalds to find her lacking.

She dressed in her wedding finery and descended the stairs an hour later. The hall was bustling with activity, and Ewan stood talking with his brothers near the high table.

When she entered, Ewan looked up and saw her. The approval in his eyes made her spirits soar. He gestured for her to come to him and she hurried over to stand next to him.

"You're just in time to greet our guests with me," he said. "They arrive in a few minutes' time."

Ewan led her from the hall, his brothers following behind. When they reached the courtyard, the McDonald soldiers were filing over the bridge and through the courtyard arch.

She was of course biased, but the McCabes presented a much more impressive sight.

Ewan stood on the steps with Mairin by his side, as the man in front dismounted and gave Ewan a nod.

" 'Tis good to see you again, Ewan. 'Tis been far too long. When last I was here, your father greeted me. I sorely regret his passing."

"As do we all," Ewan said. "May I present my lady wife, Mairin McCabe?"

Ewan escorted her down and she curtsied in front of the other laird.

Laird McDonald took her hand and bowed, pressing a kiss to her knuckles. "'Tis a great pleasure to meet you, Lady McCabe."

"The honor is mine, Laird," she said. "I offer you and your men refreshment, if you would come into the hall. The meal is set and ready to serve at your leisure."

The laird smiled broadly and then gestured behind him. "May I present my daughter, Rionna McDonald?"

The young woman was reluctant in both manner and expression as she edged forward. So this was the woman whom Laird McDonald wanted Ewan to marry. It was all Mairin could do to keep the frown from her face. The lass was quite beautiful. Indeed her hair shone in the sun like spun gold and her complexion wasn't marred by a single blemish. Her eyes were a peculiar amber color that caught the highlights in her hair and seemed similarly gold in the sunshine.

Mairin cast a quick glance at Ewan to judge his reaction. The last thing she wanted was for him to feel regret that he'd missed an opportunity to wed this woman.

Ewan's eyes glimmered with amusement. He probably saw right into Mairin's head and plucked out her thoughts.

Mairin turned and smiled to the other woman. "Do come in, Rionna. I'm sure you must be fatigued from your travel. You can sit by me at the table and we can become acquainted."

Rionna offered a faltering smile of her own and allowed Mairin to take her arm to lead her inside.

The meal was a lively affair. Laird McDonald was a loud, boisterous man, and he ate with an enthusiasm that appalled Mairin. Why, if she had to feed this man on a regular basis, the McCabe hunters would be hunting night and day with no rest in between.

Gertie frowned her disapproval as she refilled the laird's trencher for the third time. Mairin caught her eye and shook her head. It wouldn't do to insult the laird.

The talk centered around mundane topics. Hunting. Raiding. Concerns over protection of their borders. After a while, Mairin tuned out, struggling to suppress the yawn that threatened to overtake her.

She tried in vain to engage Rionna in conversation, but the lass focused on her food and kept her head down during the entire meal.

When finally the men were finished eating, Ewan caught Mairin's eye, and she rose to excuse herself from the table. The time had come for the men to discuss whatever they discussed in meetings like this, and they no doubt had no desire for women to be present.

She thought to invite Rionna outside to take a stroll about the keep and perhaps indulge in play with the children, but as soon as Mairin excused herself from the table, Rionna hastened away.

With a shrug, Mairin went in search of Crispen.

When the women departed the hall, Laird McDonald nodded toward Ewan. "Your wife does you proud. The meal was magnificent and the welcome was warm."

"My wife is a credit to our clan," Ewan agreed.

"I was dismayed to hear of your marriage," the laird continued. "I had hopes of a match between you and Rionna. It would seal an alliance and bind our clans."

Ewan lifted his brow but didn't say anything. He eyed McDonald to see where he was going with the current conversation.

McDonald looked over at Alaric and Caelen before returning his gaze to Ewan.

"I would speak plainly with you, Ewan."

Ewan motioned for his men to leave the table. Alaric and Caelen remained behind along with Ewan, Laird McDonald, and a few of his men who stood to the side.

"I want this alliance," McDonald said.

Ewan pressed his lips together in thought. "Tell me, Gregor, why do you seek this alliance? Goodwill is not something I associate with our relationship since my father's death. And yet, you were loyal to him and he to you."

McDonald sighed and leaned back in his seat, his hands covering his protruding middle. "'Tis necessary now. Duncan Cameron threatens my holding. We've become embroiled in a few skirmishes over the last months. I think he's testing the might of my army, and I'll be honest, we've not faired well in the battles we've fought."

"Son of a bitch," Ewan muttered. "Your lands adjoin Neamh Álainn. The bastard is planning for the day he thinks to take over Mairin's lands."

"Aye, and I can't hold him off by myself."

"What are you proposing? 'Tis obvious I can't marry your daughter."

"Nay," McDonald said, drawing out his words. Then he looked over at Alaric. "But he can."

CHAPTER 25

Alaric nearly choked on his ale. Caelen looked relieved that McDonald's remark hadn't been intended for him, but he glanced sideways at his brother with sympathy written all over his face.

Ewan shot Alaric a warning look and turned his attention back to McDonald.

"Why is it so important that we seal this alliance with marriage? Surely there are important enough factors at work that we would ally ourselves for the common good."

"Rionna is my heir. My only heir. I have no sons to take over when I die. The man she marries must be willing to assume the duties of laird as well as be strong enough to protect the holding from threats like Duncan Cameron. If our clans are allied not only through agreement but marriage, your loyalty to your brother won't allow you to ever break with our agreement."

Ewan stiffened and glared at the older man, outraged by the insult. "Are you saying my word isn't good?"

"Nay, I'm saying I would feel more secure in the alliance if there were more at stake than mutual protection. I don't want my lands in the hands of a man like Duncan Cameron. He's a greedy, power-hungry bastard who'd betray his own mother to further his cause.

"There are rumors, Ewan, more now than ever, that

Duncan plots against the king. And I've heard that he might throw in his lot with Malcolm to support another uprising against the throne."

Ewan drummed his fingers on the table and looked again at Alaric, who wore what could only be described as a pained look of resignation.

"I'll have to speak to my brothers. I won't make any decision that affects Alaric without hearing his thoughts on the matter."

McDonald nodded. "Of course. I would expect no less. Separately, we are strong clans. But together we would be a force to be reckoned with. Think you the McLauren clan would join in our cause?"

The McLauren clan, though small, did have well-trained soldiers. Together with the McCabes and the McDonalds, they would form a formidable alliance that would only be strengthened when the McCabes controlled Neamh Álainn.

"Aye, they will," Ewan replied. "With the three of us united, it might sway Douglas to our side. He controls the lands north and west of Neamh Álainn."

"If we plant the idea of Duncan Cameron sniffing around Neamh Álainn, he'll come around fast enough," McDonald said. "He alone can't stand up to a force like Cameron, but with us, Cameron doesn't stand a chance against our might."

"Duncan Cameron doesn't stand a chance against *me*," Ewan said softly.

McDonald's eyebrow lifted in surprise. "That's a heavy boast, Ewan. You don't have his numbers."

Ewan smiled. "My men are better trained. They're stronger. They're more disciplined. I don't look to this alliance to defeat Cameron. I'll defeat him with or without allies. I look to alliances to cement the future."

At McDonald's disbelieving look, Ewan leaned back in his seat. "Would you care for a demonstration,

Gregor? Perhaps you'd like to view firsthand those you ally yourself with."

McDonald's eyes narrowed. "What sort of demonstration?"

"Your best men against my best men."

A slow smile spread across the older man's face. "I like a good contest, I do. You're on. What shall we wager?"

"Food," Ewan said. "Three months' store of meat and spices."

"God's teeth, you drive a hard bargain. I can't afford to part with that kind of bounty."

"If you're concerned about losing, we can of course call off the contest."

Knowing an opponent's Achilles' heel was all-important, and for Gregor McDonald, his weakness was a challenge. Suggesting he was afraid of losing a wager was like summoning hounds to a carcass.

"Done," McDonald pronounced. He rubbed his hands in glee and his eyes gleamed triumphantly.

Ewan rose from his seat. "No time like the present."

McDonald leaped from his chair and gestured for one of his commanders. Then he peered suspiciously back at Ewan.

"You and your brothers aren't allowed to participate. Only your men. Soldier against soldier."

Ewan smiled lazily. "If that's what you prefer. I would not have a man under my command if he weren't as worthy as I am with a sword."

"I shall enjoy raiding your stores when my men prove their mettle," McDonald crowed.

Ewan kept his smile and motioned for McDonald to precede him from the hall.

When McDonald hurried out to his men, Alaric hung back. "Ewan, are you giving consideration to this marriage business?"

Ewan eyed his younger brother. "Are you telling me you're not?"

Alaric frowned. "Nay, it isn't at all what I'm saying. But hell, Ewan, I've no desire to be saddled with a bride."

"'Tis a good opportunity for you, Alaric. You would be laird of your own clan. You'd have lands and sons to hand that legacy down to."

"Nay," Alaric said quietly. "*This* is my clan. Not the McDonalds."

Ewan put his hand on Alaric's shoulder. "We'll always be your clan. But think. My brother will be my closest neighbor. We'll be allies. If you stay here, you can never be laird. Your heir will never be laird. You should grab on to this with both hands."

Alaric sighed. "But marriage?"

"She's a bonnie lass," Ewan pointed out.

"Pretty enough, I suppose," Alaric grunted. "I couldn't see much of her face during the meal because she had it pointed down the entire time."

"There'll be plenty of time to see her face. Besides, 'tis not the face you need to concern yourself with. 'Tis the rest."

Alaric laughed and then looked quickly around. "Better not let your bride hear you say that. You might be sleeping with your men tonight."

"Are you ready, Ewan?" McDonald boomed across the courtyard.

Ewan held up his hand. "Aye, I'm ready."

"What on earth are they doing?" Mairin asked as she heard the roar from the courtyard.

Crispen grabbed her hand and tugged her toward the hill. "Let's go up the hill so we can see!"

The other children followed suit and soon they stood atop the hill. Mairin shielded her face from the sun so she could see the goings-on below.

"They're fighting!" Crispen exclaimed.

Mairin's eyes widened at the sight of so many warriors gathered in a tight circle. In the middle stood two soldiers, one a McCabe and one a McDonald.

"Why, that's Gannon," she whispered. "Why is Gannon fighting the McDonald soldier?"

"'Tis the way of things," Crispen boasted. "Men fight. Women tend the hearth."

Gretchen punched Crispen in the arm and gave him a fierce glare. Robbie in turn shoved Gretchen.

Mairin frowned and stared down at him. "Your father told you that, no doubt."

"Uncle Caelen did."

She rolled her eyes. Why didn't that surprise her?

"But why are they fighting?" she persisted.

"'Tis a wager, my lady!"

Mairin turned to see Maddie heading up the hill, several of the McCabe women on her heels. They carried a basket between them.

"What wager?" she asked, as the women approached.

Maddie plunked the basket down and the rich smell of bread wafted through the air. Despite the splendid meal in which she had partaken, Mairin put a hand to her rumbling stomach.

The children leaned forward eagerly, their expressions hopeful as they circled Maddie.

"Our laird and Laird McDonald have a wager as to whose men can best the other," Maddie said, as she began passing out bread to the women now sitting on the ground. Then she passed a hunk to each of the children. She motioned to Mairin. "Join us, my lady. We thought to have a picnic and cheer the McCabe warriors on."

Mairin settled onto the ground, spreading her skirts about her legs. Crispen plopped down next to her and began devouring his treat. Mairin took a piece of the bread and tore a piece off. As she placed the bit to her lips, she frowned. "What's the wager?"

Maddie smiled. "Our laird is cunning! He wagered three months' stock of food. If the McCabes win, we'll collect meat and spices from the McDonald stores."

Mairin's mouth gaped open. "But we don't have three months' stock of food!"

Bertha nodded sagely. "Exactly. He wagered the thing we need the most. 'Twas brilliant and well thought out of him."

"But what if we lose? We can't possibly afford to part with such riches. We don't even have it to lose."

One of the older women *tsk*ed under her breath. "Our warriors won't lose. 'Tis disloyal to think they would."

Mairin scowled. "I'm not being disloyal. I just thought it was odd the laird would wager what we don't have."

"Since we won't lose, it really isn't an issue," Maddie said, patting Mairin's arm.

"Oh, look, Gannon's won his bout and now 'tis Cormac's turn!" Christina exclaimed. "He's ever so handsome, isn't he?"

The women around Christina smiled indulgently. Maddie leaned forward and whispered conspiratorially. "Our Christina has eyes for Cormac."

Mairin observed the way Christina's cheeks went pink as soon as Cormac strode into the circle. His shirt was off and the muscles bulged and rippled in his arms. He did make a fine sight. Not as fine a sight as Ewan, but still not bad at all.

Christina gasped when Cormac took a particularly hard blow and fell back. She covered her mouth with her hand and stared as the warrior picked himself up and lunged forward again. The sounds of clanging metal pierced the air as Cormac fought with renewed vengeance.

It was over seconds later, when Cormac's opponent's sword went flying through the air. Cormac raised his sword over his head and then slashed downward until the point rested under the other man's chin.

The man held up his hands in surrender and Cormac extended a hand to help him to his feet.

"Our men are making short work of the McDonald warriors," Bertha said smugly.

Indeed the McCabe soldiers quickly dispatched the next two. The match was over, given that four of the McDonald warriors had already fallen, but the fifth stalked into the ring fully adorned with protective armor and helmet.

"He's a small one!" Maddie exclaimed. "Why, he can't be more than a lad."

Evidently, Diormid, who'd been chosen to go last, agreed, because he stood to the side, a perplexed look on his face. When the smaller warrior raised his sword, Diormid shook his head and strode forward.

Though he was a great deal smaller than Diormid, he proved to be extremely nimble and agile. He deftly avoided blows that would likely have knocked him from his feet.

The McDonald warriors, inspired by the best performance thus far, surged forward, shouting encouragement to the lad. He was quick to parry and he had Diormid fighting to remain on his feet.

Mairin found herself holding her breath, impressed by the smaller man's courage. She leaned forward as Diormid dodged a barrage of thrusts and she held her breath when the lad jumped to avoid Diormid's sweeping kick.

" 'Tis so exciting," Gretchen whispered beside her.

Mairin smiled at the little girl who was so enraptured by the spectacle in front of them.

"Aye, it is. It looks like Diormid has his hands full with the lad."

The fight wore on and it was apparent that Diormid was frustrated by his inability to make the much smaller man yield. Diormid's movements became more desperate and wild. It was clear he wanted to end the fight and just as clear the lad was having none of it.

Then an amazing thing happened. Diormid lunged and the lad's leg shot out, tripping Diormid. In an instant, the lad leaped on top of Diormid with a yell worthy of the most seasoned warrior. Sword held high, he slashed downward until the point rested against the vulnerable flesh of Diormid's neck.

Diormid glared up at the youth but finally dropped his sword in concession.

"The lad has bested our Diormid," Maddie whispered.

Slowly the lad rose and extended his hand down to Diormid. He pulled himself up, nearly knocking the lad off his feet as he struggled with the weight of the much larger warrior.

The McDonald man staggered back then sheathed his sword. Then he yanked his helmet from his head and a mass of golden hair spilled from the confines.

Rionna McDonald stood in front of the assembled men, her hair flashing in the sun. The women next to Mairin gasped in astonishment.

"'Tis a lass!" Gretchen exclaimed in delight. She rounded on Robbie, her eyes gleaming with unholy light. "See? I told you that women could be warriors!"

Crispen and Robbie were both staring at Rionna with a mixture of awe and grudging admiration.

Rionna's father was apoplectic. He shoved through the crowd of men, his face mottled in rage. He waved his arms and shouted at Rionna, and Mairin strained to hear his words.

Rionna bowed her head, but not before Mairin saw the flash of anger cross her face. Rionna's free hand curled into a fist at her side and she took a step back from her ranting father.

Mairin was on her feet, her heart going out to the woman despite the fact that she'd donned man's garb and humiliated a McCabe warrior. Indeed, Diormid was furious, his face as dark as a storm cloud.

Still, Mairin found herself hurrying toward the courtyard, intent on rescuing the lass from a horde of angry men. Murmuring pardons, she elbowed through the men, ignoring their irritated murmurs when she shoved them aside.

Getting through the last line was difficult because the warriors were all shoulder to shoulder. She poked and prodded without success and finally she kicked one in the back of the knee, causing it to buckle.

He turned with a snarl until he saw who was behind him. His expression turned to one of shock and he hastily stepped aside to let Mairin through.

Relieved that she'd made it into the ring, she realized she didn't have a plan beyond getting there. Ewan didn't take her presence well and he stared holes in her from across the ring of warriors.

Mairin tucked Rionna's hand into hers, ignoring Rionna's look of surprise.

"Curtsy," Mairin whispered.

"What?"

"Curtsy then back away with me. And smile. Really big smile."

"Begging your pardons, Lairds. We'll be going now. The children of the keep need our attention, and we must see to the evening meal," Mairin said. She offered them a dazzling smile and dipped into a curtsy.

Rionna flashed a smile, and Mairin marveled at how stunning the lass was. Her mouth spread into a wide smile, showing perfectly straight, white teeth and a dimple in the smooth skin of her cheek. Rionna also dipped low in a curtsy and then allowed Mairin to drag her toward the perimeter.

The men tripped over themselves to move as Mairin gifted them with another sweet smile. She dragged Rionna off, fully expecting Ewan's roar at any moment. When she managed to exit the courtyard, she breathed a sigh of relief.

"Where are we going?" Rionna asked.

"There is a little girl who would dearly love to meet you," Mairin said cheerfully. "She was most impressed with your performance."

Rionna shot her a puzzled look but allowed Mairin to take her all the way up the hill where the others sat watching with avid interest.

Gretchen could contain herself no longer. As soon as Mairin and Rionna drew near, Gretchen jumped to her feet and fairly danced over to Rionna.

She curtsied but bubbled over with excitement and proceeded to bombard Rionna with a dozen questions in succession.

Seeing Rionna's complete befuddlement, Mairin took pity on her and laid a hand on Gretchen's shoulder to staunch the flood of chatter.

"Gretchen wants to be a warrior," Mairin explained. "It was explained to her that women couldn't be warriors, and now she's decided that 'tis obviously an untruth since you defeated Diormid in swordplay."

Rionna smiled, this time a genuine smile, and knelt in front of Gretchen. "I must share a secret with you, Gretchen. 'Tis not a popular opinion, but I firmly believe that a woman can be whatever she wants to be if she sets her mind to it."

Gretchen was aglow with delight. Then she became somber as she looked beyond Rionna to the courtyard. "Your papa wasn't happy that you fought Diormid."

Rionna's eyes darkened from the light gold to an amber hue. "My father despairs of ever making a lady of me. He's not impressed with my skills as a warrior."

"I'm impressed," Gretchen said shyly.

Rionna smiled again and took Gretchen by the hand. "Would you like to touch the hilt of my sword?"

Gretchen's eyes rounded and her mouth dropped open. "Could I?"

Rionna guided her hand down until it hovered over the jewel-encrusted hilt of the sword. " 'Tis smaller than a normal sword. 'Tis lighter, too. Makes it easier for me to wield it."

"That's amazing," Gretchen breathed.

"I want to see!" Robbie said belligerently.

He and Crispen both shoved forward, their eyes bright with wonder.

"Can we touch?" Crispen whispered.

As reticent as Rionna had been over the meal, she was open and friendly with the children. Mairin decided she must just be extremely shy.

As the children gathered around Rionna, chattering and exclaiming over her sword, Mairin chanced a glance back at the courtyard to see Ewan standing in the distance, hands knotted at his waist as he stared at her.

She offered a small wave and turned away before he got any ideas about summoning her.

When the children drifted away from Rionna, Mairin eyed the other woman. "Would you like to have a bath drawn before the evening meal?"

Rionna shrugged. "I usually swim in the loch, but I suppose it would horrify my father if I were to do so here."

Mairin's eyes widened. "Are you mad? The water is frigid!"

Rionna smiled. " 'Tis good training for the mind."

Mairin shook her head. "I have no understanding for someone who would forego the joys of a tub full of hot water for a hellish swim in an icy loch."

"Since swimming in the loch isn't a possibility, I'll gladly take you up on your kind offer of a hot bath," Rionna said with a grin. Then she cocked her head to the side and looked at Mairin with an odd expression on her face. "I like you, Lady McCabe. I don't appall you as I do others. And the way you waded through the men to rescue me was very well done."

Mairin flushed. "Oh, do call me Mairin. If we're to be friends, 'tis only appropriate that you should address me thusly."

Maddie cleared her throat behind Mairin, and Mairin turned, horrified that she'd forgotten her manners.

"Rionna, I want you to meet the women of my clan."

Each woman stepped forward in turn and Mairin went down the line, introducing those whose names she remembered. Maddie supplied the names that Mairin hadn't learned as of yet.

When they were done, Maddie directed the women back to the keep so they could heat water for Rionna's bath.

After showing Rionna to the chamber she would occupy, Mairin went below stairs to check on the plans for the evening meal.

She was nearly to the kitchens when Ewan entered the hall. Laird McDonald accompanied him and Mairin quickened her step.

"Where is my daughter?" Laird McDonald demanded.

Mairin paused and turned to face the surly laird. "She's above stairs seeing to her bath and dressing for the evening meal."

Apparently mollified by the idea that his daughter wasn't out battling more warriors, the laird nodded before turning back to Ewan. Mairin waited a moment, fully expecting Ewan to reprimand her for her interference, but he looked past Laird McDonald and winked.

It was done so fast that she was sure she'd seen wrong. The idea of the laird doing something like winking was too much to contemplate. Sure she'd imagined it, she headed for the kitchens once more.

CHAPTER 26

Mairin was long asleep when Ewan came to their chamber that night. He stood by the bed and watched as she slept, so burrowed under the furs that only her nose peeked out.

Talks with McDonald had rapidly deteriorated as more ale had been consumed. Instead of talking marriage and alliances, the men had sat around the table in the hall drinking and engaging in bawdy tellings of tavern wenches and old battle scars.

Ewan had excused himself, more interested in slipping into a warm bed with his wife than engaging in ribald boasting. It should bother him that even asleep the lass had such a hold over him that all he had to do was imagine her above stairs in his bed and he grew restless and ready to depart the men. But he found that it didn't bother him at all.

While the rest were in the hall fondly recounting nights spent in the arms of a woman, he'd be above stairs holding his in his arms.

He undressed and carefully pulled back the bed covers. She immediately stirred, frowned, and then yanked the furs to bring them back up. He chuckled and slid into bed beside her.

The shock of her warm body against his brought him

instantly and fully to awareness. She stirred again, murmured something in her sleep, and proceeded to burrow underneath him.

Her nightdress fell down one arm, baring the curve of her neck and the smooth skin of her shoulder. Unable to resist, he pressed his mouth to her flesh and nibbled a path to the column of her neck.

He loved her taste, loved the way her scent filled his nose as his tongue laved over her softness. She emitted a sigh that tickled over his car.

"Ewan?" she asked sleepily.

"Who else were you expecting, lass?"

"Oh, I don't know. It seems every time I wake, there are people in our chamber."

He chuckled and nipped at her earlobe.

"You aren't angry with me?"

He drew back and stared down at her. "What have you done now?"

She huffed, and her lips twisted into a disgruntled line. "I've done nothing. I was referring to earlier today. When I took Rionna off with me. I know I shouldn't have interfered but—"

He put a finger over her lips. "Nay, you shouldn't have. But I'm fast discovering that you do many things you shouldn't. It was a good thing that you removed Rionna when you did. Her father was angry, and you diffused the situation. My only complaint is that you placed yourself in a potentially explosive situation, not to mention you waded through a bunch of men who were caught up in the excitement of a battle."

She slid her hands down his middle, lower, until she found his hardness. Her fingers circled his shaft and he groaned as he swelled within her grip.

"But you aren't angry," she said in a whisper-soft voice.

His eyes narrowed even as he pushed farther into her hand. "Don't think I don't know what you're about, lass."

Her eyes widened innocently as she stroked him from his cods to the very tip of his cock. He leaned down to kiss her, breathing in her very essence. He inhaled, holding and savoring the air that had been hers and then he returned it and it danced around their lips and tongues.

"This won't get you out of trouble every time," he warned.

She smiled. "I'll settle for most of the time."

He was about to lose himself in her hand. Her soft exploration was driving him to the brink of insanity. He had to have her. Now.

He reached down and clutched the hem of her night dress.

"Don't tear—"

The sound of material ripping muffled her warning. He shoved the material up over her hips and rolled until he was positioned between her splayed thighs.

He found her heat, felt her silky warmth spread over the head of his shaft and with one push he was inside her. She gasped and arched into him, her belly trembling beneath his.

She was so tight around him, a fist gripping and squeezing, holding him so intimately that he began to unravel.

"Ah, lass, I'm sorry."

"For what?"

Her hands trailed over his shoulders, her nails scraping at his flesh. He closed his eyes, knowing this wouldn't last long at all.

"I seem to lose all control when I'm with you. This will be fast. I cannot hold back."

"'Tis all right," she whispered. "For I find I cannot hold back either."

She lifted her hips and wrapped her legs around his waist. It was too much for him to bear.

He thrust hard and already he felt himself letting go. Again he thrust, plunging mindlessly into her willing body. His seed spurted forth and he kept driving, over and over, until her passage, so slick with his passion, released him.

Unwilling to deprive himself of her sweetness just yet, he tucked his shaft back to her opening and eased inward, riding the aftershocks as she trembled and spasmed around him.

He leaned forward, resting his weight on her while he remained inside her warm sheath. She was breathing hard, her puffs of air blowing over his neck and chest. Her body was tangled around his, arms and legs clutching him and holding him close as if she'd never let go.

He liked that. Aye, he liked it a lot.

Finally he rolled to the side but kept her limbs entwined with his. He wanted her a part of him. He liked the sight of her much smaller body secured by his. She was his.

She gave a lusty yawn and nuzzled into his chest. He knew she was asleep in a matter of moments, but he remained awake, liking the feel of so much feminine sweetness in his arms.

When he finally slept, he was careful to keep her as closely linked to him as possible.

The next day, Mairin busied herself with the women to prepare the noon meal while Ewan was occupied with Laird McDonald. The two men had gone hunting that morning, and much to Rionna's displeasure, she'd been left out of the hunting party.

She sat in the hall dressed in man's garb, a loose-fitting tunic swallowing the upper half of her body, looking bored and faintly terrified by all the bustling going on around her.

Rionna was a bit of a mystery to Mairin. She wanted to ask the lass about her apparent fascination with the duties of a man, but she was afraid of insulting the woman. Mairin had heard from Maddie that Laird

McDonald sought to marry his daughter to Alaric to seal the alliance with the McCabe clan, and that in fact, the lairds were in talks of just such an arrangement.

Mairin pitied Rionna because she gained the distinct impression that Rionna had no desire to marry, and Mairin could only imagine Alaric's reaction to the proposed arrangement.

What did the lass hope to accomplish by engaging in such shocking activities that obviously brought her father's ire down on her?

And Alaric, surely he wouldn't be accepting of his wife's wish to engage in swordplay. Ewan would be appalled, and Alaric was no different in his thinking. All the McCabe brothers had firm ideas of a woman's role, and it was definitely not the path that Rionna had chosen.

Rionna needed someone more . . . understanding, though Mairin couldn't imagine any warrior allowing his wife the freedoms that Rionna apparently enjoyed.

Mairin shook her head and allowed Rionna to remain sprawled in one of the chairs to watch the goings-on around her.

"Is everything prepared?" Mairin asked Gertie as she entered the sweltering heat of the small cooking area.

"Aye, I've just taken the bread from the fire and the stew is simmering. As soon as the men return, I'll begin putting out the food."

Mairin thanked Gertie and then retraced her steps into the hall. A noise at the entrance told her that her husband had returned and she went to greet him.

She stood back, waiting for him to enter fully. He came in, Laird McDonald just behind him, with Caelen and Alaric bringing up the rear.

"Welcome home, husband. If you and the laird would take your seats at the table, the meal will be served."

Ewan nodded his acknowledgment and she retreated to tell Gertie to begin the serving.

More of Ewan's men filtered in, mixing with Laird McDonald's soldiers. The three tables in the hall quickly filled up while the men who hadn't gained seats waited at the entrance to the kitchen for their portion.

Unsure of any marriage arrangement since Ewan hadn't seen fit to share Laird McDonald's proposal with Mairin, she opted to seat Rionna beside her, with Laird McDonald across the table on Ewan's other side. Alaric and Caelen would occupy the two seats next to Laird McDonald.

The meal was a loud, boisterous event as the morning's hunt was recounted for all to hear. Food and serving dishes went everywhere and Mairin found herself confused at one point as to which goblet was hers. She reached for the goblet between Ewan and herself and took a sip to chase down her food.

She wrinkled her nose at the bitter taste and hoped that the entire batch of ale hadn't gone bad. She set it aside so Ewan wouldn't drink it and motioned for Gertie to bring the laird another cup in case it was indeed his.

Laird McDonald kept Ewan engaged in talks of border protection, increased patrols, and the plan to strengthen their alliances by talking with Douglas.

Mairin paid only partial attention to the chatter as she watched Rionna pick idly at her portion. She was wondering what topic she could engage the other woman in when a cramp rippled across her belly.

She frowned and put a hand to her abdomen. Had the food been bad? But surely it was too soon to feel the effects, and the meat was fresh, brought in just two days ago. She watched the others but saw no sign of discomfort. In fact, everyone dug into their food with seeming satisfaction for the taste.

She reached for the goblet that had replaced the bitter

ale when another cramp viciously seized her stomach. She gasped for breath but the pain was so intense that she doubled over.

Another pain knifed through her, gripping her middle in an unrelenting knot. Her vision blurred and she felt a sudden urge to vomit.

She shot to her feet and in her haste, knocked over Ewan's goblet. The liquid spilled over the table and into Ewan's lap.

Ewan jerked his head from his conversation with McDonald, a frown marring his lips. She swayed and then doubled over, a cry escaping as fire twisted her innards.

Rionna jumped up and bent anxiously over Mairin, her face creased with concern. Around her, murmurs arose as everyone focused on their mistress and her obvious distress.

"Mairin!"

Ewan was on his feet, his hands reaching to steady her. She would have fallen had he not hauled her up against him. She went limp, her legs no longer able to sustain her weight.

"Mairin, what's wrong?" Ewan demanded.

"Sick," she gasped. "Oh God, Ewan, I think I'm dying. The pain."

She sagged again and Ewan went down with her, easing her weight to the floor. Above her, Alaric's worried face appeared.

"What the hell is going on, Ewan?" Alaric demanded. He shoved Rionna back and maintained a protective perimeter around Mairin.

And then she turned her head and retched all over the floor. The sound was awful even to her own ears, but it felt ten times worse.

It was as if she'd swallowed a million pieces of glass and they were shredding her insides.

She curled into a ball on the floor in so much pain that in a moment of weakness, she prayed for death.

"Nay!" Ewan roared. "You won't die. I won't allow it. Do you hear me, Mairin? I won't allow it. You will obey me, goddamn it! For once you will obey!"

She whimpered as Ewan hauled her from the floor. She winced as his shouts rung in her ears. He yelled orders and the hall was alive with the sound of scrambling feet and answering exclamations.

She was jostled about in Ewan's arms as he charged up the stairs. He burst into their chamber, all the while shouting demands to the rest of his clan.

He wasn't gentle as he laid her on the bed. Her stomach heaved again as the smell of her own vomit seared her nostrils. Her dress. It was ruined. Now she couldn't even be buried in it.

Ewan clasped her face in his hands and leaned down until their noses were nearly touching.

"No one is burying you, lass. Do you hear? You will live or, so help me, I'll follow you to hell and drag you back kicking and screaming the entire way."

"I hurt," she whimpered.

His touch gentled as he smoothed the hair from her face. "I know, lass. I know you hurt. I'd bear it for you if I could. Promise me you'll fight. Promise me!"

She wasn't sure what she was supposed to fight, and the pain screaming through her insides made her want to curl into a ball and close her eyes, but when she tried, Ewan shook her until her teeth rattled in her head.

"Ewan, what's wrong with me?" she whispered, as another wave of pain overwhelmed her.

His face was grim and going more blurry by the minute. "You've been poisoned."

CHAPTER 27

It had been many years since Ewan had prayed. Not since the birth of his son, when he'd prayed over his wife's bedside as she struggled to bring forth the life within her.

But he found himself offering fervent prayer now as he stood over Mairin's bedside. Maddie flew in behind him with Bertha on her heels.

"You must make her vomit, Laird," Bertha said. "There's no time to waste. We don't know how much of the poison she took in and she must rid her stomach of all its contents."

Ewan bent and grasped Mairin by the shoulders, rolling her to the edge of the bed so her head hung over the side. He took her face gently between his hands and pried her mouth with his thumb.

She twisted and fought against him but he tightened his grip, refusing to give way.

"Listen to me, Mairin," he said urgently. "We must rid your stomach of its contents. I must make you vomit. I'm sorry, but I have no choice."

As soon as her lips parted, he thrust his fingers to the back of her throat and she gagged and convulsed. With only one arm to hold her, it was difficult.

"Help me hold her," he barked to Maddie. "If you can't do it, call one of my brothers."

Bertha and Maddie both leaped forward, pressing their full weight against Mairin's body.

Mairin gagged again and she vomited onto the floor.

"Again, Laird," Bertha urged. "I know 'tis difficult to see her in such pain, but if she's to survive, it must be done."

He'd do anything to keep her from dying, even if it meant causing her agony. He held her head and forced her to retch. Again and again she heaved until nothing more would push itself out. Her entire body was so rigid, it was a wonder she hadn't broken any bones yet.

Still he pressed on, determined to keep her alive. Finally Bertha touched his arm. "'Tis done. You can release her now."

Maddie got up and wet a rag with water from the washbasin and thrust it at Ewan. He wiped Mairin's mouth and then her flushed, sweaty forehead.

Carefully he eased her back onto the bed and then stripped the clothing from her body. He tossed the garments aside and instructed the women to clean the chamber to rid it of the noxious smell.

He sat by Mairin's side as he pulled the covers to shield her nakedness. He watched anxiously, feeling so helpless that it kindled a rage so deep that he burned with it.

He could hear the commotion outside his chamber door, knew his brothers were there, and others, but he wouldn't take his eyes from Mairin.

The women rapidly cleaned the mess from the chamber and removed the offending clothing. Moments later, Maddie returned, shutting the door firmly behind her.

"Laird, let me take over her care," she said in a soft voice. "She's emptied her stomach. There's naught to do but wait now."

Ewan shook his head. "I won't leave her."

He ran a finger through her limp hair and touched her cheek, alarmed by how cool her skin felt to his touch. Her breathing was shallow, so light that many times he'd leaned his head down, afraid that no air escaped her nose any longer.

She'd slipped into unconsciousness. She hadn't moved, hadn't stirred or cried out from the vicious pain assaulting her. He didn't know what was worse. Hearing her helpless cries or seeing her as still as death.

They both frightened the hell out of him.

Maddie stood by the bed for a long moment, and then with a sigh, she turned and left the chamber.

Before Ewan could recline on the bed beside Mairin, his brothers burst into the chamber.

"How is she?" Alaric demanded.

Caelen didn't speak, but the storm was there in his eyes as he stared down at Mairin.

Ewan touched Mairin's cheek again and ran his fingers underneath her nose until he felt the light exchange of air on his skin. There was so much turmoil churning in his gut. Rage. Fear. Helplessness.

"I don't know," he finally said. The admission twisted the knife in his belly until he had the same urge to vomit as Mairin.

"Who did this?" Caelen hissed. "Who could have poisoned her?"

Ewan glanced down at Mairin as anger knotted his chest. His nostrils flared and he curled his fingers into tight fists. "McDonald," he said through clenched teeth. "Goddamn McDonald."

Alaric reared back in surprise. "McDonald?"

Ewan stared hard at his two brothers. "I want you to stay with her. The both of you. Summon me if there is any change in her condition. Right now I trust no one but you until I discover who is trying to kill my wife."

"Ewan, where are you going?" Caelen demanded, as Ewan stalked from the room.

Ewan turned around as he reached the doorway. "To have a word with McDonald."

He stormed down the stairs, his sword drawn as he entered the hall where the majority of his soldiers were now assembled. They came to attention when they saw Ewan's sword at the ready.

McDonald stood to the side, surrounded by his guards. Rionna was next to him and the two were conversing in urgent tones. Tension knotted the air in the hall, so thick that Ewan's skin prickled with it.

Rionna looked up in alarm when she saw Ewan approach. She drew her sword and stepped in front of her father, but Ewan shoved her aside and she went reeling.

The hall erupted in chaos.

The McDonald men lunged for Ewan, and Ewan's men reacted fiercely in protection of their laird.

"Protect the woman," Ewan barked to Gannon.

Ewan was on McDonald before he could draw his sword. Ewan grabbed the older man by the tunic and slammed him against the wall.

McDonald's face purpled with rage and his cheeks puffed out as Ewan drew the collar of his tunic tighter around his neck. "Ewan, what is the meaning of this?"

"Just how badly did you want me to marry your daughter?" Ewan asked in a dangerously low voice.

McDonald blinked in confusion before realization set in. Spittle peppered his lips as he huffed and made sounds of outrage. "Are you accusing me of poisoning Lady McCabe?"

"Did you?"

McDonald's eyes narrowed in fury. He shoved at Ewan's hands in an attempt to dislodge Ewan's hold, but Ewan only slammed him into the wall again.

"This is war," McDonald spat. "I won't let this insult go unanswered."

"If you want war, I'll be more than happy to accommodate you," Ewan hissed. "And when I've wiped the earth with your blood, your lands and all you hold dear will be mine. You want to speak of insults, Laird? You come into my home, partake of my hospitality, and you try to kill my lady wife?"

McDonald paled and stared hard into Ewan's eyes. "I did not do this thing, Ewan. You have to believe me. Aye, I wanted Rionna to marry you, but a marriage with your brother will do just as well. *I did not poison her.*"

Ewan's jaw twitched and his nostrils flared. Sweat broke out on McDonald's forehead and he looked nervously left and right, but his men had easily been staved off by Ewan's soldiers.

Rionna stood several feet away, her arms held by Gannon. She was spitting mad, and it took Gannon's all to restrain her.

There was no guilt in McDonald's eyes. Did he tell the truth? The timing of McDonald's arrival and Mairin's poisoning was too coincidental. Or was it only made to appear that way?

Ewan relaxed his hold and eased McDonald away from the wall. "You'll excuse my rudeness but I want you and your men off my lands at once. My wife lies deathly ill and I know not if she'll survive. Know this, McDonald. If she dies and if I discover you did this thing, there is no rock in all of Scotland that you can hide under, no corner you can seek refuge in."

"W—What of our alliance?" McDonald babbled.

"All that concerns me right now is my wife. Go home, McDonald. Go home and pray that she lives. We'll speak of our proposed alliance another day."

He all but threw McDonald toward the door leading from the hall.

"Ewan! The lass is sick again. She's retching something fierce. Nothing Caelen and I do seems to help."

Ewan whipped around to see Alaric standing at the entrance to the hall, his expression haggard.

"See to their departure," Ewan snapped at Gannon. "Escort them to our border and make sure they don't linger."

Then Ewan broke into a run, shoving past Alaric as he thundered up the stairs.

He burst into the chamber to see Caelen holding Mairin over the side of the bed as she gagged and heaved. Caelen looked desperate, and yet he held Mairin protectively against him, anchoring her as her entire body shook with the force of her retching.

Caelen looked up as Ewan charged toward the bed. "Ewan, thank God you're here. I can't make her stop and 'tis killing her!"

Ewan took Mairin's limp body and cradled her in his arms. "Shh, sweeting. Breathe with me. Through your nose. You must stop the retching."

"Sick," she whimpered. "Please, Ewan, let me die. It hurts so much."

His heart turned over and he hugged her tighter against him. "Just breathe," he whispered. "Breathe for me, Mairin. The hurt will go away. I swear it."

She clutched his tunic so tight that the material drew uncomfortably across his arms. Her body tensed, but this time she managed to hold back the urge to vomit.

"That's it, lass. Hold on to me. I won't let you go. I'm here."

She buried her face against his neck and went limp. He lowered her to the bed then looked up at Caelen who stood by the bed, his face drawn in helpless fury.

"Wet a cloth so I can wipe her face."

Caelen hastened to the washbasin. He wrung out the cloth and shoved it in Ewan's direction. Ewan wiped

Mairin's brow and then ran the damp material over her mouth. She sighed but didn't open her eyes as he cleaned the rest of her face.

She seemed to be over the spasms that wracked her stomach. She cuddled into his side and wrapped one arm around his middle. And then with a sigh, she slipped back into a deep sleep.

Ewan cupped the back of her head and pressed his lips to her forehead. The fact that she'd awakened was a good sign, but he hated to see her in such pain. Her body was trying to rid itself of the poison, and she was valiantly fighting the effects.

"Live," he whispered. "I won't let you die."

Alaric, who'd followed Ewan back to the chamber, and Caelen looked discomfited by their brother's uncharacteristic display of emotion. In that moment, Ewan didn't care who saw him at his weakest.

"You care for her," Alaric said gruffly.

Ewan felt something inside him loosen and unfold. Aye, he loved her, and he couldn't bear the thought of losing her. By God, she was going to wake up, sass him, and then he'd seduce her into giving him the words he most wanted to hear.

Aye, she'd live, and then the difficult little lass was going to love him every bit as much as he loved her.

He looked to his brothers, who watched him with odd fascination. "I have need of your help. Someone tried to kill her. As much as it pains me, it has to be someone from our clan. We have a traitor in our midst and he must be flushed out or Mairin will never be safe. I can't lose her. Our clan can't lose her. She represents our salvation—and mine. If you won't do it for her, your sister, then do it for me, your brother."

Alaric went down to his knees by the bed and reached out and placed his fingers into Mairin's limp hand. Caelen squared his shoulders and then he, too, got on his knees at Alaric's side. He touched Mairin's shoulder and his gaze softened as he stared down at her.

"You've always had our allegiance, Ewan," Alaric said in a grave voice. "Our loyalty belongs to you. Now I pledge my allegiance and my loyalty to Mairin as well. I'll protect her as your wife and my sister. I'll place her safety above my own."

Alaric's solemn declaration sent a fierce surge of pride through Ewan.

"She's a good lass," Caelen said gruffly. "She's a good mother to Crispen and a loyal wife. She's a credit to you, Ewan. I would protect her with my life and seek justice for the wrongs committed against her. She'll always have a place of honor in my eyes."

Ewan smiled, knowing how difficult it must have been for Caelen to recite such a pledge. "Thank you. This means much to me. We must make sure she is safe from this day forward. She won't be easy to contain when she is back on her feet."

"You sound sure of her recovery," Caelen said.

Ewan looked down again as hope burned in his gut like brimstone.

"Aye, I'm sure. The lass is too contrary to give in to death."

Ewan met with his brothers late into the night. They sat in the hall with only a single candle to illuminate the dark room.

"We've questioned everyone who served, everyone in the kitchen, everyone who came into contact with the food, and everyone who was gathered in the hall," Caelen reported.

"Gertie is distraught," Alaric said grimly. "She's sick that Mairin was poisoned. I don't believe for a moment that Gertie was behind it even if she would have had the easiest opportunity of anyone. She's been with our clan since before we were born. She was loyal to our father and has been steadfast since his death."

Ewan didn't believe it either, but he'd be a fool to discount the possibility. He couldn't imagine anyone in his clan trying to kill Mairin. Why would they? She represented hope. She was their salvation and there wasn't anyone who didn't know that.

But someone had.

Gannon and Cormac entered the hall, their expressions grim. Fatigue lined their faces and they made a direct line toward Ewan.

"Laird, we have a report."

Ewan gestured for them to sit.

Cormac took a seat but Gannon opted to stand, his agitation evident in the way he clenched and unclenched his fists.

"We've determined the source of the poison," Gannon said.

"Tell me," Ewan bit out.

"It wasn't in the food. We tested pieces from all the remaining plates, including Lady McCabe's. The poison was in a goblet. It was nearly full, so she didn't drink much of it."

"Thank God," Ewan breathed. There was hope yet.

"Laird," Cormac said painfully. "We don't believe the goblet was Lady McCabe's."

Ewan thumped his fists on the table and leaned forward. "Whose was it then?"

Gannon blew out his breath. "We believe it was yours, Laird."

At that, Caelen and Alaric nearly unsettled their chairs. "What the hell do you mean?" Caelen demanded.

"We spoke extensively with all the serving women. There were three goblets. One that Lady McCabe upended when she rose from the table. That was her goblet, but it wasn't placed correctly and we don't think she ever drank from it. She took your goblet and drank a small portion. It must have tasted badly to her because she pushed it to the side and summoned one of the serving women to bring you another goblet. Soon after, she grew ill."

"But why . . . ?" Ewan's voice trailed off, and he looked up at his most trusted men and his brothers. "The arrow. The arrow wasn't intended for Mairin at all. It was meant for me."

"Jesu," Alaric said in agitation. "Someone is trying to kill *you*, Ewan. Not Mairin."

"It makes more sense," Caelen said grimly. "No one gains if Mairin dies. That's not the case if Ewan dies and leaves Mairin without a husband and without child."

"Cameron is behind this and somehow, someway he's infiltrated our clan. Someone here is doing his bidding. Twice he's tried to kill me and twice Mairin has nearly died as a result." Ewan's fist met the table with a sickening crack as he snarled out the realization.

"Aye, but who?" Alaric asked.

"That's what we must find out," Ewan said. "And until we do, Mairin must be watched closely at all times. I won't have her injured by another attempt on my life."

CHAPTER 28

Harsh shouting interrupted Mairin's nice, hazy dream. She couldn't be sure it was a dream, but it was all nice and floaty and she wasn't feeling any pain. She much preferred the nice, quiet float over the alternative.

Then she found herself being shaken until her brain seemed to rattle inside her head. The pain was back and she heard Ewan's voice.

Oh, but the man did love to roar. He seemed to enjoy a good lecture, particularly when it was aimed at her.

"You are the most disobedient lass I've ever had the misfortune to meet," Ewan snarled. "I order you not to die and you're determined that you'll do just that. You're not the lioness who championed my son. She would never give up as you're giving up."

Mairin frowned at his insult. It was just like him to act so shamefully when she was sick and dying. He acted as though she'd done it apurpose.

She heard him chuckle.

"Nay, lass, you might well be sick, but you're not dying. You're going to obey me this time or, as God as my witness, I'm going to turn you over my knee."

She glared, or at least she thought she did. The room still seemed incredibly dark to her, and her eyelids felt like someone had laid stones over them. Sudden panic hit her. Maybe they were preparing her for burial. Didn't they put stones over the eyes of the dead to keep them closed? Or was that coins? Either way, she didn't want to die.

"Shh, lass," Ewan soothed. "Open your eyes. You can do it for me. No one is burying you, I swear it. Open your eyes and look at me. Let me see those beautiful blue eyes."

It took all her might but she managed to crack her eyelids. She winced as sunlight speared through her head, and she promptly snapped her eyes shut again.

"Cover the window," Ewan barked.

Mairin frowned. Who was he talking to? It was getting to be a regular occurrence for them to have visitors to their chamber.

She heard a chuckle and she opened her eyes only to see a fuzzy shape that resembled Ewan. She blinked rapidly and then looked beyond him to see Alaric and Caelen in front of the now covered window.

"'Tis good you returned home when you did, Alaric. Ewan would need you for the funeral."

Alaric frowned. "Whose funeral, lass?"

"Mine," she said.

She tried to lift her head but soon discovered that she was as weak as a newborn kitten.

Caelen laughed and Mairin turned to offer him a frown of displeasure.

She sniffed. "'Tis not a laughing matter. Ewan would be most displeased if I died."

"Which is precisely why you aren't going to do anything of the sort," Ewan drawled.

She turned her head to look at Ewan again and was startled to see him look so . . . haggard. His hair was unkempt, his eyes were red, and he had what looked to be several days' worth of beard growth on his jaw.

"I am ever obedient, husband. If you command me not to die, then I will of course not deny your wish."

Ewan grinned and as he looked down at her she saw such relief in his eyes that her breath caught in her throat.

" 'Tis a sin to lie, wife, but 'tis God's truth that I don't think He or I will mind this one untruth."

She *hmmph*ed. "I try to be obedient."

"Aye, lass, I did command you not to die, and it was very accommodating of you to obey me this once. I'm so pleased that I might consider not shouting at you the next time you see fit not to obey me."

"The both of you are daft," Caelen grumbled.

Alaric moved closer to the bed and reached to squeeze her hand. "Welcome back to the land of the living, little sister. You gave us all quite a scare."

She laid her other hand over her stomach. "I feel no pain. 'Tis quite odd, really, but I'm hungry."

Ewan laughed and then leaned down and pressed his lips against her forehead for the longest time. He trembled against her skin and smoothed his hand over her hair as he slowly drew away.

"You should be near to starving, lass. You've been abed three days and you emptied the contents of your stomach on day one."

"Three days?" She was appalled. Utterly appalled.

"Aye, lass, three days." His tone grew more serious and the lines reappeared in his face. He looked . . . tired.

She reached up to trace the lines at his brow and then let her fingers fall to his cheek. "You look tired, husband. I'm thinking you need a bath and a shave and then a long rest."

He cupped his hand over hers, trapping it against his cheek. Then he turned his mouth inward and kissed her palm.

"Now that you're awake, I will indeed sleep. But don't be thinking that just because you've awakened that you'll be scurrying all over the keep. You'll stay abed until I say you can get up and not a moment before."

She gave him a look of disgust but held her tongue. It wouldn't do to start an argument with him the moment she awoke. After all, she could be accommodating on occasion.

Ewan laughed. "Aye, lass, it would appear that on occasion you can be very accommodating."

"I really must learn to control my tongue better," she muttered. "I can't go about blurting out my every thought. Mother Serenity said I'd rue the day I ever began such a terrible habit. I'm thinking she has the right of it."

Ewan leaned down and kissed her again. "I'm thinking your tongue is perfect."

Both Caelen and Alaric laughed and Mairin was scandalized. "Ewan!"

Mortification tightened her cheeks and she yanked the blankets up to cover her head. Ewan joined in their laughter while she huddled there wishing the floor would open up and take them all.

Ewan eventually shooed everyone from their chamber and then ordered food brought up to them both. He sampled every bite of food himself before he passed it along to her.

In truth, it scared her spitless. She didn't want him to die for her and she told him so.

He didn't look impressed with her concern. "'Tis my duty to watch over you, lass."

"And a fine job you'll do if you die in the process," she grumbled.

After they ate, she lay back on the pillow and closed her eyes. She really was quite weak, and it was the truth that the food didn't settle all that well in her stomach. After three days of not eating, she supposed it was only natural.

She started when she heard the door open, and a parade of serving women came into the chamber bearing pails of hot water.

"I thought you might like a hot bath," Ewan said.

In that moment she wanted to throw herself around him and hug him until he had no breath. And she would if she didn't find that even moving her arms was incredibly taxing. So she lay there like a pile of useless flesh and watched with mounting excitement as steam rose from the almost-full tub.

When the last of the water was poured from the pails, Ewan bent over the bed and began to unlace the ties on her sleeping gown. She didn't have enough energy to protest, not that it would have done her a bit of good anyway. Soon enough he had the gown off her body and he gently gathered her in his arms and carried her over to the tub.

He eased her down into the hot water, and she moaned in delight as the heat lapped over her body.

Instead of leaving her as she'd anticipated, he knelt beside the tub. He reached for the pitcher on the floor and filled it with water before pouring it down her back to wet her hair.

When his fingers dug into the strands to wash her hair, she closed her eyes at the simple pleasure of having him take care of her needs. She was weaker than she could have ever imagined she would have been after her ordeal, and she was grateful for his regard.

She moaned softly as he turned his attention to the washing of her body. He took his time, rubbing her shoulders and her arms. His hands plunged into the water and he cupped her breasts, rubbing his thumbs over the hard tips.

He didn't tarry overlong but continued his relentless quest to wash every inch of her body. By the time he reached her feet, she was shivering with raw pleasure. He picked up one foot and water sluiced up her leg. Then he began a meticulous massage of each part of her foot, going from bottom to top. When he reached her toes, she tried to jerk her foot away and shrieked at the tickling sensation.

He laughed but grabbed hold of her ankle so she didn't slip away.

"I had no idea you were so ticklish, lass."

He held her foot in both hands and ran his hands over her ankle and then, to her shock, he kissed the arch of her foot. He caressed a path up her leg, over her knee, and down to the juncture of her thighs.

His hands were like silk on her flesh. The combination of the soothing water and his heated caresses were a balm to her tattered senses.

He was thorough in his wash. No part of her went untouched. By the time he was done, she was limp, her vision hazy, and she was so lethargic that she couldn't have risen from the tub if she'd wanted to.

Ewan picked her up and held her over the tub while the water rushed from her body. He set her by the fire and promptly wrapped a large blanket around her, tucking the ends between her breasts.

"As soon as your hair is dry, I'll tuck you back into bed," he said. "I don't want you to get cold."

Just when she couldn't imagine being more shocked by his gentle regard, he began to dry her hair with one of the drying cloths. His hands worked through the strands and when he'd blotted the excess moisture from the heavy mass, he began to work a comb through the knots.

They sat in front of the fire, her nestled between his thighs, facing the blaze. He was exceedingly patient, pausing when he reached a particularly difficult snarl.

The warmth from the hearth wrapped around them until her skin glowed pink. Heat seeped into her bones and she found herself nodding off as he combed her hair.

When he was done, he set the comb aside and wrapped his arms tightly around her. He pressed his cheek against the side of her head and rocked slightly as she stared into the glowing embers.

"You scared me, lass."

She sighed and melted deeper into his embrace. "I scared myself, Laird. 'Tis the truth I had no liking of the thought of leaving you and Crispen."

Crispen slept in your bed each night you were ill. He on one side, I on the other. He was just as determined as I that you not die."

She smiled. " 'Tis nice to have family."

"Aye, lass, it is. I think you and Crispen and I make a fine family."

"Don't forget Caelen and Alaric," she said with a frown. "And Gannon, Cormac, and Diormid, of course. They do annoy me, but they have good intentions and they are ever so patient. Oh! And Maddie and Bertha and Christina."

Ewan chuckled against her ear. "Our clan, lass. Our clan is our family."

Oh, she liked the idea of that. Family. She gave a contented sigh and leaned her head back on his shoulder.

"Ewan?"

"Aye, lass."

"Thank you for not letting me die. 'Tis the truth I was close to giving up, but your bellowing made it quite impossible to give in. You do like to bellow. It probably made you happy to have an excuse to carry on so."

He squeezed her to him and she felt the tremble of his body that signaled silent laughter.

"When you are well, we're going to have a long talk."

She tried to sit up but he held her tight. "Talk about what, Laird?"

"Words, lass. Words I intend that you'll offer me."

CHAPTER 29

He'd given her an entire fortnight in which he bullied her into resting, showered her with affection—privately, of course—and the loving . . . Ah, the lass had quickly recovered and Ewan had spent each night driving her, and himself, mad with pleasure.

Yet she'd never spoken of loving him. She was free with her compliments, he had to give her that much. She told him in the sweetest tones that he was handsome, bold, arrogant . . . though he wasn't certain that she meant all of these as compliments.

She was certainly impressed with his skills at loving, and she'd developed some of her own that he still hadn't fully recovered from.

She had to love him. He couldn't countenance that she felt only passing affection for him. She sure as hell wasn't obedient, nor was she particularly respectful. But he saw the way she looked at him when she thought he wasn't watching. He saw how she fell apart in his arms night after night in the darkness of their chamber.

Aye, she loved him. There was no other explanation. He just had to get her to see it.

The poisoning had made Mairin more wary, and as much as Ewan liked that she took his requests seriously, he did miss their fiery exchanges—usually spawned when she disregarded an order. He didn't like that Mairin's spontaneous charm had been curtailed by her near death.

Only Ewan, his brothers, and Gannon, Cormac, and Diormid knew the truth. That Mairin hadn't been the intended victim. There were many reasons for Ewan to keep the information to himself.

One, his clan had become fiercely protective of Mairin since the incident. They all looked after her with a keen eye, and she was never alone. That suited Ewan's purposes perfectly, because whether someone was trying to kill Mairin or not, she still faced the threat that was Duncan Cameron.

Two, he had no desire for Mairin to worry, and if she found out that Ewan was the intended victim, not once but twice, there was no telling what the lass might do. Ewan had discovered in a short time that she was fierce in her protection of those she considered hers.

And the lass did consider Ewan hers, much to Ewan's smug satisfaction. She may not have given him the words he wanted to hear, but there was no denying her possessiveness when it came to him. He remembered well the look she'd given him when Rionna McDonald had been introduced.

He looked forward to the day when they would be free of threats. The shadow hanging over the keep had affected not just Mairin, but everyone. Mairin . . . well, Ewan hadn't had a single report of her causing a ruckus since she'd gotten up from her sickbed.

He should have known that wouldn't last . . .

"Laird, you must come quickly!" Owain said as he ran up to Ewan.

The younger man panted as he came to a stop. It looked as if he'd run the entire way from where he came.

Ewan turned from the sheepherder, who was giving

him a detailed accounting of McCabe stocks, and frowned.

"What is amiss, Owain?"

"'Tis Lady McCabe. The entire hall is in an uproar. She's ordered a group of your men to take over the women's duties!"

"What?" Ewan demanded. Then he put his fingers to the bridge of his nose and took in a deep breath. "Tell me exactly what goes on, Owain."

"Heath angered her but I don't know what transpired, Laird. She's ordered him and the group of men with him to do the washing! And the cooking! God help us all. And cleaning the kitchens and the floors . . ."

Owain broke off, winded, and then plowed forward again. "They're all ready to revolt because your brothers can't control the lass."

Ewan frowned and swore under his breath. Heath was a hotheaded young soldier who'd only recently come to the McCabes. He was a bastard son of Laird McKinley—one of many—who'd been unacknowledged by his father before the laird's death. The result was that he had no home. Ewan had gathered such men over the years, adding to his numbers when so many of his own clan had been eliminated by Duncan Cameron's attack.

Ewan had already had problems with Heath and a group of younger, cocky, arrogant soldiers who had allied themselves with Heath shortly after his arrival.

They'd been disciplined before, and Ewan had already decided that it would be his last effort to turn them into McCabe warriors.

If Heath was involved, it couldn't be good. Match him to Ewan's equally hotheaded wife and an explosion was sure to follow.

"Where are my brothers?" Ewan demanded.

"They're with Lady McCabe in the hall. 'Tis a very

tense situation, Laird. There was a moment that I feared for the safety of Lady McCabe."

That was all Ewan needed to hear. He ran for the hall, and as he rounded the corner into the courtyard, he saw all of his men, who had been out training, standing still, their heads cocked as they listened to the din coming from inside the keep.

Ewan shoved past them, vaulted up the steps, and barged into the hall.

The scene before him was chaos. A group of younger soldiers was across the room, surrounded by Ewan's brothers and Mairin and Gertie.

Cormac and Diormid were being roundly scolded by Gertie. Gertie was so riled that she shook a spoon at the two men and managed to hit them with it about every third stroke. Alaric and Caelen both wore expressions of fury as they sought to place Mairin behind them. But she was having none of it.

What caught Ewan's attention, however, was Mairin, who stood in the middle of the fray, her face so red from anger that she looked fair to exploding. She was on tiptoe, shouting insults at Heath from around Gannon, who was also valiantly trying to keep her at a distance.

Heath's face was purple with rage. The lass had no idea the danger she'd put herself in. But Ewan knew. He'd witnessed the younger man's brash temper more than once. Ewan had already started across the room when he saw Heath raise his hand.

Ewan let out a roar, drew his sword, and launched himself over the remaining space. Mairin ducked, but Heath's fist still grazed her jaw as she turned away. She went flying back just as Ewan slammed into Heath.

If Caelen and Alaric hadn't pinned both Ewan's arms back, he would have killed the younger man on the spot.

As it was, Heath lay sprawled on the floor, blood dripping from his mouth.

Ewan twisted in their grip but they wouldn't let him go. "Leave off!" he roared.

They wrestled him back several paces before he finally managed to break their hold. He yanked his arm away and went to where Mairin was picking herself up off the floor.

He caught her elbow and helped her to her feet. Then he cupped her chin and turned it up so he could see her jaw.

"He barely touched me," Mairin whispered. "Truly, Ewan, it doesn't pain me at all."

Fury sizzled over his skin. "He had no right to touch you at all! He'll die for this offense."

He dropped his hand from her face and then turned to fix the rest of the room with his glare. "Can someone tell me what in God's name is going on?"

Everyone started talking at once. Ewan closed his eyes and then roared for silence. He turned to Mairin. "*You* tell me what happened here."

She glanced down at her hands but not before he saw the betraying quiver of her lip.

"I'll tell you, Laird," Diormid said loudly as he stepped forward. "She ordered Heath, Robert, Corbin, Ian, and Matthew to take on the tasks of the women." The disbelief and outrage Diormid felt on behalf of his men was evident. "She instructed them all to do the cooking and the cleaning and the scrubbing of the floors!"

Ewan watched as Mairin's expression went flat. Her lips drew into a thin line, and then she simply turned away and would have walked out of the hall if Ewan hadn't quickly caught hold of her arm to prevent her departure.

"Lass?" he asked pointedly.

Her chin wobbled, and she blinked furiously. "You'll

just yell, Laird, and I have no desire to be humiliated again in front of my clan."

"Tell me what happened," he said in a stern voice. He was determined that he not show weakness in front of his men. What he wanted to do was pull her into his arms and kiss those trembling lips. She was on the verge of tears, and he'd do damn near anything to prevent her crying.

But what he had to do was be fair and disciplined. He had a duty to everyone involved to be fair and impartial, which meant that if his wife had hatched another of her hare-brained schemes, he was destined to make her cry.

Her chin went up, which relieved him. He far preferred her belligerence to her tears.

She pointed at Heath. "That . . . That idiot struck Christina."

Ewan stiffened and jerked around to see Heath helped to his feet by Diormid.

"Is this true?" Ewan asked in a low voice.

"The bitch was impertinent," Heath growled. "She deserved my reprimand."

Mairin gasped in outrage. She would have flown at Heath again but Ewan caught her by the waist and yanked her to his chest. Her feet kicked at his ankles but he wouldn't let her go. He turned to Alaric and thrust Mairin into his arms.

"Do *not* let her go," Ewan ordered.

Alaric wrapped his arm around her waist and simply held her against his chest, her feet inches from the floor. Mairin looked outraged, but Ewan was more interested in Heath's explanation.

He turned back to Heath once more and pinned him with the full force of his stare. "You will tell me everything."

Mairin struggled in Alaric's arms but he held her fast.

"Ewan, please," she pleaded. "I would tell you all that happened."

She was beyond furious. She was so sickened by the men's treatment of the serving women that she was ready to take Ewan's sword and gut them all. If she could lift it, she'd do just that.

She turned to Alaric when Ewan continued to ignore her. "Alaric, may I borrow your sword?"

Alaric raised a startled brow. "Lass, you couldn't lift my sword."

"You could help me. Please, Alaric, I've a need to shed some blood."

To her surprise, he laughed outright, the sound loud in the quiet room.

Tears of frustration pricked her eyes. "Please, Alaric, 'tis not right what he did. And now he'll make excuses to Ewan for his disgraceful behavior, for all their behavior."

Alaric's gaze softened. "Ewan will take care of this, lass. He is a fair man."

"But he's a man," she persisted.

Alaric shot her a puzzled look. "Aye, I just said so."

Before Ewan could again demand an explanation from Heath, the hall erupted once more. Women poured into the room, their cries rivaling that of any warrior. To Mairin's astonishment, they held an assortment of makeshift weapons, from pitchforks and sticks to rocks and daggers.

Ewan's mouth gaped open just as Alaric finally let Mairin loose from his grasp. She landed with a thump on the floor and cast a disgruntled glare in Alaric's direction. But he, like every other man, turned to stare in astonishment as the women converged on them.

"Lass, are you all right?" Bertha demanded from the front of the crowd of women.

Christina hurried over to Mairin, grabbed her hand,

then gestured for Maddie before pulling Mairin to the assembled women.

Mairin squeezed Christina's hand as she stared at the darkening bruise on Christina's cheek. "Are you all right?" Mairin whispered.

Christina smiled. "Aye, thanks to you, my lady."

"Laird, we be wanting a word from you," Bertha bellowed.

She waved her pitchfork for emphasis as Ewan continued to stare at the women in astonishment.

"What the hell is going on?" Ewan demanded. "Has the entire world gone mad?"

"Your men behaved reprehensibly," Mairin said.

The women voiced their agreement by waving their weapons and stomping their feet. Ewan's men looked as if they didn't know whether to be afraid or angry.

Ewan folded his arms over his chest and looked sternly at her. "What did they do, lass?"

Mairin glanced at the other women, drawing courage from their support. Then she jutted out her chin and pinned the laird with her best impression of his scowl. It must have been a worthy impression because he lifted an eyebrow as he stared back at her.

"The women were all doing their duties, just as you expect the men to do. That *idiot* over there decided to test his charms on Christina and the lass refused him. He was so furious over the rejection that he began to criticize her work. You see, she was serving the soldiers their afternoon meal. Thus began an effort to belittle and demean the work of every woman in this keep. They made jests and grew louder and louder in their criticism. They bellowed at Maddie when the food wasn't served soon enough. They complained about Gertie's preparation when they felt the food was not savory enough or it was too cold."

She drew in a long breath before she spilled forth the rest of her ire.

"And when Christina sought to diffuse the situation, Heath tripped her. She spilled ale everywhere and then he had the nerve to chasten her for ruining his clothing. When she protested, he slapped her."

Mairin's hands curled in fury as she stepped forward, her entire body shaking with rage. She pointed at the group comprised of Heath, Robert, Corbin, Ian, and Matthew. "And not one, not *one* of them stepped in to help her. Not one! No one moved a finger to stop his abuse of Christina. They were too busy laughing and criticizing women's work."

She stopped in front of the laird and poked her finger into his chest. "Well, I say if 'tis so easy and the men are so critical, they can take over the women's duties for the day and we'll see how well *they* perform the women's tasks."

She held her breath and waited for Ewan to denounce her.

"I would speak, Laird!" Bertha yelled out, her voice so loud that more than one woman winced.

"You may speak," Ewan said.

"I'll not go overlong with my comments, but hear this. As of this moment, the women are not lifting a finger in this keep. And we're keeping Lady McCabe!"

Ewan lifted his brow again. "You're keeping her?"

Bertha nodded. "Aye, she's going with us. We'll not have her chastised for her defense of us."

To Mairin's surprise, he smiled.

"There's a bit of a problem with that, Bertha."

"And what is that?" Bertha demanded.

"*I'm* keeping her."

That statement caused a series of murmurs to race through the hall. Both the men and the women leaned forward, curious as to which way the laird would rule. It was clear he was displeased.

"I will not be swayed by blackmail and demands," he said.

When Bertha puffed out her chest and prepared to launch into another angry tirade, he held up a hand to silence her.

"I will hear what both sides have to say before I render judgment. Once I do, the matter will be final. Is that clear?"

"Only if you decide the right way," Mairin muttered.

Ewan shot her a quelling look.

The laird turned and it was the truth that he didn't look pleased as he stared at Heath and the four younger men who stood defiantly by his side. Then he looked to Gannon, who was the most senior of all his men.

"Have you an explanation for this?"

Gannon sighed. "I'm sorry, Laird. I was not present. I was in the courtyard with some of the other soldiers. I had informed them they wouldn't eat until they performed their maneuvers correctly."

"I see." He turned to Cormac, who stood to the side of Diormid and Heath. "Cormac? Have you anything to offer?"

Cormac looked furious. He glanced between the men, who stared expectantly at him, and Ewan, who also awaited his word.

" 'Tis as our mistress reported, Laird," he said through tight lips. "I came into the hall just as Heath tripped Christina." Anger rippled across Cormac's face as he glanced over at Heath. " 'Twas not Christina's fault. The men grew louder with their insults and when Christina offered disagreement, Heath struck her. 'Tis God's truth I would have killed him myself, but Lady McCabe intervened before I could act, and then my foremost concern was her safety."

Ewan nodded his agreement over Cormac's assessment, then looked over to where Diormid stood beside Heath. "And do you defend his actions?"

Diormid looked torn in his loyalty to the young men directly under his command. "Nay, Laird. 'Twas not the tale as he told it to me."

"So you weren't present for the happenings?" Ewan asked.

Diormid shook his head. "I entered the hall as Lady McCabe was issuing orders for the men to take over the women's duties for the day."

"And do you commend his actions? Do you stand by them?" Ewan asked.

Diormid hesitated before finally saying, "Nay, Laird. I am shamed by them."

Then Ewan turned to Bertha. "You may take the women and retire to your cottages. Or however else you'd like to spend your day of leisure. Robert, Corbin, Ian, and Matthew will see to your duties."

Mairin frowned at the omission of Heath, but the cheers from the women prevented her from voicing her displeasure.

Equally explosive were the shouts of dismay from the four Ewan had sentenced to the women's work. They looked so appalled that it was all Mairin could do not to smile her satisfaction.

Bertha beamed at Mairin. "Come, lass, you must celebrate with us."

Mairin turned to leave the hall with the women when Ewan cleared his throat. Slowly she turned around and peeked up at the laird. Surely he wasn't angry with her. Not after having heard the full story.

His expression was still stern as he crooked his finger at her. With a sigh, she left Bertha to go to her husband. The women remained in the hall, either curious over what the laird wanted or to defend Mairin from reprimand. Mairin wasn't sure, but she was grateful for their support.

When she was a respectable distance, she stopped and folded her hands in front of her. "You wanted me?"

He crooked his finger again, and she huffed as she moved even closer. He stretched out his finger and touched her chin, prodding until she was looking directly up at him.

"You have instructions for me, Laird?"

"Aye, lass, I do."

She cocked her head farther back and waited for his order.

His fingers trailed over her chin to her jaw where Heath's fist had grazed her. Then he delved into the hair over her ear, his hand cupping the back of her head in his possessive grasp.

"Kiss me."

CHAPTER 30

Mairin was so relieved that she threw herself into Ewan's arms and fused her mouth hotly to his.

"You didn't trust me, lass."

His voice was reprimanding as he tasted her lips again.

"I'm sorry," she whispered. "You did look as if you wanted to yell at me again."

"Laird, you cannot mean for us to do the women's chores!"

Ewan turned sharply at Robert's protest.

"Indeed, I do. If any man has a problem with my command, they are free to leave the keep."

Heath's lips turned up into a snarl and Mairin automatically moved farther into Ewan's hold. The man made her nauseous, and the hatred in his eyes frightened her.

"What of Heath?" she whispered. "Why was he pardoned from the women's work?"

The scowl that blackened Ewan's face terrified her. "Stay with Alaric."

He actually deposited her between Alaric and Caelen before stalking over to where Heath stood. Their shoulders closed in front of her and she stood up on tiptoe, bobbing left and right in an effort to see over or through the two brothers.

When Ewan reached Heath, he didn't say a word. He drew back and rammed his fist into Heath's face. Heath fell like a rock. He groaned piteously when Ewan gathered his shirt in his hands and hauled him back up again.

"That was for Christina," Ewan snarled.

Then he rammed his knee right between Heath's legs. Alaric and Caelen both winced. Gannon turned white and Cormac flinched and looked away.

"That was for my wife."

He dropped Heath on the floor, where he promptly curled into a ball. Why, Mairin could swear the man was weeping.

"I'd be weeping, too, lass," Alaric murmured.

Ewan turned and addressed Gannon in chilling tones. "He dies. Take him away."

Heath blanched at the death sentence and began begging in hoarse tones. The assembled warriors winced and showed their disgust at the piteous way Heath behaved.

"Aye, Laird. Immediately."

Gannon bent and hauled Heath to his feet, and he and Cormac dragged him from the hall, Heath still hunched over in pain.

Ewan then turned his attention to the celebrating women. "My apologies, Christina, that you suffered such injustice. I do not condone, nor will I accept such behavior from my men. Enjoy your free day from your duties. I doubt my men will do the job you would do in their stead, but the work will be done."

Mairin's heart swelled with pride. She was so thrilled by the sincerity in Ewan's evenly voiced words that her eyes stung and watered. She gripped Caelen's and Alaric's arms until her knuckles turned white.

Caelen carefully pried her fingers from his elbow and

then rolled his eyes when he noticed her tears. "What on earth are you crying for, lass?"

She sniffled and scrubbed her face against Alaric's shirt sleeve. " 'Tis a wonderful thing he's done."

Alaric pushed at her head and scowled until she stopped wiping her tears on him.

"He's a good man," she said.

"Of course he is," Caelen said loyally.

Having settled the matter, Ewan walked over to where Mairin stood. Uncaring of how it looked or the fact that he hadn't invited her this time, she launched herself around Alaric and Caelen and catapulted into Ewan's arms. She peppered his face with a barrage of kisses and latched onto his neck and squeezed for all she was worth.

"Let me breathe, lass," Ewan said with a laugh.

"I love you," she whispered into his ear. "I love you so much."

And suddenly he was squeezing her every bit as hard as she squeezed him. To her utter shock, he turned and hauled her out of the hall. He took the stairs two at a time and burst into their chamber just moments later.

After he kicked the door shut with his foot, he stared fiercely down at her, his grip so tight around her that she couldn't squeeze out a single breath.

"What did you say?" he asked hoarsely.

Her eyes widened in surprise at his vehemence.

"Just a moment ago. In the hall. What did you say into my ear?"

She swallowed nervously and fidgeted in his arms. Then she gathered her courage as tightly around her as he held her. "I love you."

" 'Tis about damn time," he growled.

She blinked in confusion. " 'Tis about time for what?"

"The words. You finally said them."

"But I only just realized," she said in bewilderment.

"I knew it already," he said with smug satisfaction.

"You did not. I didn't even know it, so how could you?"

He grinned. "So tell me, lass, how did you plan to spend your afternoon of leisure?"

"I don't know," she admitted. "Perhaps I'll go find Crispen and play with him and the other children."

Ewan shook his head.

"Nay?" she questioned.

"Nay."

"Why?"

"Because I've decided that an afternoon of leisure sounds extremely appealing."

Her eyes widened in astonishment. "You have?"

"Mmm-hmm. I wondered if perhaps you were willing to be leisurely with me."

"'Tis a sin to be slothful," she whispered.

"Aye, but what I have in mind has nothing to do with being a sloth."

She blushed furiously at the suggestion in his voice. "You've never taken the afternoon off from your duties."

"My most important duty is to see to the needs of my wife." He cupped the area of her cheek where Heath had struck her, and his gaze darkened.

"Do you really mean to kill him, Ewan?" she whispered.

Ewan scowled. "He struck you. You are wife to the laird, mistress of this keep. I tolerate no disrespect and I damn sure will kill any man who ever touches you."

Mairin twisted her hands, guilt surging through her. "I provoked him shamelessly. I called him terrible names. I used words no lady should ever use. Mother Serenity would wash my mouth out with soap."

Ewan sighed. "What would you have me do, Mairin?

He's been a problem before today. He'd already used up his allotment of chances. Even if he hadn't struck you, I would not tolerate him raising a hand to another woman in this clan."

"Can you banish him? I would think that a man with no home and no means would suffer far more than if you offered him a quick and easy death. Maybe he'll starve to death or a pack of wolves will descend upon him."

Ewan reared back in surprise and then he laughed, the throaty sound sending prickles of delight down Mairin's spine.

"You're a bloodthirsty lass."

She nodded. "Aye, Alaric said as much."

"Why is it important that I not do the killing, Mairin? 'Tis my right as laird and as your husband."

"Because I feel at fault for provoking him so. If he hadn't struck me, you wouldn't have ordered his death for striking Christina. Not that you wouldn't have punished him," she rushed to say.

"So you'd rather he be ravaged by a pack of wolves."

She nodded.

He chuckled. "So be it, lass. I'll have Gannon escort him off our lands with the order never to return."

She threw her arms around him and squeezed as hard as she could. "I love you."

He pulled her away and then leaned down to kiss the tip of her nose. "Say it again."

She twisted her lips and scowled up at him. "You're a demanding man, Laird."

His lips found hers and he drank deeply, rubbing his tongue over her mouth until she opened to let him in.

"Say it," he whispered.

"I love you."

With a low groan, he gathered her in his arms and

walked her back until her legs hit the edge of the bed. He swept her down and then rolled until she was sprawled indelicately atop him. He pushed at her clothing, baring first her shoulders and then her arms. He gripped her upper arms and pulled her down so that he nuzzled her neck. Ah, but his lips were magic.

Determined that he wouldn't be the only one doing the torturing, she bent and ran her tongue over the thick cords in his neck. Smiling when he flinched and went rigid underneath her, she sank her teeth into his flesh, inhaling his male scent. She savored his taste, rolling her tongue over every line and dip.

"Mairin?"

She leaned up so she could look down into Ewan's eyes. "Aye, husband?"

"Do you have a particular fondness for this dress?"

She frowned. "Well nay, 'tis a work gown after all."

"Good."

Before she could think on his meaning, he ripped the material from her bodice all the way past her waist. It fell away, baring her breasts to his eager touch.

" 'Tis not fair," she grumbled. "I can't rip your clothing."

He grinned. "Would you like to, lass?"

"Aye, I would."

Chuckling, he rolled until he was on top and he began shrugging out of his clothing. As soon as he was naked, he pulled the remaining tatters of her dress from her body and then rolled her back on top of him.

" 'Tis an odd position, husband. I'm sure you don't have the way of it."

He traced a line from her temple over her cheek and to her lips. "Aye, lass, I have the right of it. Today the women are in charge and the men are doing the work. It only seems right that you should be on top. I am your humble servant."

Her eyes widened. She thought on what he'd said, pursed her lips, and then finally shook her head. "I'm not at all sure such a thing is possible."

"Oh aye, 'tis possible, lass. Not only is it possible, but 'tis a marvelous experience."

He gripped her hips, lifting to position her over his groin.

"Put your hand down, lass. Guide me in."

She trembled with excitement and anticipation. Her legs quivered and jumped against his sides as she reached down and grasped his hardness.

"Oh, aye, lass, just like that. Hold me just right there. Let me fit you to me."

He moved her, holding her still as the tip of his cock brushed through her damp heat. Then he found the entrance and slid in the tiniest bit. Her eyes flew open and she tensed as he began to breach her opening.

"Relax," he soothed.

He guided her down and she removed her hand and placed both palms on his chest. She leaned forward as his fingers slid from her hips over her buttocks. He gripped her flesh and spread her wider as he slid deeper.

With one final push, her bottom met the tops of his thighs. It was an unsettling sensation, being speared, so full with no relief. Her body hummed with pleasure. Her nipples tightened into hard points, pouting and begging for his touch.

He obliged her, leaving her hips and feathering his fingers over her belly up until he cupped both breasts in his palms. Little sparks of fire sizzled through her body when he thumbed the taut buds. He teased and coaxed until they were painfully rigid.

"Ride me," he said huskily.

The image of doing such a thing exploded in her mind. A hot flush worked through her core until she squirmed and gripped him even tighter in her sheath.

Eager to do his bidding, she began to move, tentatively at first. She felt awkward and shy but the look in Ewan's eyes gave her all the confidence she needed to continue.

Back and forth she rocked, rising up and then easing down. They both made contented sounds that became more desperate and urgent as she picked up her pace.

Delighting in her newfound freedom, she proceeded to drive them both beyond the bounds of reason. She smiled seductively down at her husband when he pleaded with her to stop tormenting him.

With her lips fused to his as tightly as their bodies were joined, they found their release. She swallowed his cry of triumph as he swallowed her cry of ecstasy. His fingers dug into her hips and he pulled her down, holding her there as he emptied himself into her body.

With a sigh, she collapsed on top of him and burrowed into his warmth. His heart pounded frantically against hers until she wasn't sure whose beat harder. He wrapped his arms around her and kissed the top of her head.

"I love you, Mairin."

For a moment she didn't think she'd heard correctly. Aye, she loved him. More than she'd imagined loving a man. But she hadn't dreamed that he'd return her feelings. He was affectionate with her. Loving, even. But she hadn't ever expected that he'd offer her his heart.

Tears filled her eyes as she rose up, her hair falling over his chest while she stared down at him in wonder.

"Say it again," she said huskily.

He smiled at hearing his own words tossed back at him.

"I love you."

"Oh, Ewan," she whispered.

"Don't cry, lass. I'd do just about anything to keep you from crying."

" 'Tis happy tears." She sniffed. "You've made me so happy, Ewan. You've given me a home and family. A clan to call my own. And you stood behind me today when I feared you'd denounce me in front of everyone."

He frowned and shook his head. "I always stand behind you, wife. I may not always agree with you, and there will be times that I may not make a decision you agree with, but I always stand behind you."

She hugged him again and pressed her face into his neck. "Oh, I do love you so, Ewan."

He rolled until they were on their sides facing each other. He touched her face, stroking the wispy tendrils of hair from her cheek. "I've waited a long time for you to say those words, lass. And now that I have, I'm never going to grow tired of them."

She smiled. " 'Tis a good thing, Laird, for I have this problem with saying the least thing that runs through my mind, and 'tis a fact I'll be thinking of how much I love you often."

"Perhaps you should show me," he said in a husky, aroused voice.

Her mouth dropped open. "Again?"

He smiled and kissed her. "Aye, lass, again."

CHAPTER 31

Mairin slowly dragged herself out of bed and headed straight for the chamber pot where she vomited what little remained in her belly from the night before.

It was a miserable occurrence and had happened like clockwork every morning for the last fortnight. Only it didn't end there. She vomited promptly after the morning meal, then again after the noon meal, and usually at least once before bed.

She'd hidden her condition from Ewan for as long as possible, but with all the vomiting and the way she eyed food as if she were being poisoned again, it was inevitable that he found out.

She would tell him today of her suspicions. Not that they were actually suspicions because it seemed obvious to her that she was carrying his child, and God knew, Ewan had put enough effort into the task of impregnating her.

The entire clan would greet the news with joy. With her dowry to be delivered at any time, prosperity would finally visit their keep. A pregnancy and safe delivery of a child would seal the McCabe control of Neamh Álainn.

She fairly danced with excitement over the idea of telling Ewan the news.

After washing out her mouth and getting dressed, Mairin headed below stairs where she was met by Gannon. She raised her eyebrows in surprise when she saw him because since her poisoning, Ewan had made it a point to have either himself or one of his brothers guarding her every moment of every day. It was a fact she was resigned to and had accepted with good grace.

"Good morning, my lady," Gannon said cheerfully.

"Good morning, Gannon. Tell me, what have you done to anger your laird?"

Gannon blinked and eyed her with confusion. Then he laughed as he realized she was jesting with him over his duty.

"Nothing, my lady, 'tis the truth I volunteered for the chore of looking after you today. The laird and his brothers have gone out to greet the McDonalds."

Her eyebrows rose again. Any talk of the McDonalds had been dispensed with after her poisoning. Why, she'd even forgotten the matter of an alliance herself. The McDonalds' departure was not on pleasant terms, so the idea that they had returned made her very curious.

"Where are they?" she asked.

"Unloading the stores of food from the wagon," Gannon said with a smile.

Mairin clasped her hands in delight. "So they made good on that ridiculous wager?"

Gannon rolled his eyes. "Of course. 'Tis a peace offering, too. The two clans must soothe over any bad feelings if we are to ally ourselves."

"Oh, that's wonderful. Surely this will carry us to the winter months."

Gannon nodded. "And beyond, if the hunt continues to be successful."

And if her dowry would come, the clan would have warm clothing for the winter. The children would have shoes. They would eat instead of worrying about where their next meal would come from.

This was very welcome news.

"Where might I find Ewan?" she asked Gannon.

"I'm to escort you to him when you rise."

She frowned. "Well then, I've risen, so let's go."

He chuckled and guided her outside to where the McDonald wagons had been driven into the courtyard. Men were unloading the supplies and taking them to the larder.

Ewan was absorbed in conversation with McDonald, and Mairin frowned as she scanned the people littering the courtyard. Then her gaze fell on Rionna and she brightened.

She started to call out and wave when Ewan caught her eye and motioned her over.

He pulled her to his side when she approached. "Laird McDonald wished to give you his regards. They aren't staying and have only arrived to deliver the supplies. Since we are in agreement over Alaric's marriage to Rionna, we'll meet later in the summer to celebrate the arrangement and announce their betrothal."

Mairin smiled at the laird, who took her hand and bowed.

"I'm relieved that you are back in full health, my lady. I look forward to the time that our clans are united not only by alliance but by marriage bond."

"As do I," she said. "Safe journey to you and I look forward to seeing you when you return."

When one of the men walked by with the gutted carcass of a stag, Mairin's stomach revolted. Her cheeks puffed out as she sucked air through her nose to keep from vomiting there in front of Ewan and Laird McDonald. There'd already been far too much drama the last time the laird visited, and she had no desire to start another fracas by losing the contents of her stomach all over his boots.

She hastily made the excuse that she needed to see Gertie so she could supervise the storing of the provisions and bolted before Ewan could remark.

Once inside the keep, she took in long, steadying breaths and then made her way to the kitchens. It wasn't a complete fabrication. She did want to know Gertie's plans for the sudden surplus of food, and she also thought it would be a nice surprise to plan a special meal for the occasion.

Predictably, Gertie was grumbling over a large cauldron of stew when Mairin entered the kitchen. Gertie stopped periodically to taste, then she'd groan and add another vegetable.

Gertie looked up and frowned when she saw Mairin. "You're looking peaked, lass. I saved you a bowl from the morning meal. Are you still feeling poorly every time you eat?"

Touched by her thoughtfulness, Mairin placed a hand on her stomach. "Aye, I'm afraid so. 'Tis the truth, not much seems appetizing to me these days."

Gertie *tsk*ed and shook her head. "When are you going to tell the laird that you're carrying his child?"

"Soon. I wanted to be sure."

Gertie rolled her eyes. "Lass, no one retches as much as you have for as long as you have if they're ill. By now they'd either die or get better."

Mairin smiled and put a hand to her middle. "Aye, 'tis true, still I didn't want to chance telling the laird something that was false. So much rides on this little one's shoulders."

Gertie's expression softened. "You have a good heart, lass. Our clan has much to be thankful for since you came to us. It almost seems too good to be true."

Embarrassed by the other woman's praise, Mairin directed the conversation to the matter at hand.

"I thought to plan a special meal since Laird McDonald made good on his wager. It seems all we've eaten of late is rabbit stew. I'm sure the men would love to have fresh venison and vegetables. Surely we could spare a little for celebration without depleting our stores to dangerous levels again."

Gertie smiled broadly and reached over to pat Mairin on the arm. "I was thinking the same thing myself, lass. I already had in mind to make venison pies, with your permission, of course. With the salt that Laird McDonald provided, we no longer have to spare every grain for preserving. 'Twill make the meal taste delicious."

"Wonderful! I'll leave the planning in your capable hands. I've promised Crispen that I'd throw skipping stones over the loch with him this afternoon."

"If you wait but a moment, I'll give you some bread to take. It will settle your stomach and give you and Crispen a snack for the afternoon."

Gertie wrapped several small loaves into a cloth sack and handed it to Mairin. "Off with you now, lass. Go and have a good time with Crispen."

"Thank you," Mairin said as she turned to go.

Her heart light, and giddy over the idea of telling Ewan of her pregnancy, she went outside to find Crispen.

The sun's rays shone bright and she turned her face up, seeking more of their warmth. She paused for a moment to watch the McDonalds file across the bridge to the other side of the loch. Her gaze sought Ewan but he was already off on another duty.

She headed around the corner of the keep, searching the shores of the loch for a sign of Crispen. He was standing on a rock outcropping a distance away, his small body outlined in the sun. He stood alone, throwing stones across the surface of the water. He'd watch as the stone traveled, seemingly mesmerized by the way it progressed across the loch. His laughter rang out so pure and untarnished that Mairin's heart seized. Was there anything more beautiful than a child's joy?

She looked to the day when Crispen would lead his brother or sister to the loch to throw stones. The two would laugh and play together. Like a family.

Smiling, she started forward, looking on the ground for appropriate stones as she went. She gathered half a dozen before arriving to where Crispen stood.

"Mama!"

There was no description for the sheer joy that gripped her whenever he called her *mother*.

He ran into her arms and she hugged him close, spilling her rocks in the process.

Laughing, he bent down to help her retrieve them, exclaiming over the perfection of one or two stones as he examined them.

"I want to throw this one," he said, holding up a particularly flat rock.

"Go on then. I wager you can't make it skip more than eight times."

His eyes lit up as she knew they would at the challenge she'd set forth. "I can do nine," he boasted.

"Oh ho! How you boast. Deeds are much stronger than words. Let me see your prowess firsthand."

His chin set and concentration knitting his eyebrows, he lined up his shot and then set the rock flying. It struck the water and skipped in rapid succession toward the other bank.

"One! Two! Three!" He paused for breath but his gaze never left the progression of the rock. "Six! Seven . . . eight . . . nine!" He turned. "Mama, I did it! Nine times!"

"Surely a record," she said, acknowledging his feat.

"You try now," he urged.

"Oh, I can't hope to best someone as skilled as you."

He stuck his chest out and he smiled smugly. Then he brightened and took her hand. "I bet you do well . . . for a woman."

In response she tussled his hair. "You must stop listening to the ideas of your Uncle Caelen, Crispen. It will not endear you to the ladies in the future."

He wrinkled his nose and stuck out his tongue, making a gagging noise. "Girls are awful. Except you, Mama."

She laughed and hugged him to her again. "I'm ever so happy that I'm not considered an awful girl."

He tucked a perfectly flat, smooth rock into her hand. "Try it."

"Very well. After all, the honor of all women rests in my hands."

Crispen giggled at her dramatics as she elaborately lined up her shot. After a few test swings of her arm, she let fly and watched as the rock sailed far, hitting the surface and kicking up water as it bounced.

Beside her Crispen counted under his breath. "Eight! Mama, you did eight! That's brilliant!"

"Wow, I did it!"

They hugged and she whirled him around until they were both dizzy. They collapsed onto the ground in a fit of giggles, and Mairin tickled Crispen until he begged for mercy.

On the hillside that overlooked the loch, Ewan walked up behind Gannon and Cormac, who stood watch over Mairin and Crispen. He watched as they wrestled on the ground, hearing the joyous sound of their laughter ring out over the land. He smiled and pondered how fortunate he was. He had gained so much in such a short time. No matter that multiple threats shadowed their existence. He took moments like these and held them close.

Love was very precious indeed.

Ewan trudged wearily up the stairs and let himself quietly into his chamber. Some of the fatigue dissipated and the strain he'd been under lifted away as he gazed upon his sleeping wife.

She was sprawled indelicately, facedown, her arms spread out over the bed. She slept just like she did everything else. Full out. No reservations.

He stripped out of his clothing and climbed into bed with her. She snuggled into his arms without ever opening her eyes. She was exhausted often these days, a fact that hadn't gone unnoticed by him. Neither had all the retching the poor lass had done over the last few weeks.

She had yet to tell him of her pregnancy, and he didn't know if it was because she didn't want to burden him with how ill she was feeling, or if she truly hadn't yet realized it herself.

He rubbed a hand down her side and over her hip before sliding it between their bodies to rest over her still slim abdomen where their child rested. A child that represented so much hope for the future of his clan.

He kissed Mairin's brow, smiling as he remembered her and Crispen skipping stones on the loch. She stirred against him and sleepily opened her eyes.

"I wasn't sure you were coming to bed tonight, Laird."

He smiled. "'Tis actually quite early. You just went to sleep much earlier than usual."

She yawned and burrowed closer, twining her legs with his. "Has an agreement been made regarding Alaric's marriage?"

Ewan stroked a hand through her hair. "Aye. Alaric has agreed to the match."

"You'll miss him."

"Aye, I'll miss having him here as my right hand. But this is a great opportunity for him to rule his own lands and clan."

"And Rionna? Is she satisfied with the match?"

Ewan's brow crinkled. "I don't concern myself with what McDonald's daughter is satisfied with. The marriage is set. She'll do her duty."

Mairin rolled her eyes, but Ewan, unwilling to be at odds with her on a night he wanted only to hold her in his arms, kissed her long and deep. "I prefer to discuss other matters, wife."

She pushed back just a little and viewed him with skepticism. "What things, husband?"

"Like when you're going to tell me that we're expecting a child."

Her eyes went soft and glowed warmly in the light from the hearth. "How did you know?"

He chuckled. "You've been sleeping far more than usual. You're usually unconscious by the time I come to bed at night. And you can't keep anything you eat down."

She wrinkled her nose in distaste. "I hadn't intended for you to know of my retching."

"You should know by now that you can't hide anything from me, lass. Everything you do is my concern and I'd rather hear it from you when you aren't feeling well."

"I'm feeling quite well now," she whispered.

He raised one eyebrow before capturing her lips in a long kiss. "Just how well?" he murmured back.

"I don't know. I might need some loving to make me feel completely myself."

He cupped her cheek and tenderly rubbed his thumb over her mouth. "By all means, we can't have you feeling anything but yourself. The keep wouldn't know what to do if you weren't driving them daft at every moment."

She balled her fist and pounded him on the chest. He hugged her tightly to him and their laughter filtered through their closed door.

Down the hall, Alaric quietly closed his door so the sound wouldn't invade his sanctuary. He sat on the edge of the bed and stared out the window at the stars hanging low on the horizon.

He envied his brother. He took such delight in his marriage and his wife. Mairin was a woman like no other.

He'd told the truth when he told his brother that he wasn't ready for marriage. Perhaps he'd never be. Because he'd decided as soon as he watched his brother fall hard for his new bride that he'd never settle for less in his own relationship than the one Ewan and Mairin shared. Only now he wasn't offered a choice. His clan needed him. His brother needed him. And he'd never refuse Ewan anything.

CHAPTER 32

Over the next weeks, the weather grew warmer and Mairin spent as much time outside the keep as she could. Though she wouldn't admit as much to Ewan, she kept a sharp eye to the horizon, watching for when her dowry would be brought by the king's escort.

Ewan's missive to the king had gone unanswered thus far, but Mairin held hope that any day they would hear the news that the dowry had been carried to McCabe land.

Her belly had pooched ever so slightly. It wasn't noticeable under the full skirts of her dress, but at night, naked, beneath Ewan, he delighted in the tiny swell that harbored his child.

He couldn't keep his hands or his mouth from the mound. He'd palm and caress it and then kiss every inch of her flesh. His obvious joy over her pregnancy brought Mairin great satisfaction. Her clan's joy over the announcement warmed her to her toes.

When Ewan had stood during the evening meal and announced Mairin's pregnancy, the hall had erupted in cheers. The word raced throughout the keep and a celebration ensued, lasting well into the night.

Aye, life was good. Nothing could mar this day for Mairin. She patted her belly, breathed in the perfumed air, and set off for the courtyard, eager to get a glimpse of her husband training.

As she descended the hill, she looked up and caught her breath. Her heart pounded furiously as she watched the distant riders galloping toward the McCabe keep. Unfurled and flying, held by the front rider, was the king's banner bearing the royal crest.

Her haste was unseemly, but she didn't care. She picked up her skirts and ran for the courtyard. Ewan was already receiving word of the imminent arrival of the king's messenger. Word had raced like wildfire around the keep and her clansmen popped from every corner, crowding into the courtyard, the steps of the keep, and the hillside overlooking the courtyard.

The air of anticipation was thick and sparked like fire as the excited murmurs buzzed from person to person.

Mairin stood back, her bottom lip clenched so tightly between her teeth that she tasted blood. Ewan's brothers flanked Ewan as he waited the approaching riders.

The lead rider cantered across the bridge and pulled his horse up in front of Ewan. He slid off his mount and called a greeting.

"I bear a message from His Majesty."

He handed a scroll to Ewan. Mairin surveyed the remaining riders. There were only a dozen armed soldiers, but there was no sign of trunks or anything that might signal the arrival of her dowry.

Ewan didn't immediately open the scroll. Instead he extended hospitality to the king's men. The rest dismounted and their horses were taken to the stables. The McCabe women brought refreshment to the men when they gathered in the hall to rest from their travel.

Ewan offered them lodging for the night, but they refused, their need to return to Carlisle castle pressing. Mairin died a thousand deaths as she hovered, waiting for Ewan to open the message. Only when the messenger was seated with drink and food did Ewan also sit and unroll the missive.

She whispered to Maddie to fetch quill and ink, knowing that Ewan would need to pen a reply if one was necessary before the messenger took his leave.

As his eyes moved back and forth, his jaw clenched and his expression became murderous. Mairin's chest tightened in dread as she watched anger gather like a storm in his eyes.

Unable to restrain herself, she rushed forward and touched Ewan's shoulder. "Ewan? Is something amiss?"

"Leave me," he said harshly.

She instantly recoiled from the fury in his voice. Her hand dropped and she took a hasty step back. Ewan raised his gaze to the others assembled and barked an order to clear the hall.

Mairin turned and left, avoiding Maddie's look of sympathy when she passed her by.

Ewan read the missive again, unable to believe what was before his eyes. He scanned the signature at the bottom, noting that it was signed by the king's closest advisor, not the king himself. He wasn't sure what to make of that.

Regardless of whether it was signed by the king or his advisor, it bore the royal seal and was carried by a contingent of the king's royal guard. Ewan was compelled to obey, despite the fact that the accusations were laughable and an insult to his honor.

"Ewan, what has happened?" Alaric demanded.

The king's messenger eyed Ewan warily as he shoved his goblet aside. "Will you be penning a response, Laird?"

Ewan's lip curled and he barely restrained his urge to wrap his hands around the man's neck. Only his knowledge that it was hardly fair to slay the messenger for the words of another kept him from venting his rage.

"You may bear my response back verbally. Tell our liege that I will come."

The messenger stood and, with a bow, signaled his men and beat a hasty retreat.

The hall was empty, save Ewan and his brothers. Ewan closed his eyes and brought his fist down on the table with a resounding crack.

"Ewan?" Caelen's concern was sharp, as both he and Alaric leaned forward in their seats.

"I've been summoned to court," Ewan began. He still couldn't believe the contents of the missive.

"To court? Why?" Alaric demanded.

"To answer charges of abduction and rape. Duncan Cameron has taken his suit to the king and claimed that he married Mairin, consummated the marriage, and I abducted and abused her sorely. He put in a claim for Mairin's dowry that predated my own, and now he demands the return of his wife and the immediate release of her dowry."

"What?"

Both Caelen and Alaric roared their outrage.

"I'm to bring Mairin to court, where the king will decide the matter."

"What are you going to do?" Caelen asked.

"I'm sure as hell not taking my wife anywhere Duncan Cameron is in residence. She'll remain here under strict guard while I travel to court."

"What do you want us to do?" Alaric asked tightly.

"I need you to watch over Mairin. I trust you with her life. I'll take a contingent of my men with me but the bulk of my army will remain here. Mairin's safety is paramount. She's more vulnerable than ever now that she carries my child."

"But, Ewan, these charges are serious. If the king doesn't rule in your favor you'll face stiff sanctions. Possibly even a death sentence, since Mairin is the king's niece," Caelen said. "You need more support. If you leave the majority of your army here, it puts you at a disadvantage."

"Perhaps it would be best if you took Mairin with you," Alaric quietly suggested.

"And expose her to Cameron?" Ewan snarled.

Caelen's lips tightened. "We would go with the might of the McCabe clan behind us. We may not be as large an army as Cameron's, but he's already suffered one crippling defeat against us, and he has to know, judging by the way he tucked tail and ran like the bastard coward he is, that he'd commit suicide by challenging us to a fair fight."

" 'Tis too convenient that you're summoned away, Ewan," Alaric added. "It divides our might. If you go with too little protection, you could be ambushed and killed on your way to court. If you take too much, it leaves the keep vulnerable and Mairin as well."

Ewan considered Alaric's words. As much as it pained him, after his initial vehemence over taking Mairin anywhere Duncan Cameron would be in attendance wore off, he knew that the best course was not to let Mairin out of his sight. If he went, so would she, and he'd carry the might of the entire McCabe clan.

"You're right. I'm too angry to think straight," Ewan said wearily. "I will call on the McDonalds and the McLaurens to provide troops to protect the keep in our absence. Mairin needs to be close so I can see to her protection at all times. I don't like to think of her traveling now that she is with child."

"We can take a slower pace and bring a litter so that she is comfortable," Caelen suggested.

Ewan nodded, and then he remembered snarling at Mairin to leave him, when she'd asked him what was amiss. He'd been so furious that he'd needed a moment to process the ludicrous charges that had been laid out against him.

"Jesu," he muttered. "I must find Mairin and explain. I fair bit her head off before she left the hall, and now I must tell her that we have to travel to court to answer a summons from the king. Our future depends on the whim of our king. Her dowry. Neamh Álainn. My child. My wife. Everything could be taken away in a moment."

Alaric raised an eyebrow and exchanged glances with Caelen. "Are you going to allow that?"

Ewan pinned his brothers with the full intensity of the emotion brewing in his chest. "Nay. I'll send missives to the McLaurens, to the McDonalds, and to Laird Douglas to the north. I want them to be ready for war."

Mairin paced the floor of her chamber until she was ready to scream her frustration. What had the message from the king contained? Ewan had been furious. She'd never seen him so angry, not even when Heath had struck her.

She was so sick with worry that for the first time in a fortnight, her stomach seized and nausea rose in her throat. She sank onto the stool in front of the fire and gripped the goblet of water that Maddie had brought up moments before. She sipped the liquid in an effort to settle her stomach, but the tension was knotted too thickly.

As soon as the water went down, her stomach lurched and she stumbled toward the chamber pot, retching the liquid right back up. She registered the door opening and closing, but she was too embroiled in her current misery.

"Ah, sweeting, I'm sorry."

Ewan's hands soothed up her back and her stomach convulsed painfully. He gathered her hair at her nape and put his palm over her belly in an effort to soothe her.

Sweat poured from her forehead and she sagged into Ewan's arms as she finally stopped the horrible gagging. He stroked her hair and held her tightly against him. He pressed a kiss to her temple, and she felt the roll of tension flash through his body.

She turned, so worried that for a moment she had to battle back the urge to heave again.

"Ewan, what is it?" she whispered. "I'm so scared."

He palmed her face and stared down at her, his green eyes flashing. "I'm sorry I yelled at you in the hall. I was greatly unsettled by the contents of the missive and I took out my anger—and fright—on you. It was unfair."

She shook her head, unconcerned with his earlier outburst. It had been obvious that he had been upset over the news, whatever it was.

"What was in the message?" she asked again.

Ewan sighed and leaned forward until his forehead touched hers. "First I want you to know that everything is going to be all right."

That statement only worried her all the more.

"We've been summoned to court."

She frowned. "But why?"

"Duncan Cameron launched a claim for your dowry before my request was received by the king."

Her mouth fell open. "On what grounds?"

"There's more, Mairin," he said softly. "He claims you were married, that he bedded you, and that I stole you away and sorely abused you."

Mairin's eyes went wide with outrage. Her mouth opened and shut as she tried to gather an appropriate response.

"When he learns you carry a child, he'll claim he fathered the babe."

Mairin clutched her belly, suddenly terrified as the implications hit her. Ewan had been summoned to answer to those charges. The king would decide the matter. What if he decided against Ewan?

The idea that she would be handed over to Duncan Cameron sent her straight back to the chamber pot. Ewan held her, murmuring words of love and reassurance as she was sick all over again.

When she was done, he scooped her in his arms and carried her to their bed. He gathered her close in his arms and cradled her against his chest as they lay on their sides.

She was terrified. Utterly terrified.

He tipped up her chin until their gazes were locked. "I want you to listen to me, Mairin. No matter what happens, I will never hand you over to Duncan Cameron. Do you understand?"

"You can't go against the king, Ewan," she whispered.

"The hell I can't. No one takes my wife and child from me. I'll fight God himself, and be assured, Mairin, I won't lose."

She wrapped her arms around Ewan's waist and laid her head on his chest. "Love me, Ewan. Hold me tight and love me."

He rolled until he was atop her, staring down into her eyes. "I'll always love you, Mairin. King and Duncan Cameron be damned. I'll never let you go."

He made sweet, fierce love to her, drawing out their pleasure until Mairin was senseless, until she knew nothing other than his love. Until she believed the words he'd uttered so fiercely.

"I won't let you go," he vowed as she fell apart in his arms. He found his own completion and cradled her to his chest, whispering his love for her and their child.

CHAPTER 33

"I have bad news, Laird," Gannon said in a grim voice.

Not liking his commander's tone, Ewan looked up with a frown as Gannon strode toward him, still dusty from his travel.

"Did you bring Father McElroy?" Ewan demanded. Time was of the essence. Ewan had sent Gannon to fetch the priest so that he could bear witness to the wedding ceremony performed for Ewan and Mairin. They only awaited the priest's arrival before they departed for court.

"He's dead," Gannon bit out.

"Dead?"

"Murdered."

Blasphemies spewed from Ewan's lips. "When?"

"Two days past. He was traveling between McLauren land and McGregor land to the south when he was set upon by thieves. They left him to rot and he was discovered by McGregor soldiers the next day."

Ewan closed his eyes. Thieves? Not likely. Priests had nothing to steal. A thief wouldn't have bothered. It was more likely that Cameron had arranged for the priest's murder to prevent his testimony before the king.

The one card that Ewan held was the fact that Mairin

was David's niece, and surely he would listen to her accounting of the events. Women weren't heard in such matters, but Ewan couldn't imagine the king ignoring the word of his own blood.

"Ready our horses and the men," Ewan ordered his brothers. "I'll go tell Mairin we're to leave posthaste."

Two hours later, with the arrival of McDonald and McLauren men to fortify the McCabe keep, Ewan and his men set off. Mairin rode in front of Ewan. A litter was carried at the end in case she wearied of the horse, but until such time came, Ewan wanted her as close to him as possible.

The clansmen gathered to see them off, worry marring each of their faces. The farewell was somber and tense, and prayers were whispered for the safe return of their laird and his lady.

They didn't travel as hard as Ewan might have in other circumstances. They stopped for the night before dusk fell and set up the tents and built several fires around the perimeter.

Ewan posted guards in turns around the area, as well as outside his and Mairin's tent. Mairin didn't sleep well, nor did she eat well. She was nervous and on edge, and the closer they got to Carlisle Castle, the deeper the shadows were under her eyes.

Ewan's men were just as tense and silent, as if they were mentally preparing for war. Ewan couldn't dispute that they might very well be going to war. Not just against Cameron, but against the crown.

Such an action would brand them as outlaws for the rest of their days. Life hadn't been easy for the McCabes these last eight years, but it would only get worse once there was a price on their heads.

On the fifth day of their journey, Ewan sent Diormid ahead to announce their impending arrival and also to find out if Cameron had already arrived and what the mood was at court.

They paused in their travel and Ewan coaxed Mairin to eat while they awaited Diormid's return.

"I don't want you to worry," he murmured.

She raised her head until her gaze met his and her blue eyes shone with love. "I have faith in you, Ewan."

Ewan turned when he heard a rider approaching. He left Mairin to greet Diormid who'd returned from the castle.

His face was set into a grim line. "I have instructions from the king's man. You're to leave your men outside the walls of the castle. You and Mairin are to be escorted inside at which point Mairin will be placed under the protection of the king until the situation has been resolved. You will have your own quarters until you are called to give testimony."

"And Cameron?" Ewan demanded.

"Also housed in separate quarters. Mairin is to be held in the king's private wing under heavy guard."

Ewan didn't even consider that dictate. "She does not leave me. She will take up residence in my quarters." He turned to his brothers and his three trusted commanders. "You will also accompany me inside the palace walls. There will be times when I must leave Mairin to attend our king, and I don't want her without protection for the barest of moments."

"Aye, Laird. We'll guard her with our lives," Gannon vowed.

"See that you do."

They rode the hour's journey to the castle and when they neared, they were met by a small contingent of the king's soldiers and escorted to the castle walls.

On the east side of the walls, Cameron's men had taken up residence, their tents bearing Cameron's insignia and the banners flying from atop the structures.

Ewan gestured for his men to camp on the western side and instructed them to remain alert at all times.

When his men departed, only Ewan and Mairin, Caelen and Alaric, and Ewan's three commanders that he had charged with Mairin's safety were left.

They rode down the long bridge over the moat and through the stone, arched gateway leading into the courtyard. Court was well attended at present and many stopped to watch as Ewan and his men came to a stop.

As the king's man-at-arms surveyed those in attendance with Ewan, he greeted Ewan with a frown. Ewan lowered Mairin down to Alaric and then swung from his saddle and pulled Mairin to his side.

"I'm to escort the Lady Mairin to her private quarters," the man-at-arms said as he approached.

Ewan drew his sword and pointed it at the man, who stopped in his tracks. "My wife stays with me."

"The king has not issued his judgment on the matter."

"It matters not. My wife will not leave my sight. Are we understood?"

The soldier frowned. "The king will hear of this."

"I expect he will. You may also tell him that my lady wife is with child, and that she has journeyed a long way for this farce of a hearing. I am not pleased to have taken her from our home in a time she should be cared for."

"I will of course bear your message to His Majesty," the soldier returned stiffly.

He turned and motioned for several women who stood on the perimeter awaiting orders.

"See that Laird McCabe and his men are shown to their quarters and have refreshment after their travel."

Ewan aided Mairin up the winding steps to the section that housed chambers reserved for guests. Alaric, Caelen, and Ewan's commanders were directed to an open common room with an array of cots for sleeping. Ewan and

Mairin were directed into a larger chamber at the corridor's end.

Ewan pulled her into his arms and eased her down onto the bed. "Rest, sweeting. We must be at our best during our sojourn here."

"What will we do, Ewan?" she asked against his neck. "I have no wish to mingle at court. I have no finery in which to attend the dinners. I cannot pretend indifference when the very idea of sharing a meal at the same table as Duncan Cameron makes me ill."

"We must act as if we are in the right. If we hide, people will say we have something to hide. If we avoid Duncan Cameron, people will say I fear him."

He stroked Mairin's cheek and gazed down into her eyes. "We must be on our guard and allow no one to think even for a moment that the claims Cameron launched are anything but false. If I can gain an audience with the king soon, I have faith that this will all be cleared up and we can be on our way home."

"I understand," she said quietly. She snuggled tighter into his embrace and yawned broadly. He kissed her brow and urged her to sleep. The travel had taken its toll along with her stress and unease. She would need her strength for what was to come.

A knock sounded at the chamber door, rousing Ewan from sleep. Mairin was still soundly asleep, her face tucked into his neck. Gently he pried himself away from her and rose, pulling on his tunic.

When he opened the door, a servant bowed and extended a jeweled plate with a scroll on top. Ewan took the scroll and nodded at the servant.

He carried the missive inside the chamber and sat at the small desk where a half-gone candle flickered, casting shadows on the wall. He unrolled the scroll and read the summons. He was to attend the evening meal at the king's table in the great hall.

He glanced over at Mairin, who had succumbed to her exhaustion. He didn't want her to endure the strain of a meal where Cameron would likely be in attendance, but it was also important to maintain the public appearance of having done no wrong. Mairin was his wife. His beloved wife. She carried his child. The king and his advisors needed to see firsthand the absurdity of the charges against Ewan.

With a sigh he went to wake her. He had no jewels to adorn her with, but her beauty shone all the more brightly, undistracted by the glitter of riches. Her dress was a simple confection that the ladies had hastily sewn when they'd learned of the impending journey to court.

A castle maid fashioned Mairin's hair, braiding and then coiling the heavy braid atop her head. The maid would have left off, but Mairin caught her hand. " 'Tis unseemly for a married woman to show her hair at court, and I am married to Laird McCabe. Please fashion the wimple around my hair."

Ewan felt a surge of pride at how steady and composed his wife sounded even though he knew how afraid she was. When the maid was finished, Mairin stood and turned to her husband.

"Are you ready to escort me to dinner, Laird?"

"Aye, wife."

He took her hand, tucked it under his arm, and covered it with his other hand as he guided her from the chamber. His brothers waited just down the hall with Gannon, Cormac, and Diormid flanking them. They made an impressive sight, moving down the halls of the castle toward the great hall. Indeed, when they entered the hall, conversation quieted as everyone turned to see Ewan's entrance.

As Ewan escorted his wife toward the high table on

the dais, murmurs rose and raced from table to table. Mairin went rigid against him and her chin jutted upward. Her eyes narrowed and a deep calm worked over her features. As on her wedding day when she'd entered the hall with all the airs of a princess, she now walked beside Ewan as he guided her toward their seats.

Another buzz of murmurs rose, this time louder, and Ewan turned to see Duncan Cameron striding toward them, wild relief on his face. Ewan tucked Mairin behind him and Ewan's brothers stepped forward, but Cameron stopped and dropped to his knees at Mairin's feet.

"My lady wife, finally. After so many months, I despaired of ever seeing you again."

Mairin stepped back, distancing herself from Cameron and clutching Ewan's hand even tighter. Ewan saw the speculation—and the sympathy—that Mairin's rejection inspired in the crowded hall. Cameron was playing the victim to the hilt, and he'd obviously gained the support of many by humbling himself at Mairin's feet.

Cameron rose, grief engraved in the lines of his face. The man was a consummate actor; he even managed a gray pallor as he retreated, seemingly in defeat, to take his seat on the other side of the table.

Ewan had no sooner seated Mairin and himself when the trumpet sounded, signaling the king's arrival. Everyone stood and turned their attention to the door, but it wasn't King David who entered. It was a bevy of his closest advisors, including the king's cousin, Archibald, who'd issued the summons for Ewan to appear.

Archibald nodded pompously and took the seat usually reserved for the king. He first eyed Duncan Cameron and then turned his gaze on Ewan before letting it slide to Mairin on Ewan's right.

"I trust your journey was not too taxing, Lady Mairin. We have only just heard of your being with child."

She bowed demurely. "I thank you for your regard, my lord. My husband has taken great care with me."

"Where is the king?" Ewan asked bluntly.

Archibald had no liking for the question. His eyes narrowed as he stared at Ewan. "The king has other matters to attend to this night."

He turned to survey the many people seated at the tables in the hall. "Let us eat," he announced.

The servants lining the wall burst into activity, filling goblets with wine and setting out the trenchers of food. The aroma was tantalizing and the tables overflowing with bounty.

"Eat," Ewan whispered to Mairin. "You must keep your strength up."

Ewan and Duncan's presence at the same table made the tension so thick that the rest of the noblemen seated around them remained silent. Archibald suffered no ill effects and ate grandly, gesturing for seconds and then thirds of the roasted chicken.

Ewan was ready to be done with the meal so that he and Mairin could retire to their bedchamber, but Archibald kept up a steady stream of mundane and tiresome chatter that made Ewan's head ache.

He had no patience for games played by courtiers. Everyone knew why he and his men were there, and the air was charged with anticipation over the potential confrontation. The people assembled were all but licking their chops over such an event.

"The king is considering the matter put before him," Archibald finally said, as he leaned back in his chair. "He intends to summon the both of you to present your side on the morrow. He understands that this is a stressful time for Lady Mairin and it isn't healthy for a woman in her delicate condition."

"Her name is Lady McCabe," Ewan bit out.

Archibald raised his eyebrow. "Aye, well that does

seem to be the pressing question. His Majesty will decide the matter on the morrow."

"In that case, if you would excuse me, my lord, I would take my lady wife back to our chamber so that she may rest."

Archibald waved his hand. "By all means. I know this must be an ordeal for her."

Ewan rose and then helped Mairin to her feet. Again she donned a cool, regal air that radiated from her in waves. She passed each table, head held high, until many of the people who stared at her averted their gaze in discomfort.

"You did well," Ewan murmured. "This will be done with tomorrow and we can return home."

"I hope you are right, Ewan," she said anxiously, as he closed the door to their chamber. "Duncan Cameron makes me uneasy. It isn't like him to adopt such a meek demeanor and play the snubbed. I do not like the king's man," she said bluntly. "I will be glad to put the matter before my uncle, the king. I have heard he is a fair man and a religious man, as was my father. Surely he will render a just judgment in accordance with God's will."

Ewan had less faith in the piety of men and their willingness to act in accordance to God's laws, but he didn't say as much to Mairin. He wanted her to have faith that it would end quickly and in their favor. But already Ewan was silently preparing for the worst.

The next morning, Ewan was up before dawn. He paced the floor of the chamber, waiting and worrying. He'd spoken to his brothers after Mairin had fallen asleep the night before and they had planned for every contingency.

A knock sounded at the door and Ewan went quickly to answer so Mairin wouldn't be awakened.

One of the king's guards stood outside the door. "His

Majesty requests the presence of the Lady Mairin in his quarters. He will send a guard for her in an hour's time. You are to await his command to appear in the great hall."

Ewan frowned.

"She will be well cared for, Laird."

"I will hold you personally accountable for her safety," Ewan said menacingly.

The guard nodded and then departed down the hall.

"Ewan?"

Ewan turned to see Mairin up on her elbow, her hair streaming over the shoulders.

"What is happening?"

Ewan crossed the room and sat on the edge of the bed. Unable to resist, he ran his hand along her side and then to the tiny swell of her belly.

"Have you been able to tell if our child moves yet?"

She smiled and cupped her hand over his. " 'Tis just a flutter, almost like a tiny brush over my skin. But aye, I can feel him."

Ewan pushed up her nightdress until the smooth expanse of skin was bared to his sight. He leaned down and pressed his mouth to the curve of her belly. The swell was firm, the evidence of the child she sheltered within her body. Ewan was sure he'd never seen a more beautiful sight. He was captivated and wholly entranced. He could spend hours enjoying the silky smooth pale skin and the beauty of the woman who carried his child.

Mairin's fingers tangled in Ewan's long hair as he kissed the shallow indention of her navel.

"What did the messenger say?" she asked quietly.

Ewan raised his head and stared into her eyes. "He summoned you to the king's chamber in an hour's time. He's sending a guard to escort you and then he will summon me to the great hall."

Nervousness fluttered in her eyes and her lips tightened into a thin line. She tensed beneath the hand he held cupped over her belly and he began stroking her to alleviate some of the tension.

"I do not feel he will allow any harm to come to you, sweeting. You are his niece, his blood. For him not to ensure your safety reflects badly on him. His rule is too tenuous with the threat of Malcolm and Malcolm's followers for him to do anything to lose support."

She leaned forward and cupped his face, her thumbs running over his cheekbones. "You always know just what to say. I love you for that, my mighty warrior."

He turned until his mouth slid over her palm and he pressed a kiss to the tender skin. "And I love you. Remember that."

"Summon the maid. I will need help if I am to be ready to see the king in an hour's time," she said with a grimace.

He rose and helped her from the bed. "I'll summon her at once."

She stood at his side and turned her face up so that she looked deep into his eyes. "Promise me that we will leave the moment this matter is settled. I've a need to be home with my clan."

"You have my word."

CHAPTER 34

Mairin walked down the hall, surrounded by four guards. She was more nervous by the minute at the idea of coming face-to-face with her uncle. She was prepared to plead Ewan's case and tell him all that Duncan had done. After hearing all she had to say, the king couldn't possibly rule in Duncan's favor.

The guard knocked and the door was opened by Archibald, who motioned them inward. He smiled and took Mairin's hand and guided her to a comfortable chair in the lavishly decorated sitting room.

"I'm afraid the king is not himself today," he said smoothly. "He's been forced to retire and conveys his deepest regrets that he is unable to speak with you privately as he'd hoped. I will act on his behalf and render judgment on the matter before the crown."

Alarm beat in Mairin's chest as she settled more comfortably in the chair. Her hands shook and she hid them in the folds of her skirts so as not to betray her unease.

"I do hope His Majesty's ailment is not serious," she said politely. "I had looked forward to making the acquaintance of my only blood relative."

"That's not entirely accurate," Archibald said. "I am the king's cousin, so that makes us related by blood."

"Aye, of course," she murmured.

"I would ask that you wait here, cousin, until you are summoned to the great hall. I will, of course, provide refreshment. You'll want for nothing during your confinement."

The way he said *cousin,* and then his casual reference to confinement, made the hairs on Mairin's nape prickle. Still, he viewed her kindly and seemed genuinely concerned over her well-being, so she smiled and offered her thanks.

"I would speak to you, if permissible, about the matter before you, my lord."

He patted her arm. " 'Tis not necessary, dear lady. I am sure the experience has been trying enough and 'tis my duty to get to the bottom of it by hearing both men's accounts. I assure you, I will have the right of it."

She had to force herself not to argue. The last thing she wanted was to anger the man who held her life in his hands.

"Now, if you will excuse me, I must make my way to the great hall and summon the lairds to bear testimony. I will, of course, call for you when they are ready."

She nodded and clenched her hands together in her lap. As the king's cousin left the room, she offered a fervent prayer that justice would prevail this day and that Duncan Cameron would be consigned to hell where he belonged.

Ewan stood outside the great hall with his brothers and commanders and awaited his summons. Down aways stood Duncan Cameron with his men, and it took all Ewan had to not launch himself at the man and kill him on the spot.

Cameron was summoned first, and he walked by Ewan with a look of smug satisfaction. It wasn't just the snideness that bothered Ewan. It was the supreme confidence in both look and manner. Cameron was a man who feared not the outcome of today's hearing.

Caelen put his hand on Ewan's shoulder. "No matter what happens, we're with you, Ewan."

Ewan nodded his appreciation, then he murmured in a low voice that only his brothers could hear. "If things go badly, I want you to leave the hearing, find Mairin, and take her from the castle. Her safety is the most important thing. Whatever you have to do to secure her, do it."

Alaric nodded his understanding.

Next, Ewan was called to make his appearance and he walked into the hall, his brothers shoulder to shoulder behind him. He knew his warriors made an impressive sight. They were larger, more muscled, more fierce looking than any other warriors in attendance.

They stalked down the cleared path in the middle of the hall to the dais where Archibald sat in David's throne. The hall was packed full of people, all insatiably curious as to how the king would rule.

Excited murmurs greeted Ewan's entrance, and his brothers and commanders got many a scrutinizing look from the other soldiers present.

At the front of the assembled people, Ewan stood on the left side of the hall and Cameron stood on the right as they awaited David's arrival.

Instead of the king's arrival, soldiers filled the room, lining the pathway to the dais so that everyone was contained behind the line of warriors. More soldiers filled the front of the room, surrounding the dais and standing in a firm line in front of Archibald.

Ewan frowned. It was as if they expected a battle.

And then his wife entered the hall, flanked by David's soldiers. She slowly made her way up the aisle toward the dais where Archibald watched her approach. He gestured for her to take the position on his right and she gracefully sank into the seat. Her gaze instantly found Ewan's, and no one in the room could discount the instant flash of emotion that arced like a bolt of lightning between them.

Archibald held his hands up and addressed the assembled crowd. "His Majesty, King David, is indisposed this day. He is ill and our prayers should be with our king in his time of need. He has asked that I preside over today's hearing and that my word be received as his."

Ewan turned sharply to his brothers to see the same incredulity etched on their faces as was on his. This was wrong. It was all wrong. Ewan curled his fingers into fists and glanced over at Duncan, who only had eyes for Mairin.

"Laird Cameron, you've leveled serious charges against Laird McCabe. Come forward. I would hear all from the beginning."

Duncan walked confidently toward the dais and bowed low before Lord Archibald.

"Mairin Stuart arrived at Cameron Keep from Kilkirken Abby, where we were married by the priest who has tended to the souls of my clan for two score years. I have a letter written from him to the king attesting to this fact."

Ewan's eyes narrowed in outrage that a man of God would be a willing party to this deception. Duncan handed over the scroll to Archibald, who unrolled and read it before setting it aside.

"Our marriage was consummated." Duncan pulled from the pouch that hung at his side the sheet bearing Mairin's bloodstain. "I offer this as proof."

Ewan's fists clenched in rage. Aye, the blood was Mairin's blood. It was the sheet that Ewan had ordered Cameron's man to bear back to his laird, the proof that Ewan and Mairin's marriage had been consummated.

The sheet that Duncan now offered as proof of his bedding of Mairin.

Archibald turned to Mairin, whose face was as pale as death, her gaze fastened on the sheet. She looked up at Ewan in bewilderment, and Ewan closed his eyes.

"Can you attest to the fact that the blood on the sheet is yours, Lady Mairin? Do you recognize the linen?"

Her cheeks colored and she looked at Lord Archibald, clearly unsure as to how to proceed.

"I would have your answer," Archibald prompted.

"Aye," she said, her voice cracking. " 'Tis my blood, but 'tis not Duncan Cameron's sheet. 'Tis from the bed of—"

"That is all I require," Archibald said, slicing his hand in the air to silence Mairin. "I require an answer, nothing more. Be silent until I've given you permission to speak again."

Fury settled in Ewan's chest, boiling, at the manner in which Archibald addressed Mairin. He showed her blatant disrespect as both the wife of a laird and cousin to the king.

She looked as though she'd argue, but Ewan caught her gaze and quickly shook his head. He had no desire for her to be punished for speaking out in the king's court. The punishment for such was steep, and more so for a woman daring to speak out.

She bit her lip and looked away, but not before Ewan saw the rage in her eyes.

"What happened next?" Archibald asked Cameron.

"Mere days after my marriage to Lady Mairin, she was abducted from my keep by men acting under Laird McCabe's orders. She was taken from me to where she has remained, on McCabe lands. The child she carries is mine. Laird McCabe has no claim. Our marriage is valid. He has kept her prisoner and forced her to his will. I ask for his majesty's intervention so that my lady wife and my child are returned to me and her dowry is released to me as requested in my missive to the king informing him of our marriage months past."

Mairin gasped at the accusations that spilled from Duncan's lips. Ewan started forward, but Caelen gripped his arm and held him back.

"Cousin, please," Mairin pleaded. "Let me be heard."

"Silence!" Archibald roared. "If you cannot hold your tongue, woman, I will have you removed from this hall."

He turned back to Duncan. "Have you witnesses who support your accounting of what happened?"

"You have the statement from the priest who wed us. That predates any claim Laird McCabe makes on Mairin, her dowry, or her lands."

Archibald nodded and then turned his cool stare to Ewan. "What say you to these claims, Laird McCabe?"

" 'Tis complete and utter horseshit," Ewan said calmly.

Archibald's brows drew together and his cheeks reddened. "You will hold a civil tongue in your head, Laird. You would not speak thusly to the king, and you will not speak in my presence as such."

"I can only speak the truth, my lord. Laird Cameron speaks falsely. He stole Mairin Stuart from the abbey where she'd taken refuge for the last ten years. When she refused to wed him, he beat her so badly that she could barely walk for days afterward, and she wore the bruises for an entire fortnight."

The hall broke into a series of murmurs. The buzz rose and grew louder until Archibald shouted for order.

"What proof do you offer?" Archibald asked.

"I saw the bruises. I saw the fear in her eyes when she arrived on my lands, that I would treat her as she was treated by Cameron. My brother Alaric tended her for the three-day journey from where he found her after she escaped Cameron's clutches until they arrived on

McCabe land. He, too, saw the bruises and witnessed the pain that the lass endured.

"We were married a few days after her arrival. She came to my bed pure and her virgin's blood was spilled on my sheet, the one that Cameron has offered to you this day. The child she carries is mine. She has known no other man."

Archibald leaned back in his seat, his fingers pressing together in a V as he surveyed the two men in front of him. "You give a very different accounting than Laird Cameron. Have you witnesses who can speak as to the veracity of your words?"

Ewan's teeth snapped together in a snarl. "I have given you the right of it. I need no witness to verify my claim. If you want to ask someone, ask my wife. She will tell you exactly what I have told you."

"I would speak, my lord."

Ewan turned, surprised to see Diormid step forward, his gaze focused on Lord Archibald.

"And who are you?" Archibald demanded.

"I am Diormid. I have commanded under Laird McCabe five years past. I am among his most trusted men, and I myself was charged with the safety of Lady Mairin on many occasions after her arrival on McCabe land."

"Very well, approach and give your accounting."

Ewan glanced back at Gannon, who shook his head at Ewan's silent question. Diormid stepping forward wasn't at Gannon's instigation. Ewan had instructed them to say or do nothing during the hearing.

"I have no knowledge of what transpired before the lady Mairin arrived on McCabe land. I can only speak as to the events that transpired afterward. 'Tis the truth that she was sorely mistreated under Laird McCabe's hand. He guarded her jealously and, 'tis the truth, she was most unhappy during her time at McCabe Keep. I witnessed her tears on more than one occasion."

A gasp went up from the crowd. Ewan saw a haze of red that buzzed in his ears and clouded his eyes. Bloodlust hit him so hard. He'd never wanted to kill another man as much as he wanted to kill Diormid at that moment.

Ewan's brothers were equally furious. Gannon and Cormac looked horrified by Diormid's calm recitation of blatant lies.

"During the time she was on McCabe land, she was shot at by an archer and poisoned. She nearly died. It should also be noted that the priest who was called to marry the laird and Lady Mairin died under suspicious circumstances less than a fortnight ago."

Ewan could stand no more. His roar shook the entire room as he lunged for Diormid. Mairin screamed his name. His brothers dove after him. Chaos reigned as the king's soldiers leaped in to separate the two men. It took seven of the guards to pry Ewan away from Diormid.

"How could you betray us this way?" Ewan demanded as he was hauled back from Diormid. "How could you stand before God and king and give false witness to events you know to be untrue? May God consign you to hell for this sin. You have betrayed me. You have betrayed Lady McCabe. You have betrayed your clan. And for what? A bit of coin from Duncan Cameron?"

Diormid refused to meet Ewan's gaze. He wiped the blood from his mouth where Ewan had struck him and turned to face Archibald. " 'Tis as I have said, as God is my witness."

"You lie!" Ewan roared.

Duncan Cameron moved to stand by Mairin's side. Her eyes were haunted and fixed on Diormid. Her hand covered her mouth that was agape with shock.

"This is disturbing," Archibald declared. "You will

restrain yourself, Laird McCabe, or I'll have you taken to the dungeon."

When Duncan put his hand on Mairin's shoulder, Ewan erupted again. "Don't you touch her!"

"I would protect my wife from Laird McCabe's outburst," Duncan said to Archibald. "Allow me to take her away from this."

Archibald held up his hand. "I believe I've heard enough to render judgment in this matter. I rule in Laird Cameron's favor. He is free to take his wife and return to his lands. The dowry entrusted to the crown until Mairin Stuart weds will be released to Laird Cameron and taken to his lands under palace guard."

A cry rippled across the room as Mairin shot to her feet. "Nay!"

Ewan was in a state of shock. A man he'd trusted with his very life, with Mairin's life, had betrayed them all in the cruelest fashion possible. It was also apparent that Ewan had never had a chance from the start. Archibald was in league with Duncan Cameron. What wasn't clear was whether the king was also in league with Cameron, or whether Archibald boldly plotted against his cousin.

"My lord, please hear me," Mairin pleaded. " 'Tis not true. None of it is true! My husband is Laird McCabe!"

"Silence, woman!" Duncan roared. He backhanded her in reprimand and she fell into the chair she'd just risen from.

"She is distraught and clearly not thinking straight, my lord. Please forgive her impertinence. I will deal with her later."

Ewan could not be contained. As soon as Cameron struck Mairin, Ewan went crazy. He exploded across the room, hitting Duncan in the chest. The two men went down as, once again, chaos reigned.

This time his brothers did nothing to stop him. They were fighting their own battle against the king's guard.

A battle they couldn't hope to win. They were hugely outnumbered, more than a dozen to one. Without their swords, they were at an even greater disadvantage.

Ewan was hauled off Duncan and went to the floor under the weight of four soldiers. They pulled his arms back and pressed his face to the floor. Mairin flew to his side and knelt down, her hands reaching for him. Tears slid freely down her cheeks.

"Imprison Laird McCabe!" Archibald ordered. "And his men. Laird Cameron, take your wife and be gone from this hall."

Duncan bent over and grabbed Mairin by the hair as he hauled her upward. She fought like a wildcat and Ewan roared his fury as he broke free and tried to attack Duncan again.

The soldiers grabbed him, holding him back even as he bucked and strained against them.

Mairin was being pulled away, her eyes filled with tears, her arms outstretched to Ewan.

"Mairin!" Ewan called hoarsely. "Listen to me. Survive. You survive! Endure. No matter what. Endure what you must but survive for me. Survive for our child. I will come for you. I swear it on my life. I will come for you!"

"I love you," she said brokenly. "I will always love you."

The hilt of a sword crashed down on his head. The pain blurred his vision and his head snapped to the side. As he slid toward the floor, blackness closing in around him, his last image was of Mairin being dragged, screaming, from the hall by Duncan Cameron.

"I love you, too," he whispered.

CHAPTER 35

Mairin found herself thrust into Duncan Cameron's chamber ahead of him. He barked orders to those around him as she stumbled toward the bed. When he neared the bed where she was sprawled, she hastily backed away, prepared to fend him off in whatever way necessary.

He sat on the edge of the bed, his expression calm as he surveyed her. One of the servants pressed a goblet into his hand and then Duncan waved them away. One by one, his men exited the chamber until he was alone with Mairin.

She edged up onto her elbow and inched backward to put more space between them.

He gave an exaggerated sigh of resignation. "I regret what transpired between us the first time we met. I realize my actions were reprehensible and my wooing skills are sorely lacking."

Wooing skills? Reprehensible? His words swam through her muddled mind. Was he insane?

"Your actions *now* are reprehensible," she said hoarsely. "You lied. One of Ewan's own men lied and betrayed our clan. I can only assume at your instigation."

"It would benefit you to make the best of your situation," Duncan said, his voice carrying a hint of dark warning.

"Please," she said, her voice breaking. She hated that she was reduced to begging before this man. But for Ewan, she had no pride. There was nothing she wouldn't do. "Let me return to Ewan. I am married to him truly."

Duncan shrugged. "It matters not whether you are married to him or me. That is of little consequence as long as I receive your dowry and control of Neamh Álainn." He transferred the goblet to the hand closest to Mairin and extended it in her direction. "Now here, drink this, dearling. 'Twill solve our immediate problem. I regret that it will cause you pain, but hopefully it won't last overlong."

She stared at the cup hovering close to her lips. She sniffed and recoiled from the bitter smell.

"What is it? Why will it cause me pain?" Did he think her daft?

He gave her a gentle smile that sent a cold shiver down her spine. "'Tis necessary to rid your body of the babe you carry. Don't worry, I'll give you sufficient time to heal before I make demands. I don't want to wait overlong, though. 'Tis important that you carry my child as soon as possible."

Terror hit her in the stomach. Nausea rose, billowed up into her chest until she gagged and had to turn away. She buried her face in the pillow.

"I'm sorry," she muffled out. "'Twas not well done of me but I find myself ill at the oddest times ever since learning of the babe I carry."

"'Tis the way of things," Duncan offered generously. "When you carry my child, you'll not lift a finger. You'll be waited on hand and foot."

Until you deliver. The words weren't spoken but they hovered heavy in the air. Aye, she had no doubt she'd be treated like a queen until the day she bore the heir to Neamh Álainn.

He meant to kill her child. Ewan's child. And replace

it with his own seed. The mere thought had her gagging again, and she inhaled sharply through her nose to prevent vomiting all over the bed.

"Here, 'tis better to have it done with. Drink it down. I'll summon the palace healer to help you through the worst of it. 'Tis said it can be very painful."

He was so calm about it. How could he discuss murder with a tender smile? The man was a monster. A demon from hell.

"Why would you waste valuable time?" she choked out. She tried frantically to come up with a plan, something, *anything* to sway him from murder.

He frowned. "What mean you?"

"You seek to rid my womb of the child I carry when I am already nearly half done with the carrying. Losing a babe at this advanced stage can render a woman barren. 'Tis no guarantee I'll become pregnant right away or at all. You've already claimed to all that the babe I carry is yours. If it matters not who I'm married to, why should it matter whose babe I carry? As long as I deliver a child, control of Neamh Álainn is yours. Why would you wait and risk my not becoming pregnant again?"

His frown deepened, as if he hadn't considered such a possibility.

"I want my child to live," she said softly. "Regardless of who it calls father. I'd do anything to protect him. In that regard you have the advantage, Laird."

Duncan stood and paced restlessly in front of the bed. He stopped every once in awhile and eyed her as if trying to determine the truth of her words.

" 'Tis often said a mother's love knows no bounds. All right, Mairin Stuart. I agree to your terms. I'll spare your child's life, but from this day on you are mine. You'll not fight me when I seek to avail myself of your body. You will never utter a single word to contradict the account I have given Lord Archibald. Are we understood?"

May God forgive me.

"I agree," she choked out.

"Then be prepared to depart the castle. We leave in an hour's time to return to Cameron land."

"Ewan! Ewan! Wake up for God's sake."

Ewan found himself shaken roughly as he gained awareness of his surroundings. He cracked an eye open and glanced around only to find himself cloaked in darkness.

"Caelen?" he rasped.

"Thank God."

The relief in Caelen's voice was staggering.

"Mairin."

The single word sent grief splintering through his head and chest. Bile rose in his throat at the knowledge that right now his wife was with her tormentor.

"Mairin," he said again. "Where is she?"

The silence was oppressive. He heard his brothers' breathing in the darkness, knew they dreaded the telling they must do.

"I'm sorry, Ewan. Duncan departed hours past, bearing Mairin with him," Alaric said in a grim voice.

Ewan sat up, pain ripping through his head. His brothers caught his shoulders and guided him back down again when he nearly fell.

"Where are we?" he demanded.

"The king's dungeon," Caelen said, fury laced in each word. "The little bastard Archibald had us all tossed in here after his soldiers bashed you in the head."

"Cormac and Gannon?"

"Here, Laird," Gannon returned.

Ice filled Ewan's veins as everything came back to him in a rush. "Diormid. Where is he now?"

"I'm not certain, Laird, but he'll have gone from here. He knows any of us will kill him on sight. 'Tis possible he went with Cameron, since it looks that he was working with Cameron all along."

"The attempts on my life. The arrow. The poison. It must have been him. He had orders from Cameron to kill me. When that didn't work, he put his petition before the king."

"I suspect he had the petition working even before Diormid's attempts on your life," Alaric said. "He had every angle covered from the start."

"The question is, if David is involved in this along with Archibald or if Archibald acts alone with Cameron," Caelen mused.

Ewan put his hands on the rough floor of the dungeon and pushed himself into a sitting position. "Archibald said that David was indisposed and castle rumor confirmed that the king is very ill. I wouldn't be surprised if Archibald is behind that as well."

"Are you all right, Ewan?" Alaric asked. "Does your head pain you overmuch?"

Ewan touched the side of his head, felt the warmth of blood, but it was thick and it no longer flowed freely. "I'll be fine. What's important is that Mairin not stay in Cameron's grasp a minute longer than she has to."

"I've sent a message to our men," Caelen said. "'Tis my hope we hear from them soon."

Ewan stared around the darkened dungeon. "How did you send a message to our men?"

"I might have threatened one of the guards who tossed us into the cell," Caelen admitted. "I told him that unless he informed our men of our fate that I would spit him on my sword, castrate him, and feed his cods to the buzzards."

Alaric chuckled. "The man couldn't leave us fast enough to bear Caelen's message to our men."

"How long have we been down here?" Ewan asked as he rubbed more of the blood from the side of his head.

Caelen sighed. "Several hours. One of the guards who

obviously feels 'tis best to remain on my good side informed me of Cameron's departure a few hours past."

"Son of a bitch," Ewan swore. "I can't believe that bastard allowed Mairin to fall into Cameron's hands. This was all a setup from the beginning. Archibald never had any intention of presenting this matter before David, and he damn sure never had any intention of listening to Mairin or to me. Diormid's testimony just gave him the sway of public opinion so that when he rendered his judgment, there was no backlash from the other lairds who might have thought he intervened unfairly."

"I'm sorry, Laird," Cormac said, devastation in every word. "I should have seen it. I spent every day in Diormid's company. I fought with him. Ate with him. We trained together. We were as brothers. I would have never dreamed he would betray us."

"'Tis just as much my fault as anyone's," Ewan said bleakly. "I trusted him with Mairin's safety many times."

Ewan rubbed his hand tiredly over his face and tried to put the memory of Cameron's hands on Mairin out of his mind. He couldn't imagine Cameron hurting Mairin because it would drive him insane. The only way to survive this was to turn it off. Turn off his emotions. Turn off the images flashing through his mind with torturous precision.

"Cameron will expect a full-scale attack on his holding," Caelen pointed out. "He'll know that Archibald cannot hold us in the king's dungeon forever, and he knows you'll come for Mairin. He'll know it and expect it, so he'll be prepared."

"I can't risk Mairin's safety by attacking his keep with the might of my entire army. If she was not in residence, I'd give him the fight he expects and not give a damn that he expects it. I'd swarm over his lands like the plague and decimate everything in our path. But I won't take the risk that Mairin would be caught up in the battle. And if Duncan knew all was lost, he'd kill her out of spite."

"Aye," Alaric agreed. "What then do we do?"

"We steal into his keep and take Mairin back."

Caelen let out a deep breath, the sound loud in the quiet of the dungeon cell. "You make it sound like a simple raiding mission, Ewan. Cameron will expect such a trick as well."

"We'll succeed. We have no other option."

Caelen, Alaric, Gannon, and Cormac voiced their agreement. Silence fell once again as they waited.

An hour later, a sound outside the cell stirred them to action. Caelen leaped to his feet and charged toward the iron bars as a guard shuffled down the corridor, torch in hand.

"You must hurry," the guard whispered in an urgent voice. "Your men have staged a distraction. Follow me. I'll show you to the northern gate."

Alaric helped Ewan to his feet and they hurried from the cell and up the stone staircase to the first level of the castle. The guard rushed down the long corridor, past the great hall, and beyond to the kitchens.

They exited the castle through the small door where rubbish was discarded and approached a small wooden gate carved into the imposing stone wall that jutted upward. The guard produced a key and hastily unlocked the large metal padlock.

"Go," he urged.

Ewan's men filed out of the doorway and Ewan paused at the end. "You have my thanks," he told the guard. "You need to watch over your king. Archibald plots against him. I've heard rumor the king is unwell. Examine his food and drink."

The guard nodded. "Go with God, Laird McCabe. I'll pray for the safe return of your lady wife."

Ewan ducked out of the doorway and followed his men into the night. They raced across the terrain, heading for the distant cover of the forest.

CHAPTER 36

Ewan trilled a soft birdcall, the sound echoing over the still night. In the distance, an answering call sounded and Ewan crept stealthily forward, his brothers on his heels.

They'd waited four days for the new moon, after taking three days to arrive on Cameron land and carefully survey the layout of the keep. Ewan couldn't wait a single moment longer. There had been no sign of Mairin in several long days as they watched and waited. Duncan was keeping her under tight wraps.

After singling out the chamber that Mairin was most likely housed in, Ewan and his men circled the keep. Along with his brothers, Ewan crept inside the stone skirt, past the sleeping guards to the tower that loomed overhead.

Now in the darkness, Ewan tossed the rope with the hook up the wall. It took five attempts before he hooked the sill. Tugging on the rope to make sure it would hold, he began a quick hand-over-hand scale up the wall to the window.

Mairin stood in her window and bowed her head, as the shame of her circumstances fell over her shoulders. A devil's bargain. Her child's life for her own. Her child's life for her life with Ewan. She didn't regret the decision she'd made, but she mourned all she had lost. All she'd never have.

The strain of the last week was too much to bear. She was at her wit's end. She was afraid to eat lest Duncan change his mind and go back on his word. She feared at every turn that he'd put a potion into her drink or food that would cause her to lose her child.

She lived in constant fear of having to give herself to the man who now called her *wife*. She swayed wearily and turned in the direction of the bed. She couldn't continue on in this manner. It wasn't good for her child, and yet she had no choice.

Tears glistened on her cheeks as she gave in to the overwhelming grief welling from the depths of her soul. How could she live when she'd known a love so deep that she ached at the memory? How could she ever willingly lie with a man after knowing Ewan's touch?

Finally, in her exhaustion, she crawled under the covers and buried her head in the pillow so no one would hear her sobs.

She had no idea of the passing of time. When she felt a hand slide over her arm and to her shoulder, she flinched away and turned over, prepared to defend herself from Duncan's attack.

"Shh, lass, 'tis me, Ewan," he whispered.

She stared up at her husband in the darkness, unable to believe that he was here, in her chamber.

He touched her wet cheek and wiped away the trail of tears. His voice was tortured and the words seemed ripped from his very soul. "Ah, Mairin, what did he do to you?"

"Ewan?"

"Aye, lass, 'tis me."

She rose up and threw her arms around his neck, holding on for dear life. If she was dreaming, she never wanted to wake up. She wanted to exist in this dream world where Ewan's arms were securely around her and she could smell his strong masculine scent.

He crushed her to him, his hand stroking her head, shaking and making a mess of her already unruly hair.

"Ewan," she choked out. "Oh God, Ewan. Ewan."

His lips found hers and he kissed her desperately, as if it were the last kiss they'd ever share. Their lips tangled and her tears slipped onto their tongues. She breathed him in, the last breath she wanted to take. She lived in this moment, reaching for everything she'd lost, for everything she wanted most.

"Shh, don't cry, lass. You're breaking my heart. We don't have much time. I've got to take you from this place."

His words penetrated the heavy grief surrounding her. She stared up at him, afraid to believe he was real, that he was there and not a figment of her dearest fantasies.

He picked her up from the bed and carried her toward the window. He leaned out and she clutched at his shoulders as she stared down at the dizzying distance between her sill and the ground.

"Listen to me, sweeting," he said in a gentle voice. He brushed his lips over her temple and held her tightly against his chest. "We're going down a rope from your window."

She raised her head in alarm. "Ewan, I can't! The babe. I'm too big and clumsy."

He cupped her chin and stroked his fingers over her cheek as he stared down at her. "I'll be with you every step of the way. I'm going to lower you down first. Alaric and Caelen wait for us at the bottom. If you fall, they'll catch you. I need you to trust me."

She reached up to touch his face, her love and faith soaring in her soul. "I'd fly if you asked me to."

He kissed her hard and then lowered her to the floor.

He wasted no time securing the rope around her foot so that it fit her like a stirrup. Then he strung the rope from her foot to her hands, looping it around her wrists and palms so she gripped it tight.

The other end he tied to his waist and he took position just inside the window.

"Step onto the sill, sweeting. Very carefully put your feet against the wall of the castle and keep them there so you don't scrape against the stone as I lower you. Try to remain upright."

'Twas insanity, what he was asking her to do, and yet she climbed onto the ledge, holding on to his shoulders for dear life.

He grabbed the rope just inches from her hands and braced himself as she started to climb over. Inch by inch she lowered her foot until it scraped against the side of the stone wall.

"That's it, lass. Go slow and be careful. I've got you. I won't let you go."

Sliding over the sill was the hardest thing she'd ever done. And then she simply let go. She spiraled downward, hitting her feet against the wall as she struggled to gain her footing. She threw back her head and saw Ewan fighting with all his strength to slow her descent. The rope had to burn his hands and yet he hung on.

She jammed both feet against the wall and gripped the rope with all her might. Halfway down she finally managed to control her descent by walking down the wall with her feet. When finally she neared the bottom, Alaric and Caelen reached up and grabbed her waist. They lowered her to the ground and quickly untied the rope so Ewan could pull it back up.

"How will he get down?" she whispered urgently.

They ignored her and stared upward, waiting for Ewan. Several long minutes later, she saw his dark figure coming down the rope, hand over hand, his feet against the wall as hers had been.

When he reached a safe distance, he dropped the rest of the way, landing with a soft thump beside her. She reached for his hands and, as she suspected, they were torn and raw. Her throat swelled and she kissed each palm, holding them reverently in her own hands.

"Let's go," Alaric hissed. "Gannon is waiting with the horses."

They ducked and ran toward the stone skirt in the distance. Alaric tossed up another rope and the hook hit the stone ledge at the top with a *clink*. Wasting no time, Alaric scrambled up the wall and lay along the top, his hand extended down for Mairin.

Ewan hoisted her high over his head and urged her to reach for Alaric's hand. Their fingers glanced off each other before Alaric finally captured her hand and slid his fingers down to grasp her wrist.

Ewan pushed upward and Alaric pulled her up with incredible strength.

"Grab onto the ledge and pull yourself over," Alaric hissed.

As he swung her up, she lunged for the top of the wall and rolled up so she was head to head with Alaric.

"Listen to me," Alaric said. "Sit up and straddle the wall. As quietly as you can, scoot back until you give Caelen enough room to scramble over. He'll go down and then you'll drop down next. I'll stay up to help Ewan over. His hands are too damaged to climb up another rope."

With some hesitation, she swung one leg over so she straddled the wall and quickly pushed herself back until there was enough space for Caelen to climb the wall.

Moments later, he swung over the top and then dropped down on the other side.

"Take my hand and I'll lower you over the side. Listen for Caelen and when he tells you, let go. He'll catch you," Alaric instructed her.

Swallowing back her fear, she grasped Alaric's hand and slid over the side. She dropped, her feet scraping the side of the wall to slow her momentum. Alaric caught her wrist and nearly pulled her arm from its socket.

"Let go," Caelen called up. "I've got you, Mairin."

She closed her eyes, kicked away from the wall, and let go of Alaric's hand. She needn't have worried. Caelen didn't even stagger under her weight as he caught her against his chest. Still she threw her arms around his neck, hugging him with fierce gratitude for not allowing her to fall.

He gently pried her arms away from his neck and set her down on her feet. Her knees buckled and she clutched at his hand so she wouldn't fall.

"You're all right now," Caelen said in a low, reassuring voice. He caught her to his side to steady her as they waited for Ewan and Alaric to descend.

Ewan dropped down first and Mairin threw herself into his arms. She hugged him so fiercely that he likely couldn't draw breath, but she didn't care. She was in his arms. He was taking her from Duncan Cameron.

"Come," Alaric urged when he dropped to the ground. "Gannon is waiting with the horses."

They raced for the cover of the trees. Just inside the forest, Gannon stood with their horses and Ewan urged her toward his steed.

Alaric and Caelen swung into the saddles. Cormac was already astride his horse and Gannon mounted his. Ewan took to his saddle in one quick motion and then he simply reached down, plucked Mairin off the ground, and settled her in front of him.

She laid her head on Ewan's chest and slipped her arm around his waist. Tears fell freely now, but she did nothing to distract him from his concentration. If Cameron discovered her gone, he would pursue with the might of his entire army, and Ewan would be slowed by bearing her with him.

Only when they were miles away did she turn her face upward. "Ewan?"

He dropped a kiss on the top of her head. "Not now, sweeting. We'll talk when we reach McCabe land. We aren't stopping until we reach our border. Sleep now."

It was on the tip of her tongue to ask him how he thought she'd sleep now, but before they'd gone another mile, her exhaustion caught up with her. After so many nights of not sleeping for fear of what Duncan might do, she was now safe in her husband's arms. She laid her head back on his broad chest and allowed the steady motion of the horse to lull her into sleep.

Ewan rode with one hand holding the reins, the other wrapped solidly around his wife. He set a grueling pace that his men were only too happy to keep. They would not stop to sleep or eat until they reached their border.

CHAPTER 37

True to Ewan's word, he didn't stop for more than a few minutes until they were just outside the border of McCabe land. They pushed through the nights, the pace that Ewan set inhuman.

Mairin rode with Ewan, and when she wasn't sleeping, Ewan was feeding her from the burlap sack attached to his saddle. His men looked gray with exhaustion but no one offered a single complaint. The journey was eerily silent, with neither Caelen nor Alaric offering conversation. They were too focused on making sure they weren't pursued.

"Ewan, I have need to stop," she whispered.

"Can you wait just a few more miles?" he asked. "We'll be on McCabe land soon."

She grimaced. "I'm afraid not. The child I carry makes it hard to hold it in."

His smile was fleeting as he called a halt. He eased her down from the saddle, and she nearly went down in a heap. Gannon was there to catch her and she nearly wept in gratitude when he offered her a reassuring smile.

To Gannon's utter shock, she threw her arms around him and hugged him fiercely. His hands went up and he stammered as he tried to ask her what she was about.

"Thank you," she whispered. She pulled away and smiled at him.

"For what, my lady?" he asked in confusion.

"For coming for me."

She turned then and went in search of a private area to relieve herself.

Ewan smiled and watched as his wife ducked behind a tree in the distance. She had stunned Gannon with her gratitude. If he had to guess, all his men would be the recipients of her affection before it was over with.

A moment later, Mairin returned and Ewan absorbed the vision of her holding a protective hand over her small, round belly. It staggered him just how relieved he was to have her home, or nearly so. He'd pushed his men hard, afraid that Duncan would pursue them and Mairin would be caught solidly in the middle as they would do battle. He wanted her safe. He wanted her far removed from the inevitable bloodshed between him and Cameron. The bastard's days were numbered, and no matter that Ewan defied the king himself, he'd avenge his wife.

As he was reaching down to pull Mairin into the saddle, he realized that he no longer sought vengeance for the wrong done to his father and their clan. He sought vengeance for a beautiful lass who had more hurt in her blue eyes than he ever wanted to see in a lifetime.

"We're nearly home," he whispered in her ear.

She turned and looked up at him with sadness and pleading in her eyes. "As soon as we cross over to McCabe land, can you send your men ahead? I must talk with you, Ewan. 'Tis important that I do so before we arrive at the keep. Once we ride into the courtyard, we'll be pulled this way and that. We have to settle this. We must."

He touched her face and tried to smooth the lines of worry from her brow. What on earth worried her so?

Dread gripped his heart at the depth of sadness in her gaze. He prayed for the strength to endure the telling of it all. "Aye, lass, we'll talk."

An hour later, he reined in his horse and then motioned the others to go ahead.

Caelen and Alaric approached on their horses and stopped beside Ewan and Mairin.

Alaric frowned. "I don't like leaving you alone, Ewan."

"We're far enough onto our land now. I have need for some time alone with my wife. We'll be along in a while. Go ahead and announce that I'm bringing her safely home."

With reluctance, Alaric and Caelen rode ahead. Their pace picked up as they started down the mountain toward the last stretch home. Soon the others followed suit, spurring their mounts to a gallop and then a run.

Shouts filled the air. *Whoops* and cries of triumph filled Ewan's ears, and he couldn't help but smile. But when he looked down at Mairin, her eyes were troubled and filled with grief.

His heart turned over and he closed his eyes as he prepared to hear of all that Duncan had done to her. A part of him didn't want to know. He wanted to forget it— wanted her to forget it—so they could put it solidly in the past. But he also knew she'd have need of telling it, so she could rid her system of the poison Cameron had inflicted.

He got down from his horse and then reached up to gently take her from the saddle. He carried her to a patch of thick grass that was warmed by the sun. He sat down on the ground and nestled her firmly into his arms.

He could scarcely credit that they were on his lands and she was back in his arms. The last week had been a test of his endurance. At his lowest point, he wondered if he'd ever see her again. He never wanted his faith tested in such a manner again.

"I did a terrible thing," she choked out.

Ewan pulled back in surprise, his brow furrowed in confusion. "What are you speaking of?"

"I agreed. God help me, I agreed to a devil's bargain in order to keep our child safe. I was disloyal to you, Ewan, for I vowed I'd lie and support Duncan's claim in exchange for our child's life."

Ewan swallowed back his own grief at the desperation in her voice. "Shh," he whispered. "I'll never believe for a moment that you were disloyal to me."

Pain filled Mairin's eyes. "He wanted to make me miscarry our child. He was going to force me to drink a potion. I would have said and done anything to save our baby. I convinced him that if I miscarried, as far along as I was, that there was a chance I wouldn't bear another child. I convinced him that the logical thing to do was to carry on the avowal that it was his child, for as long as I delivered a child, he would control Neamh Álainn regardless whose babe it was. He agreed, but even then I was afraid to eat or sleep because I worried he'd go back on his word and eliminate our baby."

Ewan gathered her in his arms and rocked her back and forth, his eyes closed at the terror she'd lived in. No wonder she was so thin. She hadn't eaten for fear she'd lose her child. His child.

"Your brilliance amazes me, lass. To have thought of a solution so quickly. I'm humbled by your courage and daring. No child could have a fiercer mother. Our son or daughter will be blessed beyond measure."

She stared up at him, hope lighting her eyes for the first time. "You aren't angry?"

"How could I be angry at a woman who'd sacrifice everything to keep my child from harm?"

"Oh, Ewan," she whispered. And then her eyes clouded again and she looked down.

He nudged her chin upward with a tender gesture. "What is it?"

"I agreed to be his wife. I agreed to never deny him." She closed her eyes as tears slipped in silvery trails down her cheeks.

For a moment Ewan didn't breathe. He couldn't imagine such a sacrifice. His chest ached as he finally sucked air into his lungs. But if she could find the courage to tell him all, he would find the courage to hear it. "Tell me, sweeting. Did he . . . Did he hurt you?"

The words spilled painfully from his lips. His throat threatened to close at what he imagined she might have endured.

"I . . . I vomited on him the first time he tried. I blamed it on my pregnancy, but it was God's truth the idea of him bedding me made me ill. Afterward he seemed afraid I'd repeat the insult so he stayed away from me."

Ewan's relief was so great that it made him light-headed. He gathered her in his arms and held on, just absorbing the feel of her in his grasp after so many weeks. And then he chuckled, the image of her retching all over Cameron amusing him to no end.

She looked up at him, her eyes shining so brightly that he lost himself in the deep pools. The light dimmed for a moment and she frowned.

"Ewan, what about the dowry? Is it lost to us forever?"

Ewan sighed. "It was awarded to Cameron. I've no doubt that he'll receive it whether you're in residence or not. Archibald, and possibly the king himself, is in league with Cameron."

Tears filled her eyes and she hung her head. "Everything you married me for hasn't come to pass. Our clan needs food and clothing. Our soldiers need supplies. We have need of repairs. How are we going to survive, Ewan?"

He caught her face between his hands and stared down into her eyes. "*You* are everything to me, Mairin. I can go without food. The keep can crumble. But I can't live without you. We'll make it. We've always made it. Somehow we'll see it through. But I cannot live my life without you. If the dowry never comes to pass. If we never claim Neamh Álainn. As long as I have you, lass. As long as I have you."

She threw herself around him and hugged him until he couldn't breathe. Her body shook as tears slipped down his neck. He didn't chide her, though, because it was God's truth he wanted to cry himself.

"I love you, Ewan. Thank God you came for me."

He pressed his forehead to hers as their lips danced ever closer to each other. "I'd battle the fires of hell to bring you home, lass. Now let's ride on. Our son misses his mother and our clan misses their mistress."

The entire clan was assembled in the courtyard when Ewan rode across the bridge, Mairin held solidly before him in the saddle.

Her head rested against his chest and her hair streamed down her back, the ends lifting in the slight breeze.

His clansmen all leaned forward, and their need to see that their mistress was well was visible on each of their faces.

Ewan came to a halt and pulled back the blanket that shielded Mairin from view. The courtyard erupted in a chorus of cheers.

Mairin straightened in his hold and smiled back at her clan. Tears shone in her eyes and she offered a reassuring wave.

"Mama! Mama!"

Crispen bolted through the crowd and ran straight for Ewan's horse. Ewan smiled down at his son.

"Stay right there, lad. I'll hand your mother down."

Crispen's and Mairin's smiles lit up the entire courtyard. Something inside of Ewan shifted and clenched until his chest ached. With love.

Alaric and Caelen came forward and Ewan handed Mairin down to them while he dismounted. As he'd expected, she threw her arms first around Alaric and squeezed until he laughingly begged for mercy. Then she let him go and turned to Caelen, who already had his hands up to ward her off. Paying him no mind, she launched herself at him and he had no choice but to catch her so she didn't fall. She hugged him fiercely, babbling her thanks all the while.

"You daft woman," Caelen muttered. "Did you honestly think we'd leave you to that pig?" He tweaked her chin and she beamed up at him before hugging him all over again.

Caelen groaned and turned her around in her husband's direction. Ewan was only too happy to gather her in his arms and swing her around.

"Put her down, Papa! I want to hug Mama."

Chuckling, Ewan set her on her feet and Crispen promptly threw his arms around her waist. Tearfully, Mairin gathered him in her arms and proceeded to kiss every inch of his hair.

Alaric and Caelen looked on indulgently, but Ewan could see in their eyes the clear affection they had for his wife. She had conquered them all. Ewan. His brothers. His men. Their clan.

He held up his hand to silence the uproar around them.

"Today is a truly glorious day," he said to the gathered clan. "Our lady is returned to us at last. She made incredible sacrifices to keep our child safe and the McCabe legacy alive. She worried that the loss of her dowry would somehow dampen our enthusiasm for her return when indeed she is our greatest treasure."

He turned then to Mairin and slowly went down on one knee in front of her. "You *are* my greatest treasure," he whispered.

Around him, his men also went down on one knee, their swords drawn and pointed in her direction. Alaric and Caelen both stepped forward. Ewan saw the question in her eyes. Then they both went on bended knee in front of her.

It was too much for his tenderhearted wife. She wept as noisily as a newborn babe. No one seemed to mind. Smiles shone on the faces of his exhausted men.

"Oh, Ewan," she cried, as she launched herself toward him.

He had no choice but to catch her, though they still landed on the ground in a tangle of arms and legs. She loomed over him and peppered his face and neck with kisses.

She was crying so hard that twice her lips slipped off his face and glanced off his ears.

"I love you," she wept. "Never did I dream that I'd find a man like you."

Ewan caught her in his arms and gazed lovingly into her eyes.

"'Tis a known fact that you were God's gift to this clan, lass. And to me. Especially to me," he whispered.

A resounding cheer nearly deafened him. Mairin clapped her hands over her ears, but her smile was enough to light up the darkest winter night.

Not caring who saw him or what conclusion they drew, he rolled to his feet, swung her into his arms, and started for the steps of the keep.

"Ewan, what are you doing?" she demanded.

He silenced her with a kiss as he walked inside the hall. "Hush, wife. Don't question me. I have a pressing need to experience my wife's indecency."

CHAPTER 38

Mairin stared longingly over the rolling terrain, the earth bursting with green, and inhaled the sweetly perfumed air of summer. She itched to leave the keep, even if just to walk about the courtyard, but Ewan had expressly forbidden her to leave the safety of the walls, and he had enough worries without her adding to them.

The McCabe clan readied for war. It wasn't an outward cry but rather a quiet readying of the men and their weapons. They were resigned to their fate as enemies of the crown and of Duncan Cameron.

Mairin left the window and descended the stairs to the hall, where she found Gannon and Cormac eating the noon meal with their soldiers. She waved her hand for them to continue eating.

"I'm just going into the kitchens to see Gertie," she called as she walked by. "I won't venture farther than that."

Gannon nodded but kept an eye on her progress. "Stay where I can see you, my lady."

She smiled and stepped inside the door but remained where Gannon could see her from where he sat.

Only, Gertie wasn't tending the fire as was her habit. Mairin sniffed the air. No bread was baking either, which was unusual given that Gertie always had a loaf baking, day or night. Mairin often wondered when the woman took her rest.

Perhaps she'd stepped into the larder. Aye, that was likely, and if so, she'd return in a moment's time. Gertie wouldn't leave an unattended fire for more than a few seconds.

But when Gertie didn't return, Mairin frowned. A noise that sounded like a moan coming from the larder spurred her into action. She rushed through the kitchen and stepped inside the small room, her gaze seeking Gertie.

There crumpled on the floor lay Gertie, blood trickling down her temple. Mairin rushed forward to kneel by the older woman. Then she turned, prepared to call for Gannon, when a hand clamped over her mouth and an arm jerked her from the floor against a hard body.

"Not a sound, my lady."

She managed to free her mouth. "Diormid?"

"Silence," he bit out.

Her shock wore off and gave way to burning rage. "You dare to show yourself on McCabe land? You'll not live to see another sunrise. My husband will kill you."

"You are my passage to freedom," he gritted out next to her ear.

The unmistakable feel of a blade cutting into her dress over her belly sent a shiver up Mairin's spine. He held the knife so close she could barely move for fear of being cut.

Diormid's grip tightened on her and he laid the flat of the blade against her now bare belly. "Listen well. If you do anything foolish, I'll slice open your belly and spill the babe onto the ground. If I fail to bring you back to Cameron, I die. If I'm caught on McCabe land, I die. I have nothing to lose, Lady McCabe, and I assure you, if you draw attention to us, I'll kill you and your babe before I die."

For some reason his words infuriated her rather than

struck fear in her heart. She was tired of the endless fear they all lived in. She was tired of seeing the worry in Ewan's eyes. He didn't sleep well. He wasn't eating properly. All because he feared the implications of the choices he'd made as laird.

She fingered the dagger attached to her belt. Caelen had gifted it to her upon their return to McCabe keep. His thought was that there was no reason a lass shouldn't be able to defend herself if the situation arose.

She found in this moment she was in complete agreement.

Careful not to upset Diormid in any way, she nodded her agreement. "Of course I'll do whatever you wish. I've no desire for harm to come to my child."

"We go out the back, where the skirt crumbles. My horse waits in the trees. If anyone sees you, you are to call out that Gertie has need of the healer."

Mairin nodded. Diormid's hand closed around her nape while his other hand still gripped the knife against her belly. As soon as she felt the metal leave her flesh, she whirled, her dagger in hand.

In Diormid's surprise, his knife swung up, slicing her upper arm. But the pain barely registered, so intent was she on her task.

She rammed her knee right between his legs and at the same time sank her dagger deep in his belly. He staggered back and then went down hard, his hands going to his groin. He was crying far more piteously than Heath had done when Ewan gave him the same treatment.

Wanting to make sure he was incapacitated, she grabbed one of the heavy cooking pots from the floor and bashed him over the head. He went immediately still, sprawled on the floor, arms and legs thrown wide. Only the hilt of her dagger shone against his belly. No part of the blade was visible. It was buried too deeply in his flesh.

Satisfied that he wasn't going anywhere for the moment, she turned and fled, yelling for Gannon as she went.

As she entered the kitchen, she ran full tilt into Gannon and bounced off. She would have fallen had he not grasped her arms to steady her. Then he saw her torn dress, and his expression grew stormy.

"What is it, my lady? What's happened?"

Before she could respond, he shoved her behind him and drew his sword.

"There is something I must show you," she said urgently. "Well, that is, I need you to stand guard while I fetch Ewan."

Without awaiting his response, she ran around him and tugged at his hand, pulling him into the storage room. She pointed at Diormid sprawled on the floor. "I must fetch Ewan. Can you make certain he doesn't move until I get back?"

Gannon's face clouded with fury as he looked on the man he'd trusted and called brother-in-arms. Then he looked up at Mairin in astonishment. "My lady, what did you do to him?"

At his question, the events of the last moments caught up to her hard and fast. Realization set in as to just how close she and her babe had come to harm. Her hands began shaking and her stomach rebelled. She turned and retched violently. She bent double and held her middle as she heaved onto the floor. Tears burned her eyes as she sucked in steadying breaths in an attempt to quiet her roiling stomach.

"My lady, are you hurt? What has happened?" Gannon asked worriedly.

She straightened and put her hand on Gannon's arm to steady herself. "Do I have your promise, Gannon?

You'll make sure he doesn't move until I return with Ewan?"

"I'm already here, lass. The entire keep heard your bellow," Ewans' voice sounded behind her.

She whirled in its direction to see him and his brothers standing in the doorway and promptly regretted her action. Nausea billowed up her throat and she bent over once again.

It was Caelen who put an arm around her and held her as spasms overtook her. Ewan was too busy surveying the scene in front of him.

"What in God's name happened?" Ewan roared. "How did he get into our larder?" He turned on Gannon. "Have you an explanation for this?"

"Nay, Laird, I do not."

"Gertie," Mairin choked out. "Ewan, she's injured."

Ewan motioned for Gannon to see to Gertie, who still lay on the floor a short distance away. Gannon lifted Gertie in his arms and carried her from the larder. She was already coming around and protesting loudly that she could walk under her own power. Ewan turned to Mairin, who shook like a leaf against Caelen's side.

"Tell me what happened, lass."

"He cut my dress," she said, as she held up the tattered material of her skirts. "He threatened to cut the babe from my womb if I didn't cooperate."

Alaric stared at her in astonishment. "If he held a knife to your belly, how in God's name did he wind up unconscious on the floor with your dagger in his belly?"

"I took a page from Ewan's book," she said primly.

Ewan raised an eyebrow and exchanged glances with Caelen.

"This I've got to hear," Caelen muttered.

"I kneed him . . . down there. And well, I plunged my dagger into his belly at the same time. When he fell, I wanted to make sure he didn't escape, so I bashed him over the head with a pot."

Alaric winced. "I don't think he was going anywhere, lass."

She shrugged. "'Tis the truth I wanted to kill him. He threatened my child."

Caelen chuckled. "I don't think Crispen or your other children will ever have to worry about coming to harm, Ewan. Your wife will single-handedly take on any threat to her young."

Ewan pulled Mairin against his side and kissed the top of her head. "Are you all right, sweeting?"

"He didn't hurt me."

He took his hand away from her arm and frowned when he saw blood on it. "Then what is this?" he demanded.

She shrugged, remembering now that Diormid had cut her in the scuffle. "'Tis naught but a scratch, Laird. I will wash it later."

"What's to be done with Diormid, Laird?" Cormac asked from the doorway.

Ewan's expression blackened, but then he glanced at Mairin, likely remembering her aversion to having Heath killed for his infraction.

"I think he should be fed to a pack of wild wolves," Mairin muttered. "Perhaps tied between two trees and left to bleed to attract predators."

Ewan and his brothers gaped at her in astonishment.

"Or we could simply drag him behind a horse for a few miles?" she asked hopefully.

Caelen died laughing. "Bloodthirsty lass. I love it! She's fierce, Ewan. I like your wife very much."

"You would," Ewan muttered.

Ewan looked at his wife in exasperation. "I was going to suggest we kill him and get it over with since he's not going to survive your dagger to the belly anyway."

" 'Tis too quick a death," she said with a sniff. "I think he should be made to suffer."

Ewan frowned and she relented with a sigh. "Oh, very well. Kill him quickly. But he's not to be buried on McCabe land. You can feed his corpse to the buzzards, can't you?"

Ewan shook his head and laughed at her hopeful tone. He gathered her in his arms and squeezed her until she couldn't breathe.

"Aye, lass, we can feed his corpse to the predators. Will it make you feel better to imagine his eyeballs plucked from their sockets?"

Her stomach recoiled at the image and she put a hand to her mouth to staunch the urge to retch again. Then she glared up at her husband. "You did that apurpose!"

He grinned and then turned to his brothers. "See to his body. I'm taking my wife back to the hall."

Mairin let Ewan guide her away but then she stopped and called back. "I'll be wanting my dagger returned, Caelen."

CHAPTER 39

"Laird! Laird! The king approaches!"

Ewan dropped Mairin's hand and hurried into the hall where Owain was shouting for him. The young man had obviously run the entire way, for he stood panting for breath as he frantically searched the hall for Ewan.

When he saw Ewan, he hurried over and once again repeated his announcement.

"Hold!" Ewan bit out. "Tell me all. How far is the king? Does he ride with his army?"

Before Owain could answer, another of Ewan's soldiers ran into the hall. "Laird! McDonald rides through our gates!"

Ewan stalked toward the courtyard, Mairin on his heels. He got to the steps as Laird McDonald slid from his horse. Beyond the gates of the keep, what looked to be McDonald's entire army spread out over the terrain.

"Ewan!" McDonald called. "My men brought news that the king's army approaches."

Not a moment after Laird McDonald's pronouncement, the McDonald army parted to allow Laird McLauren to ride over the bridge and into the courtyard. In the distance, McLauren's army gathered at the rear of McDonald's men.

"Ewan," McLauren greeted as he approached the two lairds. "I came as soon as I heard."

Ewan looked at the two men in surprise. The sight of so many soldiers on horseback was an impressive sight, spreading as far as the eye could see.

"Do you realize that by your actions, you actively rebel against the crown? You'll be branded outlaws," Ewan said.

Laird McLauren scowled. " 'Tis wrong what he did, Ewan. If he takes a man's wife, what's next? His lands? I stand beside you, as do my men."

Laird McDonald nodded his agreement.

Ewan grasped the forearm of Laird McLauren and then turned to do the same to McDonald. Then he threw his fist in the air and gave a war cry that was picked up by his men and spread to the McDonalds and the McLaurens. Soon the hills surrounding the keep echoed with the sound of impending battle.

He turned to Mairin and took her hands in his. "I want you to take Crispen and remain behind the walls of the keep. Do not come out until I've summoned you. Promise me."

She nodded her understanding, her eyes wide with fright.

He bent and kissed her. "Do not be afraid, Mairin. We will prevail this day. Now go tend to that cut on your arm."

She touched his face. "I know we will."

She turned and called for Crispen. Then she issued a sharp order for all the women of the keep to retreat behind the walls.

"We'll greet our king at the border of my lands," Ewan declared. He ordered his men to mount their horses and they rode out, the McDonald and the McLauren men behind them.

Ewan was sick at heart but resolute in his position

against the crown. The life he was forging for himself and Mairin and their children wasn't an easy one. Their name would forever be associated with dishonor. A hero to some, an outlaw to most.

If keeping the woman he loved by his side was a cause for dishonor, he was prepared to wear the mantle for the rest of his days.

When they arrived at their border, Ewan was surprised to see the king mounted atop his horse with only an escort of half a dozen men. He waited beyond the border, making no effort to cross over onto Ewan's lands.

"Is this some trick?" McLauren murmured beside Ewan. "Where are the rest of his men? 'Tis suicide to come without his army."

"Remain here," Ewan said grimly. He motioned for his brothers and Gannon and Cormac, and rode forward until he was just before the king but still on McCabe land.

The king looked tired and as if he still suffered the effects of his illness. His face was drawn and pale and his shoulders sagged precariously.

"Your Majesty," Ewan acknowledged. "Why have you come to my borders?"

"I've come to correct a wrong. And to thank you."

Of all the things Ewan thought his king might say, that wasn't one of them. He cocked his head to the side but didn't say anything, instead waiting for the king to explain.

"You come with the might of not only your army, but that of the McDonald and the McLauren clans," the king said. "Tell me, Laird McCabe, would you have fought me this day had I come under the declaration of war?"

"Aye," Ewan said without hesitation.

Amusement gleamed in the king's eyes. "By doing so, you would brand yourself an outcast for the rest of your days?"

"Only if I lost," Ewan drawled. "And I didn't plan to lose."

The king shifted on his saddle. "I would meet my niece, Laird McCabe."

Ewan leveled a stare at King David, unflustered by the abrupt change in topic. "I'll not allow Mairin outside my walls."

The king nodded approvingly. "Which is why I hope you invite me within. We have much to discuss, and as I stated, I have much to thank you for."

"It could be a trick," Alaric muttered.

"You'll enter alone," Ewan said. "Your men remain outside the walls."

The king arched one eyebrow. "You're asking me to have that much trust in a man who's admitted he has no issue with killing me?"

"If all I wanted was to kill you, you'd already be dead," Ewan said calmly.

David studied him for a moment longer and then slowly nodded. "Very well then. I'll ride with you into the keep. My men will escort me as far as your gate."

Ewan turned and gave his men the signal to hold. Then he motioned for David to follow him. Ewan's brothers flanked the king as they rode back toward the keep.

True to his word, David signaled his men to halt when they reached the bridge across the loch. The McDonald and the McLauren men remained behind while Ewan's men tramped across the bridge behind their laird.

They dismounted and David slid from his horse and wavered unsteadily on his feet. Ewan frowned but did nothing to shame his king by offering aid in front of his men.

"Laird, shall I send for Lady McCabe?" Cormac whispered.

Ewan shook his head. "Nay, and in fact, I want you to

go to your mistress and make sure she remains in her chamber until I summon her. Protect her well, Cormac, until I know all that transpires here."

Cormac nodded and hurried away.

The men entered the hall and Ewan called for ale and light refreshment. They sat at the high table and David was quiet as he sipped his ale.

After a moment he looked at Ewan over the rim of his goblet and chewed his lips in a thoughtful measure.

"I've need of men of your ilk, Ewan. You had every reason to despise me and yet you warned my guard of your suspicion that I was being weakened by men I trusted. 'Tis because of that warning that I am alive and in front of you today. Archibald indeed plotted against me with Cameron. Archibald slowly poisoned me over time so it would appear as if I sickened and died of natural causes."

The king sighed and set his goblet down. "I would apologize for the wrongs done to you and especially to your lady wife. I would like to meet my niece with your blessing."

Ewan regarded his king for a long moment but saw only sincerity reflected in the older man's eyes. Then he turned to Caelen. "Go and escort Mairin to the hall so that she may meet her uncle."

Mairin clutched at Caelen's arm as they started for the stairs. She'd instructed Crispen to remain behind in her chamber with Maddie, but right now she'd give anything to have someone else to hold on to.

Caelen paused at the top of the stairs and then he produced her dagger in the small leather sheathe he'd fashioned to attach to her belt.

"I thought you might like this back," he said in amusement.

She reached for the knife and attached it to her belt. "Thank you, Caelen. 'Twas very thoughtful of you."

He smiled and squeezed her arm reassuringly. "Chin up. A fierce lass such as you bows to no one."

They traveled down the stairs and turned the corner into the hall. Across the room, Ewan and the king rose from their seats in acknowledgment of her presence.

Mairin's knees knocked together in abject terror. Not terror in that she was afraid the king might harm her. Nay, Ewan was standing right beside the king, and he'd never allow such a thing to happen.

This was her family, though. Her flesh and blood. Her uncle. And he was the king of Scotland.

Caelen came to a stop just before the king and loosened his hold on Mairin's arm, stepping back to allow her the moment with her uncle.

Remembering that she should show respect for the king, no matter Caelen's thought that she should bow before no one, she hastily dipped into a sweeping curtsy and prayed she wouldn't fall at his feet.

She waited for his permission to rise, but to her surprise, he knelt down in front of her and took her hands in his. He pulled her to her feet, and she was further shocked to see a bright sheen of moisture in his eyes. Eyes that reminded her of her own.

He looked haggard. Pale and exhausted as if he'd fought a long battle with sickness and had only just begun his recovery. Lines etched deeply into his forehead, and wrinkles marred the corners of his eyes.

He kept a firm grip on her hands as he held them in the space between his own. "If I ever had any doubt, I don't now," he said in a gruff voice. "You have the look of my mother, may God rest her soul."

"I do?" Mairin whispered.

"Aye, she was a beautiful woman, kind in spirit and devoted to those in need."

Mairin swallowed, overwhelmed by the enormity of this moment. After so long in hiding, of living in fear, she was openly acknowledged by her father's blood.

Ewan stepped to her side and wrapped his arm around her waist. The king reluctantly let go of her hands and directed his gaze at Ewan.

"You did a good thing, Ewan. The thought of the lass in Duncan Cameron's hands . . ." He cleared his throat. "I will work to correct the wrongs done to you and your wife. I'll give public blessing to your marriage and I'll have her dowry transported immediately under heavy guard from Neamh Álainn."

Mairin gasped. "I thought my dowry lost to Duncan Cameron."

The king shook his head. "Archibald awarded the dowry to Duncan, but he knew not where it was held. Only I have that knowledge as only I was entrusted with Alexander's legacy bequeathed to the firstborn of his daughter. It has been under lock and key at Neamh Álainn since Alexander made the bequest so many years ago."

"Oh, this is wonderful, Ewan!" she exclaimed as she nearly danced in Ewan's arms.

She turned back to her uncle, concerned by his pallor and apparent weakness. "You would do us great honor if you remained here until your health is restored."

The king's eyes widened in surprise and he looked up to Ewan for confirmation. Ewan shrugged. "I have long determined the foolhardiness in denying my wife anything. Besides, she has the right of it. Until you are at full strength, the threat is still strong to you. You need time to ferret out those who worked with Archibald. We would be honored if you spent the time with us."

David smiled broadly. "Then I would be glad to accept your hospitality."

In the end, David stayed on for a fortnight, until Mairin's dowry was delivered. Her husband and the king, after a wary start, actually got along quite famously. They hunted many of the evenings, going out with Ewan's brothers and returning to drink ale in the hall and argue over who brought in the biggest kill.

David's health rapidly improved with Gertie's cooking and Mairin's nagging for him to rest. When he rode out with the contingent of soldiers who delivered her dowry, Mairin was actually quite sad to see him go.

That night, in the privacy of their chamber, Ewan made sweet love to her, and afterward she giggled at the memory of telling her laird he was unskilled at loving.

"What amuses you, wife? 'Tis a sin to laugh right after a man has indulged in loving."

She smiled and snuggled into his arms. As he always did, he cradled her to him, protectively surrounding her burgeoning belly.

"I was remembering certain inaccurate assessments I made about your prowess."

"Damn right you were wrong," he growled.

She laughed again and then sighed in contentment. " 'Tis a wonderful day, Ewan. Our clan is saved. We can feed our clan, clothe our children, and supply our men with the weapons and armor they so desperately need."

"Aye, sweeting, 'tis a wonderful day." Then he turned and kissed her until she couldn't draw breath. He gazed down at her with such tenderness in his eyes that her heart fluttered in her chest. "Almost as wonderful as the day you first stepped onto McCabe land."

*Read on for an exciting preview
of Maya Banks's next novel*

SEDUCTION OF A HIGHLAND LASS

Alaric McCabe looked out over the expanse of McCabe land and grappled with the indecision plaguing him. He breathed in the chilly air and looked skyward. It wouldn't snow this day. But soon. Autumn had settled over the highlands. Colder air and shorter days had pushed in.

After so many years of struggling to eke out an existence, to rebuild their clan, his brother Ewan had made great strides in restoring the McCabes to their former glory. This winter, their clan wouldn't go hungry. Their children wouldn't go without proper clothing.

Now it was time for Alaric to do his part for his clan. In a short time, he would travel to the McDonald holding where he would formally ask for Rionna McDonald's hand in marriage.

It was pure ceremony. The agreement had been struck weeks earlier. Now the aging laird wanted Alaric to spend time among the McDonalds, a clan that would one day become Alaric's when he married McDonald's daughter and only heir.

Even now the courtyard was alive with activity as a contingent of McCabe soldiers readied to make the journey with Alaric.

Ewan, Alaric's older brother and laird of the McCabe clan, had wanted to send his most trusted men to accompany Alaric on his journey, but Alaric refused. There was still a danger to Ewan's wife, Mairin, who was heavily pregnant with Ewan's child.

As long as Duncan Cameron was alive, he posed a threat to the McCabes. He coveted what was Ewan's—Ewan's wife and Ewan's eventual control of Neamh Álainn, a legacy brought through his marriage to Mairin, the daughter of the former king of Scotland.

And now because of the tenuous peace in the highlands and the threat Duncan Cameron posed not only to the neighboring clans but to King David's throne, Alaric agreed to the marriage that would forge an alliance between the McCabes and the only clan whose lands rested between Neamh Álainn and McCabe land.

It was a good match. Rionna McDonald was fair to look upon even if she was an odd lass who preferred the dress and duties of a man over those of a woman. And Alaric would have what he'd never have if he remained under Ewan: his own clan to lead. His own lands. His heir inheriting the mantle of leadership.

So why wasn't he more eager to mount his horse and ride toward his destiny?

He turned when he heard a sound to his left. Mairin McCabe was hurrying up the hillside, or at least attempting to hurry, and Cormac, her assigned guard for the day, looked exasperated as he followed in her wake. Her shawl was wrapped tightly around her, and her lips trembled with the cold.

Alaric held out his hand and she gripped it, leaning toward him as she sought to catch her breath.

"You shouldn't be up here, lass," Alaric reproached. "You're going to freeze to death."

"Nay, she shouldn't," Cormac agreed. "If our laird finds out, he'll be angry."

Mairin rolled her eyes and then looked anxiously up at Alaric. "Do you have everything you require for your journey?"

Alaric smiled. "Aye, I do. Gertie has packed enough food for a journey twice as long."

She alternated squeezing and patting Alaric's hand, her eyes troubled as she rubbed her burgeoning belly with her other hand. He pulled her closer so she'd have the warmth of his body.

"Should you perchance wait another day? It's near to noon already. Maybe you should wait and leave at dawn on the morrow."

Alaric stifled his grin. Mairin wasn't happy with his leaving. She was quite used to having her clan right where she wanted them. On McCabe land. And now that Alaric was set to leave, she'd become increasingly more vocal in her worry and her dissatisfaction.

"I won't be gone overlong, Mairin," he said gently. "A few weeks at most. Then I'll return for a time before the marriage takes place and I reside permanently at McDonald keep."

Her lips turned down into an unhappy frown at the reminder that Alaric would leave the McCabes and, for all practical purposes, become a McDonald.

"Stop frowning, lass. It isn't good for the babe. Neither is you being out here in the cold."

She sighed and threw her arms around him. He took a step back and exchanged amused glances with Cormac over her head. The lass was even more emotional now that she was swollen with child, and the members of her clan were becoming increasingly more familiar with her spontaneous bursts of affection.

"I shall miss you, Alaric. I know Ewan will as well. He says nothing, but he's quieter now."

"I'll miss you, too," Alaric said solemnly. "Rest assured, I'll be here when you deliver the newest McCabe."

At that, her face lit up and she took a step back and reached up to pat him on the cheek.

"Be good to Rionna, Alaric. I know you and Ewan feel she needs a firmer hand, but in truth, I think what she most needs is love and acceptance."

Alaric fidgeted, appalled that she'd want to discuss matters of love with him. For God's sake.

She laughed. "All right. I can see I've made you uncomfortable. But heed my words."

"My lady, the laird has spotted you and he doesn't look pleased," Cormac said.

Alaric turned to see Ewan standing in the courtyard, arms crossed over his chest and a scowl etched onto his face.

"Come along, Mairin," Alaric said, as he tucked her hand underneath his arm. "I better return you to my brother before he comes after you."

Mairin grumbled under her breath, but she allowed Alaric to escort her down the hillside.

When they reached the courtyard, Ewan leveled a glare at his wife but turned his attention to Alaric. "Do you have all you need?"

Alaric nodded.

Caelen, the youngest McCabe brother, came to stand at Ewan's side. "Are you sure you don't want me to accompany you?"

"You're needed here," Alaric said. "More so as Mairin's time draws close. Winter snows will be upon us soon. It would be just like Duncan to mount an attack when he thinks we least expect it."

Mairin shivered at Alaric's side again and he turned to her. "Give me a hug, sister, and then go back into the keep before you catch your death of cold. My men are ready and I won't have you crying all over us as we try to leave."

As expected, Mairin scowled but once again threw her arms around Alaric and squeezed tightly.

"God be with you," she whispered.

Alaric rubbed an affectionate hand over her hair and then pushed her in the direction of the keep. Ewan reinforced Alaric's dictate with a ferocious scowl of his own.

Mairin stuck her tongue out and then turned away, Cormac following her toward the steps of the keep.

"If you have need of me, send word," Ewan said. "I'll come immediately."

Alaric gripped Ewan's arm and the two brothers stared at each other for a long moment before Alaric released him. Caelen pounded Alaric on the back as Alaric went to mount his horse.

"This is a good thing for you," Caelen said sincerely, once Alaric was astride his horse.

Alaric stared down at his brother and felt the first stirring of satisfaction. "Aye, it is."

He took a deep breath as his hands tightened on the reins. His lands. His clan. He'd be laird. Aye, this was a good thing.

Alaric and a dozen of the McCabe soldiers rode at a steady pace throughout the day. Since they'd gotten a late start, what would normally be an entire day's ride would now require them to arrive on McDonald's land the next morning.

Knowing this, Alaric didn't press and actually halted his men to make camp just after dusk. They built only one fire and kept the blaze low so it didn't illuminate a wide area.

After they'd eaten the food that Gertie had prepared for the journey, Alaric divided his men into two groups and told the first of the six men to take the first watch.

They stationed themselves around the encampment, providing protection for the remaining six to bed down for a few hours' rest.

Though Alaric was scheduled for the second watch,

he couldn't sleep. He lay awake on the hard ground, staring up at the star-filled sky. It was a clear and cold night. The winds were picking up from the north, heralding a coming change in the weather.

Married. To Rionna McDonald. He tried hard but could barely conjure an image of the lass. All he could remember was her vibrant golden hair. She was quiet, which he supposed was a good trait for a woman to have, although Mairin was hardly a quiet or particularly obedient wife. And yet he found her endearing, and he knew that Ewan wouldn't change a single thing about her.

But then Mairin was all a woman should be—soft and sweet—while Rionna was mannish in both dress and manner. She wasn't an unattractive lass, which made it puzzling that she would indulge in activities completely unsuitable for a lady.

It was something he'd have to address immediately.

A slight disturbance of the air was the only warning he had before he lunged to the side. A sword caught his side, slicing through clothing and flesh.

Pain seared through his body, but he pushed it aside as he grabbed his sword and bolted to his feet. His men came alive and the night air swelled with the sounds of battle.

Alaric fought two men, the clang of swords blistering his ears. His hands vibrated from the repeated blows as he parried and thrust.

He was backed toward the perimeter set by his men and nearly tripped over one of the men he'd posted as guard. An arrow protruded from his chest, a testimony to how stealthily the ambush had been set.

They were sorely outnumbered and although Alaric would pit the McCabe soldiers against anyone, anytime, and be assured of the outcome, his only choice was to call a retreat lest they all be slaughtered.

He yelled hoarsely for his men to get to their horses.

Then he dispatched the man in front of him and struggled to reach his own mount. Blood poured from his side. The acrid scent rose in the chill and filled his nostrils. Already his vision had dimmed and he knew if he didn't get himself on his horse, he was done for.

He whistled and his horse bolted forward just as another warrior made his charge at Alaric. Weakening fast from the loss of blood, he fought without the discipline Ewan had instilled in him. He took chances. He was reckless. He was fighting for his life.

With a roar, Alaric's opponent lunged forward. Gripping his sword in both hands, Alaric swung, slicing through his attacker's neck and completely decapitating him.

Alaric didn't waste a single moment savoring the victory. There was another attacker bearing down on him. With the last of his strength, he threw himself on his horse and gave the command to run.

He could make out the outline of bodies as his horse thundered away, and with a sinking feeling, Alaric knew that they weren't the enemy. He'd lost most, if not all, of his soldiers in the attack.

"Home," he commanded hoarsely.

He gripped his side and tried valiantly to remain conscious, but with each jostle as the horse flew across the terrain, Alaric's vision dimmed.

His last conscious thought was that he had to get home to warn Ewan. He just hoped to hell there hadn't been an attack on the McCabe holding as well.